Acclaim for Steve Amick's

THE LAKE, THE RIVER & THE OTHER LAKE

"Thoroughly believable. . . . Few first novels manage to satirize their milieu with as much affection." —*The Baltimore Sun*

"Easygoing, rambunctious. . . . With the whoosh of a Jet Ski, the author zooms around half a dozen clusters of Michiganders. . . . You think with a contented sigh, 'Ah yes, that's my Michigan.'. . . Proust isn't the only one who had a madeleine moment." —*The New York Times Book Review*

"For the sensory pleasures alone, *The Lake, the River & the Other Lake* is a great book to tuck into your vacation tote." —*Detroit Free Press*

"Charming. . . . Refreshingly nuanced. . . . As Amick skips from story line to story line like a flat stone on the titular body, he never fails to keep your interest. His crazy-quilt patchwork of indelible characters, superb dialogue and oftentimes wry humor [are] truly satisfying." —*The Washington Examiner*

"A rollicking tale. . . . Extremely funny. . . . Amick juggles the different plot threads extremely well, with a storytelling voice that's sharp, funny and genially affectionate." —*The Capital Times*

"By turns humorous, tender, and tragic, Amick's debut novel features a deeply involving story that's as authentic and addicting as Mackinac Island fudge and makes perfect summer reading." —*The Flint Journal*

"Amick's a funny writer. . . . [His] Michigan village of Weneshkeen is populated with oddball characters, both lovable and crazy, and is the kind of place you'd love to spend some time in. . . . A story steeped in heart." —*Pages*

"[A] smart, punchy first novel. . . . Bitterly comic and surprisingly meaty, this roiling tale of passion, anger, regret, and lust is dark fun."
—*Publishers Weekly*

"I love *The Lake, the River & the Other Lake*. I love the rich mix of characters in the village of Weneshkeen, so alive and varied—their lives tumbling over one another and the narrative voice which has an energy and originality and humor that carries the reader on a wonderful ride, both heartening and real."
—Susan Richards Shreve, author of *Plum & Jaggers*

"Absorbing. . . . Affectionate, humorous and discerning . . . lovingly crafted. . . . Amick is a talented storyteller, whose characters come alive on the page and almost demand our involvement. . . . It's an impressive debut and a great book to take along to the cottage for a weekend."
—*The Grand Rapids Press*

"Fully peopled and richly plotted and one of the greatest summer reads ever. Smarter than most big blockbusters, more emotionally involving, it's wonderfully readable and very satisfying."
—*Sullivan County Democrat*

"Thrilling. . . . Move[s] from the hilarious to the heartfelt. . . . Amazingly rich and colorful, the writing flows so smoothly that one's only regret might be that the novel has to end."   —*Library Journal*

"The novel's real appeal is its characters. . . . [They] will make you laugh, and a few of the people will make you cry. . . . Amick's particular gift to his readers is to show us the local mysteries we tend to overlook. He makes ordinariness exotic."   —*Ann Arbor Observer*

"Worth cherishing. . . . The storytelling has an old-fashioned air. . . . You won't find Weneshkeen on any real map, but when you come away from *The Lake, the River & the Other Lake*, you'll know you've been to the real world all the same."
—*The Washington Post Book World*

STEVE AMICK

THE LAKE, THE RIVER & THE OTHER LAKE

Steve Amick's short fiction has appeared in *McSweeney's*, *The Southern Review*, *The New England Review*, *Playboy*, *Story*, the anthology *The Sound of Writing*, and on National Public Radio. He has an MFA from George Mason University and has been a college instructor, playwright, copywriter, songwriter, and musician. He lives in Michigan, dividing his time between his hometown, Ann Arbor, and a family cottage on a famously clear lake along the northern edge of the Lower Peninsula.

Please visit Steve Amick on the Web: www.steve-amick.com.

THE LAKE, THE RIVER & THE OTHER LAKE

THE
LAKE,
THE
RIVER & THE
OTHER
LAKE

A Novel

STEVE AMICK

Anchor Books
A Division of Random House, Inc.
New York

FIRST ANCHOR BOOKS EDITION, MAY 2006

Copyright © 2005 by Steve Amick

All rights reserved. Published in the United States by Anchor Books,
a division of Random House, Inc., New York, and in Canada by
Random House of Canada Limited, Toronto. Originally published
in hardcover in the United States by Pantheon Books, a division of
Random House, Inc., New York, in 2005.

Anchor Books and colophon are registered trademarks of
Random House, Inc.

The Library of Congress has cataloged the Pantheon edition as follows:
Amick, Steve.
The lake, the river & the other lake / Steve Amick.
p. cm.
1. Identity (Psychology)—Fiction. 2. City and town life—Fiction.
3. Summer resorts—Fiction. 4. Michigan—Fiction. I. Title: Lake,
the river and the other lake. II. Title.
PS3601.M53L35 2005
813'.6—dc22
2004056600

Anchor ISBN-10: 1-4000-7994-2
Anchor ISBN-13: 978-1-4000-7994-0

Book design by M. Kristen Bearse

Map by Steve Amick

www.anchorbooks.com

Printed in the United States of America
10 9 8 7 6 5 4 3 2 1

for Sharyl

WENESHKEEN

IF YOU HOLD UP YOUR RIGHT HAND, with your palm facing you, and you say that's the state of Michigan, then somewhere along your pinky would be Weneshkeen. All along that left side of your hand is the Gold Coast, the eastern shore of the most popular Great Lake, Lake Michigan. (From the Ojibwe *michigami*, or "great lake." So, redundantly, "Lake Great Lake.")

Weneshkeen lies on the Oh-John-Ninny River, a short reedy squiggle that connects Lake Michigan to the west with Lake Meenigeesis, only two miles inland to the east. Today, the "Oh-John," as it is now generally short-handed, is mostly used by people with big fancy boats to get inland and gaze on all the cute, tiny, far shabbier boats on whose decks they would never set foot. In lumbering days, the village of Weneshkeen boasted one of the nation's largest smelters, turning Upper Peninsula ore into pig iron, and the narrow river served as the main water route for timber to fire the smelter. For centuries prior, it was known as the *ojaanimi ziibii* or *Ojaanimiziibbii*—the "busy river"—not because of a particularly swift current, but because of the swirl of activity along its banks. The small band of Ojibwe whose name became synonymous with the river made their summer encampment there, and the shores were often brimming with fishing, trading and merrymaking children.

Officially, the area was "discovered" in 1672 by Marquette. Brief mention of the site in Marquette's writings offers meager explanation for the name: "it is [a] Village called Weneshkeen for that is what [the] Savages call it."

However, to the degree that being European and simply showing up is any sort of achievement, the credit more correctly goes to a Greek named, variously, Argus or Anastasius Mulopulos, way back in 1634. Mulopulos was not in the New World out of any sense of God or gold. He was simply pulled from a Marseille prison at the bayonet-prodding of a Royal press-gang and sent in a brig across the Atlantic to Quebec and then farther in. Though he was not a trained polyglot, Mulopulos was ordered to help act as interpreter/general pack mule under Jean Nicolet, one of Champlain's "young men of promise" bent on pursuing a route to the Orient. In 1634, Nicolet passed through the Straits of Mackinac and sailed into what is now Green Bay, Wisconsin, so convinced he was close to China, he actually dressed up in what he considered Oriental finery—silken robes and damask, brocaded with flowers and birds. There were several among the expedition who thought this route misguided and the dressing-up part just plain nuts, and this contingent grew nervous and rancorous. Mulopulos shared their opinions but kept them to himself. One moonless night, he stole away on the inflated bladder of a wild boar, recently killed by a hunting party, and drifted southeasterly for three nights, during which he saw no sign of shore in any direction. His third dawn on the bladder found him smashing into an outcropping of rocks at what is now probably Sumac Point.

And soon he was surrounded. In canoes and scrambling out along the rocks, they gathered around him. Red savages. There was a long channel or river winding in from the rocky spit where he lay, and he saw them all in there along its high banks: the men nearest, alert, *en garde,* the women and children farther back, all of them turned his way, watching—a whole summer village of brown healthy people with fish strung on leads and cookfire smoke and general signs of plenty.

The nearest ones had sticks, spears, cudgels. They sniffed at him cautiously. He raised his empty hands to indicate he was friendly. He asked them, in French and then Greek, where he was, what the name of this place was, hoping it was one of the villages farther north, along the straits, that he might recognize.

"Weneshkeen," was the unanimous answer. They all said it. Several kept saying it. He had never heard the name mentioned back among the expedition, but now it rumbled from man to man all along the rocky point, deeper into the village, carrying over the water.

What actually happened was that when Mulopulos asked where he was, they asked, in return, "Wenesh kiin?" meaning, "Who are you?" They kept asking, demanding to know. Though Mulopulos believed *his* question had been answered—repeatedly—it seemed to them *he* was ignoring their one direct question. The more he failed to explain who he was, the more peculiar he appeared—and irritating. But Mulopulos left long before he could figure this out. Perhaps he grew tired of being poked and sniffed by the curious savages, without any real welcome as compensation. Maybe it was frustration at the repetition of their conversation. Their civic pride seemed to border on the lunatic. It's possible he felt threatened, was struck, shoved, pushed around—but whatever his reason, he left in the middle of the night after only two days, stealing a canoe, some jerky and some skunk pelts. Following the polestar, keeping the shore within sight, to the starboard side, he headed north and eventually reached the Straits of Mackinac, where Jean Nicolet, returned from his failed meeting with the Chinese of Wisconsin, had him flogged for desertion. The punishment injured Mulopulos so severely, affecting even his spinal cord, that he died of his wounds, but not before telling the priest who was administering last rites, of the Indian village called *Weneshkeen* and the narrow river passage into another, smaller lake and the strange reddish drink he was given. His tale was passed, in turn, to Nicolet, who made mention of it in his log but felt he could not officially claim the site for France, since no one had knelt on the ground and placed a flag and asked for the Lord's blessing. Besides, he wasn't about to rely on the word of some criminal foreigner who was a thief and a deserter and probably a liar.

The tale grew among the Ojaanimiziibii people as well. For years, long before Marquette's appearance at the mouth of the river, they told and retold the story of the strange "bloodless man" who came to them from another world and wandered around their village for two days, and would not answer when they all demanded, "*Wenesh kiin? Wenesh kiin?*" An easy question: "Who *are* you?" They gave him some sumac steepings and not much else and finally he got the hint and left, returning, they hoped, to someplace far away. But he never once answered the simple question of identity, and because they had never before seen a man like this, with that bloodless skin—dark in a way, though not bloodless as a ghost, with dark eyebrows but hair on the head the color of sand—there was much discussion about whether his visit was a singular event, like the creation of the great Sleeping Bear Dunes far to the north, or whether it was something that would happen again and again, like the hard week of rain that came at the start of each summer. It was eerie, everyone agreed—and very troubling, because what kind of man does not tell you who he is?

MAY INTO JUNE

1

THERE WAS A HEAVENLY TIME, a sliver-thin window of peace that Roger Drinkwater cherished every year on Meenigeesis—those early days when the water warmed just enough for him to bear but all others steered clear and he could swim in peace and hear nothing but the water and his breath and the birds and the distant road: the way it had once been on this lake. It was a time before jet-skis; before the idiot boys on their idiot toys, as he thought of them in the little singsong chant that drummed in his head the rest of each summer.

One misty predawn in late May, he got his first indication that the lake was now warm enough for at least a few intrepid others. Kids, of course, tended to brave the waters sooner than their finicky parents, and the evidence he found was something that obviously came from a child. It was floating, half-submerged, at the end of his dock, and he bumped his head against it on the return lap of his morning swim: an underwater toy in the shape of a flattened megaphone, purple plastic with a green mouthpiece. If it hadn't had a brand name, Sub-Speaker, stamped on the side, he might not have known what it was for.

He stood there in the water, examining it, disgusted. Plastic toys lost in the lake were essentially just pollution. Still, he wondered how well it worked. Glancing around first to make sure he was alone, he knelt to the waterline and put the mouthpiece to his lips. What came out was Chief Joseph One-Song's famous words to Congress: *"Nimaanaadendam gaa zhi binaadkamgiziik . . ."*

The water was so still, the sound waves would carry as if across a drumhead. It's funnier, he decided, if no one can see me, and so he dropped lower in the water, the toy just nosing above the waterline, and he repeated the phrase, making it more guttural and ominous and spooky. He imagined some dumb cluck on the other side, those rich weekend warriors with the matching hot pink jet-skis and that pontoon boat, looking out and shuddering, unable to spot him, unable to understand the words, just knowing that the words were ancient, foreboding, and they would feel very, very uneasy. It was hard to do it without snickering.

ROGER DRINKWATER was actually only seven-eighths Indian (Ojibwe or Chippewa—or Anishinaabe, if you wanted to get precious about it, which he never did—of the Ojaanimiziibii band). The little bit left over was actually Polish, his mom's grandmother having come up as a young girl from Hamtramck, outside Detroit, back in 1914. She thought she would be spending just the one summer—out at Cliffhead, the place people now called "the bootlegger's"—working as a nanny for the Fifels, the family of the man known at the time as the Rumbleseat King. She once told Roger she thought that at most she might learn to swim that summer. But much more than that happened. She got involved with Roger's great-grandfather, John Birchtree, a leather-dark Indian boy who helped out in the Fifels' stables, and she got in trouble and knew she could never go back home and so they got married, both of them still teenagers. Even if she hadn't gotten in trouble, it would have been damaging enough just to have been briefly mixed up with an Indian boy: there were other Hamtramck girls in the household staff and they would return with the Fifels, bringing sordid stories of the summer, and she would be ruined back home. Beyond ruined, she might be in actual danger there.

So, though she never returned and never spoke to her family again, Grandma Oshka carried on the only traditions she knew, filling the many grandchildren and great-grandchildren that followed with golabki and pierogi and tales of Smok Wawelski, the dragon from the Wawel Castle in Kraków, and how a poor shoemaker killed the evil dragon with trickery and a river.

But seven-eighths was still pretty damn pure in 2001 and it was good enough for Roger to qualify for a dividend check with the area casino. Thirty grand a year for doing nothing more than being a member of the regional band. He could make much more if he chose to actively participate in the actual operation, but he didn't. The casino was at least two hours away and besides, having been to Nam, Roger figured he'd had enough gambling to last a lifetime or three. Besides, the casino money was only part of his income. There was the jerky business, the product sold as Schmatzna-Gaskiwag® at stores all over the county and as far north as a froufrou specialty foods store his grade school buddy, Eric Revels, ran up in Petoskey called Gourmet Gobbles. (No one ever came in and asked for it by name. The combination of the Polish *smaczny*—"delicious"—and the Ojibwe *gaskiwag*—"dried smoked meat"—amounted to more than a mouthful for most Fudgies, the weekend tourists from downstate. But they managed to figure out to ask for "that local stuff. The . . . *you* know. That authentic stuff? The stuff in the Baggies?" and sales did not seem to suffer.)

During the summer, he periodically taught at the short-term dive school camps a mile out on Lake Michigan aboard a restored nineteenth-century schooner, and year-round, classes for the National Guard up in Grayling. During the school year, he was the high school swim coach. He got great results from those kids, producing two state champs in the past ten years, and the school board kept trying to get him to coach more, especially water polo, but Roger said no way. First of all, he did not believe the water was a place for games. Even without the aid of an internal combustion engine or oversized floaties, as used in the more obvious sins of water-skiing, jet-skiing, parasailing. Even water polo—just flouncing around hitting balls and carrying on—Roger deemed unacceptable. The water, he felt, was for meditation and sustenance and life. And in extreme times, battle, which was part of life. But his official bottom line for declining was the water polo headgear. "You shouldn't wear something on your head when you're in the water," he would say. "Against my religion." If they looked at him blankly, he would shrug it off with, "Hey, it's an original people thing. You wouldn't understand." The truth was, nothing with the word "polo" in it could possibly be tolerable.

THERE WAS A SONG of his people that told, "If you follow the river inland through the village, you come to the other lake." And lately, it seemed nearly everyone was coming to the other lake. Years ago *National Geographic* had praised it for its clarity and beauty and, more recently, *Lifestyles of the Rich and Famous* had called it "a local gem."

To Roger Drinkwater's people, it was just *Miinigiizisigami*—literally, "berry moon lake." But what they had meant was "lake of the moon when berries are picked," not because there were ever spectacular amounts of any kind of edible berries right around the lake, but just because that's how you say *August* in Ojibwe. Due to the shade of its densely wooded banks and the deep center of the lake, it never got very warm at all, and August was the only month the unaccustomed could manage getting in the water without a lot of silly shrieking. Maybe a more accurate translation would be "That Lake You Can Really Only Stand During The Moon In Which Berries Are Picked—Where They *Are* Picked—Meaning August, Basically," but that wouldn't work on a map.

Unlike most of the place-names in the area, this was one the whites somehow managed to translate fairly accurately, and for about a century it was known officially as Lake August. The name change, leaning back *toward* the aboriginal, more or less, actually predated considerably the PC era (as well as this era of influence from the Indian casino lobby). And it had less to do with being accurate and more to do with being American: it was World War II and someone—no one remembers who—took the floor during the "new business" part of a half-empty village meeting and proposed that "Lake *August*" sounded awfully Germanic. Never mind that it was the name of a month—the month, specifically, when one's testicles were less likely to retreat into one's abdominal cavity during a dip—and had nothing to do with any Austrian baron or Bavarian prince, real or imagined. But somebody seconded the motion and it soon became *Meenigeesis*. In recent years, there had been a small group, mostly of outsiders (those itching to pave the road that encircled the lake—or worse, Roger strongly suspected: *develop*—slap up subdivisions, build more cell towers and time-sharing condos), who had lately been floating the idea of again changing the name. These jackasses were favoring the more lyrical *Berry Moon Lake*. But, as one old-timer pointed out, when he had the floor at the village meeting, "Where the fuck do you see berries?" The nearest berries in any great quantity were a few miles out of town, at vonBushberger's (an orchard, incidentally, so much a part of Weneshkeen that no one, even back during the war, ever questioned *its* Germanic derivation). So for the time being, the Berry Moon Lake suggestion had mostly been kept at bay by hoots and jeers and—appropriately, Roger felt—derisive, Archie Bunker–style raspberries.

Besides, the Indian thing was hip. In fact, the bigger, newer houses on Lake Meenigeesis—the ones that had recently jacked up the property taxes—the overblown, rambling four-bedroom affairs that seemed, to Roger, to make a mockery of the term "cottage"—were mostly on the side of the lake referred to as "the Indian side." It was a term that had been around before he was a boy and had nothing to do with the heritage of anyone living in the million-dollar homes that stood there now. Traditionally, as recently as a hundred years ago and uncountable time before, this section was the summer campgrounds of the Ojaanimiziibii band. And then, when they were Westernized and dragged to the white man's churches and schools and given haircuts and biblical first names and Anglican surnames and shoved into pants, the "Indian side" was where they homesteaded with year-round housing, very humble one- and two-room shacks. These shacks and the slight improvements that followed—stone porch affairs like Roger's—were the beginnings of the summer cottages on the lake. As the Ojaanimiziibii population dwindled in the nineteen-twenties and thirties, whites from town began to buy up these little houses as summer, weekend homes. More cottages were built around the rest of the lake—fancier homes compared to the "Indian side," but humble by present standards. Sometime in the late eighties and early nineties, when real estate boomed, Roger's neighbors started having to sell off. These were middle-income whites—skilled tradesmen, public school teachers—too practical-minded to hang on to property that was growing rapidly out of their league. But this boom had coincided with the advent of the casino, and so for Roger, the money was less an issue. So far, he'd resisted selling. But the rest of the "Indian side"—the cheaper lots with shabby historical cottages similar to his own—were snatched up by a whole new breed of summer people, people of wealth on a level that had not yet been seen in Weneshkeen and hailing from strange locales: a Detroiter who owned his own security alarm company, the first importer of chai tea in the state of Arizona, an Ohio man who held the patent on a revolutionary golf club, and a woman from Santa Monica thought to be the "Father of the Fruit Smoothie." They constructed cathedrals of glass and exotic wood, with wraparound decks and paved driveways that sluiced non-point-source runoff right into the lake. (Or rather, had it done on their behalf, rarely actually setting foot on the property, as far as Roger could tell. These money dumps were almost always just overrun with younger, more annoying people who couldn't possibly be footing the bill, while the breadwinners were somewhere else—or at least inside, online—earning more bread.) They "grandfathered" their way past zoning restrictions by demolishing everything but, say, the original stone fireplace and chimney, then rebuilding around it, as high and as close to the water as they wanted, using the twisted loophole that they were "remodeling" an existing pre-code structure. And when the houses got more valuable, everyone's taxes went up and up, squeezing out more of the merely moderately well-off and their modest cottages. Some moved over to the increasingly smaller section of the lake that had once been "the nice side" where the "better people" lived. Now Roger was the only Ojaanimiziibii still living on the lake. Ironically, though he lived on the "Indian side," with his "quaint" little cottage and his nose-thumbing disdain for the lives of excess all around him, he was considered very misplaced. If a seven-eighths Indian, one-eighth Pole belonged anywhere at all on this tony lake, it was certainly not on the "Indian side" but maybe only on the "nice side." If even there.

He was well aware of all this. Things, he felt, were getting so ridiculous here he wasn't sure how long he could stand it.

2

THERE WAS A POLICY on Lake Meenigeesis regarding jet-skis: a curfew limiting their use to ten A.M. till dusk. It was a bit of a gentleman's agreement, making enforcement sketchy if the offender was truly hell-bent on being a jackass. By the time you called the sheriff's office and someone drove out, the kid could be docked and back inside his air-conditioned palace, playing video games or downloading porn.

It galled Roger to think what they were doing to this famously clear lake: jet-skis, with their two-stroke engines, could dump as much as thirty percent of their fuel straight into the water. He'd read somewhere that the fuel in the water from jet-skis each year amounted to fifteen times the *Exxon Valdez* spill and that one hour zipping around the lake was the equivalent, pollution-wise, of driving a car for a year. But he didn't need to read these facts to know them to be true: he could see it. He remembered, as a kid, making lemonade right off the dock. Grandma Oshka would give him a slice of lemon or, in a bind, a bit of sumac, and one of those old aluminum drinking glasses they used to have, and a long wooden spoon, and he'd sit there, feet dangling off the side, and scoop up a glassful and mash it all together and drink it down with a grin. No way would he be doing that now. It was still a beautiful lake, sure, but he knew the difference from how it had once been, B.J.—Before Jet-skis. Before Jackasses.

If you lived on a cul-de-sac, Roger always liked to point out, and the neighbor kids—some too young to drive a car—rode around in circles endlessly on whiny two-stroke minibikes right in front of your house, there would be no question it was wrong and illegal and you could take action, pronto. And yet, there were no real laws against them doing this with the marine equivalent. The problem with jet-skis was that the technology developed much faster than the law. Sometime back in the late eighties, jet-skis were everywhere, almost overnight, with no rules in place to govern them. It was a case of the gizmo catching on long before the legislators did—by the time lawmakers heard any backlash, the things already had a strong foothold in the summer culture. Plus, they were tied to big motorcycle companies, which meant they contributed significantly to political campaigns and had a lot of PAC money in their corner. It was all nasty business, rotten politics.

And besides the noise and pollution, there was the danger. Since jet-ski operators were usually either sugar-addled teenagers trying to impress some prepubescent girl by acting out a Mountain Dew commercial or weekend warriors or their guests who wanted to "take it for a spin" and therefore had no experience in handling the thing and no knowledge of the rules, this all added up to real peril during his morning swim. Because, despite the etymology of the lake, Roger got in that water not just in August but every single day from usually mid-May to

Halloween. And not just a quick shrieky "double-dare" dip, howling and carrying on like the rest of those pussies and outsiders and white men: he *swam*. From his dock, straight across to the Petersons' and back, over a mile total, every morning starting at six forty-five. The way over was never a problem—not even the craziest teenager was out plowing the water that early—but on the way back, when he was weary and perhaps more loglike, sometimes they were out. They weren't supposed to be out, but sometimes they cheated and snuck out early. When he'd ask around later, he'd find it was a renter, just up for the week, who didn't know the rules, or somebody's nephew who supposedly would never do it again, but inevitably, they lied. They always did it again. Still, you had to call them on it. It was the principle of the thing.

And they got close, on occasion, probably just as surprised to see him as he was alarmed to see them. He usually heard the roar starting up as a low, leaky sound underwater, long before they approached, but still, it rattled him, the thought of that jockeyed torpedo, essentially, clipping him even in passing, cutting an artery or the hull itself cracking his skull, sending him sinking deep into the blue, a purple cumulus cloud, like a streamer, the blood leaving his body and joining the lake.

It made his teeth ache, just imagining it; made him puff harder than he should, pushing his stride; made him break entirely, treading water to heads-up and reconnoiter the asshole's position every five seconds: generally, a pain in the ass. So there was no reason he had to dirty his hands dealing with such things. Not when they paid taxes for a sheriff's department.

Of course, if the kid insisted on being an irredeemable little turd and denied he'd been out there or if the parents didn't care or weren't around, the sheriff would be useless. But that didn't mean you could just lie back and take it.

Just a few days after he found the first lost toy of the season floating in the lake, he had his first narrow miss of the season. In the home stretch of his morning swim, no more than fifty feet short of his own dock, he surfaced to the wake and roar of a jet-ski cutting right across his path. The kid was wrong on three counts: he was less than one hundred feet from Roger's dock, wasn't yielding to swimmers, and was out at least two hours too early. Roger watched him arc over to the Petersons' place, whooping and grinning. He thought of the Plains peoples, like the Sioux, and their need to "count *coup*"; the pride they took getting physically close to their enemy. Perhaps it was because his own people were more settled and domesticated, but those Plains traditions always struck him as foolish.

He stood and walked in the rest of the way to shore, glaring over at the asinine little savage. Roger waited for some response, an acknowledging glance. The kid seemed intent on ignoring him, so he went inside and called it in.

He pictured one of the deputies, Janey Struska, taking the call. Her coming out would at least improve the situation. He'd always thought highly of Struska, whom he'd known since she was a smart-alecky member of the girls' swim team and he was her coach. He hadn't had a lot of dealings with her since, but she was clearly well liked and respected by both the locals and the summer people. She was practical and diplomatic and even pleasant—which made it even more stupid that she hadn't been made sheriff. Typical white man politics had ruled the day when the sheriff recently retired and she was passed over in favor of the new and untried Jon Hatchert, some outsider who met the minimal, unspoken requirements of being white and male. Roger had yet to speak to the man and didn't particularly care to.

But when the cruiser pulled in, crunching gravel, he saw from the angular shape at the wheel that it wasn't Janey Struska. It was Hatchert, responding personally. And uselessly—all he agreed to do was talk to the kid in real general terms about operating his craft more safely and making an effort to give swimmers the right-of-way. He wasn't about to enforce the curfew policy.

"This curfew you people have," he said, shaking his head. "See, it's not truly a law. It's sort of a handshake agreement. Between the Department of Natural Resources and this 'lakes association' you people put together and old Don Sloff. But he's not the sheriff anymore, and frankly, I don't know as this lakes association represents all the homeowners so evenly. What I suggest is you get yourself a bathing cap. They make them in all kinds of Day-Glo colors—orange and red. Like that."

Roger mustered his best stone face and told the new sheriff, "Don't fuck with me."

"Hey, I'm not kidding. They'll see you a mile off in a bathing cap." He smiled, got in his patrol car and drove away.

IT WAS MOMENTS LIKE THIS Roger wished he could be as eloquent and succinct as the legendary Chief Joseph One-Song. That guy knew how to make a statement.

Back in town, in Scudder Park—between the drinking fountain and the little shed that supposedly housed the missing tennis nets and the badminton equipment you used to be able to rent (only someone lost the key years ago and no one had bothered breaking open the padlock to check if it was there or rotten or what)—there was a statue of this last great Ojaanimiziibii leader, whose real name was *Bezhik-Nagamoon.* The plaque at the base commemorated his appearance before the U.S. Congress in January 1837, making him what was believed to be the first Native American to ever address that assemblage. He was invited, along with a retinue led by the acting Territorial governor, the twenty-five-year-old "Boy Governor" Stevens T. Mason, to appear at the granting of Michigan's statehood. The chief's speech was actually only two lines—eight words plus a healthy helping of wheeze and spittle: *"Nimaanaadendam gaa zhi binaadkamgiziik. Aaniishpii ge nimaajaa yin?"* In translation from the Ojibwe, roughly: "You have all been a great disappointment. When are you leaving?" And then he walked back to the Hotel Liberté and laid himself down on the floor in his room, skipping the fine goosefeather bed, and died. That evening, when President Jackson was debriefed on the day's events and informed of the short words from the old "Chippeway" from Michigan, Jackson insisted he would "thrash that ingrate savage" and "flay his red hide." Half in the bag, the old Indian-fighter tore out of the White House and rode bareback across the Mall, straight to the Liberté. But upon arrival, when he was informed by the house doctor that the great elder had been declared dead, the president cooled somewhat and retired instead to the hotel bar where he confided, to the aides that finally caught up with him, out of breath, that the thrashing "would likely prove mostly ineffectual, at this late juncture . . ."

Roger loved the idea that at least *once* it was the white man left holding his dick, realizing he was just a little too late to do anything to correct the situation. And he loved Chief Joseph One-Song—wrote papers about him when he was in grade school, stopped and paid his respects every time he passed the statue in the park, thought he might even name a son *Bezhik-Nagamoon* (if the theoretical mom didn't think it was nuts)—because the chief never quite, as they used to say when Roger was a Navy SEAL, went along with "the program."

HE DID TRY THE BATHING CAP. Once. Gave it a fair chance, he felt. He didn't actually go out and buy one, just borrowed one from the high school. They had a bunch in the supply closet in the coach's office that he doled out for the girls' swim team.

It wasn't one of the flamboyant Day-Glo colors that that asshole Hatchert had described. White, he decided, should be sufficient. It shouldn't be necessary to dress up like a highway traffic cone just to avoid getting creamed by a jet-ski.

It was tight getting it on, but the hardest part was pushing the image of Esther Williams out of his mind. He felt like any minute there'd be strings and a full orchestra and he'd be expected to swim with one leg up and do his part to imitate a chrysanthemum in mid-bloom. It felt weird, the way he cut through the water, no sensation of his own hair. He worried, too, that it might be even more dangerous, the way it covered his ears. Everything took on a dull hum underwater. Midway across the lake, he wished he'd started out even earlier in the morning. If anyone saw him they'd laugh themselves silly. He imagined then what his old Navy SEAL buddies would say if they could see him, if they weren't in a million pieces in the afterworld. If they weren't already dead, he'd probably have to kill them just to keep them silent.

By the time he reached the far side, he was disgusted with himself. He remembered his claim to the athletic department that it was against his religion, wearing something on his head in the water. He peeled off the rubber cap, wishing he could fling it, but polluting the lake was not an option. He looked around for a place to put it and realized he was very near that giant A-frame with the his-and-hers jet-skis, in matching pencil eraser pink. An idea was forming.

He dove down and swam underwater parallel to the shore, toward their dock. He came up for breath once, just his chin and nose, employing the stealth swimming techniques he still practiced when he taught Guardsmen up at Camp Grayling, and dropped down again till he touched the dock pilings. He came up under the dock where no one would see him. Water lapped against the jet-skis. He doubted the owners were awake yet, if they were even in town, but he was on automatic now, working in that old cold way that, innately, made him err on the side of caution rather than regret. He reached around along the planks overhead till he found a spot where the point of a ten-penny nail poked through and, gripping the cap in both hands, ran it against the nail till he got it to tear. Working carefully, he continued until he had one long jagged strip of rubber. Dropping down again, he took only two dives to feed the long strip of rubber snugly into the jet-ski's intake pump and then he was out of there, hugging the lake floor and swimming hard away.

It was sort of a kick. He only wished he'd worn two bathing caps.

3

AT THE MAIN ENTRANCE to vonBushberger's, the big fruit orchard north of town, on one side of the main driveway stands a big wooden sign, visible a half-mile off by even the speeding Fudgies who whip up 31 every summer weekend. The sign features scrolled black lettering—oddly old-fashioned and Old World if you really examine it—on a familiar lemon yellow background, and it reads, simply, *vonBushberger's*. Then, in smaller letters below, though not that much smaller: *Local Fruits Since 1907*. On eyehooks below hang removable slats that outline what these local fruits currently are, nicely lettered in the same font. This information is almost just quaint trivia because the main crop is always cherries—sweets, blacks, Royal Anns, Rainiers, tarts . . . At times, you can also get peaches and melons and berries and they're good enough. But what the name *vonBushberger* has come to mean—what the original homesteader there, Emil vonBushberger, first envisioned, planting trees by hand back in 1907—is cherries.

The sign, constructed by the current head of the vonBushberger family, is surrounded by a beautifully terraced arrangement of lake rocks and pansies and geraniums and August Moon hostas. Von, as he is known—his real name is *Hubert* but everyone, including his wife, calls him *Von*, since when your last name is *vonBushberger,* that's more than enough—also installed two all-weather spotlights on either side of the sign to light it at night. His wife, Carol, found this extremely aggravating and vain, since the workday was over by sunset.

"Just because we're not open at night," Von told her, "doesn't mean we can't advertise to people driving by at night."

Carol never bought this argument. "Is it your hope they'll start wandering up to the porch, knocking on the door, waking us up?"

"My hope," he said, "is to just keep the vonBushberger name in their mind."

Carol just saw it as an added boost to their electric bill. "You want them to know we have fresh fruit . . . that they won't be able to buy till tomorrow."

They didn't always turn the lights on.

Directly in front of this sign, in a smaller circle of flowers where the rock border formed a figure eight, there stood a wrought-iron signpost, taller than Von. If you weren't from Weneshkeen and didn't know the man behind this post, you'd probably think that something had been swiped and just never replaced. Not so. The pole was, as yet, a sign-virgin. It was waiting for its sign.

The vonBushberger family had been owners, operators, and residents of the orchard for nearly a century—just a hair short of qualifying for Centennial Farm status, which was granted by the state of Michigan to farms that had been in the hands of one family for a hundred years. The tangible benefits of this were tax breaks and the moderate increase in revenue from the heightened prestige and public awareness that would be enjoyed by both their product, making it more of a name brand, and their on-site sales, making the place more of a destination, like taking the family to a museum or historical battlefield. (Von wasn't sure why, exactly, knowing that a pie or a lug of cherries came from a farm with an unbroken family lineage made a person want it more or made it seem more delicious, but the marketing class he'd taken at the county community college confirmed his hunch that this was so.) Plus, they sent you a very official-looking roadside marker, which was just too cool in and of itself and which was why Von already had the post.

THE MIGRANTS STARTED ARRIVING on an early June Sunday, in time to help finish up with the small berry crops and then begin the real work, picking sweet cherries from the end of June till the end of July and starting the tarts mid-July or thereabouts, the apricots the last week of July, then the peaches and nectarines about mid-August.

They mostly arrived in crews, under a workboss, and the biggest batch was Santi's bunch, the Guatemalans. Von was in front of the tractor barn, oiling and sharpening the pruning rig, when a dusty pickup—it was always a different dusty truck every year—pulled in, making a wide arc of grumbling gravel and dust, the shocks squeaking. Santi waved his straw hat, grinning, and it was clear he'd had some dental work done over the winter. (The taking-out kind, not the putting-in kind.) Von judged he had at least a dozen workers with him—the driver and his daughter, Marita, up front with him in the cab and the rest standing and squatting in the bed. Though most of them looked somewhat familiar, some were definitely new this year, squinting around at the property, getting their bearings.

The dust was still clouding up around them as Santi got out, swaying toward Von with his big brown hand outstretched to shake. Behind him, the workers looked dazed and wobbly as they dropped to the ground, getting their land-legs back. Von and Santi shook hands and then Santi was back at the pickup, helping his daughter out.

That's when Von caught sight of the belly. This was not a matter of too many greasy tortillas or a pork-rich diet. The girl was pregnant.

"Oh, no," Von said, shaking his hand in the air to help with the translation: this was no good. "No, Santi, please. I can't have this."

"No, no!" Santi said. "Is not a problem!"

Already it was starting, the headaches of summer. And it wasn't even warm enough to put away the down duvet yet. He covered his face with his hands. It made it easier to think, to say the tough things he needed to say to this man. "I know she's your daughter, I know, I know, but we can't do this, Santi. All the workers need to work."

"She works! No problem!"

"NO. No. It is a problem. I'm not having a pregnant lady out in the field, catching sunstroke. We don't do that here. Jesus, Santi. You're aware this is America, right?"

"Of course this is America. This is Weneshkeen, Michigan, United States of America! Is wonderful place here."

"Mr. vonBushberger?" The daughter stepped forward, with a little sway like she was carrying firewood. He liked that she said *Mister*, not *Señor*. He remembered her now. Pretty girl. The big, beseeching eyes. She had always been bright and lively—a good worker. But then, she'd always been someone nonpregnant before. "I understand if you do not want me in the trees, but I can maybe help around the house or at the fruit stand? Is whatever you want. I help as long as I can."

Von put his face back in his hands. He couldn't take it. All the workers were watching now. He wondered how much of the discussion the other pickers could understand. But what did they really have to understand? Migrant picker girl, big as a house, upset white landowner: it was pretty much a silent movie, he expected.

There was housework, of course, and the two roadside stands—the larger of the two had a pie oven in back and they baked and sold fresh pies. But there was Carol for that and his eldest, Brenda, and several local ladies who would get very territorial and huffy. They were German, for the most part. He knew that it would make him look like a tyrant, coldhearted because he couldn't give her some sort of meaningless make-work. But on a farm, there was really no such thing. Not if you didn't want the bank to take it all away. The only way to even make the smallest margin of profit was not to allow any waste, any deadwood or free rides or duplication. "I'm sorry, Marita," he said. "I can't do that. I don't have a job for you."

He risked looking her in the eye now, expecting she would start tearing up and there would be a lot of weeping and dramatic Latin nuttiness all around. He'd be the bad guy, the evil gringo, and have to go hide in the house. Probably his wife, Carol, would continue to scowl at him for a few days after, refer to it as "the summer you drove that poor girl off," even though even Carol would realize he didn't have any choice.

But there weren't any tears from the girl, just a flare of her nostrils. She was bold, this one. Tough. He wished she wasn't pregnant. He needed more nonflimsy people around him. She just raised her chin, slightly, like she was about to say something he wasn't going to like.

The screen door slammed behind him and he heard dirt scuffling. Startled, thinking some emergency was at hand, Von whirled to see it was just his son, Jack, laughing hard and pumping away, running straight for them. Was he actually whooping?

Jesus god, the boy was sure glad to see the pickers . . .

Jack brushed past him and practically skidded in the dust, like a runner about to slide home, cutting on the brakes in front of Marita, and then, slowly, gently, grinning, wrapped his arms around her. She threw that head of big black hair back and they were both either laughing or crying or both. Von stared as his son squeezed her very carefully, her feet lifting a few inches off the ground. It was as amazing as a magic trick. Behind them, Santi was grinning now, too, displaying his brown gums, and he stepped forward and patted Jack's arm in a small area that Marita wasn't busy squeezing and kissing. It sounded like the boy was saying *baby* over and over—as if that wasn't readily apparent to anyone with eyes and even the loosest grip on the basic concept of human reproduction.

Von, who rarely swore in front of the help, and certainly never in front of his own children, said, "What the fuck . . . ?"

THAT EVENING, while his wife continued to hustle back and forth to the little house across the yard, with dishes and armfuls of old linens, getting them "settled in," making it "nice" for "the kids," Von still was trying to wrap his head around this whole thing. First of all, he had been pretty sure, as recently as breakfast—hell, even five minutes into the migrant workers' arrival—that his only son was gay. The boy had gone on maybe three or four dates back in high school—usually unavoidable affairs, like prom and Sumac Days Cotillion—but he'd never had a girlfriend, at least any that Von had ever met. Certainly not a *girlfriend* girlfriend, the kind that hooked her fingers into his belt loops and tugged him around a shopping mall. Maybe he had down in Lansing, but who knows what goes on at college? The facts as Von knew them were the kid was twenty-two and he never talked about girls, he didn't hang any girlie posters in his room growing up, and it just seemed, whenever his great-aunt Sadie referred to the boy, fondly, as "the sensitive soul of the family," that she had pretty much nailed it on the head.

Carol, on the other hand, seemed to adjust to this news in a flash. She'd been breezing around the place humming and gathering up pillows and blankets like it was nothing more than an unexpected sleepover; Jack and a pal camping out in the treehouse.

Meanwhile, the head of the family, the goddamn patriarch, didn't have a clue. Because apparently this had all happened back in January. It was Jack's last year at Michigan State and even Von thought it might be reasonable to let the kid go have some fun during his winter break. He figured he'd earned it. Brenda, their oldest, had never done anything like that during her many years in college—road trips or Fort Lauderdale—but school came easier to her. Jack wasn't as much of a student, so it stood to reason that he might need to let off more steam or have more to celebrate.

He'd told them he was flying to Monterrey, Mexico, with a couple of friends and that they might rent a car and drive over to Cancún on the coast. At the time, Von tried not to sweat the details, because he thought, on some level, these might be gay friends and he didn't want to know about what they were up to down there with the cabana boys and the "eating the worm" and all that crap.

Christ, he remembered now, they had received a goddamn postcard, saying *"Mexico is great!"* and how much he was enjoying *"just doing nothing."* The thing was still up on their refrigerator.

It was all just a big fat lie.

It was so crazy, he had to keep repeating it to himself, just to get the order of events straight, the whole outline of it. Okay: They fell in love last summer, secretly. He snuck down there in January and decided, impulsively, to get married, because she was Catholic and her family was so goddamned important to her and if she was going to do it, she had to have every last relative there, down to the last wizened, immobile great-grandmothers and the family dogs. And then she got pregnant that week sometime and he returned and she wrote him and told him and now she was here. For good. Not just for the season. And now Jack would not be sleeping in his room downstairs but had moved across the yard with his wife—his *wife,* of all things! The two of them were out there right now in the little house, slipping into a bed together—the same bed *he'd* slept in with Carol back when they were first married.

Jesus god.

And then there was Carol and her part in this. It was only now, after a whole day of this, when it was time to go to bed and he was sitting there watching her reorganize the linen closet, that he finally put it together. She was folding their duvet and putting it away. Von thought she was being hasty, that it wasn't warm enough yet, but he didn't care about that anymore. The fact that she hadn't troubled him to stand up and help her fold the duvet—an obvious request, since he was just sitting there on the bed, doing nothing but watching—suddenly seemed like the light-stepping act of someone who felt guilty or self-conscious. The only reason she hadn't set up the little house for them ahead of time was she hadn't wanted to spill the beans. "You knew all about this," he said.

"Not *all* about it." She turned from the linen closet to frown at him. "I knew when he got back from Guatemala. He showed me the pictures."

"You mean Mexico."

"He was only in Mexico the time it takes to change planes to Guatemala. And yeah, I knew they were involved, to some degree, last summer. We didn't talk about any of it till after the wedding though. I'm just the mom. When it comes to love, I'm a neutral party. I don't promote, I don't prohibit. I just listen. And by the way, it's not my job to make you two communicate. That's something you two need to work on. This was *his* news to tell you, not mine."

Von couldn't believe what he was hearing. His own wife had kept this from him. "So you knew she was pregnant?"

She frowned. "She wasn't pregnant when they got married, Von. If that's what's bugging you."

"Right!" He knew he sounded snide, but he was beyond caring. "That's what's bugging me! My only son just eloped with some migrant picker, some wetback, and what I'm concerned about is the sanctity of the marriage bed. How'd you guess?"

She walked straight over to where he sat on the edge of the bed and stood over him. "That's the first time I've ever heard you use that word—"

He looked away.

"—and that's the last time you're going to use it." She hooked him under the chin, raising it with one sharp finger, getting his full-on attention, like a scolding mom about to dole out the time-out. "Clear?"

"Clear," he said. "I'm sorry. But I'm just not happy about this."

"You can be unhappy," she said. "Just don't be an asshole."

"That's a word I've never heard *you* use."

"Hey," she said. "New things happen all the time, Von. It's called life."

4

THIS WAS ALL ON TOP of the business of that Japanese fella, Miki. Von had known he was coming, they'd discussed it months before, but it had sort of slipped his mind, with all the preseason prep that spring, and it never really seemed a reality till one chilly day in early May, with the trees still stick-bare, when the guy pulled into the property, giddy about getting started.

The Japanese guy being underfoot was his daughter, Brenda's, doing. It was an arrangement she'd set up based on a posting in one of the agricultural alumni newsletters she received. At dinner one night last fall she had first proposed the family participate. It was some research program for a volunteer orchard to have this fancy Japanese botanist come and stay with them for the summer to study fruit blossoms and observe operations. Something to do with genetic coding and cloning or something—Von wasn't real clear. All he knew was the notion was laughable: Brenda said the guy would need to be able to make observations of and participate in the entire cherry season and all its processes, start to finish. Von had kidded his daughter pretty good as she continued to present her case on into dessert. She even got her mother on board, but Von wasn't buying it. Finally, Brenda spoke up about the ten-thousand-dollar subsidy—a card she probably should have led with. The Japanese government would actually pay them just to allow this scientist guy to loiter and ask dumb questions and collect a few blossom samples. Ten grand . . . Still, he wasn't real keen on the idea. There would probably be a lot of monkey business and headaches and nonsense. He could see it all. He imagined some Oriental following him around all day, getting in the way, bowing and scraping and saying *Very honorable–this* and *Very honorable–that*, and what would they feed the guy? His wife would make some attempt at sushi, knowing her, the way she tried to accommodate everyone. No, it probably wasn't worth the ten grand.

"They bring their own accommodations," Brenda explained. "It's this little mini lab. They sleep in it and cook in it and everything."

Von decided, after several days' rumination, that it would probably be okay, having the guy camp out.

But it was hardly camping out. He arrived on a cold day in May, grinning, in a James Bond–mobile that looked like a page out of one of those silly-ass Hammacher Schlemmer catalogues that peddle crazy crap only rich gay men with no family or responsibilities could afford. Or the Japanese government. He supposed it was a camper, of sorts, though he'd never seen anything exactly like it. Dark blue, and bulbous like a plump accessorized minivan, with gleaming built-ins to allow it to double as a lab. When Von stuck his head in and got a load of all the pop-out work surfaces and compact gadgetry that bloomed from the thing like that old movie the kids used to watch—*Chitty Chitty Bang Bang*—he thought, *Oh Christ. Half the Jap grant money's going to be blown on my electric bill . . .*

Except the guy didn't need to plug in. The thing had solar panels on the roof that ran the whole shebang.

The Jap himself was also a surprise. Von had been expecting a little fellow, especially since he was a scientist, but the guy—Miki Taki-something (it sounded like *Teriyaki*)—was tall and stocky. Not sumo fat, just big, American big—about the size of a running back. When he introduced himself, he just shook hands. No bowing.

Brenda addressed him as *Doctor Taki-whatever-it-was,* but he said, "Miki. Please." Not Mickey, like Mickey Mouse, but more like a rhyme for *squeaky.*

"Jesus god," Von said. "You're a lot bigger than—"

"Da-add." Brenda cut him off with a look like he'd said something terrible, like he'd called him *slant-eyes* or something.

"I mean, for such a little place to live in for three, four months, is all."

"My mother was a research scientist in the field of nutrient," Miki said, with no hint of a smile, as if this explained everything.

The only one smiling, really, was Brenda. Von wasn't sure he'd ever seen her looking quite like that and he had no idea what it meant.

5
———

IT WAS STILL A LITTLE COLD to be lying out—really more like yard-work weather—but Kimberly Lasco was too psyched about getting her summer started to let a few goosebumps stop her. And since it was her first weekend back in Weneshkeen, with her summer job starting in two days, it wasn't like she was dying to go hunt up some yardwork. Her dad even *told* her not to; to just relax today. So fine, she was relaxing. If there was ever any one place in the world she associated with relaxing, this little blue-edged patch of green was it.

Occasionally, she would glance up from her book in the direction she was used to glimpsing the blue of Lake Michigan and have to re-orient her view, panning from the smirking porcelain sun hanging on the side of the huge new addition that had appeared on the neighbor's house to the narrow new sliver of view her dad had made for them where those skinny, silvery trees used to be in the way. He'd said he'd "thinned it out a little" about a month before, that he wanted the place looking nice for her. It was different, but things were always different.

You live with two different parents, she figured, you can't expect the place to stay like a museum.

She barely remembered what it was like *way* before, when she lived there year-round. The divorce had come when she was only four, but she thought she remembered back when the yard rolled uninterrupted down to the lake. Back before the people from down in ritzy Birmingham, the Starkeys, bought the lakeside lot and built their giganto minimansion that made her dad's old house, she had to admit, look a little hillbilly-ish. Maybe she just thought she remembered running all the way down to the lake, in and out of those silvery trees, being chased by her dad and giggling and being scooped up by her mom, in her fur-trimmed leopard print New Wave coat and her Madonna hairdo and red fishnets. She'd seen it on an old videotape her grandparents had, but maybe she remembered it for real. Hard to say. It seemed like a totally different life, back when the three of them lived here year-round, when she wasn't this dumb summer girl from Ferndale, trying to fit in again every summer. There were a few people who remembered her and were kind enough, just being polite, probably, and she usually had no problem finding something to do, jobwise. This year, it was the fudge store again, working for Mrs. Hersha. But meanwhile, back home in Ferndale, the few good friends she had down there were all doing stuff without her, going on dates, hooking up with guys, working together at some of the same jobs . . . Having all their own inside jokes all summer that would make Kimberly feel totally left out when she saw them again in the fall. So all in all the arrangement wasn't so hot. Her parents didn't really bicker anymore, but for Kimberly, it sucked sometimes the way she now didn't really fit in either place. Sometimes it felt like she'd been put away in the basement crawlspace in the plastic bin with all the sweaters and winter clothes all summer, while everyone continued along with their lives, growing up, and she remained in deep-freeze, stuck as a little kid, reading books and selling fudge. By the first week of school last fall, three of her best friends had given guys "third" over the summer, and she'd barely done second (once—kind of—the guy's fingertips sort of grazing her chest, plus she was wearing a couple layers and a thick bra and just as it happened, she kind of breathed in too deep, feeling nervous or shocked, so it was kind of like yanking her boob away from his grasp, so did that even really count as second?). Still, she wasn't so into all that, not like her friends were, and the junk her mom was always preaching about—about being young for a while and not rushing things too soon with boys and regretting it later, how she wished she'd slowed things down herself and hadn't ended up divorced at twenty-two—made a lot of sense to Kimberly, despite its being annoying. Fine, she didn't have to act "boy-crazy," like her mom said her friends were, but she did want to have a life; be normal with people—girls or guys or *whoever* . . . Just feel like she could walk down a street somewhere and people would know her and say hello. And maybe even like her.

Not that she really wanted to hang with the local kids down at Scudder Park, slouching around on their bikes and doing nothing all summer, watching the boys build ramps for their skateboards and smoke pot. Totally dumb. She actually liked some quiet and calm and reading a good book in what breeze could still make its way to her from the obstructed lake. She'd become a great reader, thanks to summers in Weneshkeen, and she sometimes told herself that that was what she would do to compensate for not being able to learn a lot of social skills just yet. She'd develop her mind while all the other kids were developing the other, then maybe she'd get into a really good college and be all set in that department and then start learning how to interact more. Then she could have this huge group of friends and the serious boyfriend and all that good stuff, only they'd be super-smart Harvard-y types, not the lowlifes and slackers Alyssa and Chloe met working at the Target back home.

Okay, so it was a pretty lame plan and never going to happen, but what else was she supposed to do? Cry about it? It wasn't that bad a deal. There were people downstate, Fudgies, who'd pay an arm and a leg to have just one week up here and she got to stay the whole summer. Granted, she lived in a house her grandfather or great-grandfather built that looked like it needed a hound dog out front. And her dad worked on septic tanks and drove a truck that announced this fact. And she worked in a bad tourist trap with creepy old people and had to deal with the bitchy rich tourists and their bratty kids who wanted to sample every piece of fudge before even *maybe* buying anything. And the local kids acted like she didn't exist. And her dad just had lake *access* property, not lake *frontage,* which was a big diff if the neighbors built something that blocked the view you'd had for only a billion years. But still, it wasn't like she got sent to Cambodia every summer.

In the garage directly behind her, her dad was either running a compressor or sharpening some of his septic equipment. Judging by the occasional metallic shriek, it sounded like he was putting an edge on one of the bigger auger bits. In between, it was just the wobbly hum of the grinder, spinning free. It wasn't *too* distracting—by now she was starting to get used to it. Back home, she had a friend whose dad practiced the bagpipes, so she supposed it could be worse.

But then there was a new sound, in between the grindy shrieks. Someone was clearing their throat, loudly, as if in a bad high school play. She looked up to see Mr. Starkey, the neighbor, coming across the yard in a slowed sort of shuffle that seemed to be a deliberate announcement of his approach. He wore khakis and a Ralph Lauren rugby shirt and gave her an oversized wave like a birthday clown, as if to warn her that he was intruding or something. In one hand, he had a large roll of some sort of papers. A map or blueprints maybe. He helloed like someone in a Western, calling into the house and not wanting to get shot as an Indian. When he got a little closer, he apologized for interrupting her reading and asked how her winter had gone. She said fine and he said good.

"You're Kurt's daughter, right?"

"Kimberly," she said, not sure he remembered. Or if he did, he probably knew her as *Kimmy.*

"Right. You're Mark's age, I think, right?"

She said she was sixteen and he nodded. "Yeah, we called your dad last fall when we were up, right after we finished the game room. We built this addition? Thought you might want to come over and play Ping-Pong with Mark. But he said you were back home with your mother?"

"Yeah," she said. "Down in Ferndale. She has me all winter."

"Of course, now it's not really so— It's not really Ping-Pong weather and—" He looked distracted, standing over her, glancing around the yard, into the house, then finally down at her again. "Well, you're certainly getting . . ." He made a gesture lengthwise with the rolled-up papers, following the line of the lounge chair, head-to-toe. ". . . well, *long*." She could tell he'd been all set to say *tall*, but how can you tell tall when the person's not standing? It was pretty dumb. He probably said that to all teenagers, that they were getting tall. Not *Wow, you've really grown quite the rack since we last met, haven't you?* But *long*? That didn't really cut it.

But he laughed a little, shaking his head, embarrassed maybe, and so she smiled, too. At least the guy was aware he'd said something dumb. He looked away again, beyond her, into the house, asked if her dad was around. She told him to look in the garage, that he was working on his equipment (information that seemed obvious because she'd assumed, with a small sense of dread and discomfort, that he was there to ask her dad to knock off the noise), and he smiled again and told her he'd let her get back to her book.

She held it up again but still couldn't concentrate, listening as Mr. Starkey went around into the open garage door, helloing again, and she heard her dad shut off the grinder or compressor or whatever that thing was and they started to talk. She kept the book open; a prop.

It was some of the same neighborly junk again. He asked her dad how he'd been, commented on the weather and how she was growing into "quite the young lady," which made her cringe. Then she heard Mr. Starkey do that throat-clearing thing again and the whole tone seemed to change. "Listen, Kurt, I'm wondering if you know anything about the trees."

"The trees? In general? I guess I know a birch from a beech, but—"

"The trees that were cut down. The line of trees that used to run along the edge of my property."

"The poplars? Well, yeah, I thinned those out."

"You did."

"Yeah. See, I didn't have a view of the lake anymore. I used to have a little one, before you built your addition, but then there wasn't even that little view. So I thinned out that area so there's at least that little bit still. So we can see down to the lake."

"Yeah. Well. That's kind of a problem, Kurt. They weren't your trees to cut down."

"'Course they were."

"Actually, they weren't."

"Well, they might've been sort of on the line, but they were much more on my side of the line."

"They weren't really that near the line, Kurt."

"Listen." Kimberly dreaded that tone: her dad was about to get pissy. "There's stakes out there from the last time I remortgaged. Take another look."

"I've seen the stakes. That was a bank survey, yes?"

"That's *my* property," was all her dad said.

Mr. Starkey ignored this and kept going. "You're familiar with a stake survey, I imagine, working with septic systems?" There was a rattle of heavy paper, the scrolls he'd carried being unrolled. "You understand, I'm sure, that a stake survey is far more accurate than a *lot* survey, or a *bank* survey, which essentially only accounts for the approximate position of the house? Not the actual border of the property? They might leave some stakes in the ground, but it's not official and it can be pretty far off. So a bank survey's not a stake survey. There's a difference."

"I know the difference. It's just . . . Stake survey's never been necessary for most people around here. People maybe aren't as picky as they are downstate. We all just get along."

The paper rattled again. "Still, you can see on this that the line is actually a good two and a half feet on your side of the trees. The stumps, I should say now. Yes?"

Kimberly waited for her dad's answer. It wasn't quick in coming. In fact, she thought, it wasn't really an answer. After a long moment, he said, "I've always mowed all through there. For years. A good couple yards past where those trees were. You never said nothing. You ever hear of 'eminent domain'?"

"You can mow my entire lot end-to-end for all the difference it makes. See, Kurt, first of all, 'eminent domain' applies to the government. Say they want to build a railroad through here. You're thinking of 'adverse possession,' which carries all the substantive properties of Bigfoot, elves and extraterrestrial life-forms. It's something people toss around a lot, but it's pretty much wishful thinking, finding a court that'll recognize it. It requires a high and varied burden of proof. For

one thing, my property would have to have been in a state of abandonment for a very, very long time—since almost back before you could
even *operate* a lawnmower. I'm kidding—a little—but it's a very rare
ruling. It would be like getting a jail term for pot possession down in
Ann Arbor. You follow?"

Kimberly heard her dad say he wouldn't know anything about that,
that he never touched the stuff, which she knew wasn't true. She recognized the tone in his voice though—it was the one he used often with
her mom when they discussed her, shrugging things off like he didn't
know or didn't care, trying to not be agreeable; not offering a lot in the
way of helping the conversation along.

Mr. Starkey said, "You could come over and wash our windows
even, but that wouldn't make you the owner of my house, right?"

"I don't think I'll be doing that, neighbor. Washing your windows."

Mr. Starkey chuckled and it didn't sound to her like an evil chuckle,
like a villain plotting their demise. It sounded, she thought, like someone trying to keep it light; diplomatic. He said, "That's fine, Kurt. Let's
just work out a solution, okay?"

She listened for her dad to say *Of course! No problem!* to shake the
guy's hand and apologize. Any second he would do just that. Her stomach started to tighten as the moment stretched. Finally, her dad said,
"Well, it's not a big deal."

"Yeah, I'm sure it's manageable. There are few things in life that
can't be undone." There was the papery sound of Mr. Starkey rolling
up the scroll, the survey maps or whatever. "You'll need to have the
trees replaced, of course."

"What? No, I meant, it's not a big deal. I mean, look: do you honestly care? They were just poplars. Weed trees really."

Both men's voices were growing louder. "They were at least thirty,
maybe forty feet high, Kurt. Taller than the house. We're talking significant alteration of the composition of the yard, the whole house . . . So
yes, they'll need to be replaced with something of comparable height."

"Get serious!" Something metal clanged down on the workbench,
her dad making a point with his wrenches or pipes or something.
Yikes . . . She tried to sink lower in the chaise. "You know what it costs
to transplant anything over six feet?"

"You might have considered that before you fired up the chainsaw, Kurt. But at least you got some firewood out of it. You can keep that. That'll defray a little of your cost."

"I'm not going to replace any fucking poplar trees. It's not going to happen."

She couldn't hear anything for the longest time. She wondered for a second if one had done something to the other, if they'd knocked each other out. All she heard was a distant jet-ski or maybe it was a wood-chipper.

Finally, she heard Mr. Starkey say, "Sure it is, Kurt." He sounded louder, like he was halfway out the garage door.

"How?" Her dad was taunting now, calling out at the man from his workbench. "How's it going to happen?"

"Let me ask you something, Kurt." Now Mr. Starkey's voice seemed to change. He no longer sounded like a neighbor—more like a teacher. His voice got calmer, his words more deliberate. "When *your* septic tank's full or there's something wrong with the line, you handle it all yourself, right? You installed it, you maintain it . . ."

"There's nothing wrong with my system." Her dad sounded defensive. "You can look into that all you want. That's totally up to code."

"Sure, I know—"

"Or maybe you're saying now my leach field's over the line or something? 'Cause you don't know shit about—"

"No, no. I'm not saying there's *anything* wrong with it. I'm sure it's fine. I understand you're very good at what you do, Kurt. Everyone says. But I imagine, other than the wholesale cost of materials, maybe a couple extra crew hands occasionally, it essentially costs you nothing to clean out your own septic tank, replace pipes, or any of that, right?"

"What's your point, Starkey? You wanting me to do some septic work for you in exchange for the trees? 'Cause I'm not saying that I even—"

"No, I want you to replace the trees. My point is, say some guy owned a seafood store—or hell, a lobster boat—and he wanted to throw a big lobster dinner. A big bash for all his friends. That would be pretty easy for him, wouldn't it, Kurt? I mean, compared to the cost for you or me?"

"So?"

"So you do understand I'm an attorney, right? I have my own practice, my own offices downstate, my own assistants and legal aides to handle a blizzard of paperwork. I can practice anywhere in the state of Michigan. You got all that right? So you understand, it's as if I own my own law store. It costs me practically nothing to take care of this. Nothing. What would it cost you? Never mind the cost of the trees. Think about attorney fees. What would it cost you?"

"So you're threatening me, is that it?"

"I don't need to threaten you, Kurt. I'm in the right here. And eventually, you're going to have to do the right thing. I'm just trying to explain to you that if I have to *make* you do the right thing, if you don't see that I'm right and fix this on your own, unlike you, it will cost me nothing." His volume grew: he was right around the corner now, much closer, backing up, it sounded like, out of the garage. "Whereas, for you, it's going to be the equivalent of me having a big problem with my septic tank." Kimberly tried to look engaged in her book. "Which, by the way, I don't."

That was it. The conversation ended abruptly, with the hum of her dad flicking his grinder back on, and then the neighbor came around the side of the house again, stepping quickly across the patio, drawing near as he passed. He moved awkwardly, like someone relearning the use of his limbs. "Sorry," he mumbled to her this time. "Interrupting your reading and all. Sorry."

6
———

THERE WERE A LOT OF FACTORS, but the main impetus for Scott Starkey making some phone calls and getting his son the position on the river this summer was the disheartening conference he and Marcie had had with Mark's counselor at school last winter. There was nothing wrong with his behavior or grades. Academically, the kid was sharp, an A– student with great scores on the PSAT. In fact, Scott and Marcie were the ones who wanted the conference. They wanted to get a read on Mark's overall potential as a college candidate while there was still time to adjust some things, before the applications started to go out. And what they heard was not great.

Their son, Ms. Guidi claimed, was not a joiner. He participated in no extracurricular activities, no sports. He was pretty athletic, straight As in gym, but just did nothing outside the classroom. "I can't even lump him in with any one group, out in the halls," she said. "He's not a jock, he's not a computer nerd, he's not a theater freak . . ."

At first, it sounded like she was saying his son was a geeky outcast. "But he has friends, right? You're saying he doesn't even have friends?"

She smiled gently. "He doesn't seem to be *unliked* by anyone, no."

Scott's lawyerly impulse was to dismiss any and all advice or speculation made by this woman who used "unliked" rather than "disliked," but he had to admit to himself, and later to Marcie, in the car, that there was something to this; something he'd seen in his son and perhaps not wanted to see. Something missing or perhaps, hopefully, simply not yet developed. Because there were other signs that he didn't connect normally or empathize or fit in with others. Not two weeks before, a boy had fallen through the ice on Lake Saint Clair on a snow-mobile and drowned, and when the local news showed his photo and said his name, all Mark said was, "Hey, that's a friend of mine. Weird," and then changed the channel to *The Simpsons*. And the thing that still bugged Marcie was that incident back in junior high, when they busted him for vandalizing a playground. He was younger and boys will be boys, but the disturbing thing, they thought, was that he had acted alone. There was no evidence that he was covering up for his friends, unwilling to snitch. He just did it by himself.

Ms. Guidi had gone as far as to say that this lack of connection and seeming lack of passion about anything could seriously adversely affect Mark's chances with schools. "When a kid doesn't give a hang about anything? If it just *appears* that he or she doesn't? That shows up on the application. I'm telling you, they look for that, between the lines. They don't even have to interview the kid; they can tell. They know when a kid's dragging himself through life, shrugging his shoulders a lot and saying 'Whatever . . .' to everything."

She was right. Mark muttered "Whatever . . ." so much that Scott sometimes wondered if it was the way his son drew in oxygen. And he was so annoyingly lifeless about it, so devoid of any conviction, Scott almost wanted to slap off the backward baseball cap or the knit long-shoreman cap or whatever he was only halfheartedly wearing, barely pulled onto his skull as if he wasn't even sure about that.

All this was also in Scott's thoughts in dealing with the tree nonsense with Lasco. Not that he would have otherwise let that slide—of course not: he was in the right and his neighbor was absolutely wrong—but he told himself that it was probably instructive for his son to see him show some passion, act with conviction, and follow through. Yes, it would probably be a very good life lesson for Mark to watch his father pursue this matter to the full length of the law—and that would be more than enough reason not to just let it go. Like hell if he was going to raise a son who would shrug his shoulders when his property was destroyed and say "Whatever," and fail to get involved and interact with society. That simply was not an option.

7

UNTIL JUST A FEW YEARS AGO, there was an official white-on-green sign, right before you crossed the drawbridge, that announced the river's presence, declaring:

OH-JOHN-NINNY RIVER

But then, around the time the very lucrative Indian casino came to the region, along with the powerful lobbying groups that it now financed, the sign was changed to:

OH-JOHN-NINNY RIVER
(OJAANIMIZIIBII)

Originally, way back in the pre-drawbridge days, whites made a stab at recording it fairly accurately, as the *Ohjonimmizeebee* or the *Ohjohnimmyzeeby,* and, less accurately, as the *Ojohnimississibee* and the *Ohjoninnymizzy* and the *Ojohnimmy,* but soon began simplifying it on maps and in public records as the Oh-John-Ninny River.

Despite all this fiddling, the band of Ojibwe named after the river somehow managed to hang on to their name. But that is about all that hasn't changed. That and the tradition of the river pilots.

In 1901, the area's chief commodities were pig iron and pine, followed probably by lake perch. In contrast, in 2001, it was sweet cherries and fudge, followed probably by picturesque boat photos and sweatshirts that said *Weneshkeen, MI* and were sewn in Korea, embroidered in California and featured, over the breast, an algae-dripping moose the likes of which have not been seen in the Lower Peninsula probably since before the Mackinac Bridge was built, back when they would have had to swim the straits. (And even then, even probably when Teddy Roosevelt or Hemingway stomped around in area swamps, you still would have said, if you'd seen one roaming free, "God-*damn*! Is that a *moose*?!") What Weneshkeen *does*—what it *is*—is always changing; moving along like the river.

But throughout it all, always there have been the river pilots: the "pilot-boys" and the "under-boys" officially commissioned by the village to guide boats along the Oh-John. The service has become a tradition; part of the local color, though many have questioned the practical need for it. Navigational computers have changed everything, and there haven't been that many accidents in recent years, within the actual confines of the river, that couldn't be attributed in some way to alcohol consumption. It has its tricky spots, sure, but it really isn't all that treacherous or swift or anything. In fact, some say the most distinctive thing about the river is its name. Walt DeWalt, the senior river pilot, once bragged, "I'd match it mouthful to mouthful with any river in North America." And you can see that in the way the tourists gather for photos around the sign, as if they've just discovered something terribly amusing that had escaped all other visitors who came before them.

During its industrial heyday, in the latter part of the nineteenth century, one of Weneshkeen's most prominent citizens was a lumber baron named John Scudder, whose enterprises dominated these waters. Most of the town made money for him in one way or another, whether through direct labor or by rent or by custom at any of his many company stores. He was opinionated and powerful and, some say, had his battles with mental illness. The half that resented him took to calling the river the *Ninny John*. The half that feared him opted for the less inflammatory *Oh-John*. Reportedly, John Scudder himself referred to it, as close as he could manage, in the original Ojibwe, and by the time of his death, he'd taken to signing all correspondence "J. *Samuel* Scudder."

In the end, the "Oh-John" became the most common shorthand, though there are still a few old-timers alive today—sticklers and gripers—who insist on calling it the "Ninny John."

The other, more recent wisecrack commonly made about the river's name is that the new sign was put there to help separate the locals from the outsiders. If you can't pronounce the full Ojibwe version without spraining your tongue or otherwise herniating yourself, you are an outsider. But of course there are plenty of other ways to tell.

8

WHEN MARK STARKEY LEARNED from his dad that he'd been selected to be an "under-boy" that summer—an apprentice to the older river pilots, the "pilot-boys"—his reaction was less awe and more "oh." He understood it was supposed to be some sort of big-ass honor or something, a sweet deal as far as small-town summer jobs went, and the local kids hustled to lock in one of the few positions every year, getting their dads to pull some strings to get them a spot. Personally, Mark didn't really get it. Somewhere along the line, long before they'd started coming up to this town in the summer—long before he was born, even—a local status symbol had been made out of this job that was, essentially, working out in the sun all day pointing out the underwater stumps. He suspected it was like those doormen in front of hotels and fancy apartment buildings in New York, with their uniforms and rows of buttons and the epaulets, like they were in command of a goddamn battleship or something. No actual power, but prestige—in some circles, maybe, among their friends.

This was not at all how he'd hoped to spend his summer. What he wanted to do was swim and read. And go in his room and pretend to read but really be beating off. That's what summers were for, was how he saw it. And in terms of money, he didn't really need a summer job. At least not something that brought in such a small return. He had the birthday money his Gram had been giving him back before he had teeth even, that he'd put into the stock market and even with the current economy as it was, even if it was only earning him say, three percent, it was still far better than anything he could collect helping old geezers get their pleasure boats up and down the river. Granted, it wasn't an either/or situation—he'd be making money on the stocks even *with* the job—but the point was, how much walking-around money did he actually need? It wasn't like he went on a lot of dates— not in the summer, at least, stuck up in Weneshkeen with his friends downstate in Birmingham, so who would he even go to the movies with? During the school year, he'd get his weekly allowance, and as for college, which was another two years away, his parents would be paying for that, too. So why the fuck, he wanted to say to them, did he have to be a stupid pilot-boy? (Not even—an *assistant* pilot-boy. An "under-boy"—like he was going to scrape barnacles.)

When he finally asked, minus the "fuck," the answers they came up with were lame. His dad talked about "building character." His mom said she wouldn't have him "moping around the house all summer." Both of them kept coming back to the same "connecting with the community" crap, "giving back," but it was pretty clear it was just an appearances thing. Some kind of status deal for his parents, like they were blending in with the locals. Like they were legitimate, not outsiders like all the other boat people and Fudgies.

As far as Mark could tell, there were three types of outsiders you could be if you didn't happen to get born and die in Weneshkeen, like the rest of these bumfucks his dad seemed to want to fit in with. There were the "boat people," who liked to just sit on their boats in the marina, watching the village as if waiting to get the word to invade. (Except, why *would* they, he wondered, since these people already had everything. Money and looks like you'd see in a movie.) The boat people with kids hardly ever saw them because the kids had expensive bikes and rode them over every inch of the village, totally unsupervised. The grown-ups only left their boats for groceries, boat parts, booze, or maybe to purchase so-called "artwork" from the little shops—what Mark thought of as "cheesy quack-quacks": crap like his dad had in his law office back home. Stuff that told other people you were simple folks. A lot of paintings of shabby little boats they would never actually set foot on.

Then there were the "Fudgies," which were the full-on tourists—geeks who came for a weekend at a B&B or one week at a skeezy rental they saved up for for five years. They paraded around like they were at Disneyworld and planned to make every minute count, damn it. They bought a lot of sweatshirts and antiques and polished Petoskey stones and homemade fudge. Hence the name.

But there were also your basic "summer people," folks who interacted with the village a little more. These people owned a cottage or summer home and stayed for most of the warmer months. They could be either self-employed people with flexible hours or maybe distant relations or in-laws or descendants of those who built in earlier days, when everything wasn't so expensive. Or the deed was still in the name of some local, as their legal residence, so they could deduct all of their otherwise crazy-ass property taxes or some deal like that. (The state's "homestead law," his dad called it, usually in a grumbling way.) Or they could be independently wealthy or the wives and children of nine-to-five millionaires who were meanwhile stuck downstate, still slaving away all summer. Or maybe retirees with a winter home in Florida. Summer people did their own upkeep and maintenance and had a lot of projects around the house. "Puttering," his dad called it. They got their own wells running in the spring and put out their own rafts and docks. They made a big show of going in to check their rarely used mailboxes at the post office, calling people by name, signing up for library cards. Some even used the laundromat. Basically, they tried real hard to blend in and usually got their feelings hurt when they found it wasn't that easy.

Mark knew that last one was his category. Or at least his family's category. Personally, he didn't relate to any of these people—outsiders *or* yokels—so probably, you'd have to put him in his own little box. He didn't think there was any particular name for his box, but he preferred to think of it as a one-man box.

His dad, in particular, really seemed to care about this blending-in thing though it seemed like it hadn't always been that way, not when they first bought the place on Lake Michigan. It started a few summers later, around the time they winterized and started remodeling and putting on the additions. As if coming up a few more weekends after Labor Day and that one Christmas the year his dad was into snowshoeing, as if that was going to make them all of a sudden locals. So they were sometimes up here after the leaves dropped or early enough to have to buy a sack of Morton's for the driveway—big deal. They were still summer people, as far as he could tell. It wasn't like his dad had quit the firm, back home in Birmingham, where he was still a full partner, specializing in class-action law. There was a watercolor of their lake house hanging in his dad's inner office. Smack on the wall right when you walked in, ready to be gawked at with a little gallery light on top to help you be impressed. And in case you didn't get the rustic thing, the frame was made of old barn wood or something, with knots and wormholes, like evidence in an insurance investigation. The point was supposed to be *Look, I just work here. But this is not at all who I am. Deep down. In reality, I'm this authentic Up North Michigan guy and if you can't reach me for some reason, this is where I am, up at the lake, hanging out with my salt-of-the-earth fishing buddies and probably skinning a bear.*

It seemed ridiculous to Mark that with all these Opie Taylor types running around desperate for this stupid "under-boy" gig, they'd go and give it to *him,* an outsider who didn't even want the thing. How could anyone not smell a rat? Probably it was someone returning a favor to his dad, for some legal advice or for drawing up a will or helping the town council draft something. Maybe the favor came from that Mrs. Hersha lady, who owned the fudge and chocolate store and was pretty connected in town, her and her husband. They were on boards and committees and stuff. And Mark's dad had helped her a couple years back when she had to change the name of her store, back when the Hershey's company got nasty with her and sent her those cease-and-desist or whatever letters and she had to change the store from Hersha's Chocolates to T.G.I.Fudge, which was possibly the stupidest name he'd ever heard for a store, like *Thank God it's fudge and not a big turd—what a relief!* Or there were other people he'd done some law work for, too, who might have done it as a favor. It could have been anybody. Or a few different people, conniving. His dad was really busting his ass to get along with these hicks, so he probably had them all snowed into thinking he was this great guy and everything.

And though this stupid job was probably mostly meant to cement his dad's position as one of the hicks, the way his dad presented it to him, the things he said, made Mark wonder if his dad was actually buying his own B.S. Like it did honestly have something to do with the stuff Ms. Guidi, his school counselor, said about him last winter. Like his dad legitimately thought it would be good for him, as crazy as that seemed.

Finally, he just told his parents, "Fine. Whatever . . ." and left it at that.

RIGHT OFF, THE VERY FIRST DAY on the stupid job, there was way too much to keep track of. There were the three pilothouses—the outer, where the river opened into Lake Michigan, just before the long rocky point and the dilapidated lighthouse; the main pilothouse, right in the middle of the river, next to the inlet to the marina; and the inner pilot-house, where the river opened up into the inland lake, Meenigeesis (which Walt, the older of the two pilot-boys, the codger in his fifties or so, insisted on calling Lake August for some reason, just in case the whole thing wasn't confusing enough).

And none of that even began to cover the river map. The river map was the memorized route, each snag and obstruction along the way. It didn't exist on paper because the shallows and the crap under the water constantly shifted and moved around, so it had to be memorized and he would have to be able to put it down on paper, if asked. Drawing every square inch of the Oh-John-Ninny was part of the test he'd have to pass if he ever wanted to be an actual pilot, like Keith or Walt, the two sort-of bosses. Mark knew that first day on the job—even the first ten minutes on the job—that this wasn't a dream he aspired to. The goal was to get through the summer, not rise to the throne of high-exalted local hick like these assholes hopping on and off of other people's boats. He continued to hear, from Keith and Walt and from the boat owners they piloted, what a lucky kid he was to be chosen as an under-boy, and he'd nod and mumble agreement, but frankly, it sucked just exactly as much as he thought it would.

As if there weren't enough stuff they thought he should know, in between boats, while they waited in the pilothouses, Keith showed him knots. He was supposed to memorize them and be able to tie them himself, but all he heard that first day was a lot of business about the bunny going around the tree and down into the hole. They gave him a thrilling page-turner of a pamphlet called *Maritime Knots* and told him to take it home with him. There was more studying for this than there was for school. There was so much to remember, so much the guys kept repeating to him, barking at him about how important each thing was, not prioritizing at all. He wanted to yell back at them, *Hey, why don't we just agree it's* all *fucking important?* But he didn't.

There were a lot of summer people getting their boats out of the dry dock and either taking them down the river to their reserved slips in the marina or wanting to take them out for a spin—either out into the whitecaps of Michigan where they could roar and open the engines wide, or for a cruise around the other lake where they'd wave to friends opening their cottages and putting out their docks. It all seemed so brainless and *"Hey-look-at-me!"* and *"Howdy-neighbor!"*—the kind of stuff that *might* be fun if you had the water totally to yourself and didn't have to cast lines to people and say *"Hello!"* a zillion times a day. And though he knew his way around a boat, thanks to his mom's brother, who owned a sailboat and a cabin cruiser down on Lake Saint Clair, back home, he was now pretty glad, watching the summer people go through their paces, that his own dad wasn't really a boat person. Not the dorky kind like these people. They had a small boat over at the cottage, but they didn't promenade in it. They didn't take it out like it was a baby buggy you stroll with or a fancy Easter bonnet you want to show off. They just used it to actually get from one place to another, when there was a reason. It was a vehicle, not an event. His dad didn't use the boat like he was going to the prom. That was one good thing about his dad, at least.

The larger boats had to go through single-file—a situation where it seemed river pilots actually served a function. In certain spots, some of these big tubs barely scraped through and it was tricky. An extra pair of eyes from someone who knew the narrows made sense. But the rest of the time, it was clearly just a local custom: a way to tax the invading rich. The really small boats and the local good ol' boy types in good standing with Walt got a free pass, just a wave from the pilothouse. No fee, no one climbing on board for an escort.

It was clear, early that first day, why the job, despite its alleged prestige, was so poorly paid. He was redundant, not assisting with much of anything other than a few deckhand things like securing lines and radioing to the pilothouse that they were coming through, if Keith had the wheel and couldn't work the walkie-talkie. The rest of the time, he was just supposed to look at the river—just stare straight out and fix it in his mind when Keith called out the "map" to the captain—announcing each underwater obstruction like a tourist guide for things unseen.

It was hard to keep doing that, focusing, especially on such a beautiful day, with the breeze blurring the trees, girls on bikes riding along the paths of the village park, calling to each other in shrill voices that carried out along the water, and Fudgies snapping photos from the riverwalk and waving to them just because they were on a boat. It must have been these sorts of distractions that kept him from realizing, at the end of piloting a big cabin sailboat registered out of Charlevoix, that the captain was tipping them all, handing him a five.

"Kid," Keith said, and then Mark saw it. The tip wasn't surprising—most of the summer people were tipping—but he hadn't even noticed they'd reached the end of the river. Mark slipped the five into his jeans, mumbling thanks, and then they stepped off and cast loose the mooring lines and the big sailboat was free and clear, with a clang of the big brass bell, pulling away into Meenigeesis. Keith logged it in, scribbling something on the clipboard that hung by the door, recapped the tethered pen, then shoved Mark into the river.

The cold water filled his mouth and eyes and he couldn't see again till he was back on the surface, thrashing, gasping to breathe, trying to find a handhold. The river was walled here, with no natural riverbank, just the slimy pilings of the inner pilothouse, with its little wooden wharf jutting out overhead. It seemed, now, looking up into the shafting sun, that it was several stories above him.

"Starboard," Keith hollered down. "There's a ladder."

But Mark was all turned around, dog-paddling in a circle, the water still choppy from the wake of the departing sailboat. He clawed at the nearest wooden piling. It felt like he was wearing a suit of armor.

"Starboard! Jeezo! . . ."

Finally he found it, a haphazard row of wooden scraps nailed to one of the pilings, like on some kid's flimsy treehouse. He pulled himself up, fumbling and slipping. The second he reached the platform, he quickly moved into the pilothouse rather than risk standing back out on that tiny strip of dock that ran along the edge of the little shack. "Jesus," he said, "What the fuck—"

It felt like burlap, hitting him in the face. Keith had thrown him a towel. It smelled of diesel, like he'd been using it to work on an engine. "Each trip," Keith said, "you don't use your eyes, you go in the water. That's the deal. Got it?"

"Got it."

"Good. So I guess it won't happen again."

Mark went in the water three more times that day. Keith was clearly enjoying it. He told the old guy, Walt, "You ever notice how rich kids stink when you get them wet?" Mark would have argued the point about him being rich; he didn't feel that was very accurate—his family was well-off, maybe, but look around this place, look over in the marina, or just north of town, with the little airstrip and the private planes—*that* was rich. But since Keith made the cracks directly to Walt, acting like Mark wasn't even in the pilothouse, he knew it was pointless to answer back. "Me," Keith said, "I'd start wearing shorts next time, something lightweight like a normal pilot-boy, if I was going in the water so much as he is . . . Jeezo . . ."

The next day he only went in the water once. The third day he had a good day and stayed dry his whole shift.

"You're learning," Walt said. "Very good. It's all about paying attention. That's all. Keeping your eyes open, looking ahead." He actually ruffled Mark's hair. Keith looked disappointed.

The next day wasn't so good. He got shoved in twice. But overall, figuring it mathematically, Mark decided he was probably catching on.

9

2001 WAS A SUMMER OF FIRSTS for the Reverend Eugene Reecher. It was the first summer without his wife and the first summer of his retirement. He still lived in the parsonage—the little white split-level beside the First Presbyterian Church—that still faced the river, the Oh-John-Ninny, which formed the far edge of the backyard; still looked out every day at the ribbon of blue that was Lake Michigan beyond. What was different now was the free time—the long rambling days that lingered on into the night. Mary, who'd apparently been carrying cancer around in her throat for some time, secretly storing it up, blithely ignorant until the last few months, succumbed mercifully quickly, in the late fall. And soon after, he'd stepped down, after thirty-two years of service to the only congregation he'd ever known.

And now all that remained was this house that had been, for thirty-two years, temporary shelter; something they'd borrowed from the church. He'd never felt completely at home here, knowing, as most ministers know, that the house comes (and goes) with the job. But now it seemed it was the sum total of those years—all there was left—and he could not imagine leaving the house behind. Not yet.

Still, he was really starting to rattle. The house, which had always seemed meager and inadequate, now seemed overwhelming, vast and cluttered. And yet so empty. Ringingly empty, like the sanctuary on a weekday.

The place still smelled of Mary. Even after being contaminated and diluted with her medicines and the smell of death, after she was gone, her true smell, her life smell, seemed to return to the house, as if none of that—none of those ugly scents of ending—was a match for her; nothing could compete with Mary.

He'd considered potpourri, incense, scented candles, but he didn't have the heart. Nor could he throw away her clothes. Not yet. In time, but not yet. And on bad nights, nights when he played the wrong records, the Abbey Lincoln or the Chet Baker or the Mary Lou Williams, he'd wander into her closet as if he'd simply taken a wrong turn in the hallway and press his face into her blouses and inhale and then he'd call the kids.

The kids were grown and had their own lives with which to contend and he regretted calling them each time he did it, not because of their reactions or inability to help, but because he knew this wasn't the proper role for him. He was supposed to be the one giving the solace; the one taking away the pain.

His son, Ben, lived in Tucson. His daughter, Abbey, in Olympia, Washington, wasn't any closer. Ben had his work and family to keep him more than busy; Abbey had her work and her dogs and her allergies and her work and her three-days-a week analysis and more work. So he really hated reaching out to them. He knew what a bother he must be.

Ben was the one who finally spelled it out. "Dad," he said, "we really want to stay in touch with you. We do. Every day would be great. But we just don't have time for the phone." Gene noticed his son never used the word *bother,* but he had always been the more patient and polite of the children.

They sent him a computer and signed him up for Internet service. He had no idea what to do with it.

A week after it arrived, Ben called and asked how it was going and he told him he was "still figuring it out." Another week went by and Ben called again, from his cell phone, driving up to Lake Mead, and accused him of not even opening the box yet. Gene didn't appreciate the tone and besides, it was just a lucky guess.

"Dad," Ben said, "come *on.* Am I going to have to hire a tutor for you?"

Gene recalled the posture lessons he'd endured for five years as a young boy, the instructor, Mrs. Siddons, invading his home every Wednesday afternoon, with her strange liniment smell and the wooden yardstick she jammed down his shirt collar till it poked into the cheeks of his buttocks. And despite her own rigid form, her seeming steely manner, she was so easily disappointed in his lack of progress, she appeared as if she might break into tears any moment. It was unsettling. So a tutor did not sound like a good idea at all. He hoped Ben was kidding.

"They have them," Ben said. "They come to your house, set up your desktop, teach you the basics. They have them here, I mean. I don't know about back there. I suppose I could call around, maybe find someone to drive down from Traverse or up from Grand Rapids." He sighed heavily, as if they were talking now about moving a piano.

"Don't do that," Gene said. "Really. I'll figure it out."

"Like hell you will." Ben had to realize he would disapprove of such talk. Of course, it was that "P.K." syndrome popping out, even now, late in life. Even in his forties, Ben could occasionally behave like a rebellious "preacher's kid." He said, "We got the thing, frankly, to keep you busy. I can't imagine staring at the unopened box will keep you busy very much longer."

Gene pointed out that he'd managed to figure out the microwave all on his own.

"Great," Ben said, with that dry humor he got from his late mother. "They're exactly the same. Listen, as soon as you figure it out, e-mail me a frozen pizza, okay?" The line was cutting in and out. He said, "Damn! I'm in a canyon, Dad . . ." and then he was gone.

HE MADE UP LITTLE NOTICES, announcing that he was seeking to hire a tutor to show him how to work the computer. He wrote each one out by hand with an old marker he'd found in the laundry room and he thought, after about the third copy, how much easier making the notices might be if he knew how to use the computer.

But if he could already do that, he wouldn't need the notices—an amusing circle of irony that, in the past, might have inspired an idea for a sermon. Perhaps as a metaphor for material acquisition; he could even push the acceptable boundaries of the more conservative members of the congregation by slipping in a quote from Thoreau . . .

But if he were still writing sermons, he could have typed these notices. He'd typed all his sermons on an old Olivetti over in the minister's office in back of the church—a well-worn short walk through his backyard. He still had the key—they wouldn't mind. The problem was, perhaps as recently as a week before, when he went over there to type a letter to a woman Mary had grown up with down in New Buffalo— to thank her, finally, for her long and lovely letter of condolence, maybe really getting into the details of Mary's final days and his life now and updating her about the kids and all—he found the trustees or somebody had decided to replace the typewriter with another one of these shiny boxes like the one Ben had dumped on him. They were getting things ready for his permanent replacement, whoever he might be. Or *she,* he had to keep reminding himself. (Yes, possibly *she*! Very good! That would be a progressive step for ol' First Pres!)

After ten copies, his hand ached and he had to call it quits. He considered, as a sort of a joke, continuing to write a few more with the idea that the rapidly deteriorating handwriting would become such a psychotic scrawl, anyone even glancing at it would take pity on him for not being able to use the computer, thinking him perhaps a mentally retarded adult, and they'd simply have to help him.

He posted the signs in the obvious places: the library, the post office, the Spartan store, the Helpee-Selfee laundromat, the real estate office— where people stopped to look in the window at the photos of cottages for sale—and above that, B's Wax, the musty used-record shop.

The B's Wax clientele wasn't exactly right—too analog to be computer whizzes—but he tacked one up there anyway as an excuse to stop and paw through the rare jazz records. Playing on the store's stereo system was something by Abbey Lincoln—he was pretty sure it was off *Abbey Is Blue,* on Riverside Records, 1959, with Philly Joe Jones, Stanley Turrentine and Max Roach, of course, Abbey Lincoln's husband at the time—and the names of the numbers ran together in his head— "Lonely House," "Let Up," "Come Sunday," "Lost in the Stars, "Long as You're Living" . . . one other he couldn't remember . . . The sultry sounds, familiar like something deep in his bones, pried out a smile

and thoughts of Mary and how they'd listen to these records Sunday
nights when they were both very young and surrounded by clerical
friends who thought the two of them, comparatively, extremely wild—
borderline beatniks, possibly socialists.

The owner and manager, Bob Beirnbaum, squeezed up behind him
and read Gene's handwritten notice over his shoulder, breathing heavily through his nose. "Great," he grumbled. "You'll be another customer lost to eBay . . ."

Bob liked to refer to himself by his teenage nickname, which was
Mr. B. He was in his late fifties, sadly overweight. He lived alone in a
small room in back, and for years Gene found it puzzling how a little
shop like this, in a town like Weneshkeen—where most people would
tell you Ben Webster was "that dictionary guy" and Slim Gaillard made
silent Westerns—would even be profitable enough to cover the rent.
The selections seemed too esoteric for the taste of most of Weneshkeen's year-round residents and the technology too archaic for the summer people, who might have the taste and the money but probably found
even CDs quaint. Then he learned Bob owned the whole building. The
little Queen Anne with gingerbread railings was originally a private
home—Bob's parents' private home, which he'd inherited. What was
now the record shop had been Bob's childhood bedroom. Basically,
he'd just put stickers on his vast record collection and hung out a sign
down on the porch. The thing that paid for everything was the office
space he rented to the real estate agents downstairs.

When Gene turned to leave, unsure where Bob had slunk away to,
he just called out a simple goodbye and got, in response, a waggling
hand, emerging from somewhere over in the Peruvian section and a
growled, "Yeah, I'll pray for your soul, Preacher Reecher . . ."

The ribbing with the name was pretty common, but the part about
his soul was new and at first Gene found it a little puzzling—and off-
putting: wasn't Bob being a little flippant and crass with a man he
knew was still in mourning? It was only when he reached the bottom of
the stairs, and the real estate office, that he got it. He saw the new broker fellow—Barry or Bradley or something—through the hallway window, working at his computer. Ah, he thought. Bob was just making a
crack about his getting a *computer,* intimating he was about to step

into some dark, soulless netherworld. He wasn't making light of his grief. It made him smile again—too late for Bob to enjoy his reaction—but Gene enjoyed the jest, nonetheless.

Then he saw, seated across from the broker's desk, one of his flock—*former* flock—John Schank, head of the New Building Committee, and he decided to keep moving. He considered himself a friend to all in Weneshkeen, but some conversations were best avoided.

Next, he made stops at all the bulletin boards he could find along the block-long stretch of the more touristy shops, directly across from the marina—the T-shirt place, the candy-and-fudge shop, the Petoskey stone place, the ice-cream-and-fudge shop, the coffee shop and the just plain fudge shop, T.G.I.Fudge. Leaving T.G.I.Fudge, he heard someone behind him, calling after him: "Sir?"

His first thought was that he'd left his roll of masking tape behind. He turned to see it was the same little black-haired counter girl in the smudged apron who had just granted him permission, moments before, to hang up his sign. But she'd removed it. It was there in her hand. He wondered if she was going to ask him to take it back. Maybe there was something wrong with it.

But no, she was holding out her hand for him to shake. "Kimberly."

"Kimberly," he repeated, shaking it, still unsure what was going on.

"Uh . . . okay, first? I used to go to your church?"

"I'm sorry." He couldn't place the face. "You'll forgive me, but the last few months . . ."

"This was years and years ago. When I was little."

He tried not to smile at this. She was still little—a kid, as far as he could tell. Somewhere in her teens.

"It was my mom who took us. But they got divorced when I was four. I'm only up here in the summers now. With my dad." She told him her father's name and he thought he recognized it. One of the local tradesmen. A plumber or a water heater man, perhaps. "Anyways, I could help you with your computer," she said. "No problem. I'm not a gearhead or anything, but I'm sure I know enough."

The term *gearhead* caused him to look at her head and he could see now that her hair was dyed black. Perhaps it was dark to begin with but certainly not that dark. She wore it chopped in a sort of mid-length bob. He supposed they weren't calling it a *bob* these days, but he would be hard-pressed to produce the proper current terminology.

He wasn't clear at all what a gearhead might be, but he was fairly certain he probably didn't require one of those. She wasn't at all what he imagined in a tutor, but he couldn't think of any reason to object, so he asked her when she was available.

"Well," she said, rolling her shoulder and head back toward the fudge shop, "I've got *this,*" and it sounded like an admission, something she wasn't too proud of but felt compelled to fess up to. "But it's real flexible. Half-days, three days a week. It rotates, we trade shifts . . . so whenever."

Before he could think of any further objections, they were arriving at an appointment for the following day and shaking hands. When he remembered he hadn't given her the address yet, she shrugged and said of course she knew where it was; that it was just like going to church.

"Sort of," he told her. "One door over. Almost church."

When he got home, he smelled something like confectioner's sugar—maybe almond extract, mint—and realized it was his hand.

10

CREEPY was how it felt now, lying out in her dad's yard. She tried to ignore everything that was going on, neighbor-wise, and just do it, keep her face in her book, not gaze out too long toward the water, through that disputed section where her dad had cut down the trees, but it was just so unnatural and awkward and hard to concentrate. She felt like she was under a microscope now or onstage and who could concentrate on reading, really, if they were onstage?

She'd been over the same paragraph about following the landlord across the moors three times now and had no idea what she was reading. She kept thinking Mr. Starkey was up in his bedroom, watching. (Not in a lechy way, but still.) Frowning, being all feudy, like they were the Hatfields and the McCoys. Never mind that it had affected what she wore outside now. The days were getting warmer already and yet she had on sweatpants and a sweatshirt, since she was sure they were scrutinizing her now, judging everything she wore, and if she wore what she wanted today, maybe not a bathing suit but at least some shorts and a belly shirt, maybe a sports bra, they'd be up in that house thinking, *See? The guy's a tree killer and his daughter's a dirty ho*. And the son, Mark—he was her age so he'd be even harsher, saying all who-knows-what about her. Thinking it, at least.

Back home—at her mom's house, that is (both places were "home"; they'd hammered that idea into her years ago)—she and her mom got along just fine with their neighbors. They exchanged gifts, even, at Christmastime. The Hemmiters were cool: they had her call them by their first names, even though they were way old, like fifty or so. Yes, she would have no problem lying out in her yard at her mom's. Theoretically. Except, of course, that she *wouldn't* lie out in her yard—not really—because it would be the school year and too cold to do such a thing. And besides, without water nearby, it didn't feel natural. It felt sort of vain and full of yourself, like it's so obvious you're working on your tan. It's not like you're just enjoying the water and the view and the sun. Not if your view is of a bottled water plant, a convenience store and a dirty-looking park where guys went to yell at their girlfriends, like it was at her mom's house.

This, she decided, was getting a little like her mom's house. In that there was no way she was going to feel normal about lying out in the backyard. And it was really starting to suck.

She closed the book and heaved up out of the lounge chair with a sigh. No more suntanning out in the battlefield zone.

SHE WASN'T SURE WHEN the sign first appeared, but the first time she noticed it was coming home from work on a day when her dad picked her up at the fudge store. They were just about to pull into the driveway when her dad hit the brakes. She followed his stare, right at the split between the two driveways, where the Starkeys' paved wraparound bookended the mailboxes with her dad's dirt-and-gravel drive. It was a large painted wooden sign, hanging by chains from its own post and crossbeam, not unlike something you'd see in front of a restaurant. A seafood restaurant, specifically, because the whole thing was cut in the shape of some sort of blue grinning fish, wearing a red beret and horn-rimmed glasses, standing on its tailfins, beaming and pointing with one flipper to a white oval with their name in it in red letters: The STARKEYS.

"Look at that." Her dad sounded horrified. "That's gotta be a huge copyright infringement, don't you think? Wouldn't the tuna people like to know about this?"

"What tuna people?" she said. What was he talking about? Wasn't tuna an ocean fish? Obviously, it was supposed to be a perch or a lake trout, though it didn't look much like either one. But she didn't bring up all this because she wanted him to keep going, to put the truck in gear and get out of there before Mark Starkey wandered out to get the mail or something and saw them sitting there, gawking at their sign. So all she said was, "I don't get it," and gave it a shrug and left it at that.

Her dad seemed pissed at her now. "*Charlie* the Tuna? 'Sorry, Charlie'? Come on, Kimmy. Don't you watch TV?"

As usual, he didn't know what he was talking about. "This isn't from TV, Dad. Trust me. It's just a dumb fish or something. Relax."

Grumbling, her dad sprayed gravel pulling into their drive.

It made her feel so weird, his being like this and her not knowing *who* the jerk was; if he was crazy or if the neighbors were really out of line and dissing him. She wished she could just ask someone, tell one of her friends back home what was going on. She thought about calling her mom but she tried to never do that—talk smack about one to the other, get them all up in each other's faces. The summer had barely started and she could tell it was going to be a long one if things kept up like this. Because come on—it was just a stupid sign with their name on it and a big blue fish. How was that any big whoop?

She was dying to get out of the truck. The whole thing was so weird.

11

THE LAST MAN-MADE THING you would pass, heading out of the mouth of the Oh-John-Ninny into the open blue of Lake Michigan, would be not the outer pilothouse, where you dropped off the pilot-boy, but the lighthouse out at the end of the long rocky spit known as Sumac Point.

If you weren't from Weneshkeen and were wondering if the light still functioned, there would be no quick answer. Operation of the light itself was discontinued in the late forties when the Army Corps of Engineers chose Sumac Point as the subject of a study in "alternative and experimental Marine Hazard Warning Systems"—all of which meant they made the sucker glow. The entire tower was painted with a radium paint, the same used, in the war, for wristwatch hands, and sure enough, the lighthouse could be seen for miles, no power source required. The lighthouse keeper was given early retirement and a small housing subsidy, since he'd devoted himself to a real-estate-free life, and moved to the desert outside Albuquerque, New Mexico, where he had no knowledge of any of the terrain or wildlife and, it's said, less than a year after moving there, got bit by something and died. Soon after his demise, the lighthouse followed suit. It seemed to be cracking and crumbling—significantly enough that it was soon deemed unsafe to go up inside it. Which was fine—it glowed anyway, so there was no need, really, to climb the circular stairs inside the tower and change the bulbs or anything. It was roped off and entry was restricted, but it was not officially condemned, because essentially, while it was still mostly standing, it more or less did the job. It wouldn't stand forever, that was clear—big winds would knock pebble-sized pieces loose and, on moonless nights, you could make out a faint glow around the base, which was powder-fine dust falling and collecting on the rocks below.

The Army Corps of Engineers said, well, it was old to begin with and it just coincidental that it started falling apart right after they painted it. But everyone felt it was rather telling that the Corps of Engineers had not gone on to paint any more lighthouses with the stuff.

Obviously, the radium in the paint was causing hairline stress to the infrastructure, the rebars in the masonry as well as the masonry itself. And if that was the case, what was it doing—a lot of local people still wanted to know—to the lake and the town and to them? The government said, officially, it was harmless, and because it was way out there on the point and since Weneshkeen hadn't become some sort of Love Canal with outrageous medical statistics, there was probably no need, they figured, to go enlisting the aid of some Erin Brockovich type to get to the bottom of it. Besides, most people in Weneshkeen felt a certain sense of civic pride in the dilapidated lighthouse, because, hey—this was the only glow-in-the-dark lighthouse in the world.

It was also the first thing a few people pointed to as a possible explanation for the strange lights seen, by even fewer people, in the skies the summer of 2001. Though most folks dismissed this as "crazy talk, through and through," they were never explicit about which part was the crazy talk.

12

ABOUT A WEEK into his new job, Mark was working under Keith, the greasy, wiry younger one, when they came aboard a rather large pleasure yacht, moving down the river out of the dry docks to the marina. It was *The Courtney,* owned and captained by Mr. Dick Banes of Chicago. He was some big important wheeler-dealer, Mark knew—either in the stock market or maybe it was advertising—and he was so good at it, he was able to spend most of the summer up in Weneshkeen. Kind of like his own dad, Mark supposed, but on a much bigger scale. And he thought how weird that was, to be able to make yourself so indispensable that people would find a way to work around the fact that you weren't always there. It seemed like a contradiction, or at the least, a really bad way to do business, and sometimes he wondered what it would be like up here in the summer if the only people who came to Weneshkeen were underachievers and losers and people who'd declared bankruptcy.

Mr. Banes had the wife and daughter with him, and they looked like something out of a catalogue for the kind of sweaters Mark would never wear: blond and brown, all in white. Mark recognized them on sight, of course, though he'd never stood this close before and had certainly never spoken to them. It was pretty nerve-racking. Everyone knew of the Banes family.

They were summer people, like his family, and yet not at all like his family. Not by several decimal points. If it was true what Keith claimed, that rich kids stunk when they got wet, then these people would reek halfway back to Chicago. Theirs was the biggest boat in the marina, where they also stored a fleet of bicycles, a golf cart and an SUV, and they owned a condo overlooking the slip for whenever living on the boat felt too much like roughing it. The dad commuted back and forth to Chicago or stayed on the boat a lot or took it out for cruises into Lake Michigan and so wasn't as visible in town, but the daughter and mom made themselves regular summer fixtures. The girl, Courtney, had been the best-looking girl in the Sumac Days Court just about every single year she was in it, including when she was probably only four or five and crowned the Little Darling Junior Miss Sumac Days, the age class where they have to run an elastic chin strap under the tiara to keep it on and the kids usually start bawling and have to be pulled from the float before the end of the parade.

Keith was unusually polite and attentive, standing by as Mr. Banes remained at the helm. But he had Mark hopping around like a monkey—at one point, where a new snag had appeared since the last big storm, actually lying on the foredeck, hanging half over the side and reaching out to keep the upper branches from scratching the side of the boat. They hadn't bothered doing that for anyone else. Then again, no one else's boat was quite that tight a squeeze.

The wife was waving to people she seemed to know along the river-walk, but otherwise uninvolved, and the daughter looked bored and surly and Mr. Banes kept pulling her over to him and hooking his arm around her tight as he steered the boat, as if this might keep her entertained, being mashed up against him. It seemed to Mark the kind of thing a dad would do when his kid was young—a thing they used to like but had grown out of and the dad either hadn't wised up or didn't know what else to do, so just kept doing it.

When they drew up to the pilothouse to disembark, Mr. Banes shook both their hands with a hardy grip, and Mark felt the money in his palm and then Courtney, still looking off somewhere disinterestedly, squeezed past him, heading aft, mumbling something (*"Nice job,"* maybe?) and he felt something soft—the peach fuzz of her forearm?—brush against his upraised arm as he tried to minimize his presence so she could squeeze past. She wasn't even looking him in the eye, but he knew she had just handed him something. He turned to the ladder, afraid to examine what was in his palm, but it felt a lot like the feeling in the other hand, the one clutching the paper money her dad had just tipped him. Could she have tipped him, too?

After shoving the contents of both hands into his shorts pockets, he climbed, following Keith up, and as soon as Mr. Banes pulled away, rumbling, with an elephantine blast of the horn and the whole river snaking in its wake, Mark slipped into the pilothouse while Keith lingered out on the platform, grabbing a smoke, and snuck a peek, cupping the little scrap of paper close to his side and peering down to read it just in case Walt looked up from his newspaper or Keith barged in and caught him at it. The note said:

NICE ASS! ☺

He read it several times, as if it weren't in English, before putting it away. Maybe it was a crack about the shorts. They'd *said* to wear shorts, but he didn't own any new ones this summer—he'd *told* his mom he needed new shorts, that the old ones were too small, but she never got around to taking him shopping before they left Birmingham. This was her fault: she'd ignored his warnings that he'd grown out of them and now the hottest girl in town was making fun of his gay-ass too-tight shorts.

Keith reentered, coiling a mooring line, grinning through the blue haze that still trailed in his wake. "Miss Sumac Days gave you her phone number, didn't she?"

"No," he said, knowing now he must have seen her do it. "Cut it out."

"You forget you're talking to a guy keeps his eyes peeled for a living."

"Okay, she gave me a note, but it doesn't say anything."

"You mean it's blank?" He stopped coiling the line, looking genuinely confused, then frowned, as if let down. "Maybe it's just litter and she didn't want to be a litterbug. She was handing you her trash. That it?"

"She wasn't handing me her trash."

"Everyone's a servant to those people."

"Okay," Mark said. "I'll show you, but . . ." He pulled out the note and held it out between both hands, keeping a tight grip on it. Keith squinted, reaching for it. Mark backed away, but there wasn't much room to go anywhere. "Just read it," Mark pleaded. "Don't take it."

Keith stepped a little closer. He seemed to be taking his time for such a short message. "Jeezo," he said and he was strangely quiet, for him. "This is her phone number and *then* some . . ."

"Really? But she didn't give me any information or—"

"What kind of information? You don't need her phone number. You know who she is, where she stays."

A growl came from Walt. "What do you need, kid—a bloodhound? A map of the county?" Now he was piling on, too. "Shit, that boat of theirs can be seen from space."

Keith cackled, pointing at the pocket where Mark had stuffed the amazing note. "I'm telling you, the girl's already asked you out. At the *least,* she's asked you out on a date. At the very *least.* I tell you, kid, no girl ever wrote 'Nice ass' to me or to anyone when I was your age and I've only got like ten years on you. Jeezo . . ." He and Walt just kept chuckling, shaking their heads, and it struck Mark as odd seeing them react to anything as if it were exceptional.

Finally, Keith said, "Listen, I want to point out—I get some credit here for getting you to put on some shorts, right?"

13

THERE WAS ANOTHER WAY, Roger Drinkwater knew, to make himself more visible to the enemy during his early morning swim on Meenigeesis—an option that would spare him the indignity of the bathing cap.

Besides, the bathing cap had also proven ineffectual even for purposes of sabotage, having managed to disable the jet-ski for only a day—though he sure did enjoy the entertainment for the better part of an afternoon, watching from his porch through field glasses, his feet up on the rail and working his way through a whole pie from vonBushberger's. It was preseason, made from frozen cherries, but still damn good—a treat (which is what he felt the occasion called for as a pack of summer people stood around, knee-deep in the lake, trying to puzzle out why the thing wouldn't go, debating and theorizing, as if they were actually the kind of men who knew anything about anything other than which button to push to start the rider mower). But then the new sheriff stopped by and then, finally, a truck from the marina in town. Probably they were the ones who found the bathing cap.

In terms of being seen, he now had a better idea: warpaint. Much better than a stupid bathing cap.

Natural paints were easy enough to make—sumac for red, goldenrod for yellow, pokeweed berries for a midnight blue. But he decided that for the lake, in the hours he went out, white would be best. Crushed limestone, the standard white, was something he didn't have, until he borrowed a handful from the pristine driveway at the new showplace a few houses down and crushed it himself, between two cast-iron stove lids and the wheel of his truck, and then added water for a milky paste. The next step called for adding deer grease, which he had but decided, Come on—if it was going on his face, why not just substitute Vaseline? It would work about the same and tradition was no reason he had to smell like entrails. When he smeared it all on, it felt like the black camo grease they had worn on operations in Nam.

It was overcast the first morning he tried the warpaint, the sky a wintery gray, with actual wisps of fog rolling low across the flat water. Perfect for spooking kids, but not so perfect for kids being out on the lake. But sure enough, midpoint in his return lap, he heard a jet-ski start up—he judged this one as coming from over toward the big rental that was supposedly advertised in *The New Yorker*. Roger continued on underwater, nearing his own dock, and calculated that the kid was about fifty meters off and closing, about to loop across his path. It was shallow now, so he stood, in one solid motion, turning to glare, zombie-eyed, at the kid. Sure, he thought. *Now* you can see me, goddamn it. Startled, the kid made a sudden jagged correction and pitched back off the jet-ski. Roger watched as the boy floundered and yelped, the water clearly too chilly for this Fudgie. Finally, he climbed back on the bench seat of the jet-ski and sat there staring, his motor idling. Roger raised both hands, slowly, and closed his eyes, as if reciting some incantation. Peeking through slit lids, he saw the kid was shivering, mouth open, his eyes round as skipping stones, as if he was about to be flayed and dressed out like a buck. Roger gritted his teeth, clamped his jaw, kept his eyes squinted shut, trying to give the impression that he was concentrating on his hex, his voodoo spell, when actually he was just trying to keep from laughing.

"*Nimaanaadendam gaa zhi binaadkamgiziik . . .*" he chanted, in deep, deadman tones.

There was a whiny roar and the kid was gone. Roger swam around to the other side of the dock rather than wading through that area where the kid had just been. He was pretty sure he would be swimming through urine.

HE OWNED A DEPTH MAP OF THE LAKE, issued by the DNR in 1978, showing each indentation and point in the shoreline, and, in concentric organic sworls, the varying bottom of Meenigeesis. It had been created mostly for fishermen, but Meenigeesis was so cold and so deep, you hardly ever saw fish except at the far edges of the summer, early in May, late in September. Roger used the map for diving and exploring, and kept it pinned to a corkboard wall squeezed in between the door and the fireplace. Over the years, he had less need to refer to it and it had become more decoration than reference material.

But now it seemed like a good way to keep track of things. He moved some of the firewood aside so he could stand closer to the map and really see what was what. He got a work light from the shed and clamped it on the mantel so that it shone back at the wall, illuminating what he was now considering his war map.

With the colored Sharpies he used for swim meets, he drew in the cottages. He drew in the docks and rafts, occasionally stepping out through his front door to squint out at the lake, to check one or two against his memory.

With a fine-point pen, he further identified the homes—some he knew by name ("The Petersons," "Old Willoughby place") and some by inclination ("Big Fat Guy Who Screams At His Kids," "Bad Music," "Water-skiers," "*New Yorker* readers") and some he just assigned nicknames ("His & Hers," "The Freckled Family," "The Fussbudgets").

Then he fished out a box of colored pushpins he kept in a kitchen drawer and began placing them around the map. These would be the jet-skis. The targets.

He stood back and surveyed his battle plan. A lot of work lay ahead.

14

SUMAC DAYS was originally held closer to when the sumac is "on fire," as they say, or in bloom, which is closer to the autumn. But after Labor Day, with the disappearance of the Fudgies, the village council soon discovered the event wouldn't break even unless they moved it earlier in the year. Gradually, Sumac Days had crept back and back until now it was scheduled for the last week of August. Nobody actually enjoyed Sumac Days, but it was a tradition.

There would be the booths selling sumac lemonade and a small midway and the crowning of Miss Sumac Days, a competition that had engendered so many hurt feelings among the small handful of passably good-looking local girls—it almost always went to an outsider, some summer girl who didn't even live there—that now the court had expanded to include not only runners-up but also various divisions and subcategories—Miss Teen Sumac Days, Miss Preteen Sumac Days, Little Miss Sumac Days—so that essentially everyone who entered would at least place.

The whole court would ride in the parade, led by someone playing Chief Joseph One-Song. The few members of the Ojaanimiziibii band of Ojibwe who were still around generally ignored this event, so the role of Chief Joseph usually went to the next best thing, one of the Hispanic migrant pickers. The village council would slip him five bucks and a case of beer and he generally had a good time, whooping like a TV brave in buckskins and grinning back at his friends who lined up to hoot. Usually, the guy couldn't even speak English, let alone Ojibwe.

For an event billed as "a celebration of the unique history and identity of Weneshkeen," the thing had become an extravaganza of inaccuracies, lies and concessions.

For one thing, there was the whole issue of the sumac lemonade. Staghorn sumac, the variety whose tannic acids are marginally consumable, doesn't grow in vast quantities anywhere, and the amount available around Weneshkeen, even in season, in the fall, was diminishing. Inland, construction was crowding out the plant, and even out on Sumac Point, it now barely grew. Some said that maybe the experimental paint the Corps of Engineers slapped on the lighthouse back in the late forties had irradiated the plants. Some said it never should have been able to grow there anyway, so close to the water. Some said they didn't give a rat's ass. Because, fortunately, sumac had become a fairly minor component to the festival. After all, it wasn't as if they were trying to promote the stuff. It wasn't a crop or a livelihood. It was just a thing they did and few remembered why.

Those who cared to keep track of local lore would tell you that this titular beverage was originally meant to reference the story of Weneshkeen's "first visitor," Mulopulos: the small degree of succor the natives seemed willing to give the lost Greek was gourd cups of a strange reddish drink, and he reported that they kept repeating what sounded to him like "zu mach." (He considered this a crude approximation of Low German—"to make"—and theorized it was a diuretic. It certainly was bitter enough.)

But the idea wasn't really that Weneshkeen was so all-fired in love with sumac. And unlike with the Cherry Festival up in Traverse City, which often falls just before the crop comes in (causing imported sweet cherries to be rushed in from Washington State and South America), there is no commercial sumac industry and so, when there was no su-mac in bloom at the time of Sumac Days—which was becoming more and more the case each year—the ladies substituted regular lemonade with red food coloring and a few mashed raspberries, to get the pips floating around. It was actually a huge improvement on the real thing and no one complained much about the switch. When anyone first tried *true* sumac "lemonade"—the same steeped concoction that was served to Mulopulos—inevitably they stalled. They hesitated before sipping and double-checked: "Sumac? That's poisonous, right?" They would need reassuring, and then, after trying it, really need reassuring. Many contended that it didn't actually taste good, it just *seemed* tasty compared to, say, poison.

15

AT THE END OF THE RIVERWALK, on a driftwood log down on the beach, on the other side of the beginning of Sumac Point, they watched the breakers roll in on Lake Michigan. Mark still couldn't believe he was there with Courtney Banes. On a date—or sort of. He'd screwed up his nerve and called the local listing for Banes and when she finally said, after what felt like endless rambling and stumbling on his part, "Oh, right. Sure. Got it . . . ," recognizing him, she'd taken charge and done all the work and told him to meet her on the riverwalk the next night and so there he was now, actually sitting on a log with her.

Courtney Banes was actually talking to him—alone, giving him a rundown of the summer she had ahead of her—and though it sounded like it was all an ordeal to her, to Mark it sounded like the life of someone he watched on TV, not someone right there that he could reach out and touch.

She talked about being in the Sumac Days Court again this year and sighed heavily at the prospect. He'd never been involved with it in any way, nor had he cared to, but he never would have guessed being a beauty queen was such a burden. Maybe it was the part where she had to deal with so many other people—he could see that being a pain in the ass.

On top of that, during the school year, she did what she called "catalogue work" back home in Chicago. He wasn't sure what that was but she said it was boring and paid "crap." But the "bra stuff," she had to admit, was kind of fun—the idea that it was regional and kids at her school might see it in the Sunday supplement and look twice, wondering if it was really her there, smiling back at them with her top off.

She told him her uncle was Matt Banes, and said it like he was supposed to know who that was. He didn't. She explained that he was this artist guy, that his paintings were "super-hot" right now. "He has the same agent as LeRoy Neiman. You know LeRoy Neiman, right?"

"Sure," Mark said. "I mean, I know the name." Though he thought that was a clothing designer or something.

"Uncle Matt's totally different, though," she said. And when she described his process, it didn't really sound like a true painting. What her uncle did was shoot photographs of all-nude models, then painted the backdrops and skimpy clothes on them. "Maybe a cowboy hat or a captain's cap, a towel, stuff like that. They're like old-style calendar pinups," she said. "Only in reverse—he makes more out of less, is how he puts it: 'pin*downs*,' Uncle Matt calls them. And they're huge—this large-format camera. He wants me to pose for some, only he thinks we should wait another year."

"Because you're too young?"

She frowned at this. "Hardly. I'm seventeen. That's not so young. How old are you?" She didn't ask it casually. She asked it like it mattered.

He told her he was *almost* seventeen, though the truth was he'd turned sixteen only two months before. It was as much of a lie as he thought he could get away with, considering how jumpy she made him. Which was weird—normally he couldn't care less.

She got up to walk again and he followed, trying not to stare at her legs, already brown though the season was just starting, or her tight white tennis skirt, the way it flipped and shifted, or the way her posture, her slight swayback, made the small globes of her ass appear like some sort of special fruit you only got for a very short season.

"Not 'cause of my age," she said, "'cause of my boobs." She spun around and kept walking backward for a moment, facing him, tugging on the white shawl she wore draped over her shoulders, and the motion, as if on cue, caused her already proud posture to improve still further and display the topic at hand. "Uncle Matt thinks they might be a little bigger in a year. He says they're perky and nice but they're probably going to be just right in another year."

Mark thought, *And then he'll paint something over them. I don't understand.* He said only, "I see. That makes sense." He tried to imagine this sort of conversation going on in his own family and just couldn't—maybe an aunt sizing up his junk in a bathing suit, saying, *Yeah, give it another year and you'll be really packing some meat down there . . .*

And now he had a thought he couldn't get out of his head: she might take her clothes off and let her uncle take pictures and then there would be a record of it, maybe hanging in galleries in Chicago or Europe somewhere or all over the Internet. Maybe they'd appear in one of those big hernia-giving coffee-table books his mom liked to clutter up the house with. And he wondered if he'd ever have a chance to see the final product. Even if this evening turned out to be a bust and not really a date and she never spoke to him again, there was still a chance he might be able to see her someday without any clothes on. Or at least, without any real clothes on. Just painted clothes.

He had to be careful now, stepping along the water's edge. He felt like a real spaz all of a sudden, like he might trip and fall any second.

And as much as he wanted this to be an actual date they were having, to be totally honest, it was really feeling more like a job interview. True, the only real job interview he'd ever had had been meeting with

Keith and Walt before they approved his apprenticeship on the river this summer. But that was just a formality and he hadn't exactly been trying to win them over, not being all that psyched for the job to begin with. But even with only that limited experience he could recognize that that's what this felt like. He was just one of many candidates eager to be awarded the position. And if he didn't do some of the talking soon, he'd be out of the running. She'd think he was either retarded or gay or boring and move on to the next applicant.

So he sat back down on the log and started in about his new job with the pilot-boys and she sat down with him but didn't let him go on for long. "Please," she said. "I don't need to hear about all that."

"I'm sorry?"

"The Brits have a great expression I picked up in London last fall. They say, 'Less of that.'" She paused as if waiting for him to get it. He didn't. She sighed and continued. "I know all about channels and boats, okay? I've been through the Panama Canal, for God's sake. The whole thing bores me to tears. Literally. Just a big yawn."

She reached over and her hand was on his cheek. Not long, not lingering. More like she was wiping something away, some flaky imperfection, some scrap from dinner. She smiled and said, "You just don't have to do that. You don't have to talk about anything."

He didn't know what to make of this. If he wasn't supposed to talk about anything, what was he supposed to do? Hop on her? Pull her down onto the ground and roll around? This was Courtney Banes, for crying out loud. Miss Teen Sumac Days two years in a row. She'd been to the Panama Canal. He couldn't just hop on someone like that.

"Look," she said, rising from the log, standing over him. "You can fuck me. That's not a problem. You just have to know *how.*"

He couldn't believe it.

But of course he knew *how.* He'd had sex before—a few times, even. And of course he'd seen his share of porn. All you had to do was dial up the Internet and it was like training films for fucking. And then there were all those sex ed classes over the years. They hit them with the simple polywog stuff in the fifth grade, then got a little more specific in the eighth; finally gave you the thumbs-up on beating off, that it was normal, not something you had personally invented and would fry in hell for; and then in sophomore year, Human Biology, last year, the real nitty-gritty—contraception and AIDS and STDs and safe sex and anal and oral and that whole gay/lesbian thing; the stuff he'd heard about on *Loveline* since he was maybe twelve. So of course he knew *how*. But he was too stunned, at the moment, to reel off some kind of résumé, if that's what she was looking for.

She went on. "What I'm saying is, sex is really no big deal. Really. You just have to know how to *make* it a big deal. Understand?"

There were a thousand things he could say in response but what came out was, "No."

She didn't seem to understand this. "No?" She repeated it as if he'd meant he didn't want to have sex.

"I mean, not really. I don't really understand. Sorry. No offense. Could you explain? I mean if it's not too much trouble." God, he hoped he didn't sound all beggy.

She sighed, heavily; looked up at the stars, out at the waves. Mark waited, sitting there like he was in her classroom. The shawl slipped up over her head, babushka-style, and she laughed then, like she had some inside joke going. Suddenly she leaned forward, her hands on his knees, and whispered close, "Entertain me."

He stared as she pushed away and began walking off, barefoot, down the beach, humming to herself, but loud enough for him to hear. He got up off the log and started after her, but she turned and said, "Good night," and he knew he wasn't supposed to follow, he was just supposed to think about all this.

He watched her go, certain there was an old movie star he'd seen on TCM whom she looked just like, with her white tennis skirt flipping along in the moonlight, whom probably she was imitating. Part of him knew that she was being ridiculously dramatic and lah-dee-dah. But the other part, the louder part, thought it would be a good idea to try to have sex with her. And soon.

16

BRENDA VONBUSHBERGER KNEW her family respected her training. She knew it would become more and more essential, in the coming years, to the continuing survival of vonBushberger's. Nonetheless, sometimes the sacrifices she'd made for that training felt unappreciated. After all, it was her love for this place, if truth be told, more than a love for her studies, that had caused her to devote so many years to her degrees. She knew it had come at a personal price, turned her into a sort of unapproachable geek, full of "modern ideas" about the orchard. She was an unmarried woman of thirty-two, living at home, with no colleagues other than those with whom she corresponded via e-mail. Which was one reason it was going to be great to have someone around now with whom she could discuss, in a meaningful way, the more advanced elements of the horticultural sciences. The thing Brenda had not counted on was that the researcher would be so handsome.

It had never crossed her mind. The importance of his project and the degrees he'd held, the work he'd done in genetic mapping, all painted a very different picture of the man who showed up and would be camping out in their orchard this summer. And it wasn't just his appearance that surprised. If she hadn't reviewed his credentials herself, she might think this guy was sort of a flake. For one thing, there was the giddiness—about everything, it seemed. He acted like he'd arrived on some distant planet, and boy, what a great planet it was, according to him. Then there were a lot of goofy little things, like the polished Petoskey stone she spotted when he gave her the tour of his mobile lab and living quarters. He'd left the stone under the microscope he would be using for preparing slides—he'd apparently been examining the unique hexagonal shapes of the state's official fossil, which certainly had nothing to do with botany or the genetic mapping of cherry blossoms.

He caught her frowning at it and removed it—a little sheepishly, she thought—from under his microscope, explaining that he bought it at a shop in town. He asked if she knew this was the only place in the world to find a fossil like that.

She did, of course. "Any lake in the area, you find them. You shouldn't shell out money for a Petoskey stone." She considered explaining about Fudgies and the touristy crap they could actually be sold, but decided he wasn't ready to hear this. She thought, too, that the polite thing might be to offer to take him to one of the lakes sometime and help him find a few—it was sort of sad thinking about him being so lost here that he couldn't find his own Petoskeys. All it would take would be an unhurried stroll along the edge of the water with the sun high and bright, a little wading, maybe, and they'd find bucketfuls, no problem. But she held back on the offer, thinking it was a little unprofessional and that he might be offended. He wasn't here to socialize, after all, or to see the sights. The Japanese government was spending too much money on him for that.

"Already," he said, "I am knowing I will want many *souvenirs* of this place." He pronounced *souvenir* as the French would. "I already am knowing how much I will think fondly of this Michigan—even though I am only here a few days already and I am leaving not for many months!" He laughed at this, and she thought, unkindly, that if she'd passed outside the vehicle and heard his shrill laugh, she'd have assumed it was a woman laughing. "Ah!" Excitedly, he dug into his pocket. "Another *souvenir,* from a long time before." He produced a little plastic disk and handed it to her. It was an old key chain, with well-rubbed Japanese characters on one side, and clear on the other. There was a very real-looking cherry blossom encased inside.

"When I told my mother this is the profession I wished to pursue, I did so with a variance of the truth. My mother is a *kyoiku-mama.* There are no monkey businesses with her."

Brenda stared at him a moment, wondering if he'd picked up this term from her dad, who was always saying "monkey business," and had in fact said it more than once in conjunction with this very project.

But Miki went on. "As you are knowing, the cherry blossom is almost sacred in our culture. Let us at least say that we are adoring it. Very much, the cherry blossom. But that is perhaps not enough for a *kyoiku-mama,* so I told her I saw botanical genetics as an opportunity to becoming a respected, prosperous, leading man in my field, while at the same time providing a boon to our people, both for their soul and their stomach. I show her articles about how the government will always support research that will improve food production for Japan. I spoke of how one makes oneself invaluable, professionally, through constant steps of extreme specialization—very much like genetics itself. Natural selection. But that was not my real thoughts, my primary thoughts. My main reason." He grinned mischievously, as if he'd pulled a fast one on his mother.

"Which is?"

"Which is, since I was a small boy who ran off on his own one day during a school excursion to the Imperial Gardens . . ." He took the key chain back, waggling it (is that what those characters said maybe, *Imperial Gardens*?), and slid it under the microscope and flicked it on. ". . . And was scolded and shamed on the bus ride home, when they found me lying in the grass between the cherry trees—a snowing of blossoms, like the breathing in the mountains when you fill your lungs. They smell to me like running without shoes in rain. They are the softness of the neck of a loved one you dream again for many years, in your sleep." He laughed. "But these are not reasons you speak to a *kyoiku-mama*. These are reasons you keep in your heart only."

She'd never heard a man of science speak like this. His unscientific words, and perhaps his close proximity in the confining space, made her feel, for a moment, strangely unscientific, too. She put her eye to the microscope, and told herself not to look at him until she could catch her breath.

17

HE HADN'T TRULY REALIZED how disorderly and dusty he'd allowed the parsonage to become until he heard the bang of the screen door being knocked upon.

It wasn't just the kitchen and the stacked, crusted dishes and the fall-where-it-may approach he'd taken to the living room—all that he'd been conscious of and had meant to get to very soon. But it was everywhere, a recurring surprise that greeted him even in the less trafficked rooms, including the study where he intended to set up the machine, and so it was really only when he brought her in there that he saw again how cramped it was, with piles of books on the floor and scattered letters and a flank of dead or doomed potted plants underfoot. He'd managed to get over to the window one day, squeezing through the disastrous maze, and unhooked the plants from where they hung, intending to take them to the bathroom shower and let them soak, but he never got that far.

"My wife passed just a few months ago." The moment he said it he regretted it: certainly a young woman today would think him a Neanderthal, a sexist throwback, unable to keep his house clean without his wife's help. But he hadn't meant it that way exactly. He just meant that his life was a mess, that he'd been grieving, and all physical movement felt slowed by the sluggishness of depression; that everything felt topsy-turvy and who knew where even the plants should go?

But "Oh" was all she said and he saw her gaze drift up to the engagement photo he kept above the desk, he in his chaplain's uniform, Mary looking strikingly like a young Katharine Hepburn. It was black-and-white, but he always remembered it as being color, she looked that vibrant. Posed behind her, he was all Adam's apple and teeth, and he could remember, just looking at it, the exact feeling of disbelief he had when he realized that this woman was about to marry him.

"I'm sorry," the girl said. "She was very pretty."

Then she let her backpack drop to the floor and knelt down beside the big computer box, sliding the dead plants out of the way to make room, and added, more quietly, "And obviously also a really, really good housekeeper . . ."

At first, he couldn't believe she'd said it. But her smile, half-shielded now by her hair as she opened the box, seemed so tentative and unaffected, not the brazen sneer of some boat brat, some mocking teen, more the awkward attempt of the first day of school, of trying to make friends. He watched as she pulled the components from the box, each wrapped in plastic bags, like the giblets in a store-bought turkey, and he tried to remember the last time anyone had made even a small attempt to give him a ribbing. It had to be back before Mary died. Probably, it was Mary herself who'd last done it.

It was kind of nice, someone ribbing him.

THEY WERE SITTING SO CLOSE, he could smell lilac on her, and something sweet—the fudge shop?—and he fretted a little that he might be giving off an odor of which he was unaware; that she might think he smelled like an old person and wrinkle up her nose the moment she went on her way.

When she had it all hooked together and humming, she asked him what he wanted to do first: go over the software capabilities or set up his e-mail? Since he didn't know what the software capabilities were, he suggested they go with the latter. "I think that's the main thing Ben, my son, wants me to do," he told her. "The e-mail."

She sat very still and waited, then turned to him. "What do *you* want to do? This is for *you,* all right? Not your son."

"Well, e-mail still, I guess. Sure. I'd like to be able to e the kids."

She broke out laughing. "'E' them? Where'd you get that? 'E' them!"

He wasn't trying to be funny, but obviously that wasn't the term. "Send them an e-mail, I mean."

She told him it was a noun and a verb; that he should simply say, "E-mail them." The next confusing thing was when she asked him to select a user name. Of course, he told her Eugene Aaron Reecher.

But she wasn't keen on that, either. "It doesn't have to be your name exactly. You're not filling out forms for the government. Besides, if it's not weird enough, somebody might already have that name."

"My name? But I'm me. Somebody else can't take over me—"

"You can make up something fun. Like 'RadRev' or something."

He thought about it for a moment, studying that photo of his wife, then told her he'd probably prefer to just be who he was. "Eugene Reecher," he said. "Or just Gene Reecher."

"I'm saying there may already be a Eugene Reecher. We can try . . ." She sounded doubtful and disappointed, like he wasn't any fun. That's me, he thought. The old stick-in-the-mud.

"Hey," he suggested. "My initials spell out EAR. That's kind of fun, isn't it?"

She said she didn't even have to check on "EAR." There was no way that wasn't already being used. "Besides, there are times you don't want to be real obvious who you are."

He couldn't imagine a situation in which he would prefer to hide his identity from his kids, but the girl seemed to know what she was talking about, so he gave it some more thought. Next, he suggested using John 8:7, one of his favorite verses, but when she saw how he wanted to use a colon, she said it wouldn't work. "Besides," she said, "you don't want to disguise your name *that* much. You don't have to change your name to John or anything." He let it go but had to wonder if she'd ever heard *Let he who has not sinned cast the first stone.*

Ultimately he went with *reecher81757*, the numbers being the date he first made love to Mary. The girl was still partial to RadRev, but she stopped fighting him, entering it for him, saying, "Yeah . . . your birthday's always good. You can't forget those."

He didn't clarify for her, but he was a little taken aback: either she hadn't done the math or he looked only forty-four to her. He knew that was impossible. More likely, she hadn't done the math and hadn't really bothered looking at him closely.

And after they'd struggled through that whole obstacle, he next learned he had to come up with another name. This would be his password. She told him he didn't have to tell her this one, that it wouldn't appear onscreen when he typed it in, but to really think it over first. "Your password's got to be something you can always remember," she said, "but this one shouldn't be real obvious to anyone else. So *not* your birthday or your kid's birthday or your wife's first name or anything. Think about it."

He thought about it and then he typed in *CLIFFHEAD*, the name no one ever used anymore for the bootlegger's place, that white elephant of an estate out on Fifel Drive. And sure enough, the letters did not appear but ran across the screen as a line of asterisks, like the stars on a general's chest, like the top secret code for something very, very confidential.

She consulted the giant poster of instructions again. Open in front of her like an unwieldy map, it blocked his view of her completely.

"Okay . . . You've got some kind of package deal here with this ISP . . . They've got some setting options you have to decide on . . . 'Step eight,'" she read. "'Screens.'" Collapsing the instructions, she tossed them to one side, disdainful, but there was something odd about the way she asked him, "Want to put any kind of screens on this?" Her gaze seemed diverted—overly blasé, as if contrived.

If she was nervous about asking him about screens, he had no idea why. Because he had no idea what this screen business was all about. "But mine already came with this TV screen, right?" He rapped his hand against the glowing blue glass and his wedding ring made a loud click.

She snorted a laugh, though he hadn't been making a joke. "*Screens* is a stupid name, no doubt, but it's just some dumb name made up by this server you're pre–signed up for. They mean *filters,* really. It's settings you pick if you want to filter out certain content. Like . . . if you have a grandchild who might get online. Like maybe something's too . . ." She was searching for the word, or one she felt comfortable saying, so he helped her out.

"Racy?"

"Yeah. Racy or whatever. Something gross you really don't want popping up."

He tried to imagine either Ben or Abbey having enough time to come visit anytime soon. And the grandkids were both too young to travel alone.

"It's optional," she said. "We can skip it, if you want."

"Well, I guess I believe in open forums. I don't believe in censorship. I believe that if someone's seeking sin, he'll find it, regardless."

"So . . . no filters?"

"I don't think so. Not to start out."

"Cool," she said, nodding. "That's very . . . modern of you."

This amused him, being called modern. He wondered what his son would make of that. Or Mary. She was the one who insisted, finally, that he prod the board of trustees into purchasing a color TV for the parsonage when the black-and-white died. This was only in 1988.

The girl was still working on the settings, typing away.

"Just out of curiosity," he said, after a long moment, "how racy does it get?"

She shrugged as if there was no real answer to this and kept clacking away at the keyboard. "You see all kinds of stuff. It's pretty unavoid-able. But it's no biggie. You just ignore it." She flashed him the kindest smile, as if to say everything would be just fine.

THAT NIGHT HE SENT HIS FIRST E-MAIL. There was no response, but he didn't expect one right away. Ben was probably busy.

His first incoming e-mail appeared on his screen about five minutes later, unprovoked, uncalled for. He wondered for a second if it was that Spam junk mail garbage the girl had warned him about. The sender's name was FuG16. He wasn't sure he was supposed to open it—he thought of viruses, kiddie porn—but curiosity got to him and he "clicked" on it, as she'd shown him. It said:

```
Hi! Tell me if you got this!
R U enjoying the 21st century now?
HHOJ
(BTW, that means "Ha Ha Only Joking.")
Send back.
K.
PS. BTW means "by the way."
;-)
```

It was the girl.

The way she'd written it, with those clever slangy shorthands and the playful jesting, it felt like he was back in high school, passing notes in class. He had to admit, he liked it.

18

THE AGE FACTOR definitely played a part in what had happened to him. He wasn't denying he'd probably been ill-equipped to handle it properly. By the time he was nineteen, Noah Yoder had been described in *Newsweek* as "the richest person in America who can't buy a drink." The search engine he'd initially designed as a science fair project in the eleventh grade, now called Yoman!® was, at the time that article was written, worth a hundred million dollars. By the time he could drink, it was more like a billion, and, along with several tasty purchases that year, he'd begun construction on a twenty-room glass-and-metal summer home designed by none other than F. M. Mishuki to resemble, slightly, a shipwreck. Mishuki had never been to Michigan, not until they broke ground for construction, so to get a feel for the place, he said he'd been playing the "Wreck of the Edmund Fitzgerald" in his studio while he drafted. The wreck happened two or three years before Noah was even born, but he was pretty sure it was an ore boat, with lines much flatter than this spired and angular thing, and that it had gone down in Lake Superior, which was a whole other peninsula away. But when he actually saw the drawings, it put him in mind of that final scene in that really old movie, *Planet of the Apes,* the toppled torch jutting out from the sand, and regardless of Gordon Lightfoot or any of that, thought it was just cool as shit.

There was a tower, from which his guests could take in a panoramic view that stretched out into Lake Michigan, well past the defunct lighthouse on the point and the entire squiggle of that weird little river and the orchards to the north, the other lake, to the east, an emerald set in the green-spired ring of pines, and to the south, the disorder of the village and the older, meager cottages, but also the bounding range of forestland that ran far to the east and south, and the rest was haze. He'd been given, as a joke housewarming present from Richard Branson, an actual antiaircraft gun, taken off a Japanese carrier. It was permanently plugged, filled with ladlefuls of molten steel now fused to the barrel, and could never fire, but the scope still worked and could be aimed at things for interesting investigations.

During construction, the builders started referring to it as Noah's Ark. The local paper even used that as a headline once. He called up and chewed out the editor for that, smoothing it all over by buying a year of advertising (as if Yoman!® needed anything but the broadest branding now—Super Bowl spots, maybe). What he didn't appreciate was the snickering irony—it felt like they were calling it Noah's Folly, or something—but also he worried about the religious overtones. If false rumors were started that the founder and CEO was a doomsday nut, bunkering himself in some way, going Waco, Yoman!® stock could take a beating. The market was fickle that way.

But that was three years ago. And now, at age twenty-four, things had slipped drastically. He was trying to keep up a brave front, but the truth of it was, the fiscal year ending right before 2001 had been a disaster. He was now, probably, only some sort of a millionaire, and it was unclear how long he'd be able to hold on to any of this.

He had ideas of course. All kinds of new projects he hoped to develop. But the panic was on, and which one to pour everything into? That was the question. The golden days of dabbling were gone. He had to pick a lifeboat and hop in.

The metal Mishuki chose for most of the house was gleaming cold-rolled steel, burnished with rough swirls from an orbital sander and, he had to admit, driving around town, not the usual building material for a home in Weneshkeen. But it was left untreated intentionally. The idea was it would corrode and patina a far subtler rust-brown, which it did, looking much more satisfyingly shipwreck-y after the second winter. Initially, Mishuki had even floated the idea of affixing actual barnacles, farmed from some shipyard in Tokyo, but that had seemed to Noah a little much. Besides, it would get weathered and gnarly enough in no time. It didn't need any help.

The first summer, though, it was blinding, and the sheriff actually showed up, twice, warning Noah that there had been complaints. In mid-afternoon, the boats on the river got the worst of it, and late afternoon, it reflected a shaft of sunlight directly down the main drag, like the death ray beamed from the evil villain's lair in some bad sci-fi movie. A few people supposedly got into a few scrapes in their cars and were blaming it on the reflection from his house, but Noah got the idea the sheriff was talking about old people, and old people were always looking for any excuse for their lousy driving.

He asked the sheriff, very politely, he felt, what exactly he should do about that. He knew he wasn't breaking any laws. The whole thing was up to code. They'd seen to that the year before, his lawyer and financial adviser, Tony, convincing the members of the town council that rezoning his lot was in the town's best interest, that having an original Mishuki would be a source of honor and a point of interest for years to come. Tony pointed out that there were similar little towns downstate, near the Indiana border, where there were modest little Frank Lloyd Wrights that were now boasted of on official signage at the towns' entryways. "Not to mention," he told them, "the importance of Mr. Yoder himself."

But this was the old sheriff, the one who had now retired, a gruff man who never seemed very respectful to people who brought money and prosperity to his town. He didn't appear to have a solution but was merely voicing his complaint. "Well, just . . ." he said, getting back into his cruiser, ". . . just try not to be a ninny."

Noah thought he'd heard wrong. No one had spoken to him like that since probably the eleventh grade. The guy had to be saying something about that river in town. Maybe that was it. Noah stepped over to the cruiser, asking him politely to repeat what he'd said.

The sheriff cranked the window down, put the cruiser in reverse. "You know. A jackass. Try not to be one."

The steel was no longer a problem, but the plate glass still gave off significant glare. And with the green reflection of the surrounding treetops, the large windows were seen by birds as the real McCoy, and continually caused many to kamikaze into the glass. Sometimes he'd hear the bang, but usually it was a surprise he'd stumble upon later, small bundles of guts and fuzzy feathers left behind on his deck, his flowerbeds, the porch roofs, as if the workings of some practical joker, some ding-dong-ditch-it, burning-bag-of-poop-hurling teens. The groundskeeper, Mr. Much, said they were starlings, sparrows, chickadees, phoebes, mockingbirds, kingbirds and kinglets. They appeared on a regular basis, several per week, and he had to admit, sometimes, when he saw them, when they caught him off-guard, he did feel a little like a jackass.

One time there were two of them, side by side, lifeless as a pair of shoes. Mr. Much came up behind him as he was staring at the dead birds and said, "Two by two. Huh. Actually, this place is more like the *opposite* of an ark, isn't it?"

Later, he wondered, as he had done again lately, if there was some sort of research lab that might pay a small price per bird. Of course it wouldn't be much, but with the volume of dead birds produced by those windows, it might be profitable at that. Certainly, even a small income would be better than paying a groundskeeper to continually rake them away. They could be collected in one of the storage freezers in the basement and shipped all at once. There was plenty of room: knowing he'd be keeping the entertaining much simpler for a while, he'd canceled this summer's order of buffalo brauts and Omaha steaks. He made a note in his PalmPilot to look into it. *DEAD BIRDS / RESEARCH LABS? / $$?*

19

THE WAY DEPUTY STRUSKA HEARD IT, David Letterman was secretly renting some place in the area for the summer, with the idea that he would probably buy if he had a pleasant stay. If he liked the house and, of course, the town. This was probably the best news she'd heard for a long, long while. At least since she got the news that KFC was bringing back their popcorn chicken. Lately, most news had been of the other variety.

The thing was, even if she hadn't heard the Letterman rumor, if Janey Struska had to pick one celebrity she'd want to come visit her town, whether you gave her, say, a copy of *People* magazine and let her riffle through it or just said, off the top of your head ... *Go!,* the answer she'd come back with would be David Letterman. Not only because he was a scream and seemed like probably a pretty genuine guy, down-to-earth and what-not with his baseball caps and love of auto racing, and not only because she got the distinct impression, from the way he skimmed right past the so-called starlets, all glammed up and full of themselves, maybe even sniping them with a zinger or two, and then, in some dopey on-the-street thing or audience quiz game, he'd practically fall all over his boyish self getting tongue-twisted and flop-sweaty over some normal, maybe even slightly big-boned girl-next-door with a nice shy smile or freckles or real-looking curly red hair. (Okay, so she didn't personally have the freckles or the red hair, but she was certainly big-boned and could probably also muster a shy smile, if need be.) Anyway, she admired that about the guy. Thought it showed there was a real, genuine sort of deal about him.

Not that she'd expect him to *like her* like her. That would be swell, a bonus—but even if he didn't like her that way, there still might be a great opportunity here, career-wise. She knew if she had a chance to meet him—maybe not just meet him, but sit down with him and hang out, maybe have a drink—he'd see that she was wasting her talents here in Weneshkeen. Sure, police work had been fulfilling, to an extent, but she felt like she'd hit a wall lately—really, ever since she got passed over to replace the old sheriff and they brought in that interim interloper from Saginaw, Jon Hatchert. But how long could she go on being just a deputy? In the business world, they had a name for that: the glass ceiling or something.

The thing is, she could probably write jokes for him.

Letterman, that is. Not Hatchert. Hatchert wouldn't know a joke from a eulogy.

She was known for her sense of humor. In fact, a few months back, before the thaw, when they had the big farewell banquet for Don Sloff, she was the one who was asked to host the sort of "roast." And everyone loved it. They laughed their asses off (and, since it was mostly law enforcement types, with their wide frames and seat-straining girth, between them there was a great deal of ass there to be laughed off). She did some puns on his name, turning it into "sloth," working the retirement angle, like he was going to laze around all day, and then she did "The Top Ten Reasons Sheriff Sloff Is Retiring":

Number Ten . . . Wants to give doughnuts the full attention they deserve.

Number Nine . . . *Law & Order* rejected his spec script, "ripped from today's headlines," due to "lack of anything actually happening" in it.

Number Eight . . . Had his colors done. Found out he's a "winter." Winters just can't pull off brown and khaki.

Number Seven . . . He was getting so's he'd hear radio calls in his sleep (though only while napping in his cruiser).

Number Six . . . Realized how much dough he could rake in on speed traps if he doesn't have to share any of it with the village.

Number Five . . . Wants to get in on those sweet private bodyguard gigs, for someone like "that hot Eli Whitney chick."

Number Four . . . He's taking the fall for the terrible riot during Weneshkeen's last Puerto Rican Day Parade.

Number Three . . . Gentrification of much of the village's mobile home zoning, upgrading to R1 residential, will seriously hamper his chances of ever getting on *Cops*.

Number Two . . . Like *The Naked City*, there are also eight million stories in Weneshkeen. Unlike *The Naked City*, they all begin with, "So my brother-in-law comes over with a six-pack, right . . . ?"

And the Number One reason Don Sloff is retiring . . .

. . . Now he will know once and for all: is it his hot bod and continental charm that gets him so much tail or is it just the sexy uniform?

They hooted and clapped and clinked their glasses with their steak knives, and afterward everyone told her how great it was. More than one said she should do it for a living. Totally unsolicited, they said that. She didn't take it seriously, though, because she couldn't imagine any way of making that happen. Not given her age, where she lived . . .

But now, with the news of this unexpected summer guest in town, maybe she could. Maybe this was exactly the opportunity that would shift her life onto a whole new shiny avenue.

Janey spent most of her waking hours alone, in the cruiser, and it gave her a lot of time to think. Maybe too much time. She decided it wouldn't be a question of his spotting her potential. She felt pretty good about being able to make him laugh. She could really see them hanging, maybe getting a beer at the Potlicker, maybe walking their dogs together. It was just a question of exposure. Being in the right place at the right moment. Or several right moments, over time. Which should prove easy. This was a small town. With patience, she'd have plenty of chances to meet him. Even the more private residents eventually got to know everyone in the sheriff's department. Of course, this is assuming he'd fall in love with the place and stick around long enough, actually buy a place of his own. But that seemed like a done deal—as much as she loved the idea of moving on and getting a fancy job writing comedy in New York, it was hard to imagine anyone not loving Weneshkeen.

The only thing that could maybe ball it up would be if people acted like jerkoffs around him. If they pestered the guy, wouldn't leave him alone. She'd have to be diligent, run interference, make sure the man had his privacy. It was times like this she wished the old sheriff, Don Sloff, was still her boss. Don would make no bones about trolling the streets in the cruiser, using the PA, warning the people of Weneshkeen not to be jerkoffs. *"Try,"* he would tell them, *"just try . . ."*

She still carried with her, after eleven years on the job, Sheriff Sloff's basic belief about police work, what was sometimes referred to as Don's Rule on Rules, which was, "People don't have to know the exact laws, per se. Every rule and regulation. You're the average guy walking down the street, you probably don't know half of that. But if you just try not to be a jackass, you're probably not breaking any laws. Chances are good."

Old Don was a great fucking guy. A guy who knew how to be exactly the kind of sheriff a weird little bump in the river like Weneshkeen needed him to be. It was a shame, really, that the insurance doc was so jittery. The thing was, the coverage for all civil employees under the township's policy was at risk of being canceled if they didn't step in and retire Don early. It was either that or get a new carrier and hope they could raise the millage to cover the higher premiums. Their current carrier was a real bottom-basement discount house and there was no way they'd find a substitute for the same low group premium with an outfit that wasn't so picky about the fact that their sheriff, at age sixty-two, was a three-hundred-pounder. Riding around in the cruiser all day was part of it, of course, but also, he'd been operating, on the side, out of his home, a little cherry sausage industry. (He'd perfected his SloffBrauts, through much experimenting and, no doubt, personal taste-testing, to the point where they now would completely sell out in local freezer cases the same week he'd deliver them.) When the doctor at the last mandatory checkup, a new guy the insurance company was using—they all had to drive out to see him, way out in Cadillac—learned of Don's main love, the sausage business in his garage, and the fact that both Don's father and grandfather never made it to sixty, it really rattled the doctor. He told Don that he was too old a man to carry that extra weight. Supposedly, Don told him to try not to be a "nervous Nellie," but the guy filed his report with the insurance company anyway.

Everyone hated to see Don retire, but honestly, Don himself seemed a little relieved. "Life is short, Janey," he said, when he finally decided what his move would be, taking her down along the riverwalk to tell her himself. "That quack was right about one thing—I could go any day. We all could. And do I really want to be lying there on the floor, clutching my heart, wondering if I'd really done enough, tried enough different things, produced enough links in my life? Hell, I've got ideas for a venison, pecan, *wild rice* and cherries press I haven't even begun to scratch the surface on! You know? And if I go now"—he tapped his temple with one big meaty finger—"it all dies with me. You know?"

She agreed that would be a waste. They hugged and she made him consent to the big retirement blowout.

And now that he was gone, everything felt different. She still loved her hometown, but it wasn't quite the same and she really had to wonder if this wasn't a sign that she, too, should move on; if maybe 2001 could be the year—given a little help from her, a poke and shove in the right direction, taking the bull by the horns if a celebrity talk show host just happened to be hiding out somewhere on her beat—in which things might just change for her forever.

20

WHAT BURNED JANEY UP about the appointment of Hatchert was he didn't have anywhere near the qualifications she had. He wasn't even from Weneshkeen. The village council interviewed him over the phone, and the first day he set foot in town was the day before he was to officially take over. Janey couldn't believe it. She'd been a deputy for ten years, grew up in the town, knew the people. He'd had two years as a deputy in Saginaw and attended some lame-ass "leadership in crisis"

workshop down in Lansing that was supposed to shape him into something that angry, distraught or chemically addled people would shut up
and listen to—an outcome she highly doubted for the kind of events
she anyway really didn't see happening in Weneshkeen.

She hated like hell to come off as one of those types she saw as a
whiny feminist who just couldn't take the competition. She could take
the competition—hell, she could probably take him in arm wrestling—
but this was so clearly a matter of penis vs. no penis that it was almost
a hoot.

During the final day of interviews, she walked into the village offices
and asked if she could have her application back a second. Bear Eckenrod was the chair of the hiring committee. He stared at her, curious, as
she added, to the row of people who would give recommendations, the
name "Dick."

"Who's Dick?" he asked.

"No one." She dropped the pencil on his desk. "But I thought
maybe that would help even things," she explained, "since clearly it
was *his* dick put him over the edge."

IN THE SPARTAN PARKING LOT, she pulled up alongside the new sheriff, end to end in the patrol cars, so they could check in with each other.
Hatchert rolled down his window and said, "What do you know about
some Indian scaring kids over on . . . you know . . . the little lake over
there?"

"Meenigeesis." Guy hadn't even learned the names of the lakes yet.
Useless.

"Some Indian named Firewater or—"

"Drinkwater. That's not 'some Indian.' That's the Coach."

"You're saying he's not an Indian?"

For a second, she tried to recall how the Coach referred to himself, if
he bothered with the more PC terms or what, and it struck her that
maybe she didn't really know him all that well. Still, she didn't care for
Hatchert's tone. She said, "I haven't memorized the man's family tree,
okay? What exactly—"

"Guy's an Indian and can afford a house over on that fancy lake?
How's that work?"

"It's an older place," she explained. "Just a little cottage. He's been there forever. Before it got real pricey."

"Hm. Bet he gets casino money."

As a matter of fact, she happened to know he did, but she wasn't about to give her smug new boss that. He'd act like he'd won something, some big debate, when really, Coach Drinkwater, who'd been living out on that lake long before those tax-hiking log mansions, was a working-class guy with about eighty different sources of hard-earned income. Plus, he was a legitimate member of the Ojaanimiziibii band— what was wrong with that? If they were going to hand out casino checks, and he qualified, what was he supposed to do? Send it back with a note that said, *No thanks—it's been a super year for the jerky business so I'll pass*?

"If you think he's a problem, Hatchert, maybe I can see if he'd be willing to walk to Oklahoma for you. Or maybe you'd rather go with the whole infected blankets route? Your call, Chief."

"Yeah . . ." he said. "I have zero idea what that means . . ." She could see from the way he was distracted by his own mustache— wiping it straight and flat, checking himself in his rearview—that he really didn't know what it meant. And he wasn't saying it like he *wanted* to know what it meant, he said it like, *I don't want to know what that means. I have a mustache to attend to. Go away.*

So she did. And soon, maybe she *really* would.

21

THE DOWNSIDE to being just a deputy in such a small town was that she always seemed to get the bullshit jobs. Her rank made her an all-encompassing trash can for all manner of village business, including animal control and serving legal documents.

Which is why it was Janey Struska who was saddled with the task of serving a complaint on Kurt Lasco. Some nonsense about cutting down his neighbor's trees. Not that he didn't do it. She knew Kurt pretty well. Nice enough guy, but the whole thing sounded about par. She remembered when she was still a ninth-grader and Kurt was a senior, he was rumored to be one of the bunch who filled Don Sloff's old Crown Vic with about a ton of cherry pits from the old cannery south of town.

And it wasn't just because she knew him that this sort of duty was a pain. It was always a pain because they always wanted her to hear their side of the story. They never got that when she served a complaint she was essentially one notch above a carrier pigeon.

And sure enough, Kurt started in with the guff. Before she could even turn and walk back to the cruiser, he was gawking and gasping, saying, "Listen, I don't know if this thing says anything about what *really* happened, but listen—"

She held up her hand. "This isn't *The People's Court,* Kurt, and I'm not Judge Wapner. Telling me does nothing. You've got twenty days to respond—officially. There's a letter attached that explains."

"Well, I want to complain, too, then!"

This was the part they never got. Filing a legal complaint wasn't the same as simply bitching, which was all most folks were really interested in. "I'd hire a lawyer, then. At least to walk you through the counterclaims part." He gave her a sour look, as if disappointed that she'd failed to flip out her notepad and jot down his gripes. "It's not small claims, Kurt. I'm sorry. It's not that simple. This is a *civil* complaint."

"What's that *mean?*"

What it meant was he was probably going to have to hire a lawyer regardless, counterclaims or no, but she didn't say that. She just repeated, "It's all in there, Kurt. What to do, each count in the complaint that requires an answer, and . . . everything."

He still looked pissed, but now he also looked a little scared. Janey looked away. This guy Starkey could have, in fact, filed a small claims case. It was sort of a low blow, dragging him into district court. That kind of expense meant something to a guy like Kurt Lasco, as it would to anyone from around here.

"Jesus," he said.

"Sorry. I just serve the things." She gave him a weak smile and turned to leave again. "Just the messenger . . ."

"Wait a minute! Janey! Hang on."

She turned and waited for him to catch up.

"I want to show you something." He led her around the back of the patrol car to the edge of his neighbor's driveway. She thought he was about to get into a whole explanation about the property line, a thing that was none of her business—he could explain all that in court, not to her—but it wasn't the property line. It was Starkey's sign, the big blue Charlie the Tuna with their name painted up to look like the StarKist logo. Kurt wanted to know what she was going to do about it.

"Uh . . . try not to look at it if I can avoid it . . . ?" she offered.

"But I mean, this has gotta be illegal, Janey! Right?"

"You mean like a village ordinance, residential zoning rules . . . like that?"

"Yeah."

"No," she said. "Unfortunately."

"Really?" Kurt scrunched up his brow. He looked like he wanted to pick something up and swing it at the thing. "Yeah, but Jesus. Come on. It's so big and ugly and . . . stupid."

"Agreed. And very ironic, because it's in very bad taste. Which means he doesn't really remember the ads. But it's not illegal."

"What about trademark infringement? That's not illegal?"

She explained that that wasn't really her area. If the StarKist people had a gripe, they could fly their highfalutin lawyers in here and sue away, but that wasn't the kind of thing the village taxpayers expected her to pursue. Purely in terms of signage on private property, it was plenty legal. More and more, these kinds of vanity signs were popping up all over the village, to the point where Akins DeWalt, a guy she dated briefly in high school, back when he had all his fingers, now operated a sign store that specialized in hand-carved or hand-painted driveway signs. Just up the street, there was the one that said *Crash Landing*—as if that actually sounded pleasant—and featured a carved duplicate of the owner's Piper Cub. There was one a street over that said *Bea's Nest* and was owned by a woman named Bea something. A lot of them were cutesy names like that, but most of them included the family name. You could argue there was a practical application in that most of these summer people's friends were out-of-towners, too, and so they needed a little help finding the place when they drove up to visit. But really, it was just bragging, putting your brand on a big showy house.

"Sorry, Kurt," she said, getting into the cruiser. "I can't help you here."

If she were sheriff, she thought while heading to the Daisy June for a black-and-white soft swirl, she could have some deputy out doing this sort of thing for her, serving frivolous complaints and writs and being burdened with inspecting the neighbor's driveway signs.

Or . . . if she lived in an apartment right on Broadway, within walking distance of Central Park and her job, writing for David Letterman. Then, too. Then she wouldn't have to do such things, either.

22

THE LETTERMAN THING actually started with Noah Yoder.

This was back in May, during his first days in the house for the season. He'd arrived in a real panic about all the costs attached to the house, having been beaten down all winter by the alarming market slump. There were unexpected expenses waiting for him—improperly installed "scuppers" (whatever *they* were) needed to be replaced already and there was a bill for the snowplowing done to his driveway all winter when no one had even been around, and suspicions that all the glass had been improperly sealed. He'd actually spoken the thought out loud to his finance guy, Tony, that he might have to think about unloading the place.

He was standing in the gleaming metal kitchen, staring at the complicated-looking espresso machine, trying to remember when he last had to make his own—probably not since he was last in this house—and hoping he could figure it out, when he saw the firewood guy's red pickup pulling into the turnaround, arcing wide around the outbuilding to unload, and he thought, *Shit and golly. More cash I gotta hand over . . .*

He'd forgotten about the standing order of firewood. The firewood guy and his son were supposed to keep it restocked throughout the summer, a combination of ash, hickory and black cherry in an agreed-upon ratio they'd determined would produce the optimum color, flame and endurance. But it wasn't the firewood guy, just his son, some pip-squeak still in high school probably, and so Noah snatched up his cell and started making calls, trying to appear busy. This was a problem in this house, with all its glass. If you were home, it was hard to pretend you weren't. He was planning to pay them, of course. Eventually. He'd just rather it wasn't that afternoon. He just wanted to stall, not stiff them, and if he could present himself as a busy dot-com millionaire on the phone, the kid might come back later.

There weren't many calls to make, unfortunately—sure, tech support in Tacoma wanted to talk about layoffs and he knew he should also probably get the latest abysmal news from his broker, but these weren't calls he relished making just then. So he hit speed dial to his sister in Minneapolis and got the nephew, David, and they discussed the game David was playing at the time, Lara Croft—Noah explaining how hot she was and David saying *gross!* but listening (he'd get it soon enough). Then he called the Weneshkeen *Identifier* and told the editor he wouldn't be placing any ads this year, sorry.

There was a bang from outside, the kid slamming the tailgate shut. He knew he'd be coming up to the house to tell him the wood was all in, and collect his money, but Noah had run out of excuses to be on the phone.

The kid was on the deck now, foot-dragging to be polite, to serve notice he was approaching the house. He wore a smashed Gap cap, red with a *G,* and he took it off now, wiping at his nose. He looked sweaty. Lately, Noah found himself noticing sweat all the time. It made him uncomfortable.

Punching the speed dial, he called his own voice mail and pretended he was talking to someone. He knew the kid could probably hear him through the glass. It just wasn't as insulated as Mishuki had claimed it would be.

There was a copy of *TV Guide* on the kitchen counter, Letterman's dopey grin drawn in caricature, so he threw that into the conversation, ". . . when David Letterman's coming . . ."

There was a knock on the side door.

"Well, Dave's not real sure yet how long he's staying. They don't give him much of a hiatus . . . No . . ." He opened the door, the phone still to his ear, open hands thrown wide as if trying to communicate with the guy, trying to show he was caught off-guard, that he had his hands full. The kid actually stepped back a few feet, nodding like he understood. Noah gave the kid an apologetic smile and stepped half out of the door. He kept nodding to the imaginary person on the phone, saying, "Uh-huh . . . uh-huh . . ." but shrugging to the kid, holding up one finger as if he wanted him to wait, to stay. But the kid kept backing away, wincing, nodding that he understood, whispering, "Sorry!" and pointing out back where he'd stacked the new cords of firewood.

After the kid left without getting paid, Noah sat out on the deck and thought about this crazy house of his. Even if things got really bad and he did have to sell, the problem would be, of course, that he'd created such a white elephant. There were few who could afford a summer house like his, and he wasn't about to take a big loss. The idea came to him that if he was going to sell it, it might help if he spread a rumor that someone rich and famous was interested in buying. Someone like David Letterman. And hadn't he just started the ball rolling?

Because that firewood kid was, after all, a kid. In a backwater town. He'd be bursting to tell someone. Soon, Noah figured, news that Letterman was coming to Weneshkeen would be all over town.

JUNE INTO JULY

23

UNTIL WENESHKEEN GOT ITS FIRST dot-com whiz-kid millionaire, the ritziest estate was, for years, Cliffhead—more often generally referred to as "the bootlegger's"—a veritable castle perched above nearly half a mile of Lake Michigan frontage. When he first started poking around, most everyone just assumed he would be buying the crazy old heap because it had been on the market for nearly fifteen years now with no real takers and it wasn't like he'd get into a real bidding war over it. If anyone seemed in a position to buy it and fix it up, it was this Noah Yoder kid. But he wasn't interested. Instead, he built a brand-new monstrosity all his own, and so this one continued to enjoy its slow decline on the high bluff along Fifel Drive, where a deep woods of birch and beech had grown thick around it, shielding it from the indignity of onlookers.

It was built in 1910 by three dozen Italian stonemasons, using tricky, idiosyncratic rocks gathered from scattered sites all over Michigan, including the Upper Peninsula. It was said the owner actually turned away an entire barge of flawlessly cut Indiana limestone the builder had ordered, claiming it wasn't the stone of a true castle. There was no doubt the owner was eccentric, but he did have money to burn. This was three years before anyone had to pay federal income tax, when you could still be crazy-rich.

The owner was a man named Fifel, known in newspaper circles in his day as "The Rumbleseat King." That was hardly the extent of it. At the height of his run, he held a mutually exclusive contract to provide Henry Ford with automotive upholstery. His main residence was down near Detroit, but Cliffhead would be his summer home, all thirty-two rooms, horse stables and swimming pool (the first pool in the county—this one was made of those same eclectic stones, to match the house—a jigsaw puzzle of rustic rocks).

Though now a little rough around the edges, Cliffhead is still impressive, mostly because the scale seems so odd for that type of rustic architecture. It truly is a cottage-castle, with the bumpy cobbled lines of its massive wraparound porch, all stone, and the square watchtower. The tower is one area that needs significant work; almost a century of easterlies whipping straight off Lake Michigan have rendered it wobbly, the mortar crumbly and cracked. And compared to the almost over-bearing tower on Weneshkeen's newest eyesore, the summer home of Noah Yoder, this tower seems quaint, a sandcastle. But at the time of its construction in 1910, the now defunct Weneshkeen *Proctor-Venerator* referred to the structure, mockingly, as "the Fifel Tower." There are old-timers around who still call it that.

In the mid-twenties, Fifel was forced to sell, after Henry Ford spent a weekend there, took in the opulence, and decided then and there to begin manufacturing all his upholstery himself. Some felt the auto-maker did this because Fifel was a Jew (which he wasn't—the Fifels were Polish Catholics from Malva—the *Fifelskis,* originally). But Henry Ford sometimes took a lot of convincing.

The more likely scenario is simply that he saw a way to cut corners: why pay this man to provide a component he could easily provide him-self? Still, there is a photo in existence recording Ford's visit to the estate. You can see it in the Weneshkeen Heritage Museum, which is a small bay-windowed bump-out in the public library (space recently made available by the removal of the old steam radiators and the com-puterization of the old card catalogue files). Teachers on field trips point out the framed photo on the wall and explain who they are: Mr. Fifel, his wife and kids, and some unidentified guests in the pool, all in full-body bathing suits, waving. Henry Ford is perched on a wrought-iron deck chair, smiling rigidly, hands clenched in a tight little ball in his lap, his straw hat clamped on his head like a lid on a jar. Clearly, he does not want to get in the water with these people.

The next owner was the bootlegger, or the man purported to be a bootlegger. Ironically, though this is the owner most locals associate with the estate, very little is known about him. It's said his name was Rump Johnson, but no record exists confirming that and no one still alive seems to know what he looked like, where he was from or what kind of name that is. There are rumors he kept an old circus tiger in the vast basement, and let it out to prowl the grounds at night, at times when he was worried about his safety. But again, there remains no proof of this tiger's existence, no news photos of the tiger, and no one living today can personally vouch for seeing anything out there larger than a raccoon.

Most folks take, as evidence enough that he was a bootlegger, the fact that there was a lot of "ruckus" out there and loud parties and the occasional gunshot and the fact that Al Capone supposedly visited in the summer of 1926 and that, eventually, the place no longer seemed to be occupied. Somewhere in the early thirties, the bootlegger, or whatever he was, disappeared. (If there ever was a tiger, he left, too.)

In the forties, the estate was quietly commissioned by the War Department to temporarily detain certain prominent and well-to-do German- and Japanese- and Italian-Americans living in Chicago, Cleveland, St. Louis and, especially, Detroit—due to its high vulnerability as a prime industrial center in the war effort. Because of the government's shaky legal ground in this—and the fact that these were wealthy families of import, not those stunned and penniless fishmongers and greengrocers roped into pens out in California—every effort was made to provide for the comfort of these special "guests" of the government. It was sort of a combination upscale jail and five-star detainment center. There was shuffleboard and croquet and warm moist towels after the high tea. No one griped. (Reenie Huff, who is sixty-something, remembers getting underfoot in the kitchen there, "helping" her dad bake bread, and claims that the G-men in charge referred to it, among themselves, as "the Hush-'em-up Hotel," because it really was effective in this regard.)

Still, most people continue to call it "the bootlegger's place." Even in the fifties, when it was briefly owned by a Christian educational association that conducted youth retreats and religious leadership seminars on the grounds, but was later disbanded when it was revealed that certain members of the board (to be fair, only a scant two board members out of nearly a dozen—and their colleagues were shocked and horrified) were in fact members of unsavory fringe groups: one was in the American Bund, the other in something called American Purity Eventually (A.P.E.) (Even in the fifties, that sort of thing didn't fly.)

And always, throughout these times in which the estate was ping-ponged from owner to owner, it was available for rent. Few could afford such a vacation, but occasionally, mysterious visitors would fly into town on a chartered plane, and they'd be spotted, in their European-looking sunglasses, being whisked through town in the local pilot's station wagon. Not often, but it happened.

Briefly, in the late sixties and early seventies, various music promoters tried holding rock festivals on the grounds. No one seemed to be able to turn a profit at this, because they invariably had to forfeit the exorbitant deposit to the owner or holding company, besides paying out a settlement to some kid, usually high on mushrooms or acid, who would climb up on some part of the house, shinny up a tree or downspout for a better view of the stage, or totter along the stone wall leading down to the beach, and fall and break something and suddenly become far less groovy and free-and-easy and much more respectful of the American legal system and its abilities as a conduit of justice.

For six months in 1978 it became a disco called Zebra's. No one in town ever met anyone named Zebra and there weren't any zebras installed on the lawn for grazing purposes, so this one had everyone stumped. Zebra's closed its doors after a small fire in the women's restroom was revealed to be caused by someone freebasing cocaine. No one was hurt in the fire, but after everyone was evacuated, and all the customers were milling around in the yard, rubbernecking, watching the volunteer fire department secure the building, a cross-dressing nail technician from Montreal fell into an old cement birdbath in the rock garden and drowned. The village council decided they didn't need any more of that nonsense and reverted the zoning back to residential.

In between all these times, the place fell into the hands of various real estate companies, holding companies, banks and mortgage companies. It still changes hands like the lesser stock in some Far Eastern trading company, lost in a large portfolio—passed through wills and company takeovers from people who briefly own it and don't know it to people who barely know they've inherited it—because they're certainly not going to live in it, they're not going to sink money into repairing it. The result is that the average townsperson couldn't tell you on a bet who owns it at any given moment. But if you asked them if it's for sale, they'd be certain it is.

And they'd look at you funny, like you're not from around here, like you're either peculiar or filthy rich or probably both.

Still, despite all this, Weneshkeenites are proud of the big rambling heap. There's always a float in the Sumac Days parade that's supposed to resemble the famous old house, using half-dead mums for the brown stones. In any store in town where they sell souvenirs, you'll find post-cards of the grand old pile. Perhaps this is more personal nostalgia than true civic pride. Because it's said that if anyone ever invested seriously in the place again—cleaned it up with the idea of moving in—they'd first have to rent a backhoe to gather up all the virginity lost all over the grounds.

24

HE'D NEVER BEEN SO CLOSE to the old gangster castle—the bootleg-ger's place, people called it—and certainly not in the dark, trying to be cool and not stumble and look like a fool in front of maybe the hottest girl who ever set foot in this weird little town. But now that they were there, the sheer size of it filled Mark with misgivings. The place looked like some sort of gloomy fortress. Size-wise, there wasn't anything like it around for miles. This wouldn't be like breaking into a toolshed—the only other thing like this he'd ever really done.

He tried to imagine what his dad would say if they got busted. Already, just out on the lawn, they were trespassing. Sure, the estate was for sale and there were signs speared into the grass, pointing out various gardens and gazebos and features on the grounds, encouraging you to explore, take the tour. But certainly they weren't meant for two teenagers in the middle of the night looking for a thrill and hopefully— he had his fingers crossed—a place to do it.

He kept his doubts to himself, though. He could tell already, in terms of Courtney, he was doing the right thing: she squeezed his hand as he led her toward the shadowy hulk. She was into this.

The main door was padlocked, but under that main entrance they found a sort of alcove you stepped down to, and that seemed a little more promising. It reminded him of the kind of speakeasy doors under the stairs he'd seen on Turner Classic Movies. Probably a delivery entrance, originally. He tried this first, figuring it would be safer than standing up above on the big stone porch where anyone could see them if they pulled in. This way, if the sheriff happened by or swept the spotlight around, on patrol, they could duck and probably not be seen.

He kept sliding his Blockbuster card in the doorjamb but all he was getting was a very dented card. Behind him, Courtney sighed. "That's not going to work, is it?"

"It's a little tricky," he said. "Just give me a sec." The day before, he'd biked over and rode once around the turnaround for a quick look. During the day, this seemed like the most likely spot. Old latches like this, he figured it should be a snap to card.

"I'm waiting," she said, only she didn't sound like she was.

He tried harder. The card slipped and was gone. He stared at the dark door. The thing had swallowed his Blockbuster card. With his name and Birmingham address encoded on it. Great. Now they were going to have to get in there, one way or the other. He stood to remove his wallet and fish out another card. Courtney saw what he was doing, made a disgusted click with her tongue and headed back up the little stairs. He grabbed her arm.

"Just forget it," she said. "I'm not in the mood anymore. This is turning into a big yawn for me."

"Hang on, hang on." He spun around, looking for anything not nailed down, knelt and wrenched up the rusty metal storm drain piece at his feet—a perforated disk of iron, six inches in diameter—and bashed it into the door. There was a tinkle of glass. He glanced over his shoulder to make sure she was still there. She stood waiting, watching. He reached through to turn the handle but it was still too high, so he broke another panel and this time felt the door handle inside.

"See?" he said, swinging the door open for her, kicking aside the broken glass like a gentleman. "No problem."

25

ROGER DRINKWATER WAS SITTING AT THE BAR at the Potlicker. It was late afternoon on a Friday and he'd just taught a three-day dive camp out on Lake Michigan. Three days on a 164-foot schooner with male and female teenagers—not unlike sharing a pup tent with monkeys. He figured he deserved a couple beers. He was just finishing his first when he felt someone moving up behind him, someone with some size and confidence. Glancing up at the bar mirror, he saw it was the deputy sheriff, Janey Struska.

She pulled up a stool next to him and they nodded hello. She wheeled around on her stool like a kid, scanning the room, seeing who was there, waving and smiling at a few regulars, and he waited for her to do all that, check the schmoozing off the list. He knew she'd planted herself next to him for a reason. "So, Coach," she said, leaning in a little closer to him, elbows on the bar. "My new boss, the new guy? He wants me to poke around and see if there's anything to what he's hearing out on Meenigeesis."

"What's he hearing?"

"You're harassing people. Jet-skiers. Maybe some minor vandalism, monkeying with them a little. I can tell him that's not happening, right?"

He studied her for a while in the mirror. "You off-duty?"

She rolled her eyes at him. "You're not off the record, Coach. I'm not Lois Lane here. I don't have the authority to grant that kind of thing."

Roger snorted. "Jesus, Struska. I just want to know if I can buy you a beer."

She shrugged. He signaled to Dale McConkey, who brought over two fresh Bell's. He wasn't exactly *buying* Janey a beer: in junior high, Dale nearly drowned in one of Roger's drownproofing classes, because the clothes he wore were heavy-wale corduroy, and Roger had saved him, reaching into the pool and pulling him up by the collar and giving him mouth-to-mouth. So when Dale tended bar, Roger tended to drink free.

They clinked bottles in a silent toast and took a pull in tandem. "You wanna know the most I do?" he said finally. "I do kind of a proactive thing, the last couple years. With the team."

He knew she knew what team he was talking about. She'd been on his swim team, years ago. What was it—maybe fifteen years ago? He could picture her wide back, her bobbed hair, black like an Indian's, being tucked up into her school-issued cap. He recalled having some sense of the good humor she had about it all at a time when most girls her age, minus the maybe two percent who thought themselves flawless, would be hard-pressed to dream up a location more distressing than the school pool.

"What I do, during the school year, I educate them. Tell them about spirits I've seen on the lake. 'Manitous.' Indian spirits. *Pissed-off* Indian spirits, in this case."

"And they believe you?"

He shrugged. "Most of them pretend not to, but they sort of have to. They figure I must know something, I'm an Indian. And they don't see me clowning around any other time, so I must be dead serious when I'm telling them this, right? I know *somebody* believes it because I'm starting to hear it around."

"I think maybe I've even heard it, too," Janey said. "A few kids have asked me about it. They're usually young, though. Kids on bikes and skateboards and razor scooters I've chased out of the Spartan parking lot. That sort of thing."

"Yeah? Good. Don't deny it's true, okay? Do me a favor." He took a pull on his beer. "I explain it to them like this: You get too crazy with the watercraft, especially after dusk when it's supposed to be peaceful, you stir them up. All the *gamii-manidook*—the lake 'manitous,' the ancestral spirits . . . They present themselves to you and they are marked for war, man. Painted." No need to tell her, he decided, that this summer he'd started donning the warpaint himself. "I figure maybe most of my swimmers don't actually own the jet-skis themselves—they don't have that kind of money, generally—but they'll tell two kids and they'll tell two kids . . . It's like that old shampoo ad: 'And so on and so on . . .' The hope is, it eventually reaches the summer kids, the real jerkoffs with enough money to own the things, and they think twice about it now."

She was shaking her head, grinning. "You stole all that from *Scooby-Doo*."

Holding her gaze, he said, "I guess I don't follow."

He followed fine—he knew *Scooby-Doo* from his time at the VA. And he knew what she was looking for here from him: some slip that would confirm her accusation that it was all a put-on, that the lake was nothing but an inert body of water, spiritless—and in turn, implicate himself in criminal mischief. But like hell if he was going to open up about matters like personal belief systems and protecting one's home and the land and such all to Janey Struska. Especially not at the Pot-licker with a bunch of jamokes gathered around. She could think whatever she wanted to think.

But she kept coming with it. "You figure these kids aren't much brighter than Shaggy, right? Especially the summer kids."

"I didn't say that."

She smirked, setting down her beer like it was a chore just lifting it. "Yeah, Coach, I *noticed*. But you don't do anything beyond that, right? Intimidation-wise?"

He made a show of shrugging. "I'm menacing, I don't smile . . . but hey, guess what? I'm an Indian. Smiling's not required. Not a thing we're real big on, smiling."

"Yeah, I'm sure that's what I'm hearing about, Coach: you not smil-ing at the neighbor kids. I'm sure that's all it is." She was being sarcas-tic, but she clinked bottles with him good-naturedly and gave him her own half-smile, showing little lines around her mouth that he decided were relatively new, the way it dimpled like that now. She's getting older, he thought, but it wasn't bad.

HE'D ALWAYS THOUGHT HIGHLY of Janey Struska. She'd stood out even back then, on the women's junior varsity team. Not for talent or even looks, but the girl had heart. And a smart mouth, he found out one day—which he liked a lot.

He'd been trying to whip them into shape for a meet with Newaygo or someplace. They were dismal, especially on the butterfly, and so about ten minutes into practice, he called them all out of the pool and lined them up on the bench and gave them what was, for him, a pretty stern lecture. He didn't yell or stamp around or throw a bench in the pool—that wasn't his style—but he was feeling a lot of frustration and was sure it was showing that day, much more than he normally would let such things show. He didn't remember planning to get that melodramatic, but, after weighing his options, realizing they weren't going to get any better that day and that some of the girls weren't even listening—whispering out of the sides of their mouths, louder than they realized, probably, due to water in the ear—he pulled the old coach trick of telling them to hit the showers. "That's it," he said, disgusted. "Pack it in. Go home and think about what we're trying to do here."

Most seemed indifferent, hopping up and shrugging. The rest were snippy, as if he'd wasted their precious time by getting them to suit up and shower in the first place and now they had to fix their hair all over again. The only one who responded entirely differently was Janey, adopting a sort of wistful stoicism as she followed him over to the corner where he kept his satchel, and asked him if he knew "The Swimmer," by John Cheever.

He turned around and took her in. She was still dripping wet, smiling, not malevolently—cheery almost, like she was just making small talk. He told her he'd seen the movie and didn't care for it much—the way the guy smiled all the time, all that hearty laughter.

"That was just Burt Lancaster," she said. "There isn't so much smiling and laughing in the original story." He listened as she gave him her rundown. "This suburban guy decides one day he's going to swim across the county, pool by pool. Along the way, he runs into all these neighbors and friends who don't seem so keen on him and you get the idea that something's really wrong. Then at the end, when he finally gets home, the place is abandoned and boarded up—it's like the bootlegger's place, you know?—unraked leaves everywhere, and you realize he's mentally blocked the fact that he no longer has this family and marriage. And in wanting things to be the way they were, he's become delusional." It seemed to jibe roughly with what Roger remembered of the movie version, but he still didn't get what she was driving at.

"Seems to me," she explained, "the lesson there is: too much swimming makes you unbalanced. You come unhinged."

He remembered that years later, when she turned up as a deputy under Don Sloff. How she'd been basically telling him to have some perspective, only doing it with some humor, keeping it light. She was really a lot like the retired sheriff in that way and it seemed to Roger a pretty rotten thing that the idiots in charge had passed her over for that spot.

26

IN PREPARATION FOR HIS NEXT LESSON, Gene Reecher made a special trip to the Spartan and loaded up on snacks and pop. He was shocked at the options in the pop section, far more than he remembered. He wasn't sure what the girl would like to drink, so he bought a variety. Now he had Coke, Squirt, Vernors and Faygo Red Pop. "Or there's water," he offered. "Or I could make some coffee, tea . . ."

"Actually," she said, "I'm sort of used to iced coffee, from back home, but nobody sells it up here. It's kind of a chain store kind of drink, I guess, but my way works, too. Would you mind if I . . . ?"

He told her by all means, to go ahead, opening the cupboard drawers, displaying pitchers, bowls, the mixer—whatever she needed. But she was still hesitating. "You end up with a little dishwashing after," she warned. "So only if I can clean up after, okay? I don't want to add to the . . ."

"The mess?"

She grinned. "Yeah. The shambles. The pigsty. I'm kidding! I don't mind a little mess, personally. But really—you have to let me clean up after if we make the iced coffee."

He assured her it really wasn't a problem. She could make all the mess she wanted—it couldn't get any worse. The truth was, though, he'd spent a good part of an hour cleaning around the sink. Unlike on her last visit, it no longer contained one dirty dish.

He stood back and watched as she prepared her drink. He felt like a bad host, but he'd never seen this done before. He tried to pay close attention so maybe he could make it next time and have it all ready for her. While she was chipping the ice, between grinds of the mixer, he asked her what her e-mail name meant. As soon as he asked, he regretted it, a little concerned it was something off-color that he should have left alone. Because kids today made all kinds of sexual references that they never had in his day. Heck, kids didn't drink coffee in his day.

"Fudgie," she said. "You know—'cause I'm not really from around here anymore. I come up for the summer like a Fudgie." She shrugged and he could see her bra straps: burgundy. "Plus, I work at T.G.I.Fudge."

"And you're sixteen years old."

"Right," she said. "So . . . FuG16."

What she ended up with looked like a mocha milkshake, and she poured it into two tall glasses. It wasn't bad.

He announced that he could probably make these himself and she said, "No doubt. You're learning all kinds of new stuff!" She clinked her glass to his, downed the last of her drink and poured herself a refill.

When they moved into the den and got the thing fired up again and they were sitting side by side, he smelled the hazelnut coffee on her breath and it made it feel like she was even closer. It was better, somehow, that he could smell her coffee breath. It filled the house more, in the way he imagined noisy kids running around the living room would. It was nice. Less lonely.

She left it up to him what they should work on that day; asked if he was ready to work on the word processing software or if he had any questions about what they'd covered last time.

"Well," he said, "I'm e-ing out okay and people are e-ing in okay—"

"You're getting e-mail."

"Yes, but I can't seem to get to the picture part." He was reluctant to admit this, because she'd already shown him, but he just couldn't remember. It was all too much, too fast.

The girl claimed there was some sort of difference between e-mail and the Web. This began to explain some of the problems he'd been having. He'd sent and received several e-mails and yet he still hadn't figured out how to look up information. (And he certainly hadn't seen anything remotely racy.)

"It's okay," she said. "You can't take it all in at once. We can keep going over it and it'll start making sense, little by little. You'll get it, don't worry."

He loved her attitude, her confidence in him, though he was pretty sure it was misplaced. Sixty-nine might just be too old to grasp the complexities of something like a "world-wide web."

She told him, "Let's try the small-town thing. Think of e-mail like checking your box at the post office. Think of the Internet like going over to the library. Like going into the reference section at the library, only tons easier. Anything you want to look up, you just do a search."

He still didn't get it. How could you do a search if you didn't know the filing system? Of course, he'd never learned the Dewey decimal system either. He knew religion was in the 200s and jazz was 781, but that was about it. "But what are the subjects? Are there categories you look under, or—?"

"It's whatever," she said. "What do you like?"

"What do I like?" Again, he wasn't sure he knew the choices.

"Okay," she said. "It's not like a menu at a restaurant. They don't give you a list you pick from. *You* decide. You tell *them*." She looked at him, waiting, and he suddenly felt, more than ever, that this was just too difficult for him to manage. "What do you like to spend a lot of time reading about or looking at or learning more about?"

He was staring at the photo of Mary over the desk, thinking maybe he had it now.

The girl said, "Like, the Bible, maybe?"

He had to laugh at this suggestion. "The *Bible*? No, I can *read* the Bible if I want to know about the Bible. And believe me—" He stopped himself: there was no reason he should be telling this young girl how absolutely retired he felt. From all of it. No, this was for something else, this new toy. "Jazz," he said.

He could feel her studying his face. "Really. Okay. Good. You mean like Kenny G, Louis Armstrong . . . ?" She pronounced it *Louie*.

"Not particularly," he said. "But there are many different forms."

"That's something I've never really gotten—jazz."

He told her that was fine—she was a kid, she was supposed to hate it.

But she shook her head at this. "That's a dumb excuse, me being a kid. I don't want to approach things that way, based on what I'm supposed to like and not like. I just haven't found a way to connect to it, I guess. I'm sure it's not jazz's fault."

It made an almost alarming amount of sense. Her ability to size up the situation so accurately was admirable at her age. She really was special, this one. And bright. To his ear, of course, she suffered some from that malady of her generation—an almost laconic indifference toward speaking concisely—a circling and avoidance of linguistic specificity that bordered on a verbal form of shoulder-shrugging. But beyond the typical "whatever"s and "or something"s and "and stuff"s, she actually seemed to have original thoughts to express.

For a while, as she showed him how to define searches using hyphens and *and/or* and *this, not this,* he thought about what she'd just said about wanting to find a way to connect to jazz. When he asked her about her own musical tastes, she claimed she didn't really have a favorite kind of music and he had a thought. He went into the living room and thumbed through the records till he found Coltrane's *My Favorite Things.* Blowing across it, out of habit, he placed it on the hi-fi. Over in the doorway, the girl now stood, leaning, boneless, waiting. There was the scratch and pop as the needle found the groove and she made a face at the preliminary sound, asking, "What's *that*?"

"Wait," he said. "Just listen. Close your eyes."

She did. Then came the opening bars, the loopy, almost Arabian noodling, the shuffle of Elvin Jones's brushwork. He let it play before asking, "What do you see?"

She allowed one giggle, then swallowed it, turning serious. "A mountain. Tall grass. A lady with a guitar, spinning." Then the realization—a smile like an explosion. "Julie Andrews."

"Right," he said.

"'. . . these are a few of my favorite things!'"

"Sure," he said. "You can connect to *that,* can't you? Now keep listening and tell me what else you hear."

She closed her eyes again and tilted her head and the music seemed to draw her deeper into the room. As she moved closer, it seemed almost a glide, a sideways slide, with a hint of waltz, and he could picture her, in that lilting moment, standing across from him on a dance floor in decades past, in a church social hall; could picture himself singling her out for the bright aura of grace around her and approaching her and asking her to dance.

"It's still the same song," she said, her eyes still closed, "but now I'm hearing it like totally different. It's . . . exotic, like snake charmer music or something you'd hear in the market in a far-off land. Some place with goats—"

He had to tease her about this. "Goats?"

She giggled again, but kept going, "Yeah! And all the favorite things are maybe things you've never seen before—brand-new foods and experiences and stuff—whatever they're selling at this market. Colorful fabrics and strange candies and fruits. All new stuff. New favorite things. Right?"

"Maybe," he said. "Sure."

She opened her eyes and her face flushed red. "Maybe that's dumb."

"Not at all," he said. They stood there, listening. She kept tugging on her ear, head tipped. They stood there till the track was over. When it started into "Ev'ry Time We Say Goodbye," he moved to the hi-fi to turn it off.

"That's okay," she said. "Why don't you just leave it? Let it play."

So he left it on while they went back to the computer to finish the lesson. And then he thanked her.

"For what?" she said.

"Your description. Now I can hear it all over again as if for the first time, too."

She wasn't finished with her lesson when the record stopped. She stopped in the middle of showing him how to use the address book to let him get up and flip it over for "Summertime" and "But Not for Me." She seemed to like that fine, but when they were done and shutting down the computer, she asked if she could hear the first song again and he went back out and put it on. It was nice: even his own kids, who actually had some musical talent, never did much more than tolerate his tastes.

Later, while she was straightening up in the kitchen, washing out her mug and the coffee pot, he heard her humming the melody and it caused him to stop in the hallway and listen. She must not have heard him there, because she continued, uninterrupted. He almost gave himself away with a sob when he remembered Mary doing that same thing, humming in the kitchen. But this wasn't Mary. This was someone alive and real and humming in his kitchen. And the fact that it was a song he'd introduced her to, felt almost like he'd given her a present she liked, as if it were a pretty dress or a hat and it fit her just fine.

THAT NIGHT HE DECIDED TO TRY what she called "Web surfing"; just explore a little bit. He remembered what she'd said about racy sites and the first image that came to mind was a deck of pinup girl playing cards he'd had in the years before seminary: leggy girls with their scandalously dark stockings—and, sometimes, even their panties—exposed by one semi-comic mishap or another. These were pre-*Playboy,* mere cheesecake. Some fellows called them Petty girls, calendar girls, but the ones he had were all painted by . . . he could picture the draftsmanlike lettering now: Elvgren. He wasn't sure he had the spelling right but he typed this in.

Gil Elvgren. That was his name. There were several options listed and he clicked on one and there they were—those fresh smiling faces from another time, pure and vibrant as produce. They were popping up now like mushrooms—rows of little square pictures, and each one contained another cheesecake girl. He scrolled down and there were more. He clicked on the squares and each one grew massive, filling the screen. He could see the brushstrokes in the poodle skirt, the palette knife work in the bearskin rug. He couldn't imagine having this when he was a teenager. He might never have gone to seminary. Heck, he might never have left his room.

A few of these pinups he felt he recognized from the old card deck. How dog-eared and unmanageable those cards seemed now. He was always terrified he'd left one out, that it would fall down behind his bed and his mother would find it while running the sweeper and he'd come home to her sobbing in shame. Each time he looked at them he had to perform an elaborate procedure of locking the door, securing the shades, and dealing them out on the bedspread so that he could see as many of his favorites as would fit and still leave room for him.

There were more pages, more "galleries," it said. There were far more than fifty-two pinups here. He went back to the list of Web sites and opened another, and right away, he saw how many more there were. This Elvgren fellow was apparently the Norman Rockwell of cheesecake, according to the text. Very prolific, over several decades. Plus, there were options leading to other pinup girl artists, and other cheesecake sites, some even with photos. It just went on and on.

It felt like his brain might boil over. He was actually getting uncomfortably warm. He closed out of there and drafted e-mails to his daughter and his son, trying to concentrate on writing carefully and at length, giving them a detailed update on the beginning of summer in Weneshkeen, the doings at the church and his progress with his tutor. Concentrate, he told himself, on the positive benefits of this machine. Avoid the idle and base. But the pinups were still in his head and it was very hard not to go back.

27

MARK STARKEY SAT SEPARATED from the pilot-boys by a wall of potted shrubs that partitioned a small section of the deck behind Carrigan's so minors like himself could walk out from the restaurant side and enjoy the view of the river, along with the adults on the bar side. They'd dragged him along after work under the pretense of celebrating the fact that he'd gone a whole week without having "had to" be pushed into the river. But now that they were there, they were pretty much ignoring him, drinking their Bell's on the grown-up side and talking about people he'd never heard of and not even springing for a Coke for him or anything. But whatever. This was fine, since he only really came along with the hope of running into Courtney.

He was watching the patio door that led back into the restaurant, the kids in baggy shorts and young parents in matching summer ensembles corralling them in and out, when he felt something tugging at his arm and glanced down to see it was Keith's grimy finger, poking through the split in the shrubs, hooked in the sleeve of his T-shirt.

"Not bad, kid." He was appraising his upper arm. "At least you're starting to *look* like you belong on the river."

"For real? I'm getting muscles?"

"Please. You don't get muscles doing what we do. You get dark. You get—" He turned back to Walt. "What's that word?"

"Swarthy." Winking, Walt raised his beer to him in salute. "That's what makes the girls go for the pilot-boys."

"Even the puny little under-boys," Keith said. "The rich blondie girl, for example? Is it just the fine, fine booty on Ass Boy here or is it because the girls, they like 'em dark? Perhaps we shall never know . . ." He raised his beer, too, clinked into Walt's, and took a big swig that left him breathless. "*Da*-mn! Yessir . . . Say, speaking of liking 'em dark, what's this I'm hearing about someone out to vonBushberger's shacking up with the migrants?"

"Not shacking up," Walt said. "Married her. And yes, there's a baby on the way, but spare your small mind the strain of doing the dirty-minded math, Keith. Honeymoon baby maybe, but the kid's legitimate enough."

"But one of the Mex girls? Really? The guy's one of the actual family or some hired hand?" Walt then explained it was the son but Mark didn't catch the name. The whole thing was hard to follow. Keith said, "The son who's a queer?"

"Turns out he's not," Walt said. "And I don't think the girl's from Mexico."

"Well, Hispanic, whatever."

"Actually," Walt said, "when it comes down to it, the baby's not going to stick out all that much. Look at Von. Von's kinda . . . swarthy himself. In the summer at least. Don't you think?"

Keith agreed that yeah, this Von guy they were talking about *did* get dark and Walt pointed out that the man's dad had been the same. "Fred vonBushberger. Very dark features for a . . . whatever it is they are. What is that, anyway? Austrian? German?"

Keith said, "Dutch, I think. One of those. Swedish maybe?" Mark felt a sharp prick at his biceps and turned back to see Keith was flicking his arm, catching him off-guard. "Still with us, Ass Boy?"

He'd been trying to follow and, though the name rang a bell, he couldn't match it up with any of the boats. He knew that familiarizing himself with the people was part of the job; the way to get better tips. Still, he was more interested in trying to hook up with Courtney this evening.

"Whatever it is," Walt said, "for that type of extraction—Northern European, Scandinavian—they do run a little Mediterranean-looking almost. Surprisingly so."

"Still," Keith said. "Mediterranean-dark's not Hispanic-dark."

"True." Walt tipped his head the way he did on the river, calling over to Mark with a heads-up. "Whoop! Watch your starboard."

Thinking it was Courtney coming in, Mark swung around in his seat and his elbow jounced the tray held by a waitress serving Cokes to a bunch of Fudgie-looking kids at the table behind him. Keith sat up a little in his chair, calling over the shrubs to the waitress, "We apologize for our under-boy there, Joslyn. Kid's got sex on the brain."

"Do *not!*" Mark said. "Cut it out." The guy was such a jerk. The kids at the next table were snickering and the waitress gave him a big wink. Besides, he was way wrong. At least about the sex part. Okay, so maybe he'd been thinking about Courtney, wondering when he would see her next, if he was supposed to see her tonight, if she wanted him to come find her, maybe go over to her boat slip or her condo, or if he was supposed to play it cool. But it wasn't just the sex. He'd had sex before. Maybe even three different times before her. But never with a real girlfriend, an official girlfriend, and never with anyone he was really psyched about; always with just okay girls that liked him for a long time, secretly, only he knew all about it ahead of time and ended up hooking up with them at a party or studying after school after they said that it wouldn't have to mean anything, that they could just hang. They were nice enough, he guessed, just nothing to jump up and down about. And even though they'd each said they would be cool and they were just friends and all, they never failed to bug him afterward, staring at him and asking, "What're you thinking?" when really he wasn't thinking anything, just lying there wondering if that was really all there was to it, if this was the whole deal or if he was supposed to feel something more.

"So Von's okay with that, then?" Keith was saying.

Walt chuckled, but he sounded a little tired. "Being a little Mediterranean-looking?"

"Dude. The kid marrying the picker girl. Von approve?"

Walt let out a long wet stream of air, like what Keith had just asked was complete bullshit, him being quite a bit younger, less worldly at twenty-eight, twenty-nine, whatever he was. "What's to approve? There's no controlling who stirs who up. Is there? What good would approving or not approving do? You never know who's going to stop you cold, all of a sudden, stick their hand in your gut and twist it into a knot, just by looking at you a certain way, even if it's maybe the hundredth time they've looked at you. That one time it's different and then you're in, you're screwed." The old guy was on a roll. Mark had never heard him like this. "Maybe they just walk past your window a certain way, or it's the way they turn their hand, picking a piece of fruit off a tree branch or suddenly throw a bowl of soup in your face—"

"*Soup?*" Keith said, snorting. "Whoa now! That's just too specific." He parted the shrub, addressing Mark. "Hey, Ass Boy! Five bucks says Walt's slipping into the world of personal memoir here—whattaya say?" He stuck his hand through the shrubs to shake. Mark ignored the dirty palm and the offer to wager and Keith quickly retracted it.

"I'm *saying*," Walt said, sounding like he was losing a little patience, "it changes from that time on who you are and what you want and who you want to be. There's no preparing for that sort of event, legislating that. You can't control that, be blamed for it, can you? Seems like a person'd be a jackass to try."

"I guess," Keith said and the patio lights came on all at once, probably on a timer, and the two of them started talking about the strange lights that had reportedly been seen in the sky. Mark had heard enough. This was now just old-man talk, coots in their cups, with nothing to be learned about the river work, and it was probably okay now to tune them out, with their boring local gossip and their meaningless life philosophies. Besides, it looked like he would have to go track down

Courtney. He got up from the table and announced, over the shrubs, that he was leaving.

"Ah, damn," Keith said. "Here I was all set to treat you to a Shirley Temple. Well, run along then, Romeo. And uh, hey . . . 'Nice ass!'"

28

THE PART ABOUT STAYING WITH HER DAD every summer that Kimberly Lasco never got used to was this weird feeling that he never went grocery shopping when she wasn't there. Of course he must have— there weren't enough good restaurants to sustain someone who never cooked, even if he could afford to eat out every night, which she was sure he couldn't. And he didn't seem to have a girlfriend who fed him at her place—at least nothing that steady. So she knew he had to go shopping on his own once in a while. But every summer, especially on the first trip to the Spartan, the guy acted like he had no concept of what kind of food to buy. Or where anything was. And it wasn't like the store was some big-ass Kroger like back home.

"You need to pick out what you like," he always said. Which was also lame because her tastes really never changed that much, so you would think he would eventually get the hang of what to buy. But he never did. He just liked to drag her along and make her decide. And she wouldn't mind handling the groceries herself, but he always insisted they do it together. It was some sort of bonding time, she imagined, at least in his mind.

Their first trip to the Spartan this summer, they had the cart about half-full and he was walking it along slow as a grandpa, slouched on it and asking her a lot of silly questions about the sophomore winter dance—stale news by now, plus she was certain he knew all about it from her mom, who kept him updated. She could tell by the sorts of questions he asked that he already knew the answers. It sounded fake and pre-arranged, like those late-night talk shows and their pre-interviews.

When they came around a big Keebler elf display, entering the frozen meat section, he surprised her by jerking the cart back around behind the cardboard Ernie the Elf. It was like he was hiding. "Hold it!" he whispered. "Wait!"

She assumed he was just being lame. She didn't wait but stuck her head back around, peeking. The one thought she had was maybe he did have a girlfriend. But that wasn't it. It was her dad's neighbor, Mrs. Starkey, the tall thin blond lady with the strained-looking face. Kimberly felt her dad's hand on her shirt, yanking her back, and then he snuck a peek. After a second, he darted ahead, around the corner into the frozen meat aisle, almost like he was tiptoeing. Kimberly followed, feeling nervous about what he might be up to. Mrs. Starkey was gone now, but her cart was there and her dad was snooping on her big heap of groceries. He even picked up a couple items and rooted around, glancing down the aisle to make sure Mrs. Starkey wasn't returning.

"What're you doing?" Kimberly wanted to know.

He had a package of those gross sausages the old sheriff made by hand—SloffBrauts. "Spicing things up," he said and reached into the freezer with the ones from the cart. She saw the word *Mild*. He grabbed a couple replacements. She saw the words *Lava Links* as he tossed them in the crowded cart and moved a couple rolls of paper towels over them, hiding them.

"Da-ad," she said. She couldn't believe he was acting this way.

But he was pulling her back down the aisle, hustling double-time in a quick little butt-wiggle. "Come on, come on, come on!" he said like he was maybe ten. It felt like they'd just TPed someone's house or soaped a windshield on Devil's Night.

Real mature, she thought. *Realllllll mature.*

Minutes later, they almost crashed carts head-on in the produce section, whipping around between the big bins of piled fruit. Mrs. Starkey. Neither one said hello or even any actual words but both let out an exasperated sort of *tsk* that sounded, to Kimberly, like something breaking inside her own chest. It was awful.

And it didn't feel any better when, a few minutes later, they were checking out and her dad kept craning his head to see over to the other register where Mrs. Starkey was checking out, trying to see if she noticed her sausages had been swapped with spicier ones. He acted like he was going to start snickering. Kimberly wanted to elbow him in the gut.

A STRONG WIND BLEW OFF LAKE MICHIGAN, enough to clear the obstacle of the Starkeys' lakeside house and reach all the way to Kimberly Lasco's bedroom and whisper through the drapes and shake the birch at the corner of the house. She went to the window, looking out at the dark canopies of the neighbor's trees making that grass skirt sound, and she thought she heard another sound and saw a light, flickering over toward the access road, a white flash among the shimmering trees. Great, she thought, I'm about to join the ranks of those freaks who've seen lights at night . . . Just great. But then she saw it again and was relieved to see it wasn't in the sky, but lower down. She was looking at it through the treetops and ground cover that bordered the road at the end of the driveway.

It was a camera flash. It had to be. Someone was down at the end of the driveway, taking photos of something.

Oh please, she said in the voice of prayer. *Please don't let it be my dad.*

29

HE WASN'T EXPECTING the girl, but it was her, knocking at the kitchen door.

"Okay," she said, all in a rush, "I know it's not Thursday, but I'm bored and I just thought I'd pop by and see if you had any questions or problems. And also, well, I was wondering . . ." Her nose wrinkled up: she was either tongue-tied or repulsed. Or both. "How can I put this? Since it seems like you're maybe not real big on cleaning . . ."

Oh no, he thought. It was true. He did smell. She was trying to tell him he had an old-man odor. She was going to insist, if they were going to continue to work on the computer together . . .

Knock it off, he told himself. Don't be absurd. She wouldn't come over here just to tell him he stank. That is, not unless she thought it was a sign he was dying and she was saving his life by pointing it out. But wait—he'd read that somewhere himself, that signs of various fatal diseases, like cancer, can appear in olfactory form, a warning shot across the nostrils. Maybe that was true and maybe he *was* dying and maybe that's why she appeared at his doorstep with this message that was difficult to spill.

But she didn't ask him if he ever bathed. Instead she asked if he would consider hiring her to come in and help around the house a little, maybe do a little cooking, get him groceries, run the vacuum . . . He saw now that she had a bucket at her feet, stuffed with rags, rubber gloves, oven cleaner and the like.

"You wouldn't have to pay me a buttload. It's just, I don't get enough hours at the fudge shop and hey, I kind of like hanging out here."

He wasn't sure what to say to this at all, but it sounded so familiar, like the sort of arrangement Ben had been pestering him about for the past few months—someone to come in and help—that he answered, almost automatically, "Yes. That would be fine."

"Good," she said, beaming. "Great." And then, wincing, her nose wrinkled again, her wide mouth spread in a grin, "Did I just say 'buttload' to a minister?"

A few hours later, after they split a pitcher of iced coffee out on the deck, gazing out at the river, he stood alone again in his spotless kitchen, wondering what was happening to his life. Even the toaster shone, reflecting his stubbled gray chin. How embarrassing, he thought— Add a missing tooth and a pickaxe and I could play the part of a prospector. He made a mental note to pick up some razors at the Spartan. Retired or not, there was no excuse for poor personal grooming. Especially if he was going to have visitors popping in like this now. There was no reason, he decided, that he had to look like a misanthropic hermit, a creepy old shut-in.

———

ON THURSDAY, when she came for her tutorial, she showed him how to create new files and move files and how to save files and empty files into a sort of trash can, and it led naturally to the subject of his own disordered den. She had a plan that involved plastic storage bins that could be stored in the attic and the basement. She said she'd pick up a few and bring them by next time. "Just organizing it will make this shrink down a lot," she said, "but we're also going to pitch one-quarter of it. Deal?" His kids had been laying out just such harsh prescriptions for his messy den and he'd resisted their suggestions. But now, with her staring him down and nodding her head, how could he not agree? She started in on the books that afternoon, reordering the shelves and digging the strays out from under the piles of paper. They had to do it together because he needed to tell her which subjects went with which. "It's weird," she said. "These're all basically your minister books, right? It's all basically religion and stuff in that area, but still, there's a lot of different slots when you break it down, huh?"

He agreed it was a very vast and diverse field of study. "Lots of delineation and hairsplitting."

She was right: with the books all properly shelved, a lot of the clutter on the floor was cleared away. Sorting the rest into the bins would be easy.

Next she announced he was going to work on attachments. He was to compose a practice letter in Word, then send her an e-mail and attach the file. Then he should go online and find an interesting Web site and send her another e-mail with a link to that Web site. Meanwhile, she was going to work on the bathroom. He objected, thinking of the unholy state of the toilet and what else she might find, the stray pubic hairs and other disasters. But she wouldn't listen to his objections, which he could scarcely make that specific, and so he had to keep it on the "oh, please don't bother with that!" level.

"When you're done," she told him, "you can maybe make the iced coffee."

Again, they drank it out back. Summer was definitely starting. There was a warm breeze that whitecapped the waves on Lake Michigan, just beyond the river. She took off her long-sleeved shirt, revealing a snug spaghetti-strapped top that, if it hadn't been deep orange with a decal in the center of a big-eyed cartoon blob and the words *Hello Kitty,* he might have thought was a slip. It's just a shirt, he told himself. It's just hot out.

It was reassuring, feeling the sun on his face, the advent of another season, and he mentioned how it was really starting to get nice out and how he imagined pretty soon she'd probably want to come by less often; that she'd probably want to be out in the sun on her days off from the fudge shop. "So I guess I better hurry up and master the computer," he said.

She told him there was no rush at all and then she said, "Listen. I don't want to be pushy—if it's not a good idea, that's totally cool—really—but I was just thinking, would it be a problem if I lay out here sometimes?"

He didn't respond because he didn't know how to respond. He didn't know what he was responding to. He wasn't absolutely certain, in that moment, *what* she was asking him permission to do. So he said nothing and in the silence, she was already backtracking, waving her hands as if to erase the idea. "Forget it. If it's not cool, forget it. I won't do it. It's just . . . I feel funny doing it at my dad's house."

He didn't like the sound of this—not the use of his own yard, but her reluctance to use her own. He felt compelled to pry. "Is there anything . . . wrong there? With you and your dad?" He made a mental note to ask around about Kurt Lasco. He hated to think that there was something inappropriate happening there, but that sort of thing did happen, as awful as it was, and he'd made a real effort, during the years of his ministry, to put aside his own innate impulse to avoid these unpleasant realities and instead approach them honestly, dead-on. He hated discovering the darkness in people's lives, but ignoring it was no way to help either.

"It's not my dad," she said. "Really. It's just, uncomfortable. With the neighbors. They're not getting along with my dad and they have a kid and he's my age and I just feel funny sitting out in the yard now with him looking at me when they hate us and all . . ."

"I see," he said, though he really didn't. But at least it didn't sound like there was anything inappropriate going on with her dad. That was a relief.

"And plus the view's no good at home. It's not like it was when I was little. It makes me kind of sad, how it's different now."

He told her that would be fine. She was welcome to use the yard all she wanted, adding that there was a little nothing of a dock out there, too, with a wooden ladder leading down to the water. "There used to be a dinghy moored to the ladder," he said, "back when the kids were young, but I don't know if the church has it stored somewhere or if it just got too rotten and was never replaced. I could look into it, if you like."

She told him not to bother with the dinghy. The yard would be fine, wonderful. "And maybe down on that little dock. But is that okay with the church, me hanging out?"

"Never mind about them. It's okay with me."

"I just wasn't sure how much is your property and where the church's begins. There's no fence between here and the church . . . And also, how far down to the water? I just wasn't clear on any of that."

"Well, the church owns all of it. If you want to be official. The land and the waterfront and the house. But it's still my home." *As of today,* he thought. *Who knows about next week?* But he didn't see the need to admit all that. "I don't need the church's permission."

"But," she said, "you know—if I'm tanning, I'd be in a bathing suit."

He hoped he wasn't blushing. There wasn't anything wrong with a bathing suit. "I know," he said, sounding, to his own ears, defensive. Honestly, he hadn't known—he hadn't really thought it out, but the fuzzy picture in his mind had been more or less one of her dressed as she was now, in shorts and a sleeveless top. Trying to lighten things up, he said, "The only thing I can imagine the church objecting to is if you fall in the river and drown. I'm not really up to lifeguarding these days. I'm assuming you can swim, you'll be okay unsupervised?"

"Please!" she said. "I'm sixteen. I don't need a lifeguard." She bent her arm, strong-man style, grinning. "Feel that muscle."

"Okay," he said, chuckling. "So you're fit as a fiddle."

"Go on," she said. "Feel it! Like a rock!"

But he didn't feel it. He waved her off and turned away, still chuckling, saying, "Very good, Esther Williams. Very good . . ." rising and clearing away the empty glasses and the pitcher of iced coffee, heading for the house, moving quickly before she could hop up to help. There was a sense of relief at getting away from her, a sense of escape from social peril, and yet, mere seconds later, the moment gone, he felt something hard in his gut like heartbreak, like regret.

30

IT WASN'T AN ETHICAL QUESTION but rather one of logistics that had Roger Drinkwater holding off on his next attack, the move he'd come to think of as *Operation: Nozzle Muzzle*. The only doubt nagging at him was whether it would be better to hit all the jet-skis at once or space them out as a series of hit-and-run events over several nights. The former plan had the advantage that the targets would not grow increasingly alert with each strike—he would hit them all when everyone's guard was still down. The latter plan had the advantage of prolonged aggravation—a campaign of attrition. Plus, it would be less physically exhausting for him.

The plan was simple: swim underwater in the cover of night with a socket wrench and remove the plastic venturi nozzle, the thing at the end of the actual jet that directed the outtake of water and thereby controlled the steering on a jet-ski.

The only issue was the nut size. He wasn't about to carry a whole socket set with him. The first thought was to make a recon swim with a wad of putty, jam the putty over the nut on one of them, and then bring it home and measure the impression. He was planning to do that the other night but earlier in the day, while gassing up his truck at the Mobil, he turned to see, pulled up at the other side of the pump, a minivan plus a trailer with two tangerine orange jet-skis. He looked around. The driver, some mullet-head in winter camouflage warm-up pants, blacks and grays and whites, was across the parking lot, talking loudly and angrily on the pay phone about how his cell phone was "totally fucked." Roger reached through the window, removed the measuring tape from his glove compartment, stepped over the pump island and made the measurement.

That night, it was moonless and a go. He'd snorkel it, opting for the wetsuit not so much for its warmth but for the black cover it provided—he'd be a kind of wet catburglar. The wrench went into the zippered utility sleeve along his thigh. He stood in front of the mirror on the back of his bedroom door, listening to the frogs and crickets and thinking how much it sounded like he was back on the canal in Rach Soi, about to go out on a mine-clearing recon with his squad buddies, Coots and Miller. He turned to go and at the last minute decided to bring a small black nylon backpack. It would be slower moving through the water with this, but it wasn't a swim meet. He'd try one and if it went easily, he'd hit them all tonight. And if he did more than one, he'd need the backpack to haul his loot away. (There was no point in polluting the lake further, and besides, they might find the nozzles in shallow water and just reattach them.)

Three hours later, he was standing in his shed in a robe, admiring his war trophies spread out on the floor: sixteen oily nozzles, looking like the foreskins snipped off an army of robot invaders. God, he wished he could tack them up on the outside of the shed. Show them off like the rack of a ten-point buck.

But he knew better than that. This was the sort of proud moment you celebrate alone. So he ran a stringer through them all and hung them, temporarily, inside his chimney, until he could dispose of them in a better way.

And then the next morning, figuring he'd already had his exercise, he slept in. There was a little noise at first, very briefly—just enough to cause him to roll over—as the first ones out hopped on their rides and screamed out into the lake, arrow-straight, with no controls and then the others must have caught on, because it got very quiet again. He imagined he heard grumbling, swearing, yelps, teenaged whining, but that might have been something he dreamed. If there really were such noises, they weren't loud enough to wake him. He was exhausted, after all. He'd had a big night.

JON HATCHERT, THE NEW SHERIFF, was standing on Roger's porch the next morning. Other than his useless bathing cap suggestion, Roger hadn't had much previous interaction with the guy, but it was rapidly adding up to enough for him to form an opinion. Hatchert seemed to take that cop look a little too seriously, with his well-manicured mustache and crisp shirts and swagger. Like it was part of the mandatory uniform. Plus, he asked a lot of insulting questions, finally arriving at this one: "Isn't it interesting that you're one of the very few residents on the lake we didn't hear from this morning? Not a peep out of you."

"Could that possibly be, Sheriff, because I don't own a jet-ski?"

"Possibly. Which is very suspicious, by the way. You better believe I've taken note of that fact."

"The fact that I've chosen not to pollute the lake and abuse my neighbors, that puts me under suspicion? Hey, I don't water-ski or blast rap music either: you wanna get out your handcuffs?" He was starting to think the little pissant wasn't just annoying but possibly mentally deficient.

Looking past him, he watched Janey Struska moving along the water's edge from around near the old Willoughby place. He took it she'd been instructed to look around for the nozzles—as if some kid might have stashed them in a woodchuck hole or they'd washed ashore—and she looked pretty halfhearted about the task, resenting the dumb deputy jobs, or maybe she knew better, that it was a waste of time. She was moving with that sort of roll-walk, that cop thing, with the hands on the utility belt. She'd grown into a solid hunk of woman, tall and unapologetically curvy, and he admired the way she carried her weight with a confidence he didn't see in many white women. *Bik-waakaazo gi-diyenh, songan bemossewin* was the phrase from his Uncle Jimmy Two-Hands—he wasn't quite sure what it meant. Something about the rump.

When she arrived at the porch, standing just behind her new boss, a step or two down on the stoop, Roger dropped the poker-face Indian thing suddenly and intentionally, for her benefit, and made a big show of greeting her, letting this jerk see they went back, the two of them. After a few niceties, he asked her, right in front of Hatchert, "Say, Janey, you see your old boss much anymore?"

The corner of her mouth seemed to twitch. She knew what he was up to with this, he could tell. "When he's not out on his boat or out in his shed, making those braut links."

"Next time you do, tell him I said hello and we all miss him. Everybody."

With that, he turned and went back inside. End of interview.

31

THERE WAS THE MAIN HOUSE and the little house and the other house: this is the way it was with the vonBushbergers. For four generations, the head of the family and his immediate family had lived in the main house. When a son married, he moved into the little house. When the next married, he moved into the other house. When the father died and the eldest son took over, he moved back into the main house. The system had always worked out just fine.

All three houses were painted the same color, a dull yellow, almost white, like a lemon meringue made when you were running low on lemons. It was called "Clear Dawn Yellow" and the label on the can said "Manufactured by the Beavans Bros. Paint Co. of Union, S. Carol." And the address was pre–zip code. The problem was, the current holding company no longer made Clear Dawn Yellow, on account of the lead content. Apparently the color had been a favorite for henhouses in the South and traces of lead had shown up in the yolks. Roy Kunk, at the hardware store, was trying to locate a "passable" substitute, was how he put it, but Von was not convinced. All three houses could use a touch-up, but "passable" did not cut it. "It's either what it is," Von told him, "or it's not what it is." Besides, he couldn't see why they'd stop making the stuff just because of a little lead, a few dull-witted chickens. It made no sense, considering they had a whole damn lighthouse right out there on the point crumbling radioactive material into Lake Michigan and nobody gave a hoot about *that*.

A few weeks after Marita and Jack moved into the little house, Von pulled into the turnaround and saw Marita out on the front porch, painting the front door red. She'd gotten about halfway down the door.

Von stared from the cab of the truck. What the hell was that girl thinking? Never mind that you remove a door before painting—pop the pins and lay it out on sawhorses and do it right. Never mind that. But *red*?

He climbed out and as he got a little closer, now saw it was a crusty quart can she was working off of, the leftover tractor paint. He realized in that moment that he'd never explained to her about the traditional color scheme at vonBushbergers', how they were still trying to find something to match the Clear Dawn Yellow. He hadn't bothered explaining this to Marita because (A) she didn't have any paint, and (B) he just didn't think of it. If anything, he would have assumed she would be too busy getting the inside of the house orderly and cozy and setting up a nursery. There was a chronic carpenter ant problem in the little kitchen, a cracked window in the back, and the bathroom could use new wallpaper, like maybe some that would stay put on the wall. So who knew she'd go out in the barn and poke around in the old paint cans? Priority-wise, it didn't make a lick of sense.

But maybe a red door meant something in her land. He had to caution himself about making a scene, especially if he was possibly stepping on some multicultural toes here. He thought of the Amish in Pennsylvania, with those round hex signs painted on their barns, and was damn glad he wasn't Amish. That was the kind of thing they'd expect him to preserve once he got the Centennial Farm designation.

He cleared his throat and said, "Look, I don't want to be the one to question your superstitions, but—maybe this is some sort of *Guatemalan* thing, but—"

"Nooooo . . ." she said, mocking him. "Is not a Guatemalan thing, not a superstition thing. This is a . . . what you say? . . . 'cheery' thing."

"A cherry thing?" Maybe *she* didn't want to call it superstitious, but if she was thinking it would bring a better cherry crop this season, well . . .

"Cheeeeery!" she repeated. "Cheery! I say it wrong? Happy-looking! You understand 'happy' around these place? *Que pendejo* . . ."

"Hey! I understood that last bit, okay? We've only had migrant pickers up here every summer since before I even had ears to hear such garbage, so watch it!"

Her eyes closed and stayed that way. She breathed deeply, nostrils flaring, and her hands came together, as if in prayer; she spoke much slower and more deliberately now. "I am very truly sorry for the slip of my tongue. It was so very disrespectful to *mi suegro*. I am so very sorry, but I am very homogenized right now—"

"Hormonal." The way she was behaving, he had no doubt it was the word she meant.

She threw up her hands and walked into the little house. He followed her in. She flopped down on the old kitchen chair with a wheeze of exasperation and a loud groan from the legs scraping back against the floor. "Hormonal. Fine." She waved her hands in surrender. She looked like she was going to cry. "I just want to make it pretty." She studied him for a moment and tried it again: "Cheery."

"Look," he said. "Honey. I want the place to be cheery, same as you, but there's a certain paint—a certain color—that we need to use. All three of these houses? They've always been this one special yellow color. My great-grandfather painted that first one, then my grandfather added these two houses and painted them the same, and my father and I have been keeping it that same yellow. Now, I just don't feel right suddenly—"

She stared at him dumbfounded. "And you think *I* have the superstition?"

"It's not superstition that we want to use the same color," he said. "It's just . . . tradition."

She shook her head, then flopped it down hard on the kitchen table, like a weary rag doll. "My English is maybe not so good but I don't understand how those are different, *tradition* and *superstition*. I don't get it!"

He was going to try using the word *cohesive* but thought better of it. "Just wait for me to locate the color we use, okay? It'll be plenty cheery, believe me. You can't tell now because it's so faded and chipped, but it's a sort of lemon meringue. You'll like it, Marita. It's very . . . understated. But pretty. In the meantime, please don't start painting things."

She raised her head and looked at him. "Can I just ask how long you've been trying to find this special paint?"

He didn't appreciate this line of interrogation. "It's taking a while to locate, that's all."

Leaning back, she crossed her arms, resting them on the lump of her belly. "How long have you been looking for this paint? A simple question!"

"I really don't know. A while."

"More than one year?"

"Oh, yeah." It had been three years actually, but she didn't need to hear that. "This is tractor paint, anyway. This stuff you used. You know what it would cost to paint this entire house in tractor paint?"

She shrugged. "It's paint. Paint is paint! How is it different?"

He wanted to say, *For one thing, this house doesn't heat up to 200 degrees, nor does it slog through mud and kick up rocks* . . . but he thought he would be wasting his breath. So he just said. "It's different, okay? It's not cheap."

Besides, he didn't want to have one red building. Or really even one red door. But when he got up to leave, passing through the half-painted door, he stopped and stared at it, taking a deep frustrated breath and letting it out through his nose. Marita must have heard him. She called from inside, "So do I finish the door or paint it over?"

"With what?" Hadn't he just told her there wasn't any more of the Clear Dawn Yellow. "Just—finish the door, I guess. But that's *it*."

He tried not to look at it after that. It looked ridiculous. Especially from a distance, out on the road. He caught a glance of it the next day heading down 31 and it flashed in his periphery like a goddamn sore thumb. He did his best not to think about it, but it was hard not to know it was there. It reminded him way too much of the Revels dairy farm, about five miles to the east. When Burton sold it, the new guy painted the silo cap purple. Purple! A deep funky grape. It was the laughingstock. Forty years of farming and how was Burton Revels remembered now? With cracks about "The Farmer Formerly Known as Prince." Jesus god.

32

WITH TIME TO SPARE, just nineteen days after being served, Kurt Lasco entered the village offices to file his response. It didn't overly surprise him to see Bear Eckenrod at the desk, but it was a relief: they'd shared an ice shanty out on the other lake at least since before his divorce and hell, he'd power-rodded the guy's main line at least a dozen times and barely charged him the standard price, let alone the summer people price.

"Bear," he said, slumping in the chair in front of the man's desk. His what-they-called "answer to the complaint" had become kind of a tube in his hands, a scroll, and he tossed it onto the desk, where it rolled off the man's lunch, what appeared to be a leftover pasty, wrapped in tinfoil. Bear's wife made great pasties, being from the U.P., and Kurt wondered sometimes if that's where he himself made a major mistake, marrying a woman from downstate rather than farther north.

Bear's bushy brow wrinkled as he picked up the three single-spaced pages that had felt to Kurt awfully like a term paper and unrolled them on his desk, scowling for a long spell, then eyed him levelly over his scrub brush mustache. "You actually read the complaint, Kurt? And the instructions?"

"Sure," he said, feeling like he was back in high school, slouching across from the principal or guidance counselor. "But it's not at all like he says. I explained all that pretty good, I think. It's all in there."

"It is, huh? 'Cause I fail to see where you even responded to the counts. You have to answer *each* count, Admit or Deny. All's I see is counterclaims here. The judge'll—"

Kurt cut him off. "Look, Bear. I know I'm no lawyer or great writer, but I spent like three hours on it and I spell-checked the hell out of it. I know it's a little choppy, but—"

Now it was Bear's turn to cut him off. "'Choppy'? I tell you right now, the court's not going to view this mess here as a valid answer to the complaint. This isn't small claims, it's a regular *civil* case."

It was the same guff Janey Struska gave him, but he still didn't get it. "What does that mean?"

"It means you're probably going to need to hire a lawyer." He flipped through the curled pages again. "I'm looking at this ranty mess here, Kurt, I'm guessing *more* than probably . . ." With that, he tossed it on the desk, clear of his pasty. "Jesus."

Kurt picked up the form. "It was a little confusing," he said. "I didn't really get all the terms and stuff . . ."

Bear stretched mightily, then said, "Why don't you just replace the man's trees, Kurt? Gonna be cheaper than getting into it with the guy in a civil suit, with you paying some shyster whatever-an-hour and it's costing him basically nothing."

"Fuck," Kurt said, feeling totally in over his head now, which he rubbed, running his fingers up under his cap. "Fuck a fucking duck."

Bear sighed. "Tell you what—I'll file a continuance on your behalf. Buy you a little time. But that's it: from here on in, I am not acting as your attorney."

"Thanks."

"You need to get your act together, Kurt. What the hell you doing out there—Your daughter's here, right?"

Kurt nodded.

"She's a teenaged girl, Kurt. The world is already terribly, terribly embarrassing for a teenaged girl. It just is. You think she enjoys the way you heaped this Hatfield and McCoy shit on her plate?"

"I guess not." He hadn't thought about that.

"You guess not. Get it together, Kurt, and get this thing settled. And lay off the fucking chainsaw."

Kurt got up to leave. At the door, he turned, still feeling that his side hadn't been heard. "The thing is, he's not even from here, Bear. I mean, Christ!"

Bear let out a wet raspberry and looked at him sideways, his head tilted, like he was gazing upon an idiot. "Do you *know* what kind of taxes we collect from the outsiders—those big second homes? Seriously, Kurt, I could get up right now and pull a couple files and show you what the village rakes in from these summer people and I swear it would make you rethink exactly whose town this is now and who's lucky to even live here. But you're not going to make me get up and do that now, are you, on account of I've got one of my wife's delicious pasties to wolf down in the ten minutes between now and the Sumac Days committee meeting. Right?"

"Right," Kurt said. "I'm not going to do that." But he still didn't know what the hell he *was* going to do.

33

IT WAS A FRIDAY EVENING and the sky was so clear, the stars looked like ice, like they might crack and shatter. It was just the sort of night to take the radio out on the porch and see if he could pick up the Tigers.

This was something Von had been doing since he was a boy. It started with *his* dad—one of the very few enjoyments they shared—and then he picked it up in the years after he'd taken over the main house, and it became something he did with Jack. Even Brenda would listen in for most of a game, or as much of the broadcast as they could hear, and he didn't begrudge her this. Early on in her life, she'd made it evident she wasn't going to be the sort of girly daughter he'd imagined. It was supposed to be a father and son thing, but that was okay, he expected.

It was WJR, the AM station high atop the Fisher Building. Fifty thousand watts. Ernie Harwell was the guy, the voice they used to listen for—that nasal twang that trailed away, like he was talking to you from the bottom of a well. No mistaking Ernie Harwell. There was talk now of Harwell retiring, and Von wondered if it would be harder in the future to tell when he'd zeroed in on the signal, once they had a new announcer calling the game.

On a few rare nights it was clear enough for the signal to carry all the way over from Detroit, almost two hundred miles away. It was the rarity of tuning it in that made it such a treat, the nervousness that it might slip away any second that made it so precious. He knew that. If they knew for sure they could pick up the entire broadcast every night there was a game, it would take all the fun out of it. The whole event would actually seem dull, as pedestrian as a morning dump. Most nights, getting a steady signal was hopeless, but on a night like tonight, he had a shot at it.

Von set the radio down on the edge of the porch and attached the auxiliary antenna he'd designed just for this—a long spool of copper wire with an alligator clip on the other end so it could be snapped onto the metal fence that ran along the dog pen, creating an immense antenna. "Jack," he said, holding up the clip end, knowing his son was sitting over on the glider. When he was little, Jack loved that part, being allowed to go clip it to the fence. Now it was just a matter of helping out, not making his old man do it.

"Dad," Jack said. "We're kinda . . ."

Von looked up to see what he was trying to indicate, squinting in at him on the glider. The girl was slouched against him, his arm was around her, his hand down on her belly and her feet were propped up on an overturned cherry lug. They were reading something in the narrow light of the kitchen window behind them that looked like a seed catalogue. He did look sort of pinned in, squashed. "We're picking out seeds," Jack said, "for next year. Some stuff Marita might like."

Von grunted and walked the wire over to the fence himself. When he returned to the porch and started fiddling with the dial, his son was yakking about the seeds Marita was looking for. It was hard to concentrate on finding the ballgame with Jack yakking about oregano and cilantro seeds and hot peppers and all. It was as if Jack didn't remember this part of it—the part where they just sat there in the dark and listened and shut the hell up. It was a damned important part of it.

"For next year," Marita said. "No for now."

"For the garden," Jack said. "I never thought about it much before, but we don't exactly have anything very *exotic* in our vegetable garden."

"On account of we don't live in an *exotic* land," Von grumbled.

"We're just looking ahead," Jack said, like his ears were broken or something. "I know it's a year off, but we want to add a few things to the order. Zest it up a little."

Still bent over the radio, Von swung his head around to eye them there on the glider, cuddled up. The girl just stared back at him with those big dark eyes. Tougher than she lets on, he thought. "That garden," he said, "is there to feed our family. It's not there to tantalize the palate."

"It's not a matter of tantalizing, it's a matter of—"

"I understand she's got her traditional foods and she's used to what she's used to, but what she's used to, for the most part, simply isn't going to *grow* here, son. Ask your sister. Or hell, ask her little exchange student, even—he could tell you. For sure, not from a seed and not without a greenhouse and all kinds of special care. The point of the family garden is to eat economically, so we can keep turning a profit here. But if we have to design all manner of elaborate rigmarole to force a pepper to pop out, with maybe one out of fifty duds, how is that going to be eating economically?"

"I'm just going to order a *few* things," Jack said, but he didn't say it very loudly.

"We'll stock up on some of those frozen burritos," Von said. "Now please hush so we can try to enjoy the ballgame. All right?"

Jack shut up and let him try and for a few moments all Von could hear was the squeak of the glider behind him and the rustle of the seed catalogue as they continued to turn the pages. But the station was not coming in.

Brenda appeared from the murky shadows of the yard, approaching the porch with that blossom boy, Miki. They took a seat on the steps and listened for a while as he tried to reestablish the radio signal. There were a few more squelches and yelps and a fuzzy shimmering that might have been it, but then it was gone.

The Jap scientist piped up with a brilliant suggestion. "We are closer to Chicago the Windy City, as the birds are flying, than Detroit the Motor City. Perhaps you could much easier find a station playing baseball that is coming from Chicago the Windy City."

"Miki," Brenda said. That's all she said, but it sounded to Von like the same as if she'd told him "hush."

In exchange for his suggestion, Von gave the Jap a sour face, though it was too dark on the porch, he imagined, for the guy to recognize he was doing anything of the sort. He considered launching into a geography lesson, explaining that this was Michigan, damn it. They lived in Michigan, not Illinois, and as dirty and remote and unappealing as Detroit may be, it was part of Michigan and Chicago was not. And no matter if the Cubs or the White Sox were playing on a barge floating right off Sumac Point, a hundred measly feet from shore, they would either listen to the Tigers or no one.

But the whole thing was just too tiring so he settled for making the sour face and left it at that. He would just go inside to bed, leaving the porch and the night to his mixed-up kids and the mixed-up people they'd decided to drag into his life.

ANOTHER THING WAS HAPPENING around the house now that Von found particularly irksome. There seemed to be an awful lot of congregating of the help and it not infrequently seemed to involve roasting a pig. Right up in their yard area, between the main house and the little house with Marita's half-assed red door. The line between them was getting damned blurred. All other years, before this elopement thing of his son's, when the pickers weren't working, they tended to stay down in the little migrant shacks along the other side of the orchard. And they liked it that way, he was sure. They needed their privacy as much as he did. Why would they want to subject themselves to the presence of their boss during their time off? They wouldn't. Just like he didn't need to have to close his porch windows to the smell of burning pork and that mariachi-sounding squeezebox racket.

Between this ongoing fiesta and the Japanese blossom-sniffing giant, it was getting so he was feeling edgy just about everywhere he turned. Never mind that he owned the place. It felt to him as though all of vonBushberger's—a place that anyone from the four corners of the county would instantly recognize as vonBushberger's, even without the aid of that sign he had out front and the old faded shingles that spelled it out on the big barn—was rapidly being overrun by folks who just were not vonBushbergers.

But when he tried to get a little support from his wife about this, all Carol did was laugh and remind him the Guatemalans were like

Marita's family. In fact, some of them actually were her family, which meant they were *his* in-laws.

"I understand they're in-laws now. I don't like it, of course, but I understand it."

Her next response was even less helpful: "You know, Von, just yesterday, Carroll O'Connor died, so if they ever reprise that role . . . who knows, maybe you'd have a shot at it."

He didn't care to think what the hell that was supposed to mean. Jesus god, it was like he was all alone in this, like she was having her own conversation and not even involved in his. "I'm just saying," he said, "that it's going to encourage them all to come up to the house and hang around the yard *all* the time." It had already happened on two occasions—that he knew of. Soon enough, she'd have chickens and goats living right inside the little house. But he didn't say this.

Carol sighed. "Trust me, Von. They don't want to hang around our dusty old yard. They just want to see Marita once in a while. They miss her. I'm sure that in-law thing cuts both ways."

"What are you saying? Santi Santiago isn't so crazy about me?"

"Oh, I'm sure he's crazy about you. It's like Hepburn and Tracy, the romance you two have."

There she went with her sarcasm. After three decades together, she still didn't get how unproductive her smarmy comments were— especially on an orchard, where being productive was such a damn hard undertaking each day.

"Well, for the record, I've got nothing against *him*," he said. "I understand her immediate family might want to visit her up here, but isn't there some way we can keep it at that before it gets out of hand and her friends are up here with every third cousin and friend of the third cousin?"

"What do you suggest, Von? We issue security passes?"

"No . . . I mean, we could just keep a list. Just . . . maybe stop people and ask them their name and see if they're on the list."

Carol scowled and walked out of the room, making a little exasperated sound with her mouth that came awfully close to a Bronx cheer. Clearly, she didn't get that he was just trying to hold everything together for them; to keep everything from changing and spinning out of control. Everything seemed to be heading in that direction since his dad died the year before and it was probably only going to get worse. He just had a feeling.

SCIENCE HAD NOTHING TO DO with the walk under the stars Brenda took with Miki. She vowed she wouldn't talk to him about anything to do with his project, even if that felt like safe territory and anything else made her feel like she was being a jabbering fool. Well, she thought, relenting, maybe they could talk a *little* science. How could that be avoided out in the middle of all these natural phenomena—the stars, the dew, the crickets? But nothing official, no shoptalk.

They were out here, she told herself, because the night was so clear it would almost have seemed awkward and contrived *not* to wander out into it and look up at the stars. She pointed out the constellations and explained each name. He knew a few, but in Japanese, of course. He explained that, despite a relative similarity in latitude, because of pollution and cloud cover and city lights back home, when he'd been living under almost the same sky, most of what they were seeing was, to him, as new as shiny toys in a big store window. And she loved the joy she heard in his voice as he repeated back each name.

"What about this aurora borealis?" he asked. "The northern lightning you also call it?"

"Close. The northern lights. Sure."

"You can see this where we are, yes?"

"Later in the year you can. More like September, Labor Day at the earliest. But you won't be around for that."

He had no response to this and for a few minutes all she could hear was the gentle swish of his long-legged stride cutting through the dewy waist-high grass. She knew he was trying to match her shorter stride and the hesitation made a little waltzlike cadence as he kept slowing himself. Added to that was the softest snatch of an accordion drifting from somebody's boom box over in the picker shacks, and the combination made her think of Cajun two-step and how a bolder woman would speak up and point this out, maybe even get this guy dancing there in the grass. Make a game of it. But she wasn't even a slightly bold woman.

They moved through the north forty with its rows of bush-high seedlings and then dipped down, across the dirt access road, and into the Royal Anns where it was harder to see the stars, only in snatches between the rows, making little shafts of perforated night where moments before they'd seen a whole blanket. But it smelled sweeter here under the lush canopies, and the grass was kept mowed back and wasn't wet against their legs and so they kept walking. Brenda had never walked with a man like this, out here, and she wondered how long they could go on without it becoming awkward. Eventually, of course, they'd run out of property and then what would they do? Turn around and start over?

Sometimes she really had to kick herself for being such a "late bloomer" as her mom put it. By rights she should have mastered all this awkward circling years ago, as a teenaged girl. She should have had more dates—thinner glasses, less braces, less bulk, less interest in things boys found geeky, less of the awful similarity she had back then to Velma on *Scooby-Doo*. To arrive where she was now so socially ill-equipped, with such an embarrassing dearth of experience—it was as if she'd managed to earn her master's without taking a basic undergraduate requirement her freshman year.

When they reached the top of the rise at the far end of the Royal Anns, the highest point in the orchard, she pointed to the west, to the slightly darker vista below. "If there was a moon," she said, "you'd be able to see it better, but right out there, that's Lake Michigan."

He stood so close, looking out toward the dark negative of the lake, and when he sighed deeply, his size made it a demonstrative motion. "You must have had the perfect childhood—this place, your family . . ."

The laugh this produced in her came out as a yelp and she had to cover her mouth, which only exacerbated the problem. He seemed to think she was laughing at him and it was embarrassing and she was so nervous, she snickered harder, snorting snot out of her nose. It was horrible. He turned to her, seemed to stiffen, wanted to know what he had said. He sounded hurt, ridiculed.

She didn't know what to do, no idea at all. "Sorry!" she said. "I'm not laughing at you, really." She wiped her nose clean, looked up at him, that simple, open face; he was as tall as her dad. Her inclination was to study this situation some more, analyze it, but she pushed that aside and darted up on tiptoe, kissing him fast; a real short, snappy kiss, getting it over with.

She stepped back and tried to gauge his response to this experiment. It seemed as if he was still standing stiffly at attention and she felt like such a goon. But then his long arms closed around her, pulling her back in, pulling her up to him, and now it was a real kiss and now it was soft and lingering and tasted, slightly, of homemade cherry-vanilla ice cream, and this time, she felt her feet start to lift up off the ground as he dangled her in the air.

Much later, as they walked back through the sparkling dew, holding hands, he announced, "I'd like to see this aurora borealis."

34

"WHAT'S WITH THE WHALE?"

They were standing at the end of his driveway, Courtney squinting at his dad's new sign, her perfect little nose scrunched up like someone cut one. He told her he didn't think it was a whale, though honestly, he wasn't sure what it was supposed to be.

"Your mom's got a weight problem or something?"

"No."

"Your dad?"

"Not really. No. And like I say, it's not a whale." But he couldn't remember now what it was. A salmon? No, salmon were red or pink or something.

"Whatever," she said. "Kind of tacky."

She'd never been there before, never shown any interest, but when he'd mentioned that his parents would be out most of the evening, she shrugged and said, sure, whatever, what the hell did she care? And now, entering the house, even though the Denali wasn't in the driveway and his dad had said they'd be away at some annual pig roast, down at the Indian casino, till "quite late," he moved briskly ahead, calling out *Mom? Dad?* just making sure.

She glanced around, her nose wrinkled again by something. Maybe she was allergic to all the stupid Hudson Bay blankets his dad insisted they leave scattered around the living room—wool, for Christ's sake—like it wasn't eighty degrees out, like they were nineteenth-century Yoopers operating a lighthouse up on Lake Superior or French trappers hoping to do some trading with the Indians. Anyway, something was making her sniff and crinkle up her nose. "Cute," she said.

He led her to his bedroom and stood in the center of the little faux-rustic oval rug, right on the moose, hoping she wouldn't see it, and pulled her close. He wrapped his arms around her and put his mouth on hers and tipped her back, easing her down onto the narrow target of his bed. It was all so new: he'd never been with her on an actual mattress yet, in a house they were supposed to be in.

He had his fingers around one nipple when she said, "They going to be home soon?" He told her no, there was plenty of time. It was totally safe. Maybe this didn't reassure her, because when he started kissing her again, she stopped him. "All right, all right," she said, pushing against his chest, sitting up, "give it a break, will you?" He started apologizing. "Kidding," she said, though she didn't look very jokey, standing now, moving toward the bedroom door. She looked bored. "Where do I pee?" He pointed and then lay back down on his bed with a sigh he hoped she heard, and waited for her return.

This had seemed like such a good idea. They had the place to themselves, at least for a little while. The coast was clear. Only now she wasn't in the mood. He could tell.

Normally, he could hear the toilet from his bed. He heard nothing. After a while, he knew he better go investigate. He found her way down the hall, in his parents' bedroom, standing in front of his mom's dresser. She was going through stuff in his mom's jewelry boxes, trying on a necklace in the mirror. He came up behind her and she looked up and locked eyes with him in the mirror, not startled at all. She pulled open the top drawer. "Think your mom's got a special battery-powered friend in here?"

He didn't want to say stop it, but he didn't want to look either. She pulled all the drawers open and closed each in turn with a dismissive slam. The bottom one was locked, which surprised him. He didn't even know it had a lock.

She stood there staring at the locked drawer, nodding approvingly. "This is where they keep the Polaroids," she said. Then she snatched the necklace up again and held it around her neck. It was the pearls, his mother's favorite jewelry for special occasions. He was surprised she had brought them up here rather than leaving them down in the Birmingham house where she had more formal social functions.

"What do you think?" Courtney said. "Pearls and I have this thing together, don't you think?"

What he was actually thinking was how much he wanted her to put them away and go back to his room, but he said, "Yeah. Sure. It's nice. You look great."

"Uncle Matt says it's like there's these oysters, okay? Way off in the ocean somewhere? And they somehow just *know* what my skin is like. But I didn't bring any with this summer. They're all back in Chicago. These are okay. They're kind of cute, I guess." She put them back in the box and turned her attention to his parents' bed. "So this is where they do it, huh?" Turning her back to it suddenly, arms out, she flopped, Christlike, on the bed and bounced there lightly for a moment. "Big yawn, I'm sure. Don't you think?"

He didn't want to think.

"Or maybe not," she said. "Maybe they'd surprise us. Maybe they're *wild*." She started bouncing dramatically, suddenly at sea.

"Gross," he said. "My parents?"

She giggled, rolling over on her stomach, and scooched back till her legs cleared the bed and then her feet touched the floor and she angled her ass back at him, bent over the bed. "Think they do it like this? 'Yeah, come on, baby. Give it to me . . .' Only your mom's big whale ass would be bigger, of course. So big you put a whale on a sign at the end of your driveway."

Obviously, she'd never met his mom or hadn't bothered noticing that she was like a stick. He was starting to get a little mad and he told her to stop it. "That's a tuna on the sign, okay?"

She ignored him. "'Give me the big meat. Slap my big whale ass with your big meat. Ooh, yeah . . . Marky won't hear us . . . Do it, baby. Give it to me. Don't worry about little Marky . . .'"

"Little Marky says stop it," he said.

She kept moaning. "'What's a matter, lover? I'm getting too loud? Maybe you ought to fill my mouth so we don't wake Marky. Yeah, fill my mouth with your big hot meat . . .'"

Fortunately, he felt he was starting to know her better—how to deal with her, to an extent—and he saw the endgame now, the checkmate: he slapped her butt and she shrieked and giggled and pushed up off the bed, standing up straight like a normal person, mock outrage, rubbing her butt cheek, and in that moment he was able to yank her safely out of the room. He tried to pull her back into his bedroom, but she said, "Yeah, not so much. Kind of boring."

It kind of hurt his feelings. He wasn't sure it showed, but she turned and saw something on his face and she made a big cartoon boo-boo pout, sort of like she was making fun of him, and patted his cheek. "Ahhhh," she said, sympathetically. "Maybe later, though. We can come back later." She reached around and squeezed his ass.

"Well, they're going to come home *eventually*." It was like she didn't get that part. His parents were gone *now*. Why not do it now, when they wouldn't get busted?

"Whatever." She shrugged and led him out the front door and was bathed in light. It was dusk already, purple to the west, the Lake Michigan horizon at the end of their yard, and darker blue, with occasional flickers of yellow-green specks—fireflies—up the dirt road that led back to the village, but Courtney's blond hair was backlit and blinding white as she stood in front of their porch. It was his dad's new security light.

"There's a sensor," he explained. "My dad thinks the neighbor sneaks over here and snoops around, tries to cut down our trees and stuff . . ."

She said nothing, just got on her bike. It either made perfect sense to her or she wasn't really listening. When they got back up onto the main drag, they slowed down and he pulled alongside and asked if she wanted to get some ice cream at the Daisy June or hang out at Scudder Park or catch the nine o'clock at the one little movie theater, but she said no, she'd seen the movie before and besides, she didn't feel like sitting on those hard old-fashioned wooden seats and the place smelled like a dusty museum and it just completely sucked for her asthma.

Having run out of suggestions, Mark just pedaled along, following her in silence. In back of Ringwood Drugs, she pulled up next to the Dumpster, hopped off and dragged a plastic milk crate alongside. She stepped up on it and peered in. "Okay," she said, stepping down and squinting at some marking on the side. "Looks like they pick up tomorrow, so there's probably something good. I'll be the lookout and you get in there and pull out whatever looks good."

He didn't get it.

"Drugstores sometimes throw out good stuff. You never know. A friend of mine, back in Lake Forest? Scored some Ritalin once. Look for whatever—candy bars, NyQuil . . ."

Courtney was so great, but she really had weird ideas about how to spend a date. When he'd asked her to do something with him tonight, none of this was what he had in mind. Still, he knew better than to argue if she was set on something. He stepped up on the crate and did a kind of vaulting horse move, like hopping a fence, and he was in, stepping on squishy cardboard boxes and trying to make out the contents, if any, in the eerie weak yellow of the streetlamp.

"Hey," she called. "You think I looked good in that pearl necklace? Or was it too cheap?"

"No, you looked good." He corrected himself. "You looked great." He glanced up from the garbage, studying her over the lip of the Dumpster. She was grinning, the way she did whenever she'd suddenly ask if he had a condom on him.

But instead she said, "You know what a pearl necklace is?"

"Sure." He remembered a film in science in the seventh grade—how the grain of sand gets in the oyster and irritates it.

"No, I mean a *pearl necklace.*"

Oh. Now he saw. He told her he thought he did know. He'd read enough *Penthouse* Forums to know what she was talking about.

She moved closer now, abandoning her lookout. "You ever do it?"

He didn't want to answer this. He hadn't done it, but he wasn't about to let her make fun of him.

"You need some boobage to do it. Not a ton—not as much as you'd think—but some. The rest is just the girl squeezing it together." She demonstrated over her shirt, squeezing her chest together with her hands flat, and he squinted in the bad light, transfixed. He couldn't see any cleavage through the shirt, of course, but he didn't need to. He got the idea just fine. He wasn't sure if she was just talking about it or making some sort of offer, but he sure as hell wasn't going to stay in the Dumpster.

"There's nothing here," he said, heaving himself up and swinging his legs over the top. Just as he was clear of the Dumpster, a sheriff's car pulled into the parking lot, slowly, passing through on patrol, so they got back on their bikes and continued meandering through the village.

Eventually, they wound up at her family's condo and they lay on the floor and watched a video about two practically naked teenagers alone on an island together. Mark had seen it before and it was really more of a chick flick anyway and so he tried to put the moves on her. Courtney had her top off and her bra off and was lying on the floor in just her boy shorts, right in front of him, absently touching her tits. At first, maybe massaging where the bra had rubbed, then just out-and-out, plain ol' playing with her tits. *Her* doing it was fine, apparently, but every time he tried to slide closer and kiss her or reach out to help, she'd swat him away and say, *Qu-it!* or *D-on't!* or *Not now!* or *You're breathing on me!* or *I'm bored!*

When he sat up and clicked off the remote, the room suddenly turning that dark shade that made him think of the river, he asked her what he was doing wrong. She just clucked, annoyed, grabbed the remote and turned the TV back on, saying, "You are such a child. So predictable." Like she was Mrs. Mature. Like she'd done a couple tours in Vietnam or something.

They were totally unsupervised there. He didn't understand why she was pushing him away when she'd grab him in other places, get all naughty with him almost in public. Shit, she hadn't minded the museum dust and those hard seats at the movies the night she took him in there and gave him a BJ during *Pearl Harbor.*

But he didn't want to really piss her off so he lay back with a heavy sigh and watched Brooke Shields getting her cherry popped in the sand.

After it was over, Courtney hooked her bra back on and stood, pulling her top on and squinting at the clock. "Hmm," she said. "Guess my folks are staying on the boat."

It was pretty late. He'd planned on probably beating his parents home tonight—his dad usually took his time when it came to pork—but now he wondered if he'd have to give them some lame mumbly story tomorrow. They didn't have a curfew for him this summer—they just seemed glad to see he was out being social—but they did sometimes ask where he was and what he was doing.

To his surprise, Courtney knelt down and kissed him, sweet as a whisper, and breathed in his ear, "Let's go back to your place."

She left her bike and rode back double on his. The night felt cool against his skin when they got up speed down the small hills, and her hands, lying across his ribs, felt even better. At the one flashing red, where they had to stop, she slid her hand down and squeezed his junk and he almost leapt off the bike, laughing.

They got off at his road, Edgewater, where the dirt started, and he ditched his bike in the weeds so they could walk in and scout out the situation. If his parents were home, they'd have to turn around. They walked along, past the septic guy's dumpy little house, everything dead ahead silhouetted by the deep gray where the sky opened up over Lake Michigan. When they got as close as his dad's dumb sign, he could see the dark hulk of the Denali. They were home. The lights were all off. They were asleep, probably exhausted and a little buzzed and bloated on all-you-can-eat pork, but screwing in his bedroom, just across the hall from them, seemed like pushing it.

Courtney squeezed his hand, hard, like she wanted to go in anyway, but he pulled her back and they started back up the dark road, toward his bike, still holding hands. It seemed oddly datelike suddenly: just to be holding hands.

She spoke up once they were clear of the house. "Make you a deal. Get me the pearl necklace—not to keep, just to borrow till Friday."

Behind her, he saw a light on upstairs at the neighbor's and thought he saw the girl—*Cammy* was it?—working at the computer. It seemed late for this—it wasn't like she had schoolwork or anything. Some other time, he might be sort of curious, maybe even move in for a closer look, sneak up on their yard, but no way tonight, with his head about to burst with whatever the hell Courtney was up to now. "What's Friday?" he asked, and the words almost made him tired.

"You'll see. Anyway, I'll swap you—pearl necklace for *pearl necklace.*"

He had to stop walking. He stood there, trying to make her out in the dark. He couldn't see her face, just a light glow that was her blond hair, but it sounded, at least, like a better deal than climbing into the Dumpster.

"You wouldn't lose it or hurt it, right?"

She snorted. "Yeah, I'm going to shove it up my ass, Mark. I'm going to toss it in the lake."

He had to think about this. Maybe it was possible. He was trying to remember what day it was his mom went to that book club . . . Wednesdays? "Maybe I could get it some afternoon, when she's out of the house. Let me see."

"No, no, no." Courtney moved up close to him and draped her arms around his waist, palming his ass. "You need to do it tonight. While they're in the room."

"Jesus, Courtney. Why do you have to make it so—"

She was rubbing against him, growling a little. "'Cause it's *fun.* God!"

He looked back down the road at the lifeless house. It was like a crypt down there. No sign of life. He reminded himself the way they both got when they overate. A good heavy meal in them, they slept like alien pod people.

"It's *fu-un!*" She nuzzled his neck, almost whining. "And later . . . I'm going to make it *really* fun for you . . ."

Courtney waited in the road. He went around to the back deck, where the sensor light wouldn't come on, and let himself in through the sliding patio door. The hall light was on and he shut it off and stood at the edge of the living room, maybe thirty feet from the bedroom door, quietly saying, "Mom? Mom?" There wasn't any answer so he stepped lightly to the bedroom and put his ear to the door. He heard the air conditioner humming and his mom's white-noise machine, set on waves, which never made any sense to him. It was fine downstate in the winter, but couldn't she just open the window and hear Lake Michigan? And she could certainly turn off the AC, too. It got down to the sixties up here at night.

He took a deep breath and tried to let it out slowly, the way he'd once been instructed to do in some dumb theater class his counselor made him take. It didn't help much.

This was so idiotic. He told himself it wasn't like he was risking going to jail. And as far as he knew, his dad didn't own a gun. But still, what if he got caught? How could he ever explain that to his parents? Especially the part about the reward Courtney was dangling in his face. He'd never be able to look them in the eye again.

It suddenly struck him that even with the hall light off, he might create a silhouette in the doorway, and so he dropped down to his knees before slowly twisting the handle and easing the door open. Now he could hear them breathing, even over the canned air and waves. Sliding on the carpet, he worked his way over to his mom's dresser and reached up and lowered the jewelry box to the floor. It was obvious which necklace was the pearls. He lifted the box back up over his head to the dresser and then attempted to jam them in his pocket. But the way he was squatting made it difficult and so, to leave his hands free, he ended up sticking the pearls in his mouth.

As he crawled along, he expected to be busted any second, and the pearls almost dropped from his mouth when he realized he'd slid one hand along his dad's moist jockey shorts, abandoned right on the floor—a sign his normally totally anal-retentive dad, Mr. Organized, had overdone it that evening with the booze. But then he was out of the room, free and clear. As soon as he got away from the deck, he spit the pearls into his hand and began swabbing them dry with the edge of his sweatshirt. The idea of putting them in Courtney's hands still sticky with his spit was just not acceptable.

"Any problem?" she asked as she took them and put them around her neck, as casually as if he'd just borrowed them from *her*. When he told her there'd been no problem, he thought she actually looked disappointed.

"Come on," she said, and led him by the hand.

He asked where they were going and she didn't answer. She just said, "I told you what I'd do." That didn't really tell him where she'd do it, but he kept his mouth shut, afraid to say anything that would piss her off and screw up the deal.

They left his bike back in the ditch and she led him by the hand all the way back to the marina. He thought they were heading to her boat, but that couldn't be, because she'd said her folks were sleeping on it tonight. She led him down another gangplank, to a section not too far from *The Courtney,* where there were a lot of empty slips. It was *sort* of dark, despite all the old-timey fake gas lamps, but still not the place you'd want to expose yourself. Certainly not the place for any kind of complicated physical positioning. And what if someone just walked up the gangplank? It was basically like doing it on a sidewalk—if she in fact was still planning to do it. He supposed by now that the moment was gone, they were on to something new, but she said, "Right here," and lay down on the gangplank. She moved real efficiently, whipping off her shirt and stuffing it under her head as a pillow. She unsnapped her bra and reached for him, palming his crotch, pulling him down and stuffing her tongue in his mouth. It was this efficient move—this no-nonsense, businesslike rolling up of her sleeves, more than any other part of it, that made him instantly hard. More than the kissing and the grabbing and her tits right there. It was the drop-of-a-hat feeling. That's what was making him almost dizzy, afraid he'd lose his balance, roll right off the gangplank and end up splashing around in the water, alerting the whole marina.

She had him unbuckled now and was stroking him and then she stopped and squeezed her tits together. His eyes were adjusting now and he could see the whole thing. It almost looked painful how much she was squeezing them together. "Come on," she said. "Climb on."

It seemed like there could be a lot better ways to do this, ways that wouldn't be so high-pressure or uncomfortable—wasn't the wooden dock digging into her back? It certainly wasn't feeling good on his knees. And then when he tried to go where she was pulling him, tried to straddle her chest, he found that his jeans needed to come down farther, that they were pinning his legs together.

"Hold on," he said. "Sorry! Just—"

She made that exasperated sound she made sometimes and he hopped up and, staying low in case anyone was out on the deck of their boat and his untanned ass reflected the moonlight, he squatted beside her, tugging his pants down. Then he got back on her and was trying to do it, kept stroking away, but it was not at all like he'd imagined. For one thing, he couldn't look at her now. He felt so dumb and awkward and she wasn't smiling. She had a watch on and it kept bumping into his thigh where she was cupping her tits. And she kept chanting "Come on . . . come on . . . come on," only it didn't sound like it did in pornos, it sounded more like Mrs. Sanderson, the crossing guard out in front of his old elementary school. Or like an auctioneer with a barn-load of merchandise to unload. And then he saw the necklace—his mom's pearls—right there in the target zone and that really threw him off. He stopped and asked about it—didn't she want to take them off?

"They're not paste," she said. "They're real. They'll wash off. They come from the ocean, for Christ's sake . . ."

Even so, soiling his mom's pearl necklace like that . . . It just felt wrong. He kept thinking about it, wondered if it was maybe borderline incest. And then it was clear it just wasn't happening. He wasn't limp but raw and bloated-feeling, like it wasn't his dick anymore but something he'd borrowed and wasn't completely familiar with the operating instructions.

Finally, she ended it. With no fanfare or debate. She just raised up and he fell back, off her. "You're taking too long," she said, hooking her bra closed. "Maybe next time."

He didn't say anything, but he felt a sort of relief. The only thing he didn't like was the look she gave him as they walked back down the gangplank. Like he was a kid, foolish, like he'd disappointed her, like she was getting bored, like some other guy could have done it fine.

But, God, she was beautiful.

He tried to catalogue it in his head, how he would think of it: *I've* sort of *done the pearl necklace thing with Courtney Banes.* That seemed pretty good, considering.

35

AS HE APPROACHED HER FROM BEHIND, carrying the pitcher of iced coffee and two tall glasses, all he could see was her baseball cap. She had the lounge chair pointed away from the house, pulled out farther on the lawn to escape the looming shadow of the house. At the edge of the patio, he stopped and cleared his throat loudly, and then her head popped around the side of the chair and she squinted back at him. He asked if he was intruding. With a jerk of her head, she beckoned him closer. "How could you be intruding in your own yard? Give me a break."

As he drew closer, he could see over the lounge chair and felt relieved. She wasn't in a bathing suit, just shorts and a T-shirt, with the sleeves rolled up, a book collapsed in her lap. He handed her a glass and set the pitcher down on a flat spot of ground where she could reach it. "I just wanted to give you some warning I was approaching."

"A good thing too. I was buck naked just a second ago. Thanks for the warning."

He tried not to show any reaction to this comment, but he knew at once that he had: her hand shot up and covered her mouth. "I'm sorry," she said. "I was just trying to be funny. I didn't mean to offend you, Reverend."

He told her she hadn't offended him, and truly, she hadn't, just caught him off-guard. This was a girl, not a woman. An adolescent. And though she herself might very well be starting to think of herself in more adult ways—ways in which the prospect of nudity was a relevant factor—it was certainly not *his* place to think of her that way.

He diverted the conversation. "Let me take this opportunity," he said, pulling the other lounge chair closer and taking a seat, sidesaddle, "to launch into, for hopefully the last time in my life, my little speech explaining the use of the term *Reverend*."

She sat up. "Oh good! Should I take notes?"

"Do. This is for a grade. When, you ask, should you use the term

Reverend in conversation, as a form of address? Never. Just don't. Especially with me, because I'm retired."

"But you're still *Reverend,* right? That doesn't go away just 'cause you retire, does it. Isn't it like *Doctor*? Retired doctors, you still call the guy *Doctor.*"

"No," he said. "It's not like *Doctor.* Or *Captain* or *Sir.* Used properly, it's *the Reverend.* Which is less like *Doctor* and more like 'nice.' As in 'the nice Gene Reecher.' And 'the nice Mrs. Hersha.' And 'the very, very nice Kimberly Lasco.'"

"Thank you," she said, raising her iced coffee in a toast. "Right back at you, your niceitude."

"And no, it doesn't stop when you retire, because it's not really a job description. *Minister* is the position. The *Reverend* label stops when you stop being reverend, acting reverently. Like when someone you think is nice stops being so nice. You've known people like that in your short life, I'm sure."

"Hell," she said. "I'm *related* to people like that."

She covered her mouth again, wide-eyed, and apologized for saying *hell.*

"Saying *hell*'s not my concern. Creating hell is all I care about."

She was shaking her head, wistfully. "Man, I don't know why you stopped doing this minister stuff, because you seem pretty good at it to me. The explaining and going into it and being deep like that."

"I suspect, Kimberly, I've only gotten really good at it in the last five minutes, talking to you."

"Shut up," she said. He thought she might actually give him a little shove. "Now you're just trying to be smooth. Don't be smooth."

"I don't know . . ." he said. "'The Very Smooth Gene Reecher'— I might enjoy that for a while."

"If I don't call you *Reverend,*" she said, "what do I call you?"

Call me Gene, he wanted to tell her. *Call me for dinner, call me sweetheart, call me down for breakfast.* He shrugged. "Whatever you want. *Reverend*'s okay. I don't care." He realized he wasn't drinking his iced coffee and he took a sip, feeling self-conscious now.

"So how are things at the fudge shop? Selling like hotcakes?" He regretted it the second it came out: *hotcakes.* What an old-fogey thing to say.

"Better than hotcakes," she said. "It's selling like fudge during the invasion of the Fudgies. That ought to be the saying, really, not the hotcakes thing. I swear, if I suggested to Mrs. Hersha that we start selling hotcakes, just even a trial batch, she'd laugh me out of the store."

That made him chuckle. "I imagine it's kind of a fun place, though. You probably have a lot of young co-workers to pal around with. Do you get to use that big wooden paddle and smear the fudge out on the marble table? That's always fun to watch."

"I know. I get to watch. But apparently? Dewey? The old guy with the confectioner's certificate, whatever that is? He's got some kind of monopoly on the big paddle and the marble table. Mrs. Hersha had me help him cut some into squares one day when things were really busy, but Dewey yelled at me that I was doing it wrong and I had to stop. You wouldn't guess it because he's old and weird, but Dewey smokes a *lot* of pot."

This did surprise the Reverend. He knew she was talking about Dewey Furr. Dewey was a member of First Pres, on regular rotation as an usher. He had to be pushing sixty himself. Now that Gene heard it, it fit, it made sense, but he wasn't sure he liked having this private insight into a man who'd previously revealed nothing more about himself than a seemingly quiet nature and the overly sweet smell of corn syrup.

"And trust me," she said, "he is par-a-*noid*. So basically, I just sell fudge. Wait for people to stare at all the different kinds, make up their minds, then weigh a tiny slab of it, maybe just a sliver half the time, and box it up and sell it to them."

"Well," he said. "I'm sure there's some excitement once in a while . . ."

She nodded. "Oh, yeah. It's all very exciting. They'll be making a movie of my life very soon. Christina Ricci will star. She's good at those eye-rolling roles. Like, she was Wednesday Addams, remember? And *Sleepy Hollow*—member-of-a-weirdo-family roles. They'll have to strap her chest down, of course—make her flatter . . ." He turned and squinted out at the river, telling himself not to blush, uncertain it was working. She went on. "Dewey will be played by Danny DeVito. The guy from that *Twister* movie will play the part of my dad. Maybe Mike Farrell could play you. You know who he is? From that show *Providence*?"

He knew Mike Farrell as the actor who played B.J. on the old TV show *M*A*S*H*—it had been Mary's favorite show; he'd even written a sermon or two on it—but he screwed up his face and pretended he'd never heard of him. Because it was a little embarrassing—Mike Farrell was a few years younger, better-looking, probably a little taller . . . maybe a similar look, a similar build, but come on! She couldn't be serious. He said, "The only actor I'm familiar with is Buster Keaton. Him and that other new guy—Chaplin, is it?"

She laughed. It was nice to show her he could tease right back.

THAT NIGHT, HE AWOKE SUDDENLY, momentarily thrown in terms of where he was, where his wife was, what time it was. He'd been dreaming. With an erection, no less—to have one while dreaming was a notable event. He lay there, staring at the clock blinking back at him a ridiculous 2:17 and tried to recount the dream. What he remembered seemed fairly innocuous, hardly capable of producing an erection.

It was a warm, languid dream, bright with sunlight. It was something out in back of the house. The chaise lounges, the nutty liquid of the iced coffee. And skin—yes. It was a dream of touching the girl. It was that day she held out her biceps, bragging, and wanted him to feel it. He'd declined that day but in the dream he was taking her up on it, reaching out, his fingertips tingling at the touch of her Popeyed arm, the leap of her muscle tightening. Only now she was saying, "Aren't I strong?" and she was saying, "Can we swim?" and the feel of her arm was taut and smooth and he felt her muscle pop, bulge, challenging him, and she said, "Are you strong? Are you?" And he said, "I yam what I yam," like the cartoon sailor, but he wasn't making a muscle himself and he wasn't dressed to go swimming. He was just standing there in the sun, touching her arm.

It was the sheet itself, he discovered, and he was smoothing it with his hot, half-asleep hand, running it along the rounded edge of the mattress.

It wasn't a sex dream. He saw that now. Nor would it have been improper the other day. Touching her arm wouldn't have made him a pedophile. She'd wanted him to feel her biceps, to touch her only in a bonding, palsy sort of way, and that's exactly how he could have done it. With camaraderie, fellowship, humor, goodwill. There was nothing shameful in this. It was just basic human contact, something he desperately needed. He was starved for touch. And if he had it in a normal way like that, perhaps it would be less confusing, not so mixed up with less savory impulses. He was sure the erection was beside the point—possibly unrelated.

He told himself it wouldn't have been because she was sixteen, or perky or virginal or any of those qualities that would be relevant if he were a degenerate. It would be *despite* those things, not because of them. It would be because she was kind to him, she was lovely to him and he wanted to respond.

It was all so confusing. And there was no way he could fall back to sleep.

When the clock finally flopped to 2:47, he forced himself up with a groan, convinced further sleep was not in the cards. Shuffling into the den, he booted up the computer.

What he had in mind was writing her a nice note, sending her an e-mail that made some gesture of appreciation and affection, that would substitute for a friendly chuck under the chin, a punch on the arm, an *attaboy, pal.*

He started several times and deleted each time. Each attempt at a casual acknowledgment of their burgeoning friendship seemed forced at least and sort of creepy at the worst. He stared at the "TO" line, Kimberly's e-mail address blinking there as if tapping its toe, waiting for further information below. He just couldn't find the words.

Possibly, there weren't any words that wouldn't sound creepy. *Not in word or tongue,* he thought, *but in deed* . . . The First Epistle of John. He could do something; give her something. Maybe that would suffice as a gesture of connection.

He could get her something for her birthday, if he could find out when it was. Or at least as a token of his friendship. Except he had no idea what a sixteen-year-old girl liked these days.

This, he decided, would be a great use of the Internet. Now, finally, he could see some sort of practical use for the thing: picking out a present for a teenager. So he did a search. The keywords he entered were: *teen girl likes.*

The descriptions appeared: *search results 1–5 of about 33,940 con-*

taining "teen girl likes." Skimming, he spotted in the entries, scattered repetitions of the words *sex, oral sex, blowjobs*. He saw the word *cocksuckers* and one he'd never seen before: *cumshots*.

This was not what he was looking for.

He considered for a moment, hesitating, frozen, knowing he should return to the search box and enter something else, some stipulation. Perhaps *not sex,* perhaps *gifts for.* But he was curious now. He was there now. To run away from it now wouldn't be piety but actually a sort of moral cowardice and self-bunkering; spiritual stage fright. He might as well be a Catholic priest; a hermetic monk.

He opened the first entry. It was something called Guzzle Girls, part of a Web site called Ultrateen.com. A headline appeared, announcing that "Teen Girls Like Cock!" and the screen began to fill the little boxes, row after row, with photos.

But even that didn't prepare him. Even then he still wasn't quite clear on what exactly he was looking at now. These were headshots of young girls, their heads tipped, chins jutting, mouths open wide like baby birds for a dangling worm. Hard penises aimed, like big arrows—*This way! Come on in!*—right at the mouth, right at the face. The cheeks, lips, eyes, teeth—it all glistened. He couldn't look away. It was mesmerizing.

He never would have imagined anything like this even existed, let alone in such quantity. Most had their eyes lidded, as if in ecstasy, as if these girls could somehow be personally satisfied with this grotesque misdirection, this biologically irrelevant act. But others had their eyes wide open, smiling up at the unseen man, and he found these a little more palatable, more like they were having fun with it, enjoying this very extreme turn of events. Maybe not faking an orgasm but simply being playful; silly. Yes, if he had to pick a portion of these images marginally less objectionable than the rest, he supposed it would be these, with the mischievous grins, the wild young eyes like it was all a whim; a hoot.

But Lord, some of these poor young things were absolutely drenched in the stuff, not simple spatterings but draped with it, ropes of the white sticky stuff webbing their fingers. He saw one that wore braces, the metal gummed with loads of semen. Another, with a barrette, seemed to actually be blowing a bubble with it.

He could see now how that White House intern managed to get her dress soiled, a few years back. What he knew of that affair now seemed reserved, compared to this.

But the more he stared at these images, the more he could start to see the attraction. Not for these specific images, of course—coldly posed, fake and theatrical—or the crude, unfeeling manipulation behind them, but simply the basic appeal of the mouth. It did present itself, now that he really looked at it, as a wonderfully inviting portal to another person. With all the shame and hiding we attach to the rest of our body, how odd it seemed now that this one intimate organ be left fully exposed—prominently featured even, due south of the eyes, not crammed shamefully into underpants. There it was, the mouth: out in the open, wide and wet and warm. Removing for a second the issue of jamming one's privates into it, but simply considering it as an entryway—a way in, a point of contact—it did intrigue.

His late wife, Mary, would sometimes pop his fingers in her mouth, in the throes of lovemaking. At first he'd been shocked, but when he relaxed and stopped questioning it, he realized it had an effect. He felt so close, touching her tongue, her teeth. She did it to him, as well, and it didn't feel sinful or decadent. It felt joined.

That, however, had been the extent of it. The subject came up in the early seventies, when that movie *Deep Throat* became the national topic of conversation at even the most conservative dinner parties. They had several friends, in fact, who carpooled one Saturday night down to Grand Rapids to see it. He and Mary declined, but joshed with the rest of the gang about it and saw them off. They were dressed up, too, as if heading to a cocktail party or fancy restaurant. He remembered Hal Markham, that cutup, being not at all discreet about it, waving goodbye like a kid and yelling something out the window like, "You sure, Gene? Come on! Call it research for your next sermon!"

In fact, he considered doing just that—not going to the adult movie house in Grand Rapids, of course—just slipping in some vague reference to this popular film the following Sunday that Hal Markham and the rest of them would pick up on, but would be lost on the rest of the congregation. "Do it," Mary told him, and he said he would—just wait and see!—but when it came time to write it, he abandoned the idea. He couldn't figure out how to slip it in without either being really obvious and clumsy and dumb or being so obtuse even their friends wouldn't get it. A direct approach, a sermon against oral sex itself, was not something he would ever do, nor something he believed needed to be done. Besides, it was a fad—a hot topic to be giggled at, but certainly not something that was actually catching on in any permanent way. For instance, there was already a buzz about the coming Bicentennial, and he was sure this oral sex business would soon be forgotten, replaced in folks' minds with a fixation on Paul Revere, Betsy Ross and the whole Revolutionary War.

Later that night, while their friends were probably still on their way back to Weneshkeen, Mary said, in the darkness of their bedroom, as if addressing the ceiling, "That's not something you need me to do, is it, Gene?"

He denied it was. And she said she didn't need him to do it either.

There were two occasions, he remembered, in which her mouth actually touched him there. Her lips hardly passed the glans, though: just a light smoochy peck on the tip, played for laughs, clowning around. Both times, it was in the shower that this happened, both times, the kids were away at band camp, and both times she stood immediately and turned her face to the water's current.

He never thought the lack of that type of lovemaking marked either one of them a cold fish. Mary certainly wasn't. There was an arousal in her eyes alone, a wild flash that even just recalling tonight caused his cheeks to flush, his mind to grow fuzzy and unfocused, his breath to catch. And all that was just from a look she gave him. She had made him very happy. If she were here tonight, she would tell him to come to bed. If she were still alive, he wouldn't be looking at these pictures.

But he *was* looking at them, and he continued to do so, going back and opening the other entries, Web sites he could hardly believe were legal, moving slowly, patiently, through each gallery like a stranger in a foreign museum who can't speak the language or read the brochure, who can just look and wonder and tell himself he's not in a position to judge.

And later, he would look back at this night as the beginning of it all, the raft of unsolicited pornographic e-mails, invitations and links; the deluge; the fissure that opened up beneath his feet, sweeping him tumbling in.

36

ONE OF THE SUCKIEST parts of being a deputy, this time of year, was having to drive around town selling raffle tickets for Sumac Days. Hatchert wasn't doing it, but she wondered if that was less about him being the boss and more because he didn't really know anybody yet. Janey knew she should probably feel good about the fact that the village considered her well liked enough to be able to push the raffle tickets. And with select people, the merchants and more well-to-do summer people, she was supposed to ask about sponsorship. They could make tax-deductible donations to the festival or even sponsor a float. This year when Bear Eckenrod in the village offices handed her the stack of raffle tickets, he asked her to approach the billionaire with the Ark, that Noah Yoder kid. Hit him up for a big sponsorship.

There was one upside to this demeaning errand though—she thought she'd be able to feel the guy out about the Letterman rumors. One version she was hearing was that the talk show host was staying out at Noah's Ark, either as a guest of the boy genius or as a summer tenant. She was hearing other variations, too: that he was going to buy the bootlegger's place, Cliffhead, or that he had a massive cabin cruiser he was going to keep at the marina or—maybe the most unlikely, she felt—a three-masted sailboat anchored offshore in Lake Michigan and he was helicoptering in and out for the weekends, sending only his cook into Weneshkeen in an outboard dinghy for groceries and supplies.

The fact that she didn't know much more than everyone else, just a bunch of rumors and weird theories, made her question her skills as a policewoman. Never mind that she might not be so gung ho about being a cop anymore—maybe she wasn't even cut out for it. She'd been investigating, of course. Asking around. Hatchert had been no help. He'd simply said they hadn't yet received any official request for extra security from *anyone* identifying themselves as Letterman's people. And she'd asked a few of the Realtors. The only one who seemed to know something—or maybe pretended to know something—was Barry

Self, the one brokering Cliffhead. Officially, the agency he worked for had been listing that old white elephant for several years now, back before he even moved to Weneshkeen and opened the B&B with his wife, so it was fair to say it wasn't one of their more active listings. But when she'd asked him if he knew anything about Letterman visiting or renting or looking to buy in the area, he said no, and he looked genuinely puzzled, like he was hearing this rumor for the first time. But then, a moment later, as she was turning to leave, he asked if she could keep a special eye on the bootlegger's place. And when she asked why, was there a problem? he said no, he just wanted to make sure it was looked after. No special reason. So one way or the other, the guy was seriously full of shit.

At the Ark, she was a little surprised billionaire boy answered the door himself. She'd been under the impression that he had a full household staff plus quite an entourage of hangers-on. The summer before, at least, there had been so many there that Kurt Lasco said he had to go out twice in four months to empty the septic. The place seemed empty now. Surely he could afford someone to answer the door and probably a separate person to handle these kinds of solicitations? Maybe he'd decided to simplify when he's up here, enjoy a little solitude, Thoreau-style. Otherwise, why would he be standing there in his kitchen with her, offering her espresso and listening to her spiel about Sumac Days?

He'd already shot down the idea of providing a large sponsorship under the Yoman!® company name. "I'm trying to be sensitive to possible resentment among the . . . locals," he said, "toward my . . ." She thought he was going to say "money"; but he said, "company name. I don't want them to feel they're seeing Yoman!® plastered everywhere."

She said she understood and suggested he could be listed personally as a sponsor. Just his name, not the famous company name. He tipped his head, unsure. "That's trickier, accounting-wise. Plus, I think that's worse in terms of goodwill. They probably resent the pipsqueak upstart himself *personally* far more than the company that earned him all that undeserved money."

"Well . . ." She saw her opportunity now to dig a little toward her own self-serving line of inquiry. "Another thing would be if you have *guests* coming to stay with you? It might be fun to sponsor a float or something under *their* name or names and—"

He cut her off. "Not this summer. I don't think I'm expecting many guests."

With this, she was now pretty convinced she could rule out the rumor that Letterman was going to be staying in this house. Maybe the old bootlegger's estate, maybe somewhere else, maybe it was a crock . . .

"Tell me again about this Sumac Days. What goes on with that?" It felt like he was changing the subject. What the hell did he think went on? It was Sumac Days. Normal Sumac Days–type activities, of course. But she went into it, since he was an outsider and maybe a little slow, reeling off the basics—the parade, the costumes, the reenactments, the sumac lemonade stands, the fudge judging, the 10k fun run (the Sumacathon), the rubber ducky race, the raffles and midway rides and dances and the crowning of the Sumac Days Court.

"Wow," he said. "I like the sound of that sumac lemonade."

"Oh, you've tried it?"

He said he hadn't, but he was sure it was good, otherwise why would anyone make it? "That name," he said. "I love the sound of it." Then he did an odd thing: he raised his wristwatch to his lips, pressed a tiny button on the face and repeated the phrase: "Sumac lemonade."

Then he said he was going to have to pass on sponsoring anything. Something about liquid assets these days. Maybe next year.

He bought ten raffle tickets for a total of twenty dollars. She'd had better luck with Bob Beirnbaum, the creepy used record dealer. She thanked Noah Yoder for his time, put on her hat and left.

Talking into his watch like he's Dick Tracy, she thought, disgusted. What kind of world is it where a squirrelly little guy like that gets to be friends with someone like David Letterman—meanwhile I have to drive around shilling for the Chamber of Commerce? She made a mental note to shoot herself in the brainpan if she was still doing this job five years from now.

37

ROGER DRINKWATER WAS A PEACE-LOVING MAN. So much so that he made it a personal tradition to spend the Fourth of July in Canada. This despite being a Vietnam vet and, as such, entitled to a spot every year on the VFW local float, next to the WW II geezers like Arnie Stack and Gad Holsinger. He'd never stuck around and joined the parade in the twenty-five-plus years he'd had a right to, and this one coming up, July 4, 2001, would be no exception. He already had the entire holiday weekend bookended in red marker on his calendar, a whole month ahead of time. This annual retreat down to Detroit and over into Windsor was not made as a perverse comment on those who shirked their duty and hightailed it to the safety, round bacon, full-frontal strip clubs and all-night doughnut shops of that slightly foreign land, and not as a Native American, as a nose-thumbing to the holiday itself, which offered no freedom for those who were already here, indigenous, but just simply to avoid the goddamn fireworks, which drove him fairly up a tree. It was just all too loud and unnerving.

Oddly, gunshots never bugged him much. Maybe because the association for that sound went way, way back, long before Nam. He'd been hunting the woods around Weneshkeen and Lake Meenigeesis since he was just big enough to drag the gallery gun with the Bondo-ed gunstock his Uncle Jimmy Two-Hands gave him. (Sold him, really. The price: the first three birds he bagged. Which was fine with Roger, since it was all he could do to carry the gun, let alone game.) He still hunted, and the wild turkey and venison jerky he sold locally had grown to about forty percent of his yearly income. So the sound of guns wasn't a problem. It was too deeply embedded in his life, in his sense of "normal," to even register as a blip.

Part of that, too, was that he didn't actually hear a lot of steady gunfire in and around Rach Soi, where he'd operated as a Navy SEAL. They were rarely that close to the action. They had a platoon leader who didn't exactly show a lot of initiative, especially in terms of brainless bravado. They tended not to go out bushwhacking, improvising, as much as the other units. When they struck, it was tactical, usually at remote riverside installations that were necessarily not in combat mode, not on the alert. They captured the occasional VC, took him back blindfolded for questioning, kept it all fairly bloodless. Lots of demo work—blowing VC staging areas—hooches and docks and radio huts. Infrastructure stuff. *More det work, less wet work,* was how their skipper put it, referring to the fusing they used, "det cord," and the CIA advisers' term for the grisly, throat-slitting stuff—"wet work"— that they avoided. Sometimes, during these missions, floating down a river on a rubber bladder, greased black as an oil tanker tragedy, they heard the distant thrush of gunfire, skirmishes way in the hills, as menacing as a Western on the neighbor's TV.

So that wasn't what got under his skin, what gave him the jitters and made him feel like one of those cliché shell-shockers you saw on the made-for-TV movies, everything in slow-mo. There did exist certain sounds capable of triggering that in him, and he hated the way it made him feel out of control. He didn't freak and scream and do the cold sweat thing—act like someone who would be played by Mel Gibson— but still, it made him feel a little screwy.

One sound was explosions. Fireworks did it. And he was no stranger to explosions, as a former demo expert. But now he preferred to avoid them. Occasionally, he taught Guardsmen up in Grayling, and though the colonel there wanted very much to hire him to teach some underwater demo, he'd declined and stuck instead to stealth swimming, marine survival, SCUBA, snorkel and salvage diving.

The other sound that ground his nerves was the jet-skis. Not that he required a specific memory from Nam to be annoyed with jet-skis—the average human being with half a marble in his head could manage to hate the sound of jet-skis—but beyond this, and the annoyance of almost getting creamed every time he tried to go for a swim, they sounded, to Roger, way too much like the Nakon Gnat, a tiny two-stroke motorcycle manufactured in North Korea. It was like a cheap version of the little Hondas made famous, around that same time, back in the States with the Beach Boys or whoever, singing about scooting around on dates. But where the famous little Hondas had plastic leg fairings, the Gnats were made out of recycled tin, not even repainted, so that it looked, from a few meters off, like an ornate patchwork design or multicolored marbling, but if you looked closely, you could see where the tin cans had been mashed together to form the refabrication—snatches of peas and turnips and gory beets. The low purchase price was the draw: the bikes went for roughly the market value of two geese (a method of denomination he never quite got the hang of, having no point of reference since he never knew the relative goose price of any of his belongings back in Michigan). They were everywhere in Saigon, like Vespas in Rome, bicycles in Beijing. They sounded, as his bunk-mate Coots put it, "like a lawnmower trying to buttfuck a pig." In other words, like a jet-ski.

And now the sound of jet-skis drove him up a tree. It also drove him back, if he wasn't careful, to one lousy spring day in Saigon.

IT SEEMED LIKE THERE WERE BLOSSOMS in the air, even though they were in that armpit Saigon, and the only thing he could see for sure in the air were the walls and walls of laundry hanging across the streets and the sweaty-looking ducks hanging in the market, dead as something in a museum. He didn't see blossoms, of course, and didn't bring it up, because Coots and Miller, his two best buddies, whom he was on leave with, were way too involved with their discussion of what factors constitute a better blowjob and where they were going to purchase one and how much they were willing to shell out, to hear anything about blossoms. Still, he would swear he smelled something different that day. It was spring, at least according to the Playmate calendar back in his hooch, and he supposed it might be possible they were *near* some blossoms. Maybe some collateral blossomage or whatever had blown loose and entered the city.

It made him think of the cherry orchards starting up back home in Michigan, vonBushberger's and the rest, and the wild strawberry *paczki* his great-grandmother made that time of year, with "ditch berries" he gathered for her, along the paved county road, and he didn't want to think about that. So he thought instead about the blowjob debate going on and how he might politely stay out of the proceedings without looking like he disapproved and without getting razzed and called "queerbait."

And it was here that he now thought he first glimpsed something, though he could never decide if he saw it then and remembered it later, or if he only invented the image after the fact: two scowling stick-figure kids, skeleton-jawed, passing their café table on a motorbike, slow enough that the engine almost stalled, swooping by in a lolling arc, shirtsleeves flapping, heads turned, checking them out, the barrel of something long and black slung over the shoulder of the kid in back.

Some birdlike headshrinker at the VA twenty-some years ago told him she thought his brain invented this part, that he hadn't spotted the Kalashnikov at that point, but he'd convinced himself he had out of a sense of guilt. She said he felt bad for surviving and so he wanted to beat himself up that he hadn't been alert enough. Personally, Roger preferred the theory that things were just real fucked up over there.

If he did see it, it was only a flash and he was the only one. Coots and Miller were too distracted by the pair of hookers. They'd just arrived at an acceptable price for the blowjobs and the girls were trying to get them up from the table and get on with it, over to a side alley, not far, just in view of the table, where a dirty burlap rag hung for privacy. Roger kept staring at the burlap rag, wondering if anyone was waiting behind it. The burlap looked like the exact place, if there was any chance the bubonic plague still existed, that the spores might be hiding. He thought, Come on, guys. That rag alone is reason enough for me to decline.

Coots and Miller had moved past trying to razz him into joining them. They were now debating which of the girls was going to blow which one of them. The point of contention, apparently, was the teeth. Roger couldn't see it. The girls looked almost like twins to him, but Miller pointed out that one of them had some very long sharp twisted teeth up front that looked like they could lacerate some serious dong. "No way I'm going with Snagglepuss," he said, and then quoted the cartoon cougar, "I mean, 'Exit! Stage left!' on that action, pal. No thank you, man."

Coots suggested the girl he wanted could blow them both, offering it to him as if it were the gentlemanly thing to do, but Miller said, "No way. That's queer."

They were about to flip a coin when a sound rose up from above the general din—it was a Nakon Gnat emerging from an alley just down the street and raising its pitch, the flimsy engine gunned full throttle. The crowd cleared, the kid on back now sitting sidesaddle, swinging something around in his arms, leveling it.

Roger tried to scream but all that came to mind was *Exit! Stage left!* and of course he didn't yell that.

38

AS FOR BEING POLISH, there was only one time Roger had visited Hamtramck, his grandmother's hometown on the edge of Detroit. This was several years ago, returning from Canada and his yearly Fourth of July exit, stage right.

It didn't go so well.

He was thinking he'd just drive through, make a couple passes through the main drag, Joseph Campau, just take in the sights and smells. But then he saw a name he recognized: Zubreski's. Grandma Oshka had spoken of a restaurant called Zubreski's, once owned by her uncle, Peebo Zubreski. Zubreski—those were her people. Of course, that was almost a hundred years ago now. The place looked old enough to be the original building, though, at this point, it could've been owned by the Korean mafia for all he knew.

He parked and went in. It was all dark wood and bad yellow sconce lighting that was maybe supposed to resemble old-fashioned gaslight. It smelled like his grandmother's kitchen, plus cigar and beer, and seemed like a museum, the fixtures dark and wooden—a museum of bread, perhaps, with that ever-present just-baked smell in the air. Right in the front hallway, hung among the framed photos, was a *Detroit News* article from 1943, during the race riots. It showed a mob of white men, their faces twisted in rage, savagely attacking a bloody black man under a marquee that said *Roxy*. A tipped car burned behind him. Roger thought that if he put his thumb up and covered the guy getting the beating, you could convince yourself these guys were at the ballgame, cheering the Tigers. He reconsidered, just for a second. Maybe he should turn around and leave.

The place seemed to be in a mid-afternoon lull. Except for two men and a large woman in a fake inky wig, Imelda Marcos–style, at the bar at the far end, the restaurant was empty, so he seated himself at a tiny table near the front.

"What can I do for you, chief?"

A lot of people, Roger reminded himself, say *chief*. He looked up to a kid no older than twenty-two, twenty-three, reddish face, blond hair, a little heavy in a white shirt and gummy-looking apron. He couldn't judge if the guy had meant it as a generic form of address, like *skipper,* or *captain,* or *pal,* or if it was just a nasty and tired-out racial slur. He did have an order pad in his hand. But then again, he wasn't raising it to write on it. It was just in his hand, remaining low at his side. So Roger wasn't sure. He couldn't tell.

"This is Zubreski's, right?"

"You here to see someone?"

"Not really," Roger said. "Just to eat."

The guy started to take the menu away from him. "We just serve Polish food."

Roger held on to it. "Do you serve *barszcz z uszkami*?"

The guy sort of blinked. Roger thought he looked like an extra on that old TV show, *Mister Ed,* when someone heard the horse talk but wasn't sure whether or not to believe their ears. Not amazed yet, just waiting for more information. He always found that show boring and he didn't feel any less patient about it now that it was happening in real life and he himself was the talking horse. "Your *barszcz,*" he said. "You serve that *z uszkami* or is it just—?"

The guy said, "You know it's not so much *what* we serve or *how* we serve it, but *who* we serve. You follow?" He looked over his shoulder, slowly, toward the bar, then back and said, "And frankly, I don't ever recall us serving Apaches."

Roger noticed now he was chewing gum. Snapping it. It had suddenly appeared along with the attitude, something he kept tucked down under his tongue, ready to go. An optional accessory.

Where the hell did he get *Apache*? In *Michigan*?

Roger said, "Bring me the *barszcz,* however you make it, *flaczki . . . po warszawsku,* if possible . . . and maybe, if you have it, a map of the U.S., so I can show you how you're off by about, oh . . . two thousand miles or so." He squeezed out a smile, something he rarely did even when surrounded by friends, in a place where he was welcome. He folded his arms, sitting back in the chair. "And hey, easy on the cream, okay?"

The waiter winced, took a loud long breath, hissing through his nose, turning and checking over his shoulder, back toward the others at the bar. Then he faced front again and leaned on the table, putting his weight on it, rattling the silverware. "Look, if you go right now, we can chalk this up to a bad judgment call and no harm done. I mean, we don't come to wherever the hell you live and stink it up, do we?"

"Yes," Roger said, nodding for a long, deliberative time, "you do."

Roger waited for it. The waiter continued glaring.

There was movement already, a shadow in his periphery, and he wasn't going to wait for this guy's entire family to show up and pile on. They'd have to lay hands on him first—fine. He'd allow that, to establish who went first. But not much more than that. Not pinning him down.

The two guys from the bar were standing over him now, big-bellied slabs—one behind him, one beside, the waiter still right in front, grinning now. He heard him mutter, *"Scvenia poscudna"—dirty pig*—and then there it was, hands on his shoulders, firm on his arms.

Roger let the back of his chair handle the guy directly behind him, jammed back fast into the guy's nuts as he rose, elbow out, and caught the guy to his right flank under the chin, pushing this one back off his feet, with blood spurting from his nose. But the guy was lucky he just got elbow, because in his other hand, coming up, Roger held the serrated steak knife. (It never failed: any place where the idea of sensible eating was laughable, you would find the steak knife already on the table, ready to go.) His right hand clutched the waiter straight in front of him by the ear, tipping his head to the side and down, and he made one quick pass with the left and backed away.

A sound came out of the waiter as he clutched the side of his head. Roger imagined the sounds he was trying for were actually "My ear!

My fucking ear!" but what came out was more of a "nnnNNNNAA-HHH!! NNNAHHHHH!! NNNNAAAHHHH!"

The two on the floor started to get up, but he flashed the steak knife. He still had one thing to say. He repeated Chief Joseph One-Song's famous quote: "You have all been a great disappointment." Only he said it in Polish: "*Wszyscy byliscie bardzo rozczarowujący.*" The two still on the floor, the waiter bent over a chair, a red hand mashed against his sticky head—they all looked up, stunned: talking horses to the nth degree. He got the hell out of there.

He was already on I-94, well past Ann Arbor, when he realized he was still gripping the ear. It actually wasn't all that bloody. He imagined most of the arteries were more on the skull side of the head, very little in the ear itself. And those arteries were probably being closed at that moment in the trauma ward at Henry Ford Hospital. Or, if the owners of Zubreski's didn't want to cause a stir, sewn up back in the kitchen by some ethically questionable doctor they had in their pocket.

It seemed wrong to just throw it away, a human ear and all, so he hung on to it and when he got home, strung it up in his smokehouse. After about six months had passed and there were no police inquiries and no appearance in town of slabby, ruddy-faced Slavic types nosing around, he took the ear down and put it in a padded envelope and dropped it in a public mailbox, addressed to Zubreski's Restaurant, Hamtramck, MI, no return address, and with a note inside, unsigned: *Thought this should go back where it belongs.*

39

IT DIDN'T COME WITH A LOT OF FANFARE. One evening, as soon as his daughter got the road stand closed, before his wife was even ready with dinner, Brenda said they should all come down to Miki's camper because he had an announcement. Von had a feeling and he was right. Miki and Brenda stood together on the doorstep of the little mobile lab, their combined weight working the shocks, and announced they were engaged. Just like that. Then Miki broke out the saki and tiny ornamental cups.

As just plain wrong as the whole deal was, the saki was probably the worst of it. Von knew it could get you hammered, fast, but at some point, the power to inebriate becomes irrelevant—if *urine* got you wasted, he wouldn't want to drink much of that, either.

Previously, Von had always thought of Miki as being ridiculously jolly, but all that before had been nothing compared to the way he grinned and laughed his ass off now. He hugged Carol and called her "Mother" several times in a row, trying it out, then switching to "mama-san" like he'd made a side-splitting joke. Suddenly, he grew wide-eyed, like he'd just remembered something, and detached his arm from around Carol and scrambled back into the camper. He tripped on the little steps and then inside, unseen, started bumping into things, moving crap around. It sounded like he was trashing the place.

Von looked at his wife. She was just shaking her head, smiling wryly. It was like she had no stake in this, like she was just watching a movie, some foreign comedy she only understood in snatches.

Von couldn't stand it. "Jesus god, what the hell's he doing in there?" The guy seemed almost dangerous now, being that big and out of control.

Brenda rolled her eyes, covered her mouth, giggled, not at all like herself. Girlish. The saki was getting to her. "Oh jeez," she said.

"Maybe," her brother said, "he's got a really large, unwieldy engagement ring in there." Marita shoved him sideways, knocking him off his footing. She was giggling now, too, though she'd passed on the saki on account of the baby.

One of the side screen windows slid open and Miki pressed his face against the screen. "Please pardon, but the system is built into the console! It is not portable, the system!" Whatever the hell that meant, it seemed to truly distress the boy. Then his face was gone from the window.

Von caught his son's attention and repeated this, "It's not portable, the system . . ." Jack burst out laughing and Von grinned, trying to remember when they last shared a laugh like that.

Miki's face reappeared in the small sliding window and again he spoke earnestly through the screen, bending low to be heard. "But I am hoping it will reach, the system!" Then his face was replaced with a tiny audio speaker and there was more scrambling. Von heard the opening notes to something familiar he didn't quite place, a slow, unreeling kind of music box ditty, and more scrambling and bumping as Miki fumbled and careened back through the door, dragging a cord behind, down the little steps, playing out the slack. In his hand, he held a microphone.

"Karaoke and saki," Jack said. "Of course! And here I've been trying not to think stereotypical thoughts about the guy . . ."

Miki's lids hung low, his lip curled. "*Wise . . . men . . . say . . .*" He was suddenly Elvis. Flawless, gliding sideways, graceful and suave, toward Brenda, he began serenading her in a perfect, quavering tenor. "*Only fools . . . rush . . . in . . .*"

Jack whistled through his teeth with two fingers. "Whoo-whoo!" he said. "My man, Miki!"

"*But I . . . can't . . . help . . .*"

Brenda blushed, covered her face. She looked like a teenaged girl, she really did. Von didn't remember her looking like that even when she *was* a teenaged girl.

"*Falling in love . . . with . . . you.*"

Standing on the picnic table, Carol clapped and hooted.

It was hard to believe. This was going to be his son-in-law. All this right in front of him—this goofy serenading Japanese giant, this pregnant Guatemalan girl who seemed to want to change everything, and this wife of his who saw no problem with any of it and didn't hesitate to stand on picnic tables and spectate—this was it. This was the future. This was the lot they'd drawn.

Jesus god . . .

Well, there wasn't much he could do about it. Nor did he guess he *should* do anything about it even if there was some way to meddle. He knew what Carol would say if he cornered her later: was there some other potential mate they'd had in mind for Brenda? There was not. Had they ever even pictured her marrying anybody? They had not. Not honestly. She wouldn't have been the first old maid among the vonBushbergers, that was sure. So what was the loss if she married this guy? There was some consolation in the idea of gaining another egghead around the place. He doubted there was a family-operated orchard anywhere in that whole part of the state with the sort of scientific brain trust it looked like he was going to have now, right on the premises. Because certainly, they wouldn't be living in Japan. No way would his daughter spend all those years—and all that tuition money—earning an education that would prepare her to eventually run the family business and then just chuck it all for some foreigner. She was wiser than that, he was sure.

Still, he wasn't exactly ready to hop up on the picnic table and cheer. But actually, the whole thing sort of made him chuckle, watching Carol there, carrying on like a true Elvis groupie.

40

SHE AND REVEREND GENE were out on the lounge chairs, talking over iced coffee. They had the kitchen windows open wide so they could hear Dave Brubeck drifting out, but it wasn't cheering her much. She'd told him a little of what was going on, the nonsense with the neighbors, and how her dad was behaving, it seemed to her, like a real dick, making the whole situation worse, the dumb stunt at the Spartan store with the spicy sausages . . . She was hoping the old guy would have some advice for her, some tips on something she could do to smooth things over. A plan of action. But he just kept sipping his iced coffee, nodding a little, and gazing out at the river, the boats moving drowsily from one lake to the other. She wondered if he was even listening.

"I believe," he said finally, "the Lord expects us to discover what each of our own individual *strengths* and unique *opportunities* are, and then use those strengths and opportunities to make things better between us. To connect us all."

It sounded a little lame. "I don't know that I have anything you'd call *strengths*. I'm still trying to figure that kind of thing out. Like, I have no idea where I want to go to college or what I'm going to—"

He shook his head. "Don't overthink this, Kimberly. You work at the fudge shop—who doesn't like fudge?"

She had to turn and look at him. What was he saying? "So just take them some fudge? That's the answer?"

"It's *an* answer. It makes you *you*. Marks you as an individual, separate from your dad. His actions and deeds are his, not yours. He's maybe going to have to figure out what's right on his own. How to be a good neighbor, do the right thing. In the meantime, you can start making your *own* relationships with the world, following what *you* decide is right. What's right for *you*, who *you* are." His eyes twinkled. That was a nice thing about older people: that twinkly thing actually happened sometimes when they smiled. "For instance," he said, "let's say you decide that you more enjoy the jazz records of an old man, less the flash-in-the-pan barkings the other kids try to tell you are so great—Brubeck, not Beck—well, then so be it. That would be you being *you*, having your own opinion. Hold your head up, darn it!"

She *loved* that he knew Beck. Probably he'd just peeked in her CD binder once and couldn't actually name one single Beck song, and really, she liked Beck fine. Beck couldn't really be lumped in with the kind of things she knew he meant, those overnight one-hit wonders, usually rappers, that she knew in her heart were mostly hype and that she only listened to out of peer pressure. But still, how cool was he for even knowing Beck? Definitely much cooler than her own dad, despite being like a hundred years older.

"I can't tell you," he said, "how many times it's mentioned in the Bible: *Unto thy neighbor give fudge.*"

"You're a weird guy." She giggled, but knew he was right. "Really, really weird."

41

ON JULY 5, ON THE WAY BACK UP NORTH from his annual escape to Canada, passing through Ludington at about twenty-hundred hours, Roger Drinkwater spotted one of vonBushberger's trucks and had an idea. A big idea. They were pulled alongside a fruit distributor, unloading what he assumed was probably the first run of sweet cherries, which meant they'd be heading back up to Weneshkeen as soon as they were empty.

He'd been thinking how ineffectual his Operation: Nozzle Muzzle had been, in the long run (a few days of peace, but the missing jet-ski parts were soon replaced) when he saw the orchard truck from home and it all came together in a moment. Or at least most of it did.

He pulled off 31 and drove the two miles to Lake Michigan and parked his car along the dirt road, within view of the public beach and a long sandy spit that he did his best to memorize. It probably wasn't enough of a landmark, he decided, so he opened the trunk and got out a diving buoy and line of nylon rope he used to teach marine rescue and walked out to the spit. The only good anchor he could spot was a large piece of driftwood that unfortunately was already occupied by a young couple nuzzling and watching the last of the sunset. He decided they were just teenagers and told them to get up. The boy looked alarmed but got immediately to his feet. "Come on, Kristie," he said, helping his girlfriend up.

"You can have it back in just a sec," Roger told them, tying the line to a place well below the fork in the driftwood. A hunk of sun-dried beech, it looked like. Sturdy. "Okay," he said. "You can have your bench back. Resume smooching."

They started to sit back down. He grabbed the boy by the arm. "But do not—and I mean do NOT, under any circumstances—untie that rope. A life depends on it. Understand? A man could drown."

He knew it made no sense to the kid but he could tell by the gulpy look on his zitty face that it didn't really have to. "Understood," the boy said. He looked like Roger had just enlisted his aid in some brave adventure that would save the nation from Nazis or Commies or alien invasion.

He left the car and double-timed briskly, the overland stride he'd perfected in the SEALs, and got back to the vonBushberger truck just as they were loading in the empty flats. Both the driver and his partner were Mexicans or something, migrant pickers, and when he asked if he could catch a lift back to Weneshkeen, the guy nodded a lot and said, "Sí. Sí." Still, Roger wasn't convinced the guy knew what he was agreeing to. More than likely, he'd seen too many bad Mexican Westerns and was just agreeing to anything in order not to get scalped.

It was a long dark ride north to Weneshkeen, and he spent it squatting on his heels on the open bed of the truck, looking back at the tree-lined road tunneling out behind him and trying to think where he would get the materials he needed. Of course, he could do it all in his kitchen. He had the salt substitute and the bleach—that plus time and patience and he'd have potassium chlorate. But by the time he cooked all that up, it could be daybreak. Besides, he didn't need anything so fancy as plastique.

The wooden pallets moved underneath him and reeked sweetly of cherry juice. The smell took him back to the one summer as a teen that he'd worked picking at vonBushberger's. It reminded him of bee stings and backache—and an alternative, maybe, for the material he needed.

There was supposed to be a full moon, but it was so overcast, it shouldn't present a problem. He wondered if they'd had a wet Fourth; if his retreat this year had been unnecessary.

He kept low as they rolled through town, under the streetlights, and then reentered the dark, rumbling north another few miles and turning off at the orchard. He wondered if the migrants had forgotten him back there. They hadn't stopped to let him hop off in town. It wasn't surprising, being forgotten. As an Indian, Roger was long used to feeling like others couldn't see him or tried to pretend he wasn't there. Still, the fact that they kept rolling only saved him the trouble of pretending to get off and then hopping back on or getting in some big conversation with them and having to cook up some lame excuse for wanting to continue on to the orchard.

He dropped off only as they pulled in at the floodlit sign out front and stayed crouched low till they rattled on, back around the tractor barn, and he heard the truck shut off and ping and knock and the doors bang and the receding lilt of Spanish as they dragged their tired asses to the far meadow and the migrant shacks. He counted to a thousand after the last snippet of Spanish, then moved quickly to the tractor shed. Inside, he waited for his eyes to adjust, though he soon saw everything was almost exactly as he remembered it from that summer some thirty years ago.

He needed containers and quickly found two small thermoses on the repair bench. With one thermos, he slipped back outside and helped himself to probably three cents of diesel from the pump, topping off the thermos and screwing it tight. Back inside, he got some duct tape from the bench and sealed the thermos cap. With the second thermos, he moved to the metal cabinet where they kept the fertilizers, located a sack of Green Thumb, and packed the thermos with several cups. This he sealed, too, and then duct-taped one thermos to each thigh, thinking that if he attached them to his shins, he might kick them loose. At the door, he stood watching the open area between the houses, the floodlit turnaround, double-checking before he crossed it again. There was a small light and murmured voices coming from the smaller house, which surprised him until he remembered: he'd heard the son was married now. But the coast was clear, so he walked back out, passing only briefly through the pool of light, and then down 31 to the nearest access road, where he began his hike due west, to Lake Michigan.

The sun was down now, but he knew from memory that Sumac Point and the inlet into the Ojaanimiziibii were about two and half clicks south. He could just make out the dull glow of that shambles of a lighthouse. The wind was still holding, pulling waves in a southeasterly direction, so this would be a cinch. He could conserve energy during this part and just float.

Removing his shoes, he jammed them down in the pockets of his khakis, tying the laces to his belt loops as an added precaution. Stepping into the lake, he took off the nylon windbreaker with the Weneshkeen High Whos logo and, tying knots in the sleeves and cinching up the hood, held it over his head and slammed it down hard, forming an air pocket. Making an air bladder was nothing—any kid he taught on Drownproofing Day at the junior high every year could manage that much.

It was a gentle ride and he kicked to some extent, just to correct his course, but for the most part, he conserved his energy and worked it all out in his head. He had to stay focused.

Very quickly, he'd closed the distance to Sumac Point and he was right under the lighthouse. From here on in the cruise was over. Now it was warrior mode. He let the air bubble out and threw the soggy windbreaker up on the rocks, then untied his shoes from his belt loop and threw them up there, too. No one would come across the clothes that night and if he didn't get back to collect them, it would mean he'd been found out already anyway.

There would still be a few Fudgies out on the riverwalk and even though it would be hard to see him down in the water, he knew he had to be careful. He chose a frog kick till he passed the first pilothouse, then went for full stealth swimming, gliding along the riverbank, taking it slow and gentle so as not to break the water too loudly. It was tricky, because he couldn't go too deep for fear of hitting a snag, some old stump or deadhead, and the effort was already hitting him in the lungs. Easy, he told himself, no chuffing and huffing like an old man . . . But God, this was so much easier when he was a kid—even considering the occasional overhead round from an AK-47. At this point, he'd probably swap a few enemy guard towers for a pair of twenty-year-old lungs. One of the times he slipped through the surface for a grab of air, he heard a snatch of conversation—something about David Letterman—and it seemed so close, it was disorienting, like he'd slipped up and come up in the middle of a storm drain in the center of town or something.

But then there was the inner pilothouse, the hunched shape of Walt DeWalt or Keith Nuttle up there, checking out for the night—a little late, it seemed, but this was the end of a big boating holiday—and he went down again and squirmed through the narrows and he was in colder water now, back where he belonged, in the other lake, Meenigeesis.

He surfaced again, went under again, surfaced again, long enough to see his intended target was right there, docked right where he wanted it. And then next time he came up, he was right in the shadows of his own dock and he edged along it, out of the lake, and crossed his front yard, bent low and barefoot. Hugging the side of the house, he slipped around back and let himself in through a sash window in the rear that no longer quite locked.

He knew he was dripping all over the floor but he ignored that. Without turning the lights on, he stepped to the kichenette, avoiding the window, and wolfed down a very mushy banana. Grabbing the Ziplocs, he filled one with beef jerky for later and duct-taped the whole thing to his chest, keeping the opening free at the bottom so he could still get at it. Now, he told himself, was a good time to be an Indian—or really, *later,* when he had to pull the duct tape off. Less body hair was sometimes a boon.

He wanted liquids but didn't want to risk opening the fridge because of the light. Moving to the rear of the house, he unlocked his gun cabinet and, setting the bird gun aside, took out a box of shells. Prying several open, he poured the black powder onto a flyer advertising his Schmatzna-Gaskiwag® jerky. He wished he could remove the pellets but that seemed far too difficult. Opening a fresh Ziploc, he then peeled the first thermos off his leg and dumped the fertilizer into the bag, followed by the powder from the shells. Zipping it sealed, he squished it around, mixing it. Next step was the base. He unlocked the back door and eased it ajar, listening. Nothing. Still keeping low, bouncing on his heels, he scurried the short way to his shed, located the half-empty jar of putty he'd used to fix the porch windows, and poured the mixture from the bag into the jar. He removed the second thermos and topped off the concoction with diesel, stirring it with an old paintbrush handle until it began to congeal and set. He didn't want it to harden completely, just become a little more malleable, a little more adhesive, and he counted thirty more seconds before he screwed the lid on, cutting off the oxygen. He popped the whole jar back in the Ziploc and sealed it. There was the long-handled Bic lighter on the workbench, the one he used for the hibachi, and he grabbed this up and thought for a second about how exactly he was going to do this.

There was twine there. He could get far enough away so at least he wouldn't get hurt. Yeah, this would be fine. This would work. He wished like hell he had real fusing, and he had the granulated sugar and other ingredients to make some, but that would take even more time and the night was slipping away. Besides, he was starting to shiver.

Well, he thought, this'll be okay. He didn't need a timing fuse so much for getting away, for an alibi—he thought he could talk his way out of it even if it blew while he was still in Meenigeesis, but of course he'd prefer to not be around for the noise. After all, hadn't he driven all the way to Canada to avoid just such noise?

Then he remembered Jimmy Connelly.

Jimmy Connelly swam the individual medley a few years back. Strong butterfly, passable crawl, but a terrible pain in the ass. There were kids like Jimmy who forced him more into the role of gym teacher than of coach and he hated that, having to police the kids. But he heard some of the rest of the team talking in the showers, saying Jimmy had "a bomb." Roger didn't think this was true. The kid wasn't bright enough to build an actual bomb. He was more like Terry Thomas or Teri Garr than Terry Nichols. More Ted Knight than Ted Kaczynski. But he checked the kid's locker anyway. What he found was waterproof fuse—big deal. You could buy it in any hobby store that sold rocket engines, but he confiscated it anyway. He'd heard Jimmy Connelly was studying prelaw now, down in Ann Arbor. It figured.

If he remembered right, all that student contraband junk was in the bottom of his gym bag, back inside the house in the front hall, and sure enough, he found it there among the roach clips and laser pointers. Uncoiling it, gauging about five seconds per centimeter, he figured he could easily get free and clear.

He locked the back door and slipped out the same window, pulling it down behind him, then eased back into the lake.

HE WAS ALREADY OUT IN LAKE MICHIGAN, past the lighthouse, about a half-click south of town, just past that idiotic ark house, floating along on his makeshift windbreaker bladder, when he thought he heard it. Possibly. A *whump,* quick and dull.

That could be anything, though. A wave lifting a raft, letting it down solid in the water. Something blown over in the wind, a beach umbrella. He listened for sirens. Nothing.

He resumed kicking. Maybe it hadn't happened yet. Maybe it wasn't going to happen. He'd made duds before, even back when he was practicing on a regular basis. He tried to remember the last time he'd built any kind of explosive. It gave him something to do as he floated and kicked.

He decided it wasn't all that long ago. Maybe six or seven years ago. For benign purposes, too. Reenie Huff, the most bullheaded woman he knew in town, had an elm stump in her flower garden that she was tired of dressing up and camouflaging. Some kids had snatched the wrought iron sundial that formerly covered the stump and she was just sick of looking at it.

"You sick of the whole garden?" he'd asked her. "Because I don't know how to make anything quite that tactical. Something that won't muss your black-eyed Susans."

Reenie said she was ready to start over. She *was* a woman of extreme measures. She'd been head librarian with only another year to go to qualify for retirement but she quit out of protest when the village refused to finance a free reproductive clinic that would be accessible to teenagers. It had nothing to do with the job they were paying Reenie to do, really, but she was feisty and wanted to make a stand, and so she'd applied for a Planned Parenthood charter and was running, at a time she should be retired, the smallest chapter in the nation, out of her garage. It was basically a card table, a plastic jack-o'-lantern full of condoms, and a peach basket full of pamphlets on abortion and adoption and herpes and genital warts, and once a month a doctor came and did a few exams behind a Japanese screen that purportedly featured whooping cranes with fish in their beaks. More than once, Fudgies, seeing the people gathered in front of her open garage door and the card table, wandered up, thinking it was a garage sale, hoping to find a nice lamp, get a good deal on one of those quaint copper Jell-O molds.

That time, for Reenie, he didn't stoop to fertilizer but took the trouble to cook up plastic explosives with bleach and potassium chlorate. It was tricky business—like preparing baked Alaska, only trickier, since, unlike even the fanciest dessert, it could kill you—but he thought the job required a little more precision than a fertilizer bomb.

He hadn't set that one off, either. He left it in her hands, with instructions, and asked her to wait till he was out of town—he was headed up to Camp Grayling for one of those two-day classes he taught. SCUBA, it must have been. The first he learned that one had worked successfully was Reenie showing up at the lake a few days later with a thank-you plate of ranger cookies and a brochure, for some reason, on the transmission of hepatitis C. And with no missing limbs, as far as he could see.

Now he kept listening, floating farther away. He supposed it could have blown much earlier. Though he hadn't heard anything during his whole long creep back out the river, nor at his arrival at the lighthouse, on the point, taking a breather on the rocks and grabbing a bite of jerky. He'd tried counting the seconds, but it was really a judgment call. Who knew how long that fuse was? It was dark at the time and it wasn't like he'd measured the thing. And maybe the putty hadn't held. Maybe the fuse was so long, the adhesiveness gave out and the blobs of putty fell off the side of the jet-skis and plopped into the water. If that happened, it might ignite underwater—maybe—but before it did, it would also probably sink all the way down to the bottom of the lake, which had to be at least ten or twelve feet deep there, at the end of that dock, and so the underwater concussion would only make for a little raised water, a big splashy burp. Or, more than likely, if it dropped off the jet-skis and hit the water, it would lie there so long waiting for the spark to travel that long fuse, the putty would have time to get saturated with water and be about as explosive as a wet sock.

He'd stuck it on hard, one handful of the concoction for each jet-ski, scooped out of the can and molded and pressed, like a tiny volcano, smack on the hull, right above the waterline, right near the gas tank. Then he'd connected them with the green fuse and unwound it down the dock, making it as straight and as long as he could. He reached up onto the dock and hooked the fuse around a mooring cleat to keep it from dipping in the water, lit it with the long fireplace lighter, and, with the whole Ziploc bag of paraphernalia jammed, pirate-style, in his teeth, swam hard for the mouth of the river.

And now he was out in the second deepest Great Lake, probably about to drown himself, and probably for nothing—probably there had been no explosion and *would* be no explosion. Yes, they'd find his body way down in Michigan City or somewhere and much would be made of the irony of his being a swimming instructor. And as he was an Indian, they would assume he'd been drinking—how else to explain this poor slob with a stash of beef jerky duct-taped to his chest, horsing around on nothing but a puffed-up windbreaker?

He remembered how he used to be the kind of guy who didn't worry all the time. Lately, he'd sure taken to fretting. Something was really going to have to change soon or it was going to seriously cut into the calm, cool Indian vibe he'd always had going on.

BY THE TIME HE SPOTTED HIS DIVING BUOY, floating southward and still tethered to the hunk of driftwood tree trunk—the squirrelly make-out kids long gone—and caught it and stopped his drift and reeled it in and got back to his car, the replacement stick-on clock on the dash was blinking 2:05. He stripped down, threw his wet clothes in the trunk, where he snatched a towel and some clothes out of his luggage, wrapped himself around the waist and slid behind the wheel, cranking the heater up to high.

He drove north on 31 at a steady clip, stopping only once, along a desolate stretch of pine, to hop out and pull on the dry clothes. Back in the car, he rolled down his window, flipped the switch from heat to straight fan, and aimed the blowers at his head. No sense taking chances, he thought. Yet still, imagine the absolute razzing old Coots and Miller would give him if they knew he was now running the sort of "spesh op" that could be improved upon by the use of a travel-sized blow-dryer.

Coming in just south of town, it was about ten to three in the A.M., so he slowed his approach, wanting to time it just right. He pulled in at the all-night Mobil and filled up and stretched conspicuously and asked the kid working there if he had the time, knowing it was now probably three on the button.

"I've got . . . three A.M., on the money, Mr. Drinkwater." Roger was glad to see the kid was one who recognized him from the high school. This was good. He wanted the kid to remember what time he'd pulled back into town, in case he was ever questioned.

For 0300, it sure was lively. Cars were whizzing by, heading for the lake. "Three in the morning," he said, repeating it, "what the hell's going on at three in the morning?"

"Big to-do over to the lake," the kid said, jerking his head in the direction of Meenigeesis. "Somebody's dock blew up."

Roger made sure to pay him in Canadian bills.

When the kid had said *dock*, Roger's first thought was that he'd goofed; he'd done all that for nothing, just to blow up the dock. But then, as he pulled onto the county road and found it lined with half-dressed gawkers and all kinds of service vehicles—the sheriff's department and volunteer fire and even state troopers—he got the word from Deputy Struska. She waved him through with her Maglite, letting him pull into his driveway, then followed him up to the porch.

"Something going on?" he asked.

"You're kidding. Where you been?"

"Canada."

She seemed to be looking him over for a second. He wondered if there was some part of him that still wasn't dry. "Oh, right. Fourth of July. Well, you're especially lucky you left town *this* year."

"Really noisy, you're saying?"

She told him what had happened. The part of it she knew. It felt kind of strange, how she knew her half and he knew his.

It wasn't that he'd missed his target, it was just that the dock had been destroyed, too, and from the perspective of everyone else, that seemed the significant fact: a dock had been destroyed—which included everything tied to it, which was, according to a preliminary inventory, two jet-skis, an awning, two big beach towels hung out to dry, a wakeboard and tow tube (whatever that was), flower pots, a combination bench seat and ice chest, and a rowboat.

He felt a little bad about the rowboat. Rowboats were okay. But as for the rest of it, the dock and that Fudgie crap, hey, what did they expect—surgical precision? He was working with fertilizer, after all, and he hadn't had any practice in years. It wasn't like he pulled the recipe out of *Martha Stewart Living*. How exact could he be?

"I know you were away and all, but Hatchert's going to want to talk to you." As if on cue, the radio clipped to Struska's broad chest crackled and she took the call, turning away and rogering some fuzzy directive. The sound was broken by a long fizzle and a burst of light overhead, amber sparks and a report that banged in echo across the lake. Some kid with leftover fireworks, egging on the cops.

"Bottle rocket?" she asked.

"Little bigger. Maybe a skyrocket or Texas Pop."

They stood, staring up in the break through the trees, expecting more. He could feel her glancing over at him, probably wondering how he was doing, trying to gauge how unnerved the fireworks made him, but he kept his eyes straight ahead, looking up, not wanting to give her any information. He'd developed a habit, when looking up at the night sky, of first covering his throat with one hand, and he was doing this now. The idea was to protect the jugular, to not leave yourself vulnerable to someone who might slit your throat in the dark while you're star-gazing like a dope. Years ago, he'd performed this very move, without thinking, in front of a woman he had just started living with named Crystal, while they were on a camping trip out in the Manistee National Forest. When she realized what he was doing, she began weeping uncontrollably and said it was so unbearably sad (this was the seventies and her name wasn't really *Crystal:* she'd named herself after an actual crystal that she'd found in the ladies' room at an MC5 concert) and she felt terribly sorry for him but she couldn't *possibly* live with a man who had become so hardened to the world, so untrusting and "crusted," was how she put it. So there was no point in camping. All during the dark drive back home to Weneshkeen, she kept reaching across the front seat and petting his cheek like he wasn't even there, like he'd been laid out for viewing, and wept about the way "that goddamned war" had robbed him of his humanity.

The truth was he'd learned the neck move years before Vietnam, when he was little, hunting with his Uncle Jimmy Two-Hands, who'd picked it up from their Grandma Oshka. So it was actually probably an old Polish custom, or maybe just the quirky impulse of a person thrust, irrecoverably, into an ill-suited land. But he didn't bother telling Crystal any of that. She was nuts, he decided, and he just wanted his house key back.

"Hatchert's coming over," Struska said now and it sounded a little like an apology.

"I'll be unpacking," he said. He decided he'd look less like a suspect, the whole thing less like an episode of *Cops,* if he didn't wait there out on the porch. Plus, he needed to give the place a quick once-over, make sure he hadn't left any evidence out in plain view. Last time, with the nozzles, they hadn't come in, but this time, they might have a warrant.

They didn't, but the coast was clear, so he opened the door to them anyway as soon as Hatchert arrived. Struska took a casual position leaning against the kitchenette counter. She seemed to be looking around, but maybe not with the eyes of a cop. More, it seemed, with the eyes of regular company—glancing at the postcards and pictures on his fridge, perhaps appraising the curtains, assessing the sanitary level of the sponges in his sink. Meanwhile, Hatchert stalked, nosy-eyed. He was pretty direct with his accusations this time, saying he knew Roger was behind this, it was just a matter of evidence.

"Here's your evidence." Roger flashed the stack of receipts from his trip, with the one from the Mobil station on top and the Ambassador Bridge on the bottom, hoping they wouldn't notice how much time had passed between the Canadian border and stopping to refuel on the way back into town. "How do you account for the fact that I didn't get into town till three A.M.? Talk to the kid at the Mobil. How could I have blown anything up while I was out of town?"

"Timing fuse."

"Uh-huh. A three-day timing fuse. You know how long that would be? Stretch partway round the earth. *Timing fuse . . . !*" He turned to Janey. "Can you believe this guy, Deputy?"

"Well," she said wryly, "timing *is* everything."

"Especially in comedy . . . Well, *you* know that." He spoke directly to the sheriff, implying the guy was a comedian. Struska looked down suddenly, averting her eyes. "Look, if you really thought I was blowing up private property—or anyone else—you'd have called in the FBI. You'd have to, right?"

"We haven't ruled anything out."

Struska nodded. "Like for example, errant fireworks. My money's on fireworks."

"Errant ones," Roger said, feeling punchy.

Now she looked like she might start snickering. "Right."

"They're almost always errant," Roger said. "Ever notice that?"

"Which is why you exit every year," she offered.

The sheriff turned to Struska now like Roger wasn't even there, brusquely, like he wasn't worthy of direct address. "Isn't he supposed to be a SEAL or something?"

She frowned. "Not *now* he's not supposed to be . . ."

"You must be thinking of my Indian name," Roger said. "It's similar to that."

"Yeah? Your Indian name is something with 'seal' in it? What is it?"

"You an Indian?" Roger asked.

"No." This guy was really getting pissed now.

"Then I can't tell you. It's a secret."

The sheriff jabbed a finger his way, poking the air between them. "This is horseshit."

Roger shrugged. "Look, maybe if you saved my life, pulled me away from some settlers who were trying to lynch me and ravish my sister and then you and I cut our palms with a big Bowie knife and rubbed them together and became blood brothers and smoked the peace pipe, I could tell you my Indian name, but I don't see all that other stuff happening, do you?" He didn't know what it was—he was probably just punchy from the marathon swim—but something was suddenly turning him into Groucho Marx here, or at the least, instilling him with attitude, sassiness, and he had a strong feeling it had to do with Janey Struska's presence. Or maybe this new guy was just too much fun not to put on. "Yeah, that thing with the blood? Forget it. Very icky."

"I can look this all up, you know. There are records." The guy was trying to sound like this was a big threat.

"Sealed records, probably," Struska said, egging him on, too.

"Seal records?" Roger said. "Records of seals? I used to listen to those. Very big in the seventies. Not as popular as whale music or dolphins, but nice. Had them on eight-track."

"Big with the ladies," Struska agreed.

Hatchert was already leaving. He stopped on the steps and turned back, holding the screen door open, a final point to make. "And for the record, Mr. Hilarity, I know a thing or two about this Indian stuff, okay? If it's not in your environment, in the area where you live, it's not in your vocabulary. Eskimos don't have a word for cactus. So your Indian name can't be 'seal' or anything of the kind, because there are no seals anywhere around here." He let the screen door slam, even though it was close to 0400 hours already.

Struska remained leaning against the counter. They both gave out heavy sighs, almost simultaneously, as if relieved to be enjoying the sudden peace. It was very quiet, except for the creak of her leather, the holster and the belt. It was a nice crinkly sound, he thought, the sound a cowgirl might make when she wasn't busy yippeekiyaying. "He forgot about Easter seals," she said. "We get those around here every year."

Roger finally laughed with a snort. "Yeah, you better go remind him about that."

She gave him a wink and pushed away from the counter and squeaked her leathery exit. "'Night, Coach."

Of all the thoughts he might have had at that moment—bed, food, relief—the one he had was this: hey, she's okay. She's funny, she's smart, she's cute. She's all right, that girl.

42

SHE WAS OUT IN THE CRUISER, doing a routine patrol along Fifel Drive, the old unpaved road that served the older houses, like the bootlegger's place, along Lake Michigan. The sun was bright and high, with a slight breeze that shimmered the silver poplar leaves, but there was something else ahead, kids on bikes, pulling out of the unkempt driveway. They turned in her direction and she let them pass—two boys, maybe ten, and a little girl maybe seven. Janey kept going to the end of Fifel Drive, watching the kids in her rearview mirror. She thought it looked like they were stopping in the middle of the road, looking back at her, checking to see if she was following.

This is the extent of my police work, she thought, outwitting small children. I'm a regular Angie Dickinson here . . . She kept going till the dead-end turnaround, executed a sharp three-point and put it in park, giving them a full sixty seconds on her dive watch. When she drove back, they were gone. But she wasn't buying it.

It wouldn't take much to flush them out, she figured. She pulled into the dark drive, past the two stone posts now dwarfed and overshadowed by the big beech trees, staying off the siren but making the big dropped-in 427 roar, keeping it in second and letting it tach high. Thing sounded like a dragon to little kids. Then she backed out of the drive, looked to her right and there they were: still half in the trees, their front tires pointed out, little mouths gaping at being busted, unsure which way to go now, the boy in the lead stamping on the brakes and skidding, dumping his bike. She'd blocked their only exit and forced them to the woods and now they were surprised to see her.

The boys recovered fastest, cleared the underbrush and the dip in the shoulder and took off, pumping fast and screaming. But the little one in the back was stuck, her bike, bubblegum pink, hung up in the tangle of brush. She kept struggling with it, looking down at the problem, then up to yell "Tommy!" at one of the older boys, who were now in full retreat and shaking their heads, then back down at the problem, then "Tommy!" and so on.

Janey put the cruiser in park and got out, slipping off her shades to put the child at ease. It didn't help that much: she could see the panic increase tenfold in the little girl's face as she approached. Janey suspected it was that leather cop squeak, the belt and holster. She knelt down, keeping a few yards' distance till the girl relaxed a little. "Stuck, huh? Maybe I can take a look?" There was a long pause and then the girl nodded. At least she'd stopped yelling for Tommy, who was now a dot at the end of the road. Janey moved closer and saw the problem was her training wheels, which were caught in the roots of a knobby-looking birch. "Step off a second." The girl got off. Janey unhooked the bike and carried it clear of the woods, setting it down on the shoulder. "No charge." She said her name was Janey and the girl said she was Lucy.

Janey pointed out that their names sounded kind of the same. Lucy looked like she had to think about this for a while. She stared down the road, then said, very quietly, "Yes." She made no move to bolt. Janey waited. "I live here in the summertime," Lucy said. "Do you? Or do you live here in the all-the-time?"

Janey told her that she lived here in the all-the-time.

"When it's cold and snowy?" Lucy asked.

"When it's cold and snowy. So what's going on, Lucy? What're you and the boys up to today?"

"We're riding bikes."

"In the woods? Does that seem like a good idea?"

Lucy shrugged.

"Trying to hide from me, huh?"

She shrugged again. "We were going to leave anyways, 'cause we dint see him." She started to eat her finger.

Janey asked who "him" was. Lucy removed her finger and said, "David Lemmerman."

Janey wasn't sure she'd heard this right. "David Letterman. You were looking for David Letterman?"

The little girl pointed back into the woods. "Uh-huh. Down there. In the boot luggage house. David Lemmerman's staying in the boot luggage house."

"Who says?"

The girl shrugged, arms raised, fingers splayed, completely stumped on this one.

"You just heard he's staying here and you thought you'd try to see him?"

She nodded again.

"Why'd you want to do that, Lucy?"

She threw up her hands, like Janey must be some kind of a dope. "He's famous."

Well, she thought. At least it's not because she wanted to get a job as a comedy writer. Janey wasn't sure she could handle the competition. This girl was priceless. She patted Lucy on the head, right along that perfect part between the pigtails. "Get a helmet," she said. "That goes for Tommy and the other one, too. And ask them to tell you what *trespassing* means." She made a shooing motion, then rethought it, holding Lucy by the shoulder. "Wait. You're too young to stay up and watch Letterman. You sure you really know who he is?"

She was nodding, waggling those pigtails.

"Really?"

The girl shrugged, squinting back at her, repeating, "He's famous." Then she pedaled away, each stride a giant effort, as if that was answer enough.

43

IT STARTED OUT AS JUST A BIKE RIDE, following Courtney around the village. Mark knew she was bored, as usual. She even pedaled in a bored-looking way, lazily careening from side to side and narrowly avoiding getting clipped by people pulling away from the curb in trucks and SUVs. They had to squeal their brakes to avoid her, producing nothing more from her than, at the least, a roll of the eyes that said she was making allowances for the village retard or, at the most, a flip of the bird or a grab of her crotch and a *Lick me!* The biking ended pretty quickly, after a dipped cone at the Daisy June, which she only tasted, then tossed in a trash can. It got dark and she led him along the back access street that ran parallel to the main drag, River Street. There were Dumpsters back there, he noticed with a little apprehension, but also the service entrances for the bars and stores. Some were fenced off as little backyards. She seemed to have a plan, pushing her bike down into the alley that ran alongside the bar called the Wobbly Moose. She slid her bike in behind the Dumpster and he did the same, though he wasn't sure he was up for another Dumpster dive, if that's what she had in mind, no matter how much her filthy-rich friends back home thought it was cool.

There was a wooden sign over the open back door that said "Rear End of the Moose." Recorded music and voices and laughter drifted out. She stopped in front of a frosted dirty window and turned, grinning. "When I was young? This other girl and I? We'd sneak back here and stand on a crate and press our little titties up against the window. It's the men's room. The owner got mad and chased us off. Then they put in some frosted glass."

He was afraid to ask how long ago that was. He had a feeling it was probably just last summer.

"Anyway," she said, "you got some condoms, right?"

He nodded, then thought it might be too dark in the alley for her to see him nod, so he tried to say, "Yeah, sure," but it came out a sort of wet, breathy sound. Of course he had condoms—he'd quickly learned with her that it was best to have them at all times. You had to be prepared with her because she only wanted to do it at times when a person—a *normal* person—would *not* be prepared.

She took him by the hand and led him farther down the alley, toward the end where you might otherwise step out onto the sidewalk, only it was blocked with a short section of wooden picket fence, high and pointy. He could hear the voices of people milling in front of the bar, loud and clear, just a few feet away. Taking a moment to first peek out at the street through a large knothole about eye-level, Courtney then stood with her back pressed against the fence, resting one Teva-clad foot back on the low crossbeam, about six inches off the ground, so that one leg was bent, her pelvis cocked and spread. She unhooked the sarong-y wrap she wore over her bikini bottoms and raised it up around her shoulders, letting it rest there like a shawl. Then she gripped his face in her hands and pulled him to her, kissing him hard. "Come on," she said. "Let's do it."

He kissed her back. Once he'd locked on, she let go of his face and he could feel her getting ready down there, yanking aside her bikini bottoms.

"You going to take them off?" he said, into her mouth.

"No way!" she whispered back. "What if someone comes by?" She sounded excited at the prospect actually, but he was getting used to this—or as used to it as he thought he'd ever be—and knew not to question. "You can get in there," she said. When he pulled out the con-dom, she grabbed it from him and tore it open and got it on him, stroking him. Then tipped her leg a little more to the side and started trying to shove him in by hand, muttering, "Hurry . . . hurry . . ."

Mark had read a lot about foreplay and how women liked to go so slow. On *Loveline,* the radio show, they always told guys to approach a girl like you'd pet a cat, not how you'd roughhouse with a dog, and though that had always sounded good in theory, it was sort of out-the-window with Courtney.

He couldn't move in and out much because of the weird angle, the two of them standing face-to-face. And the edge of her bathing suit bottoms, the hem along the crotchline or whatever, was constricting, cutting up against his junk. Even through the condom, he could feel that thing rubbing like a piece of elastic. The fence made a creaking noise as they banged their weight into it. She was smiling now, her head rolling to one side, giggling a little and muttering something about how they were going to get in trouble. The smile was the only one he ever saw from her—that very brief sex smile. The thought flashed through his mind of maybe asking her please, as a favor, to take off her bathing suit bottoms. As if she'd really bother going to a little trouble to make it nice for him. Sure, she might have to get them back on quickly, but maybe it would feel a little more romantic. Besides, if they got busted, they'd be busted, flat out. No one would say, *Oh, I'm sorry! I thought you kids were maybe doing it back here but now I see the young lady there is wearing a tiny little bathing suit, so never mind! Sorry to interrupt your little game of whatever it is . . . Carry on!*

Suddenly she stopped moving with him, her hand clamped on his mouth, listening to the voices on the other side of the fence, her eyes wide. He was still inside her, but she held his shoulder with her free hand, indicating he should stop with the thrusting. There were several voices, laughing and talking, men and women. Mark didn't recognize any of them. They were only a few feet from the people passing on the other side, but she had known that when they started.

"Oh my God . . ." She straightened her legs and tightened and he slipped out of her like he was being shoved out, rejected. She tugged the bikini bottom back in place and, turning to peek out the knothole, swung the wrap down and back around her waist in one motion. "I knew it!" She almost squealed, something he hadn't really ever heard from her before (even when they'd been doing it, as they just had, moments before). "I knew it! It's Daddy!" She peeked through the hole some more and Mark could hear two distinct voices now, a woman and a man, as they moved away from the fence, leaving the bar. As the sound drifted away, Courtney stepped up on the bottom crossbeam, tippy-toe, and tried to peer over the top. "Looks like they're going over to that other one, Carrigan's, across the street. Probably want the next drink to be a little more . . . *in-ti-mate*." She let each syllable roll off her tongue like it was the dirtiest word in the world, and followed it up with her rendition of a cheap seventies porn soundtrack: "*Bow-chicka-bow-bowwwwww . . .*"

Mark looked now, too, just managing to see over the fence. There was a tall, tanned man with his back turned, crossing the street, his hand lightly leading, flat against the back of a dark-haired woman dressed in khakis like a forest ranger or something. Mark wasn't convinced: the guy did have the same wavy white mane as Dick Banes, but the woman seemed too short and not blond enough to be Mrs. Banes. But Courtney apparently thought it was them, so who was he to argue?

Hopping down off the fence, she moved quickly back to the rear of the building, where they'd stashed the bikes by the Dumpster. "Come on. He told me I had the condo to myself tonight, that he was going to sleep on the boat."

"So?"

She was already on her bike. "So we have to hurry if we're going to beat them there." She pedaled hard down past the rear entrances of all the nightspots and he followed her, down to the water. He didn't really get any of this, but he wasn't in the habit of asking Courtney to explain herself. They stashed their bikes at the rack behind her condo, then ran across the parking lot and down the dewy grass to the marina. He assumed, from her grin, that they were going to lie in wait and play some sort of joke on her folks. Maybe listen in on a private conversation.

On board *The Courtney*, he followed her down the narrow steps into the main cabin and turned on a light. There was a couch and a built-in entertainment system and bar behind louvered white doors. She opened a narrow closet and frowned at the contents: a bunch of exercise equipment including a long gizmo that looked like a torture rack, with a sliding seat and a series of complicated pulleys. It was up-ended, crammed in there on top of the heap. He read the word *Reformer* on its side. His own mom did Pilates and he suspected that's what it was for.

"Help me make room." Courtney dug out a big laundry bag and started stuffing it with the smaller loose things: a pink yoga mat, dumb-bells, ankle weights, some sort of big rubber ball and a Pilates hoop like the one his own mom used. "There's no place for this crap. He'll see it lying around." She cinched up the sack. "Just throw it overboard."

"No *way*," he said. "We can't do that." Spying on her folks was one thing, but wrecking their property . . .

She looked annoyed, rolling her eyes and exhaling a big huff like he was being a baby. "Fine! Tie a line to it then, we'll pull it up later. Jesus . . ." She started yanking on the Pilates machine next, dragging it out with a grunt. Apparently that was going, too. He started to explain that it would get rusty and stuff. "Piehole!" she said, musically, pleasantly, and made a closing motion with her hand, instructing him to keep his closed. So he did as commanded, hauling the bumpy sack and then the Pilates machine up the narrow stairway to the deck. It seemed like a lot of work for a prank and he wondered again why they were doing this. The best he could figure, there was probably some big parental discussion the Baneses were about to have, some important issue concerning their daughter—the kind of debate he knew for a fact his own parents had about him in the kitchen sometimes, too often, in his opinion—and that she just wanted to eavesdrop and see what they were saying about her.

He tied everything snug to a nylon mooring line, using the tugboat hitch he'd learned from Keith, and eased it all over the side with a bubbly *glub,* telling himself it wasn't very deep there in the slip, anyway. If the line broke, they could maybe still fish out the Pilates machine, at least. Maybe.

Back downstairs, there was still a big Rubbermaid bin at the bottom of the closet, full of gym outfits and larger free weights. "We're not tossing *that* in," he said.

"No, *duh*. We're gonna sit on it, dummy." She had him do just that, then closed the closet door, calling, "Can you see me through the slats?"

He leaned forward and saw a narrow slit of her, stretched out on the couch. "Yeah . . ."

She hopped up and turned off the light and joined him in the closet, sitting on his lap. It was a tight fit, but she managed to get the door closed and then it was pretty solidly dark. She whispered, peeking through the slats, "Now, let's just hope they turn the lights on . . ."

It was becoming clear that eavesdropping on a conversation wasn't what she had in mind. "Please tell me we're not actually going to watch your mom and dad having sex."

"That's not my mom. What's wrong with you? You've seen my mom—did that look like her?"

"I guess I thought she was maybe . . . doing her hair different?"

"She's doing my *dad* different—but she's not my mom. Mom flew down to Ann Arbor, for the Art Fair."

He didn't know what to say. Besides, being from Birmingham, he was not unfamiliar with the Ann Arbor Art Fair and was pretty sure it wasn't now. But he kept his mouth shut.

"Anyway," she said, "it wasn't just the dark hair that was different.

Didn't you see the khakis and the shorts and all? The chick was dressed like Smokey the fucking bear."

"I can't believe this," he said. "What are you going to do?"

"We're doing it: we're going to wait here until they show up and then we're going to watch."

"Are you going to tell her?"

"My mom? I don't *think* so."

He tried patting her shoulder, stroking the ponytail that was now tickling his nose, not sure it was a comfort. "You must be really upset, I guess."

She squirmed and reached back to flick his hand away. "Please. It's hilarious."

He couldn't see what was so funny about it. Anything remotely this crazy, with either one of his parents, he'd probably be crying or puking or both. But she was glued to the door like any minute now the circus was going to start. He pointed out that they would hear them breathing in there. She shook her head and it made his nose itch. "No chance. My dad? He's like *loud*. It's always a big production with him."

"You're kidding. You've heard your dad . . . doing it?"

"All the time. And that's just with my boring old mom. When he's got something hot happening, like tonight, I bet he's even louder. We could probably be doing it ourselves at the same time and he'd be so loud, he wouldn't even . . ." She turned around in his lap and considered him again. "Hey. Yeah. It's going to be kind of like a live sex show. Maybe we—"

Just then there were voices on the gangplank and footsteps on the deck. Mark felt a slight shift of the boat. Courtney pressed her fingers against his mouth. Then they were coming down the little stairs, into the cabin, the woman saying something about her not really being a big boat person, that she was too used to being surrounded by trees. Light came through the slats—dim and orange; the small table lamp in the corner. There was the sound of ice cubes: more drinks. The sound of the couch unfolding into a bed. Courtney's hand left his mouth, slid underneath her, between them, squeezing his crotch.

He was convinced her dad would know instantly that they were on the boat. Sure, they'd left no evidence out, their bikes were stashed up at the condo, but it was such a confined space, even if it *was* maybe the biggest boat in the marina . . . He imagined the man discovering them in there, the red rage on his face as he flung Mark overboard. Having a bigshot like Dick Banes mad at him—he might get arrested or lose his job on the river or who knows? At the very least, his parents would go mental. And Courtney had the condo to herself tonight—why the hell weren't they up there right now where they could be alone?

The stereo came on, loud—some seventies-sounding crap he was pretty sure was that guy who used to be in the Beatles. Not the one guy, but the other guy.

Courtney tipped her head to the side and forward, beckoning him to take a peek. He craned his neck, peering around her hair to see through the slats. They were doing it all right. Her dad was on top, the soles of his feet and his hairy legs and ass silvery in the dim light. All he could see of the woman was her hands on his hips, casual, like she was resting them there, and her khaki clothes folded neatly on the side of the bed like they were waiting, too.

Courtney grinned against his cheek, biting him. He could just see her eyes, looking back at him wide and naughty, like this was the Greatest Show on Earth. Personally, if they had to watch, Mark kind of wished there was more to see than her dad's hairy ass, but something about it—the idea of it, maybe—was certainly getting to Courtney. She took his hand, directing it so he was reaching around in front of her, sliding it down into her bikini bottoms. It was damp there, and he touched her where she showed him before, that spot much higher than he always thought, higher than he'd done with those few girls back home, though they hadn't complained or anything or said he was off. Maybe Courtney was just built differently, with everything way up above her vagina. She *was* a pretty exceptional specimen of human being, after all.

They were making some noise out in the room now—or at least Mr. Banes was—and Mark was pretty sure now that Courtney was right: he wouldn't hear them in there. At least not at the moment, in the middle of the act. But Courtney didn't seem to want to sit there quietly and enjoy the show. She was twisting around on him, easing to one side and trying to get at his junk. She undid his fly and started rubbing on him. He really didn't think this was a great idea, but she was already starting to work her bikini bottoms down. It didn't look like she'd have enough room to get them all the way off, but she was tugging at them, making her intentions clear, and he could feel the heat of her on his leg and with her other hand, twisted around, she was rooting around in his pockets, locating a condom. She pulled it out and bit off the corner and got it out with one hand, and tried to work it down on him, but he just wasn't ready.

She twisted around and he could tell, even in the dark, that she was glaring at him, silently pissed. But this whole thing was pretty scary—was it really that weird that he wasn't hard?

She started yanking on him, stroking aggressively, but that didn't work. Then she eased off him slightly, trying to lower her head to his lap, but she couldn't bend over that far. There wasn't enough room. So she returned to the stroking. It was no good. He wasn't going to get hard enough to do it. And he wasn't sure he really wanted to. This was just *too* crazy. Wasn't it?

Apparently giving up on him, she started doing it herself, touching that spot on herself and grinding back against his package—what there was of it at that point. She was breathing hard and he was sure her dad would hear or she'd lean too far forward, press too hard against the door, and they'd spill out onto the floor. He covered her mouth as she came and then bit his hand, not as part of her coming, but after, like giving him a shot in the ribs. It sounded, out in the cabin, like her dad was finishing, too.

The stereo was turned down and he could hear them talking now. Mr. Banes was saying wow, that was great, but man, he was suddenly really bushed, like he wanted to go to sleep. Courtney giggled into his neck, silently. Then the woman's voice, reminding him of a promise that she could spend the whole night.

"Oh yeah . . ." Mr. Banes didn't sound so thrilled. "Sure. No problem."

"Not to get heavy, really. Just— I'll get out at dawn."

Dawn? Mark thought. *Jesus Christ.* His coming home real late in the summer maybe wasn't a problem, but dawn? No way would that fly.

The stereo was turned off now and they were quiet for a long moment. And the light was still on. Mark reached around in front of

Courtney so he could press the light button on his watch. It was now almost one A.M. He waited. No one was getting up. Were they going to leave that light on all night?

As if to answer his unspoken question, Mr. Banes mumbled something like, "Hon? You gonna—?" and the woman said she needed to leave it on while she slept.

Courtney was a very slim girl. She weighed next to nothing. He kept telling himself that. Because after another half-hour of this, the weight on his legs was significant. They were tingling. A little longer, and they were definitely numb. Courtney shifted around a little, grinding that bony butt wherever she felt more comfortable, and even seemed to be dozing a little. *She* was fine. Probably bored even. But when he checked his watch again, panicked at the late hour, he wasn't sure he could even feel his legs or make them work properly. Could he even walk out of there, given an opportunity to do so? He wasn't sure. He started poking at his thighs, trying to get the circulation going, imagining the grisly amputation process, his legs two sutured stumps, the doctors shaking their heads mournfully after the gangrene set in. He rocked back and forth, hoping that might help. Yeah, he'd have to wheel himself around on a little furniture dolly. Visit other area high schools and give frightening talks to the kids about the dangers of letting your legs fall asleep . . .

Occasionally, he'd lean forward and peek through the slats and see their bodies in the glow of the bedside lamp. They didn't seem to be budging.

Maybe, he thought, maybe I can just *go* . . .

Courtney was drowsy enough, a rag doll on his lap. He slid her a little to one side and squeezed out from underneath her, still hunched in a semi-seated position and leaving her heaped on the Rubbermaid bin. He eased open the louvered door a crack. Courtney grasped his arm, but he resisted and she let go, pressing herself up against the side of the closet as best she could as he rose, painfully, to a standing position, feeling like one of those primitives midway along the chart of evolutionary man, and leaned out, moving through the door.

His legs buckled under him, useless, as he lurched toward the bed, out of control. He felt like Frankenstein, like he had two casts on his legs, and caught himself from falling with one arm on the mattress. He was leaning over it, the floor still wobbly beneath him, mushy, when the woman sat up, watching him. She was mere inches away, still clinging to Courtney's dad but wearing no real expression. She just sat straight up, staring at him, wide awake. Alarmed maybe, but not screaming, not surprised. Just unblinking, alert, like she wasn't going to take her eyes off him for a second. She looked like she'd expected him to appear. He spun and stiff-legged it up the stairs in a sort of side-to-side sashay, like a male mermaid. He managed somehow to clear the deck, but his legs weren't up to the challenge of the gangway and he lost his balance and fell, overboard. The water was colder than it should have been that far into the summer, but then he remembered how late it was and how warm, in comparison, he had been, down in the small closet with Courtney's body pressed against him. I'll drown, he thought for a second, thinking he was virtually paralyzed, but he didn't. He worked his arms and felt the slimy dock pilings and something metal—the Pilates equipment?—and grabbed at the line tied to it and pulled himself slowly back up. Standing dripping and bent on the dock, he listened for voices, alarm and chaos down in the cabin, but there wasn't any. No one had noticed or maybe no one cared and so he squished and wobbled his numb way home.

"THAT WAS PRETTY LAME," she told him the next night, after he got off work. "You just leaving like that."

Mark said again that he had to. His parents would have killed him.

"Still," she said, "I would have loved to have seen his face close up when you walked past the bed like that."

"I don't think he saw me. He looked like he was asleep." Of course, Mr. Banes very easily could have heard him falling overboard, but Mark decided not to mention that part. "Your— The woman, she saw me. Looked right at me."

"Yeah, she was kind of creepy, huh? She did the same thing when I walked out. Stared right at me, like she wasn't sleeping a wink. But my dad saw me, too."

"Shit. You're kidding."

She shrugged. "I made a little noise. I decided, fuck it, maybe he should see me, you know? What's he going to do about it—tell my mom? He didn't say a fucking word. To her *or* me. Just sat there, totally busted, his dick still hanging out."

He tried to picture it: Courtney walking out and clanging around, banging into something on purpose, maybe, glaring at her dad sitting upright, naked next to some strange woman, father and daughter face-to-face. The whole thing was just so creepy. "Listen," he said, trying to take her hand, get her attention. "Courtney. I like you. A lot." She shook his hand off but he continued anyway. "I—I like hanging out with you. And I know you got a certain way you like things and that's cool, but sometimes, in terms of just a nice evening, a nice date, you know, like a *date* date—?"

"*Nice?*" She said it like she might say *mice*.

"Like last night—that's not exactly my idea of a perfect date. I mean, you yourself—*you're* perfect and all—but the *activities*—it's not exactly how I wanted the evening to go. Sorry, but—"

"No *shit*." She frowned, practically sneered, pulled back in a sort of disdainful recoil. "That's not exactly how *I* wanted it to go. It's not exactly a big fantasy of mine to have a guy get all noodle-dicked on me in such a totally excellent situation. Pretty lame, really. Now maybe if you were *older,* if you were *my* age . . ."

She let it hang there and walked off ahead of him, toward the boats.

44

IT MADE HER SMILE, when she'd open her e-mail and see something there from *reecher81757.* Even if he had the simplest, almost babyish questions, he was so polite about it and sorry to bother her and always asked how her reading was coming and when he'd see her next or mention some new—well, new to her, ancient, really—jazz person he wanted to play for her next time.

She'd gotten online at her dad's clunky old Mac in his so-called "office," the messy mudroom between the garage and the kitchen, that he used to print out receipts and stuff for his septic business. She never liked to use it much, going to the library or getting on at Reverend Gene's instead, not because her dad was really a dick about her using it or anything, or because of the porn sites she occasionally found listed in his Web history, but because the computer itself was sort of grimy. There were black smears from his hands all over the keyboard and the side of the monitor, and though she knew it was probably just gunk and grease from the gears and motors and the tools he maintained in the garage, not actual sewage, it still made her think of that, which was pretty gross.

She finished up answering Reverend Gene's question about the *Escape* key and then shut it down, and did it the way her dad told her to, flicking the switch on the surge protector under the desk because there was something messed up about his old piece-of-crap Mac, and that's when she spotted that blue fish again—the same blue fish with the red beret and thick-rimmed glasses from the Starkeys' driveway sign. It was printed in full color on an envelope in the wastebasket. Weird, she thought. Maybe Mr. Starkey has it on his letterhead now . . . ? She slid the basket out and found the crumpled letter that went with it, also with that same big blue fish printed up near the top. It wasn't from Mr. Starkey but from some tuna company:

Mr. Kurt Lasco
Edgewater Road
Weneshkeen, MI 49660

Dear Mr. Lasco:

Thank you for your letter expressing concern about the possible trademark infringement created by your neighbor's sign featuring a close approximation of Charlie the Tuna.™

You are correct in assuming that a large corporation like The Star-Kist® Seafood Co. must remain vigilant in protecting our many trademarks. Failure to protect these can, as you suggested, cause this precious intellectual property to fall into public domain.

Our legal department has thoroughly discussed your letter and the attached photos of your neighbor's sign and upon consideration, we feel this is one of the times it is preferable not to act. The sign is not being used for a commercial enterprise, and your road (a dirt-topped "lake access road," according to our information) receives insubstantial daily traffic. In balance, therefore, the "bad press" fallout of any legal action we might take would far outweigh the advantages of pursuing this matter.

We will keep the photos of the sign on file and we thank you for calling this to our attention. Please accept the enclosed coupons toward free StarKist® product with our gratitude.

Sincerely,
Rose Anders, Esq.
The StarKist® Seafood Co.
PO Box 57
Pittsburgh, PA 15230

She put the letter back in the trash and tried to arrange it as close as possible to the way she'd found it, tucked under the envelope, which she reballed, and then slid the wastebasket back where she'd found it and went upstairs and tried to forget about the whole business.

That didn't work. Twenty minutes later, she marched back downstairs, dug the letter out of the trash, smoothed it out and wrote **REAL NICE!!** in big black marker across the bottom and left it out on his keyboard where he would have to see it.

RATHER THAN DEAL with the Starkeys in person, she decided to leave the fudge in their mailbox. It was a two-pounder she got at a discount from work—a fancy mixed sampler, in the older cloth-covered boxes that still said *Hersha's Chocolates* in vintage script rather than *T.G.I.Fudge*.

But Mark Starkey surprised her, coming up behind her on his bike and then leaning against the mailbox, asking her what she was doing. He looked tan and sweaty, probably just home from work.

She felt defensive. "It's fudge. For your parents."

He frowned and snorted, shaking his head. "My mom can't eat that stuff."

"Well," she said, "I just wanted to be . . . neighborly." She had an urge to say *It's the thought that counts,* but didn't this jerk know that? Jeez, she was just trying to be nice. Not that anyone seemed to understand that around here anymore. Except maybe Reverend Gene and a few others.

"Whatever," he said and pedaled up his driveway to the house. She put it in the mailbox anyway.

When she got back up to the house, she found her dad blocking the patio door. He'd seen the whole thing and looked angry. "What're you talking to him for? Are you that bored you have to go over there and carry on like a traitor?"

"Right," she said. "I'm a big traitor. Benedict Arnold. Jeez."

She tried to brush him off and started down the hall to the stairs, hoping to make it up to her room without further bullshit, but he called after her, "If you want to meet boys, I can introduce you to plenty. Things aren't really that dull, are they . . . ?"

She took a second, then turned and walked back into the room. "Do you ever think about why I bother here? I mean, why do I come up here every summer? Is it just to go swimming and work at the fudge shop and see people I really only knew when I was in diapers?"

What she was referring to was obvious, she thought: the fact that she continued to come up here for part of the year so that he could do his part of the raising, have his input and set an example; be an adult role model for her, along with the one provided by her mom.

But he just was not getting it. "Okay, okay! You're saying it's boring now. You're getting too old and fancy for our little town. Right? Well, I'm sorry if we don't have amusement park and rave parties . . ."

"Did I say *bored*?"

"It's because we don't have the cable, right? That's why you hate it here and you have to stir up—"

"Did I say I—? Look. Forget it. Let's just drop it, okay?" Again, she started down the hall, then decided to give it one more chance and turned and asked, "But can you just think about this one thing: What is the purpose of us spending the whole summer together? What is the purpose?"

"I'm sorry if you don't feel there's a purpose. Maybe—"

"*Not* what I said, okay? It's a question, Dad. It's not rhetorical. It's an actual question. With an actual answer that you will provide after you think about it. Got it?"

"If you're that bored up here, why don't you make a list of some things you'd like to do and—"

She growled in frustration. "Stop saying *bored*!"

They stood there glaring down the hall at each other. He wasn't getting it. She turned again and marched back down the hall but this time kept going, past him, through the patio doors and out to her bike, calling back to him, "Just *think* about it, okay?"

It was one thing, she figured, as she pedaled away, not to be a perfect parent, to fall short of the goal. It was another to not even be aware there was a goal.

MID-JULY

45

WITHOUT CALLING AHEAD, the church's New Building Committee dropped by to check on him. John Schank and Mrs. Katherine Delter and Mrs. Hiram Henderhoch. They said they were just stopping in to see how he was getting on and bring him "a few things" and collect up the pie plates and CorningWare that had accumulated after Mary passed and keep him informed about all the "latest" at the church. Mrs. Delter brought him something green-bean-and-mushroom-soup-based and Mrs. Henderhoch had a tin of ranger cookies, but niceties and casserole dishes aside, Gene could still tell it was the New Building Committee. They didn't have to spell it out.

What was going on was this (and the visits and covered dishes weren't making it any more comfortable or friendly): First Pres had recently come into a large endowment in the form of a vacant lot, adjoining the First Pres property, on the other side of the church from the parsonage. Initially, at the time of Gene's abrupt retirement at the end of last fall, when Mary's health took a turn and he decided to devote himself full-time to being by her side, the church's response was one of support and accommodation. Besides, it would only precede his planned retirement by a matter of sixteen months. At present, the ministerial duties were being temporarily filled on a rotating schedule by the many capable lay clergy—there were even two women among the bunch, which he was glad to see—and visiting ministers and even Gene himself, who agreed to take the pulpit every other month or so, "to help everyone ease into the next step" was the way the board phrased it. He was glad to do it. Though Mary's death had knocked most of the wind out of him, he could manage a simple, no-frills sermon now and again—dust off a first-year-of-seminary, connect-the-dots homily on straightforward topics like sacrifice or stewardship—and besides, it would help *him* adjust to this new phase of his life. After thirty-two years serving the same congregation, it would have been hard cutting it off abruptly, like turning a faucet, squeaking it closed.

But this limbo state couldn't go on forever. The search committee was "making inquiries" about a permanent replacement. They all agreed it would be so much easier if they could slow the hiring process down, though the reason *why* it would be easier was a sticky topic usually left unvoiced: if they could hold off, the new parsonage would be built on the new lot and they wouldn't have to kick him out of the present one. They shrank from elaborating too much on the details of this unofficial housing policy, keeping it vague. They would all "try their darnedest" to make it all work out. He wasn't going to be homeless "any time soon." They told him, "Don't you worry!" Hopefully, they said, they could keep the old parsonage there for "as long as you think you still need it."

They said that last bit like he might actually be going somewhere. But where? To stay with Ben and his fragile family? Washington state and Abbey, have her drag him around all day like one of her large dogs while she conducted her anger management workshops? Hardly. More than likely they meant a nursing home or death. That was probably it: he'd ministered to enough grieving widows and widowers to know the old maxim was true—one goes ahead, the other soon follows.

And after all, nonprofit organization or no, it made little financial sense to waste good riverfront real estate on a minister who was no longer ministering.

And all this was why he felt, to some degree, an inclination to turn his back on these people, this church that had been his family for thirty-two years. Because in the end, he was a problem for them, a burden. No different than a slobbering, doddering, pants-soiled distant relative a generation before his. The free housing was, he suspected, "really not a problem" only because they didn't believe it would last much longer.

John Schank appeared too antsy to sit, standing and strolling around the room as the ladies talked, like he was visiting a historic home in Greenfield Village and Henry Ford Museum. Gene kept glancing at him, wondering if he was looking for plaster cracks and carpet stains and other damages to the property. He peered at the titles on the bookshelves and stuck his head in the den. "Oh!" he said. "I see you have a computer now. Isn't that nice! Are you online?"

"A little," he said. "It's for the kids. They like me to e them, let them know everything's okay."

John smirked. "A little? I didn't know it was possible to be online a little." Still, Gene noticed he didn't correct him on the "e them" part. "Have you seen the church's Web site yet?"

Gene said he hadn't. He didn't even know there was one: couldn't imagine who at the church could have designed such a thing. John squinted sideways up at the ceiling and began to recite: "*Www-dot-presbyterusa-dot-org-slash-firstpres*—spell that out—the *first,* I mean, then *mich*—that's one word: *firstpresmich*—then *slash-weneshfirst-pres.*" He looked to the ladies for confirmation. "Right?"

"I think I'd have to see it written out," Gene said, making no effort to locate a pen. John slipped a fancy-looking one from his breast shirt pocket and wrote it out for him on the back of his business card from the savings and loan. Gene took it and thanked him.

"You'll be very excited to see everything that we're doing," Mrs. Delter said.

Gene said he was certain he would and smiled wide and stole a glance at the clock. He wondered if he would get them out of there before the girl arrived.

The two women glanced at each other now, as if debating something between them. "We were going to . . ." Mrs. Henderhoch began, ". . . well, offer to clean, since the last time . . . But . . ."

"Place looks real shipshape," John Schank confirmed. "Real tidy."

"We were *going* to offer some housecleaning help," Mrs. Delter said. "But . . ."

"But now it doesn't look like you really need it!" Mrs. Henderhoch added, and John gave a little smile and—unclipping his cell phone from his belt, holding it up as if by way of explanation, as if that were now a proper way to say goodbye—stepped quietly out the side door, toward the garage and the back lawn as the ladies continued to volley back and forth. "The other thing we were going to offer was—and if you're not ready for this, we completely understand—"

"No rush at all!"

"—but I'm thinking, from the way you seem to have pulled things together here a little better, with the cleaning and all, that maybe you *are* ready for it . . ."

"It's just . . . if you ever want some help sorting through Mary's things—"

"Her clothes and that sort of thing—"

"With figuring what to do with it all—"

"A charity . . . or perhaps there are some items Abbey will want one day—"

"—and you'd like a woman's help . . . well, there's no rush."

Gene thanked them and smiled but didn't say one way or the other. He wondered if John Schank had just stepped out temporarily or if he'd had to leave. He hoped it was the latter.

Mrs. Delter smiled. "It's nice to have everything a little more organized now, isn't it? More tidy like this . . . Is someone staying with you perhaps?"

At first, he thought this came out of nowhere. But of course, she was trying to make a connection to the recent improvement in his housekeeping. And though the real explanation—his arrangement with the girl—was perfectly defendable and aboveboard, he knew he wouldn't go into it with them. It was none of their darned business, truth be told. Even if he was shacking up with some chippie, it wouldn't be any of their business. This whole situation was beginning to feel like a halfway house, like his life had to be monitored and reviewed and authorized.

"Sometimes, lately," he said finally, because it was true but avoided everything they were asking, "I do things for no reason, like put my shoes in the freezer. Really. I open the freezer and my shoes are in there. I just . . . 'space,' as the kids say. I do odd things and I don't know why I do them."

The ladies made polite chuckling noises about how they were all in the same boat, how gosh, none of them were teenagers anymore, and then rose to withdraw, both of them diminishing the importance of the casserole dish and the cookie tin, as if these were things that, if they never saw again, it was just as well. They both theorized that John Schank must have had some business that called him away and that was fine, just fine, whatever was happening was fine, showing about as much concern about the return of Schank as that of the casserole dish and cookie tin.

Then they were gone. He put "Thursday's Child" on the stereo and cranked it up loud, relieved to be rid of them and looking forward to the girl's arrival. Ten minutes later, he noticed her standing out there, in her cutoffs and halter top, repositioning the lounge chair out at the edge of the patio, moving it more into the sun. She was wrestling it with one hand, the other sandwiched between the pages of a book, and he wondered why she hadn't popped in first to tell him she was there.

He opened the tin and joined her out there, holding out the ranger cookies before him. "I come bearing wondrous gifts," he announced, "that taste slightly of coconut."

"Hey," she said, looking up, selecting a cookie. "That guy earlier?"

"What guy?"

"The guy that came out of your house. With the little cop mustache?"

She was talking about John Schank. The "cop" description threw him for a second, but that's who she meant. And if she'd seen Schank, he'd probably seen her. "You were here when he left? When did you get here?"

She shrugged. "I saw you had visitors. I didn't want to bug you."

This wasn't good. "Where were you?"

"Right out here." She indicated the space she now occupied, the lounge chair, the end of the patio. "You probably can't see me from the house, the way I had it turned. And I was slouched down and all. But I've been out here a while."

"I didn't realize. Did you talk to him?"

"*He* talked to *me,* more like. Or *at* me. That guy the new minister or something?"

"Hardly."

"I didn't think so really. But he sure acted like he owned the place. What was his deal?"

"What did he say to you?"

"Oh, he was just bossy, telling me how it's church property and stuff. Only members of the congregation should be here. I started to say I used to come when I was little, when my folks both lived here, but he didn't seem to be actually looking for an answer. He just wanted me to clear out of here. Like I was riffraff. Loitering."

He felt a growl of exasperation leak out. "What is wrong with that man? That is *not* how you build fellowship . . ." What ever happened, he thought, to *Suffer the little children to come unto me and forbid them not . . . ?* He could feel real anger brewing and, thinking of the riled-up Christ cleaning house with the moneychangers in the temple, he had to question if he even *should* try to contain it. Perhaps it was all right to feel something like this. Perhaps it was appropriate. "Didn't you tell him you have my permission? That you're welcome?"

Kimberly frowned. "I didn't want to go into all that with the guy. I just acted like I was leaving. I didn't get the connection—if he was your *son* or *family* or anyone who mattered . . . So I just apologized and started gathering up my junk like I was leaving. But he kept hanging around—he was looking up at your roof and the power lines and the rain gutters and he had one of those metal tape measures like a construction guy and he was measuring stuff—parts of the yard or something. He even, like, got down on his knees a second. I think he was measuring the length of the grass!"

"You're kidding."

"I could be wrong. I wasn't totally staring. I was trying to make it look like I was packing up and leaving, you know?"

Okay, now he was angry. In the thirty-two years he'd lived in the parsonage, he'd never felt so invaded. "You could have told him to come talk to me if he has a problem. You could have told him off, for all I care. The man needs a little of that, I suspect."

"Really?" She looked surprised, as if he'd told her she could burn down the church if the mood hit her.

"Certainly. He doesn't own this church and a few clear, direct reminders wouldn't hurt."

"Darn," she said. "Now I wish I'd said something. I just assumed I was supposed to be polite to him. Else I would've come up with something good."

"Like what?"

"Something that would freak him out real good. I should have said I was your secret concubine—and I'm recuperating after having your baby so I need to sit out here and relax so please go away, else I'll scream for my *luuuuvv-ahhh,* the minister?"

"Well," he said. "That *would* be something. My goodness."

She laughed at her own audacity. "The guy bugged me!"

Gene took a ranger cookie for himself. They were terrible for his various conditions, he knew, but they were so good, he couldn't resist. "I think it's probably best that you held your tongue." He said this and yet he knew that a small part of him wished she *had* said all that and wished that he could have watched John Schank's reaction through the kitchen window and seen the horror wash over him as the man suddenly saw his former pastor in a whole new light.

LATER THAT EVENING, he got online and decided to investigate the First Pres Web site.

What came up first was a shot of the steeple, with some other doodads floating around the perimeter, labeled things like *LOCATION, HISTORY, CONGREGATIONAL DIRECTORY.* Then there was a spot in the bottom corner that read, *WE'D LIKE YOU TO VOTE!* and there was some funny clip art, a retro-looking man with oversized gloved hands and a perfectly circular fedora-topped head, sliding a ballot into a ballot box and beaming with pride.

Voting—he was sure this meant they'd already found a replacement for him. It's a short list, he thought. They're asking the congregation for input on which new minister to hire. Just great. If things were actually moving that fast, he might soon be in a position where he'd have to think about leaving his home. Because the new parsonage was still a long way off. They'd have to put the new man and his family right here. He'd be shoved out.

He clicked on this thing that said *VOTE!*

Okay, they weren't asking for input on candidates. Right away, he could see that. Because the picture now was a crude bird's-eye view of the block, with the church itself marked with a cross, the squiggle of the Oh-John up above. On the other side of the church, on the new lot, the site of the future parsonage, there was a little drawing of a hard hat. On the other side, where his house should be, there was a big cartoon question mark.

He read on. It said, *We're taking a poll. At such time as the current parsonage is no longer in use, what should we do with this property? One vote per family, please!*

There were six options listed: *PLAYGROUND, PARKING LOT, PHYSICAL FITNESS COURSE, YOUTH CENTER, VIP GUESTHOUSE* and *OTHER*. Rolling over them with his cursor provided more information: the first three plans would involve razing his home. The next two would most likely adapt the existing building to a new use. The only option, it seemed, that would not be dubbed the Eugene A. Reecher Memorial was the parking lot.

He couldn't believe it.

In the artist's rendering for the playground, there was a little merry-go-round pretty much in the exact spot where he'd slept with his wife for three decades. And right where he now sat at his desk, where he'd written almost every sermon they'd ever heard from him, there would be something you sat on that looked like maybe an elephant or a hippo, with a big industrial spring underneath to give it bounce.

He was tempted to submit something really juicy under *OTHER*, but he thought better of it. Better not to go off half-cocked but mull it over first. After all, they were being very accommodating to him, letting him stay here. This really wasn't his home anymore. Besides, they only wanted one vote per family and he didn't want to waste it on something dumb.

He clicked out of there, fast. The whole thing made him want to do something rash and such an instinct, he knew, was never sound. So, instead, he composed an e-mail to his daughter, Abbey, avoiding all mention of the Eugene A. Reecher Memorial Teen Hoodlum Hangout and Obstacle Course and all the rest of it, and then decided what he'd composed was boring and erased it, opting not to send it at all.

But he was fuming. Not wanting to stew any further, yearning for a distraction, he broke down, ignored the personal vow he'd made to stop looking at filth, and called up the first site he remembered, Ultra-teen.com.

It was shameful, he knew, but so would be showing up at his children's homes, homeless because he'd done something reckless and upset the board of trustees and gotten himself kicked to the curb—maybe e-mailed an alternative suggestion that they open a Starbucks in the parsonage. True, this was a lousy reason to look at porn, but for now, it was the best he could do.

46

NOAH YODER HAD A KNACK, he knew, for recognizing marketability. Not just things, products, ideas—but even just the names for things. He could tell you pretty much if any movie was going to be a stinker or do big box office, just by hearing the name of it—and with absolutely no knowledge of the movie itself (say, for example, he'd been out of the country, in Europe for a month). All his friends—the ones who *truly* knew him—thought maybe he should have gone into marketing and brand strategy and become some sort of packaging genius. But here he was twenty-four already—what was he going to do? Start a whole new career at that age? Please.

But it was true that the Yoman!® thing had merely been a small part of a bigger picture, the wide and varied empire he'd intended to build for himself. Besides, this might just be the thing to bring everything back on track for him financially; the thing that would save this monstrosity of a summerhouse and all his subsidiaries and his position in the yearly rankings of *Fortune* and *Forbes* and *Wired* and *Spin.* Because even during a nose-diving economy, people still got thirsty, didn't they?

Every time he heard the phrase now—*sumac lemonade*—it chimed like a mantra. Whimsical, soothing. There was something there if he just pursued it. He knew it. It was a much better plan than drumming up interest in his house with false Letterman rumors. That had been desperate hooey, he saw now. He'd been operating from a position of defeat. This, on the other hand, was productive! Fresh! Something! This was a full-blown, balls-to-the-walls *project*!

First, he brought in a marketing research planner from Chicago named Deery Lime on the recommendation of Tony, his money guy, legal counsel and roommate from his only year at college. The vibe he got when she arrived with her team, reading between the lines, was that she and Tony had been intimate at one time. He could see the draw: she had an overly attentive quality, the way she listened— "power-listened," was the way he thought of it—with her wide unblinking eyes. It was probably just an element of her professional training, gauging people's reactions, listening to their comments, but he could see it being a turn-on in a more casual setting. Theoretically, it could all translate into some fairly nonpassive monkeyshines in bed, he imagined. He didn't say anything to Tony, call him on it, but if they were in fact doing it, or had been in the past, he hoped this didn't mean she wasn't also highly qualified.

Then there was her slightly stewardess-y hairdo, the color of applesauce. Not Noah's thing—he liked them darker—but he could see the appeal for others and the way it gave her confidence. God, he hoped she was as good at this as she seemed to think she was.

Deery called him *sir*. (It always felt a little weird when people working for him who were obviously a little older called him *sir*, but he decided not to contradict it. Better to enjoy it. The days of *sir* could easily end real soon.) She said she had some tentative designs for labels and packaging but first wanted to explain her preliminary findings from a few focus groups and market surveys she'd already thrown together back in Chicago. "Bottom line," she said, "we've already determined that actual sumac lemonade—this so-called 'lemonade' as extracted from an actual sumac plant, following the steeping procedures you outlined for us—that's not going to fly. Not without a few tweaks."

Already, he didn't like the sound of this. Tweaks meant throwing more money at it. "Like what?"

"Like the name, for example. People will think 'poison sumac.' Eighty-two percent made some connection with the phrase 'poison sumac.' Besides, sumac, just as a word, doesn't sound very appealing. It's too guttural, with the soft *U* and soft *A*. It sounds like *gut-sac.*"

Noah didn't think it sounded anything like *gut-sac*.

"Well, anyway, we do. We're suggesting 'wild berry lemonade.'"

He pointed out that they weren't berries.

"Close enough," Deery said. "We'd also be interested in 'Indian Berry Lemonade.' We're going to test both, see how they scan in the twenty-two-to-thirty-five target."

"What's an 'Indian berry'? Is there even such a thing?"

"We've decided that's what sumac is. An Indian berry."

"*You've* decided. But there is no such term in common usage, right?"

"Right."

"And you're saying now it won't have sumac in it?"

"No, sir. No actual sumac. Various 'natural flavorings.'"

"Meaning . . . ?"

"Berry juices probably. Apple juice base."

"So your idea is no sumac in the name, no sumac in the bottle?"

"Essentially, yes."

"Could we have a picture of sumac on the label then?"

"Why would we do that, sir?"

"Because that's where we started out. With the sumac idea."

"Have you looked at sumac close up, sir? Not a lot of appetite appeal there."

Her assistant piped in. "It looks sort of hairy and half-dead. Even when it's in full bloom. Respondents said things like 'dust-mop,' 'ragweed' . . . They said 'ewww.'"

"They said 'oooh'?"

The assistant corrected him. "'Ewww,' actually. Seventy-three percent said 'ewww.'"

Deery checked her notes. "Two people said 'Is it a bug or something?' Two entirely different focus groups, exact same response, down to the word."

Noah sat back in his chair, limp, energy draining out of him. This was not how he'd expected this to go. *I mean,* he thought, *Is it a bug or something? . . . ?!* This was not good.

She had the mock labels on black presentation board, and she was whispering with the assistant now, reshuffling the ones he hadn't seen yet. "Let's show him the wild card idea," he heard her say and they showed him something called "Staghorn." The label was a painting of a big buck elk or something. Some massive antlered macho animal, manlier than even the Hartford deer, standing on a rocky outcropping with jagged pines in the far distance. He looked like he was deciding what he was going to mount next. "This would be if we went for the energy drink market. We add ginseng, vitamin E, taurine . . ."

Taurine was the stuff he'd heard was made from bull testicles, though that couldn't be, could it? He didn't want to appear stupid on this point.

The name was not something he liked at all, even after thinking about it, trying to give it a chance, writing it down several times on his notepad. He also wondered now if he should really rely on nomenclatural advice from someone who thought it was okay to be named *Deery Lime,* for Christ's sake.

"No, no." He scratched out where he'd written *Staghorn.* "No. Let's keep this thing on track. You're taking something unique and homogenizing it . . . Let's just . . ." But he wasn't sure what they should do.

"There's unique and quirky," Deery said, very politely, "and then there's moneymaking, there's appealing to the masses. It's a tall order to do both, usually, sir. Unique is, by definition, fairly singular. You don't say, 'Wow, look how quirky that stadium full of people is!'"

She had a point, but still. At the heart of every great success story in this country, wasn't there always an iconoclast? He thought of the Cinderella stories they used to write about Yoman!® If he could do it once, he could do it again.

She was still watching him, waiting patiently. Then she cleared her throat and told him he needed to decide if he wanted them to pack it in or if they should go to the next step, developing the prototype and creating a presentation for media and investors. She said she understood that he probably didn't actually need the capital from other investors, but in terms of PR, since he obviously had so many friends and associates with celebrity, the more star power he could attach to this venture, the better. If he wanted to continue, that is.

Noah didn't feel it was any of her business that if he did decide to do it, the investors' capital would be just as much a help as any possible PR buzz they would bring to the table. But who would he approach? The first name that came to mind was Wesley Snipes—they'd met once at a celebrity volleyball tournament for charity. And when the guy accidentally barked Noah on the shin jumping for the ball, he was very nice and apologetic. But maybe that wasn't enough to ask the guy . . .

Deery Lime said, "Say you've got a friend who can invest who's got the nation's ear, got some sort of nightly forum . . . *then* we'd really have something. You could call it *Crap Lemonade,* you get the right personality behind it."

Nightly forum? Who the hell . . . Was she talking about Letterman? She couldn't be talking about Letterman.

Why was it that everything lately seemed to be rocketing out of his control like a runaway train? Was life always like this and he'd just been lucky and shielded from it for the past few years?

I'm a smart guy, he thought. I'm the kid genius here. I ought to know what to do . . . But he didn't. More and more, he just didn't.

47

AFTER FINISHING with Brenda vonBushberger, who'd just popped in at the parsonage for some advice—she'd just rushed into an engagement with a Japanese man and was worried her father might have some difficulties with the situation—Gene walked out back to join the girl. It wasn't a Thursday, so there wouldn't be any official computer tutorial. She might do some cleaning, but she was mostly there to sun and relax.

She was reading a big hardcover book with a picture of a dove on the cover and, for some reason, Oprah's name, though she probably wasn't reading very closely, because she wore one of those personal hi-fis and had a stack of CDs beside her on the lounge. When she saw him standing over her, she splayed the book in her lap and tugged back the headphones and he could hear a rhythmic buzz like distant engine repair.

"I saw you had someone in there with you," she said. "So I didn't want to interrupt, telling you I was here."

She wore baggy shorts and a little top that seemed several sizes too small—a belly shirt, he thought it was called, though her belly was covered now with the big book.

He told her it wasn't a problem—just a parishioner who needed someone to listen. "They've been with me so long," he said, "it's perfectly natural for them to continue coming to me."

She gave him a grin. "Thought maybe it was a girlfriend."

The idea was horrifying. Brenda had to be in her mid-thirties at the most. He remembered when she was in the Junior Youth Group and he'd have to pull her out of wrestling matches with the boys. She was probably all of twelve at the time.

He frowned sternly. "She's rather young for a potential girlfriend, don't you think?"

"Seems old to me," she said. "She's got gray hair and stuff."

Brenda vonBushberger probably had, at the most, seven gray hairs. He knew he would be hard-pressed to find seven hairs on his own head that *weren't* gray. To change the subject, he picked up a CD case, found it empty, and asked if this was what she was listening to. Some sloppy buffoon posed in pants you could get lost in and there was a warning label on the front of it—something about adult content.

"It's nothing you'd want to hear. Definitely not recorded live at the Blue Note." He was impressed that she remembered the name of the famed club. She hit a button and the buzzing stopped and she reached for the case. "Not that I don't like *your* music. I do. It's just—you wouldn't go for this."

He was still trying to figure out what could be so scandalous about lyrics that were almost unintelligible. "Isn't it strange," he said, "that *Adult Content* almost guarantees only young people will enjoy it? Minors, people who aren't adults?"

He let her take the case. She was squinting at him like she was studying him. "Do you ever feel like you're the only adult—even with the other adults? What I mean is, when I was little, I thought all grown-ups were like, *grown up,* right? They didn't do anything childish or stupid or mean. But that's totally not true, right?"

"I don't follow," he said, though he thought maybe he did.

"You have to be this adult all the time for these other not-so-adult adults to turn to. That must be really lonely for you, being the only grown-up. It sucks, huh?"

He studied her for a moment. She looked bitter, personally involved, not just making an offhand observation. "What I'm hearing, Kimberly, is disappointment. How are these people disappointing you? Talk to me."

She shook her head, as if it was no big deal, then seemed to reconsider. "Okay, you know what it's like? It's like on *Loveline.* You ever listen to that call-in radio show? It comes on at like one in the morning?"

"Too late for me." The truth was, he probably could listen to it most nights, what with the insomnia and the Internet, but staying up that late was always something he regretted doing, not something he planned.

"It's mostly kids calling in. Teenagers. But grown-ups call in, too, and they're all misbehaving in these just idiotic ways? Like *they're* children, too? They're so stupid." She sounded genuinely disgusted. "A ten-year-old would know better than these alleged grown-ups. Seriously."

"Are we perhaps talking about your dad?"

She bit her lip, looked off toward the river. There was a ridiculously tall pleasure craft heading out with a gangly teenaged pilot-boy he didn't recognize up on the bridge and a woman the color of caramel fudge reclined on the aft deck. It bobbled along like a house being moved. "Maybe," she said. "For example."

He thought so. Wasn't her dad the cause of her desire to hang out in the parsonage yard, rather than at home? He was pretty sure she'd let something like that slip in the beginning, when she first asked permission. And then there was that stuff she'd confided about his feud with the neighbors. "You want to talk about it? What's he doing now?"

"Just . . . stuff. Acting like a kid. It's embarrassing."

It wasn't much of an answer. He wondered if Kurt Lasco was possibly one of the people now running around claiming they were seeing lights in the sky. That could certainly be enough to embarrass a sixteen-year-old. Especially if she was already sort of an outsider. He told her he'd like to hear about it.

"No, you wouldn't. Not two people in one hour dumping their lame problems on you. You're retired."

"I'm your friend."

She looked at him and seemed to be thinking about this. "It's no biggie. I'll spare you today. Maybe some other time."

She started to lift her book and that's when he saw it. It took him a second to understand what he was looking at, but she had a pierced navel. She caught him staring and covered it up with her book, saying, "What?"

"I'm sorry! I don't mean to stare. It's just I saw this little metal ball and I guess at first I thought it was one of those little silver decorations on a cupcake? That it had fallen onto your . . . middle there . . . and then I realized, you're not eating a cupcake."

She wrinkled up her nose at him. "You hate it, right?"

He'd seen this, he realized, on the Web sites. Not very often, though, because the stuff he kept looking at was generally more focused a little higher on the body than that, from the neck or chest up. Sometimes, in a long shot, with the girl kneeling, he saw the navel. Occasionally, they appeared, like an unpleasant sore, on the girl's tongue, an image he found horrifying. If they all had pierced tongues, he probably wouldn't have a problem because he'd never look at them again.

"It's totally normal." She seemed to want to convince him. "Really."

He wasn't sure about that. "Does your father know you have a pierced navel?"

This made her squirm a little. "*No.* I don't *know*! Maybe. I haven't gone *ta-dahh*! at him or anything. Okay? But still, it's still totally normal." He smiled because he didn't know what else to say. Even counseling both the Young Adult Group and the Junior Youth Group for all those years, he'd never run into this subject. He told her he was going to go make her some iced coffee and turned in retreat.

She called after him, defensive. "Hey! It's just like when you were young, probably, and the goldfish swallowing! It's the same thing. Just rebellion. Only everyone rebels exactly the same way, so it's normal. You know? No biggie!"

He didn't see much point in explaining that that whole goldfish thing had been roughly about the same time *his* dad was a brash young man. That wasn't what she was after here—a historic timeline of American teen crazes. "Relax!" he called back. "I'm not telling your dad!" He said it over his shoulder, too uncomfortable to look back.

48

IT WAS BAD ENOUGH, being stuck on the river, in the smelly pilot-houses or crowded onto people's boats like some unwanted guest, like one of those hippo birds that tag along for the bugs, and being stuck hanging around with that Keith, who was like the greasy older brother

Mark was glad he never had, or old dull-ass Walt, who wasn't as rude, maybe, but wasn't exactly Mr. Entertainment either—that was bad enough, that he was stuck doing all that rather than being able to run off and see Courtney all day. It was bad enough waiting around, watching the fat lazy flies spin on the pilothouse windowsill, and bang themselves against the glass, perplexed by the heat. But what really topped it off, heaping-pile-of-shit-wise, was the fact that these two lame-os weren't even really letting him in, opening up, welcoming him to the team and all. Sure, they explained what to do, pretty much, but they never bothered really explaining who people were or who they were talking about when they were just hanging around in between boats. It was super-dumb, too, because Day One, they go, *Hey, the trick is knowing people. You can't be a stranger to these people—you help them guide maybe their most precious possession down the river, you need to get to know them,* then they turn around and talk in front of him, all the time, about every last person in this stupid little town and do they explain who and what and where? No, they do not.

Mark was thinking about just this—how they conducted entire private conversations right in front of him that he couldn't follow one little bit—when they went ahead and did it again. It was a slow day—it had been raining all morning, so folks were staying off their boats. It was clear skies now, but that's how it worked. Usually kids would demand some alternate activity when it rained, so they'd either go to the one movie in town or take a long family trip somewhere for the day, drive up to Traverse or some other tourist hole. So it was both of them, Keith and Walt, in the main pilothouse and the two of them had even started drinking a little, pulling faded-looking cans of beer from a cooler Keith used as a footstool.

"Check it out," Keith said to Walt. "Tommy Dillard's at the Wobbly Moose, right? Last call, he goes home with—get this: Nancy Knecht. You know who I mean? The tree girl, the ranger?"

Walt said nothing.

"You *know*," Keith said. "Dark hair? Must be early twenties now? Used to be sort of plain and librarianish, but then she got real good-looking?"

"Sure. Nan. Pat and Sandy's kid."

Mark was stumped way back at *Tommy Dillard*. He had no face to connect to any of these names. The Wobbly Moose, he knew; could picture the carved sign, the cartoon moose; walleyed, knock-kneed. That was the bar where he'd started to do it with Courtney that one night, in the alley.

Walt added, "You pronounce the *K*, though. It's not silent."

Keith wiped at his leg where he'd spilled his beer opening it. "Whatever. Anyhow, Dillard claims he gets her home and he's thinking she's just hanging out, grabbing one more after hours, just there to shoot the shit . . . Thinks she'll be leaving soon—get in her truck and go back to the woods or wherever. 'Cause I guess she never has anything to do with anybody. Only *then* she tells him—check it out—they're not fooling around, kissing, nothing—not even flirting, Dillard says—but she goes, 'I'll stay the night and we can fool around, if you want.' Just like that. Only she's got two conditions: one, she gets to spend the whole night there, he's not going to get weird after, hustle her out, and B, they have to leave the lights on. Not just during. *After.* While they're *sleeping.* The *whole* time. Till it's daylight."

Walt seemed annoyed. "Yeah? *And?*"

"*And?* Jeezo! And so, well, Dillard tells me, 'Hey, how much could that run up my electric bill? Six, eight hours wasted electricity—cheap tail at half the price.'"

Walt grunted.

"What?" Keith said.

"Tommy's a turd. And you're a turd for passing that along."

"Hey! I'm just repeating what *he* told me." Keith threw up his hands, as if for protection. He was younger than Walt, but slight and wiry, and Mark imagined, if they ever fought, old Walt might be able to take him—though he had no idea why the two would fight, not understanding a goddamn lick of this. "This is Dillard's say-so. I'm not claiming it's true. How am *I* a turd?"

Walt considered, then made a so-so wobble gesture with his hand. "Okay, you're turd*ish* then. Maybe not as bad as Tommy, but still. You ought to keep your hole shut. I went to school with her dad. The guy got killed. In that bad fire? And Nan is a nice girl."

This was pretty much like watching Telemundo, Mark decided. You see something's going on, but it could be anything, who knows.

It was quiet in the pilothouse for a long uncomfortable moment as the two men drank their beer. Mark could hear rigging clang on boats over in the marina and gulls cry and the rumble of Walt's belly. Walt got up with a groan and moved over to the doorway and stood in it, looking down at the river.

Keith looked kind of sheepish, picking at something on his boot, then shaking and nodding his head more or less at the same time. "Yeah, you're right," he said. "I'm sorry. I just thought it was really strange, you know? Her acting like that."

Mark heard the word *strange* and had a thought. It was weird, but lately, he was starting to wonder about what the people they helped were like, what went on in their lives, what they did down in the sleeping quarters when the pilot-boys stepped off—what sentimental knickknacks they kept on board that they would grieve over if their boat ever sank and what they worried about and discussed down there at night or up at the helm, one on one, out in the crashing privacy of Lake Michigan. And it had just occurred to him: what if that woman they were talking about, the good girl gone bad or whatever, was the same ranger lady who spent the night with Courtney's dad on the boat? She did ask to stay all night and leave the light on. And what if—here's where it got real *Twilight Zone*—what if she'd seen those "strange lights in the sky" some freaks were supposedly seeing lately? She was a ranger, right? She lived out in the woods, where it was dark. Well, *maybe* she'd had some sort of alien encounter out there, the kind where there's memory lapses and big-eyed creatures looming over your bed? Or at least *thought* she *might* have, but wasn't sure, couldn't remember? Or just worried she *would*—and so she was desperate not to be alone at night—only she couldn't explain it to anyone, what she was afraid of, on account of it would seem nuts. Yeah—if that was the deal, even the girl next door would go home with a different guy every night, just anyone, and fuck him even, but make him keep the light on, just to feel safe and not feel alone. Wouldn't she? Anyone would. God, *he* would anyway, if it was him.

It wasn't a bad theory, and the idea that it could be true made him feel a little sorry for this woman, this person he'd never laid eyes on except, possibly, through the slats of a closet door.

It made sense. Sort of. But he wasn't sure it would out loud. Besides, he didn't even know Walt and Keith well enough to open his mouth. They'd either laugh at him or yell at him and he didn't care enough to give them an excuse to do either. Still, it was a weird thing, imagining about someone else like that; trying to puzzle out what a stranger was feeling and thinking. He wasn't sure he'd ever had a thought quite like that before.

In the doorway, Walt was still looking out at the river, the town, maybe the clouds moving inland to the east, and his simple shrug, the first thing to finally stir in the otherwise motionless pilothouse, was like the gavel at the end of one of his dad's cases. "People have a lot of junk going on, you know? Inside." Without looking at him, Walt was addressing Keith. "You never know what that's all about. You can't judge."

"Anyway," Keith said. "Sorry about being . . . turdish."

Walt swiveled around slow, like an old gray bear, and studied Keith with a long sort of curious look. "I knew a girl once was turdish." He tipped back the last of his beer. "Made a hell of a taffy."

Keith started to smirk. "They run a nice bathhouse, too, those people."

Walt chuckled, turning to step back out on the deck, and dropped his empty in the trash, right beside Mark. He looked him in the eye and said, "Listen, don't spread any of this garbage around, okay, kid?"

"I don't even know who you're talking about. Any of that."

"Good!" Keith jabbed a bony finger in his direction. "You don't *need* to know."

Like I care, he wanted to say. Like I really care . . .

49

NORMALLY, ROGER DRINKWATER didn't spend nearly as much time in the local bars as he had been lately. For one thing, he always felt a little too much like an outsider, like a mascot, the one token native they chose to humor or something—the "good Indian" in a bad Western. Plus, he hated contributing to the stereotype, no matter how much recent genetic studies bore out a legitimate basis for an alcoholic gene among his people. (Though probably there was more of that on the Polish side.) Inevitably, if he stayed late enough, some jackass would get shitfaced and start making drunk Indian cracks about his name, like that was the first time he'd heard such comic genius and hadn't spent six months in boot camp with a purple-faced DI who called him *Betterdrinkwaterinstead'causeyousafuckingredskin, boy!* building it into a spittle-flying scream each time. And besides, he really didn't drink all that much.

But ever since he blew up the Petersons' dock and the interim sheriff got up in his face and said he had his eye on him, he'd been trying to figure out how to do it again. And get away with it again, of course. The jerk did, in fact, seem to have his eye on him, so now it was going to be a little challenging.

The sheriff's normal daily patrols were now apparently doubled. It seemed as though every time Roger looked out the window, Hatchert was making his rounds again, slowly circling the lake. And he'd pull into Roger's little driveway, too, just to make his presence known. During his morning swim, Roger would often stick his head up and see the sheriff's car idling beside his house, the man squinting out at him. And after dark he'd pull in and swivel his spotlight around, out on his dock and even into his windows, regardless of the hour.

So, knowing the trick to pulling it off again was building a good alibi, Roger began frequenting the Potlicker and the Wobbly Moose and Carrigan's, saying hello to people to whom he'd normally, at the most, grunt and wave. He didn't have a plan yet, but he had the vague idea that the more he made his presence known, the more people might be confused, at some later date, and think he was there when he wasn't. They might at least say, "Coach Drinkwater? Yeah . . . I *think* he was here . . . I mean, he's always around . . ." Granted, it wasn't much of a plan, but until he thought of something specific, it seemed like a good policy. Besides, what better way—other than plying Janey Struska for information—to hear the latest gossip and theories about what was going on out on Meenigeesis with the jet-skis and what would be done about it? For the most part, he didn't even have to start up a conversation. Most people seemed to buy into the cigar store Indian bit. He could just sit there stone-faced on a barstool and listen. It was amazing the things people discussed openly, all around him, as if he were invisible.

He was doing exactly this one night at the Potlicker, nursing a Vernors, chuckling politely to the bartender's report that there were unsubstantiated rumors going around that folks had seen "unexplained lights in the sky" in the area. When pressed, Dale McConkey, the bartender, couldn't say where this had been, exactly, nor identify one single eyewitness, other than "some koo-koo puffs, obviously." One of the waitresses piped in with her guess that they were "summer kids on Ecstasy." Roger concurred with both theories, glad to hear there was something, no matter how bullshit, to overshadow any possible gossip about his secret jet-ski war. He nodded and smiled. It seemed like more than enough social interaction for one night, so he finished his Vernors and got up to leave.

It was a nice night and he'd walked there, so he left the back way, out onto the deck, packed with chattering Fudgies jockeying round the wire spool tables with their pitchers of beer, and down the steps to the riverwalk. Not the straightest route back home, but the Ojaanimiziibii lapped a deep mercurial blue-gray and the stars hung oversized tonight like something fanciful dreamed up by a Hollywood set designer in the thirties. At the first landing, with its bench and more stairs leading back up the hill, he paused and looked back out to the west, at the glowing lighthouse at the end of the channel. He thought about his Fourth of July marathon maneuver down under that water. Different kind of night, he thought. He heard motion on the stairs but knew who it was.

"Peaceful, huh?"

The crunch of her belt gear, something about her hardy gait, gave Struska away before he turned. "Right now it is," he said. "Here. Back home on the lake, some brat's probably breaking the curfew. Wouldn't surprise me at all."

They both seemed to think of the bench simultaneously, taking a seat with deep sighs. There was no more mention of jet-skis for a time. They sat admiring the night sky and pointing out the miraculously obvious.

"If things are that bad out there," she said after a while, "maybe you ought to think about moving."

"Where would I move to? Please."

"I'm thinking maybe inland, some place off the water."

Roger snorted. "*I'm* not. Thinking that. Jesus . . ." Though the truth was, in dark moments, he *was* thinking about just that. One idea had him maybe approaching that nutjob G. Johnny Scudder about some sort of swap. The old man, a descendant of the original nutjob, had recently acquired a lot of wooded land. (It was rumored he was planning a religious cult–based recreational community along what he considered would be the new coastline of Michigan once the floodwaters of "the Endtimes" arrived.) It was all cheap land deeper in, out toward the National Forest more. Moving might become an option down the line, but for now, he couldn't imagine that kind of a change. It would be brutal, like yanking up a morel mushroom and trying to grow it in your kitchen herb garden. He was an Ojaanimiziibii, a water-based people. And he was a Pole, a stubborn, combative people. The combination made it almost genetically impossible that he would budge. But he didn't explain this to Janey. He just told her, "Forget it. Not gonna happen."

She peered sideways at him, camouflaged by leaf shadows. "You're dug in, then? Battle stations? Reinforcing the trenches?"

Roger tipped his head in acquiescence; gave her a chuckle-y little snort. But he did not nod.

She glanced away, back out toward the lighthouse. "By the way, those are not terms you want to use in front of my new boss, okay? That military posturing. He'd see it as evidence."

"He still think I'm behind all that? Up to some sort of secret war with the jet-skis?"

"Yeah, he feels pretty sure about it. But that's where we differ."

"*You* don't think it's me."

She turned back to face him, smiling. "No, I *know* it's you—which is where Hatchert and I differ."

"What would I have to do to convince you you were wrong?"

"Well, alibis always work for me. They're not a hundred percent, but you have someone vouching for your whereabouts at a certain time, personally, I tend to look elsewhere for the perpetrator."

"Yeah? Like what kind of alibi are we talking about?"

"Well, I suppose . . . if you and *I* were . . . hanging out in a public place for a good portion of time one night . . . and meanwhile something happened on Meenigeesis at the same time, I'd probably be convinced."

"You talking about a date, Struska?"

She shrugged. "Sure. Why not? But you'd have to make it pretty convincing . . ."

It was a pretty odd thing to suggest, really—going on a date. Not something he did over much. He liked women plenty; he'd just never gotten close to many. He'd even lived with a few over the years—brief circlings and skirmishes that usually ended with a lot of steam and ruckus-raising, mostly on their part, while he sat out on the cane rocker or repaired a canoe and waited for it to pass like a thunderhead rolling inland; he waited for them to leave. He couldn't recall ever telling any of them "I love you," though he might have muttered *"Gi zah gin"* at a few, which was essentially the same thing, minus the part where they knew what he was saying.

Still, this idea of a date with Struska, even as an alibi—thinking about it after he said good night and he continued his walk back to the lake—grew more and more intriguing all way home. And then, as he stepped up onto his porch and the familiar floorboards creaked, he turned back to get a look at the stars painted on the still surface of Meenigeesis and it came to him that she had pointed out Jupiter back on the riverwalk and he'd sat right there beside her and gazed up at it, tipped his chin up, defenselessly, vulnerably exposing his jugular, his carotid artery, and hell if he could picture putting his hand up for protection, covering his throat. He'd just sat there with his hands jammed in his jeans pockets, not acting "crusted" at all, as that loon Crystal would have said.

I'll be damned, he thought. He wondered what it meant, if anything. Maybe it meant nothing. Maybe he was getting sloppy, no longer SEAL material. Or maybe it was her.

Maybe.

———

NEXT MORNING, RIGHT AFTER HIS SWIM, he made a call to Glenn Landry up at Camp Grayling: "Roger Drinkwater. Listen, you guys're still interested in getting me to teach the demo units, right?"

"Definitely." Landry sounded shocked, suddenly awake.

Roger told him he thought he saw a way that he'd be willing to do it.

50

IT WASN'T EASY for Mark to get the day off, but he wanted to take Courtney up to Sleeping Bear Dunes. He had to do some real finagling with Keith and juggling schedules with the two other under-boys, local jerks with attitude who were less than cooperative. But eventually he worked it out and so finally they were going to have a real date. They were going to be seen together in public. In the daylight, with talking and getting to know each other. Doing polite date-y things, not just screwing around. Sure, there was a lot of wild, rolling ground up there, off the trails, lots of nooks and crannies where you could hide and hump, but he wasn't really thinking they'd be fooling around today. Well, maybe in the car, on the way back, they could pull over in the National Forest somewhere. But mostly, he just wanted to have a *date* date. And because she was so geared up about "adventure" all the time, he thought the whole dune thing, the biking, would at least keep her from dozing off.

When Courtney finally showed, she was wearing her Tevas. "It's rugged terrain up there," he explained. "You're gonna need better shoes. Running shoes, at least. Hiking boots if you got them."

She shrugged, looking off toward the boats in the marina. "Whatever. Look, I just came to tell you I can't go."

"What?" They'd been planning this for over a week.

"I'm not going. I can't today."

"I can't believe you're doing this," he said, though truthfully, he sort of could. He kept staring at her, those wintry blue eyes squinting off toward the marina, the sweep of her hand, a habit of hers, through her ponytail, as if she were annoyed with her own hair. And she wouldn't look at him. "So, what—you're just standing me up?"

Her nose wrinkled like he'd cut one. "I never get that. What's that even supposed to mean—'standing you up'? I'm here telling you. How is that standing you up?"

"You show up half an hour after you say you're showing up, just to tell me you're not going. I say that's standing me up, yeah."

"Well," she said, looking at her watch, "I don't."

For a moment, he listened to the clang of rigging and turned to watch it, the spiring masts and the arcing gulls. Without looking back at her, he asked her what she had to do today that was so important.

"I don't owe you an explanation," she said. "It's a free country."

She suddenly sounded like such an idiot. "What is that—like 'You're not the boss of me'? What are you—twelve?"

She gave him the finger, then turned and began to walk away. Then she stopped and said, "My stepbrother's flying in from Chicago, okay? He got invited to something out at Noah's Ark? Noah Yoder, the, like, *zillionaire*? He wasn't going to come, but now, 'cause the weather's clear, he is. It's the weather. I have no control over—"

"No. Of course you don't." It came out cold and hard and he didn't care. He was pissed and she should know it.

She stepped closer again. "So now the weather's my fault?" She was looking at him now, directly at him, and he couldn't take it. Shoving his hands into his pockets, he stared down at his boots. Hell, he'd spent a couple hours last night just hunting down his hiking boots and now he was stuck in Weneshkeen for the day with nothing to do and hot feet. "You understand?" She reached out and touched his bare arm.

"Whatever," he said, though he didn't want to. He wanted to stand tall, give her the thousand-yard stare. "He's a pilot, your stepbrother?"

"Not like you," she said. "Not that kind of pilot."

He wasn't sure if this was a jab at him. He wasn't sure if it made any difference. He watched the ponytail whip around as she turned; watched it bob like a fishing jig as she marched off down the riverwalk.

———

"YOU AND ME, Ass Boy. We're up."

The name barely registered anymore. Keith had been calling him Ass Boy nonstop since Courtney's first note and either he was starting to say it in a more friendly way or it was just growing on him.

Keith was still futzing with the clipboard, reading the vessel name, as Mark stepped out of the pilothouse and saw Courtney's honey-colored ponytail swinging and the back of a curly-haired man in whites and shades. "Ski boat with a Chicago registry," Keith said. *The Chickenhawk.*"

He hadn't seen her for two days—not since she'd walked off in a huff on the riverwalk. They'd probably already spotted him, but Mark retreated into the shadows anyway, pulling Keith back with him, and the two of them peered out around the doorjamb like they were on a stakeout or kids playing capture the flag up in their treehouse.

The boat looked like something James Bond would use to leapfrog the ramming enemy—it was liberally dosed with red-and-black pin-stripes at rakish angles and plenty of flat surfaces upon which to bang all the exotic, slicked-hair, SCUBA-wearing goddesses that attached themselves to such a boat like those bug-eating birds on hippos whose name he still couldn't recall. They were down there, the deck bobbing low below the pilothouse, and Courtney was giggling and swatting at the guy, who was acting, halfheartedly, like he might just throw her in the Oh-John. Mark decided it was just the stepbrother. At least he hoped it was, or else it meant Courtney now had a much older boy-friend.

"I remember this clown," Keith said. "Guy's always taking teenaged girls out skiing. I think he's the guy knocked up one of the Brablec girls, the younger one."

Mark had no idea who that was, but didn't doubt it. "Listen, how old is he, you think? She says he's her stepbrother."

Keith squinted out the dusty Plexiglas pane that was held in with bent finishing nails. "He's about my age, I guess. Late twenties maybe."

"Jesus."

"What's the problem, buddy?"

Keith had never called him *buddy* or anything remotely close and at first Mark didn't register that he was being addressed. "I don't want to just stand there, being all redundant and useless." It felt as if all the air had escaped his lungs. "I'll feel foolish. Just you go ahead without me, okay? Please?"

Keith shook his head. "She already saw you. Isn't she going to wonder why you're hiding in here?" Still, he seemed to be considering. "If we knew him, we could just let him pass. Both of us stay here."

"Yeah! Do that."

"We can't, really." Keith didn't elaborate but Mark knew it was because the guy wasn't a local and so didn't get the consideration; the wink and the wave. Keith reorganized his crotch a second, apparently mulling the situation over, then said, "Relax," and stepped out on the pilothouse deck, squinting up and down the river as if checking to see if they were being watched. "Hey, folks? Listen, we're not supposed to play favorites or anything, but on account of you've got this . . . inside track with one of our best and all . . ." He yanked Mark out into the light and thumped him on the back. "We're going to let Mark here give you the special treatment."

Other than the first four days on the job, when he'd shoved him into the water repeatedly, and a couple finger flicks and pokes here and there, this was the first Keith had ever touched him. And it seemed like he was actually trying to help, not put him on the spot, but Jesus, soloing was out of the question. Mark started to object. "Keith—"

Keith clamped one hand on his shoulder and spun him around, facing away from the boat and speaking low. "Deep breaths, kid. Focus here. Here's the deal. Guy's a show-off. He's absolutely *not* going to hand the helm over to you. That's not a worry. So it'll just be navigation. Just call out the map. You know it fine." And he patted Mark's shoulder, saluted with a grin and went back into the pilothouse.

Mark had no choice but to board the boat alone. He said hi to Courtney and she gave him a little stone-faced wave, a mere waggling of the fingers—didn't move to kiss him or grab his ass, her standard greeting. He tried to tell himself it was because he was on the job and she was trying to show some respect and restraint. She was standing right beside her stepbrother at the helm, sort of leaning on his forearm as he gripped the wheel. Keith was probably right: he wasn't going to have to do anything but call the map. Mark stood on the other side of the stepbrother and tried to focus. With his curly hair and Naugahyde tan, the guy, Mark decided, looked like a certain game show host from the seventies whose name escaped him. Up close, he could see now that her stepbrother really was quite a bit older than him. And older than Courtney. He seemed more like an uncle and the thought reminded him of Courtney's uncle, the famous artist he'd never heard of who made comments about her chest and wanted her to pose nude for him. What a family she had.

The guy grinned at him and doffed his stupid Thurston Howell captain's cap. "Whenever you're ready, Mark Twain."

Mark signaled for him to start it up and they began to pull away from the mooring, creeping along. After a few slow yards, the stepbrother announced, "I hate this fucking river."

Courtney swatted the guy's hairy forearm. "Well, I like it! You get a pretty view of the town."

"It's no fun when we can't open it up. I notice your nipples get hard when we really open it up."

"Stop it!"

"Seriously, now *that's* a pretty view."

"Shut up!" It was like squealing now.

Mark felt like he was interrupting, but he had to call the map. "Your first obstruction," he said quietly, repeating the words that made him feel, suddenly, like nothing more than a glorified tour guide, one of those poor slobs—the docents?—at the art museum in Detroit that got the spiel canned in their head, "is coming up about fifty feet to your starboard side. A minor obstruction. Depth: about five meters." His own voice sounded funny to him, and he was afraid they'd pick up on it. He wished he didn't have to speak to them at all.

The stepbrother suddenly eased off the throttle and turned to Mark, all teeth. "You know what? Long as you're aboard, why don't you just take the wheel?" He was backing away now, hands in the air like a stickup victim.

"I'm sorry," Mark said. "It's a township thing, you know? If it was up to me—"

"No, no! Seriously. I'm serious. You know the waters much better, I'm sure. That's why you have the job." He removed the Thurston

Howell cap and jammed the damn thing down on Mark's head. "Perfect," the guy said, gave him a quick salute, and joined Courtney in back, sliding his arm around her.

It was just what he'd feared; just what Keith had assured him would never happen. But Courtney was looking at him funny, her lip starting to curl, and what else could he do? He took the wheel. It was stressful enough, the sheer "here-take-control-of-the-space-shuttle" aspect of it, this great rumbling beast itching to lurch ahead of him, never mind the giggly distraction going on right behind him. *Take it easy,* he told himself. *Focus.* He hated that he had to throttle back so much. Not only did it make him look like a wuss, but he could hear almost every stupid thing they said. The guy was loud, the kind of dick that comes into town and really lets you know he's there. A loud-talking guy with a big braying laugh. A jackass laugh. Maybe it came naturally to the guy, but it sure felt like he was putting it on, belting it out loud and clear to needle him. It would be so much better if he could open it up and drown him out with the roar of the giant twin inboard.

They were talking about her duties as Miss Sumac Days and all the events she had to get ready for. "You know what I hear about sumac?" the guy was saying to her. "My understanding is you've got to pick it when it's very fresh. Young sumac, that's the good stuff." He said it like it was the dirtiest thing in the world. "Delicious. Very juicy and tender and ripe. What I like is sumac pie. Taaaaaayyy-sstee!"

She was actually giggling at this, acting like the guy wasn't the major creep he obviously was, saying, "Oh, Brad, cut it out! You stop! There isn't any such thing and you know it."

"Sumac pie? Oh yes there is. Yum, yum." It had to be for Mark's benefit because the guy kept sneaking little peeks over at him. In checking bearings fore and aft, Mark caught him looking at him. He was sure of it. Eye flickers and sidelong glances, but the guy was watching him.

He wanted off the boat; he wanted to throw the stepbrother off the boat. He wanted to ram the boat into a snag, scrape the anally polished railing against the drawbridge pylons; he wanted to demonstrate flawless navigation skills and arrive at the end unscathed. He wanted to cause a scene; he wanted to get through this little trip unnoticed and forgotten. All that, all at once.

Courtney kept slapping her stepbrother on the chest, kept saying, "Oh, stop. Quit your teasing!" like she was some sort of Southern belle, *I-declaring* in a voice that echoed back off the high retaining walls. But she was also saying things Mark couldn't make out so well, whispering and biting her lip cautiously and looking around the boat as if checking to see if anyone was listening.

This, Mark decided, was the worst summer job of all time.

51

A TRANSCRIPT FROM THE RADIO SHOW *Loveline:*

DR. DREW: . . . Mark in Michigan, sixteen . . . "Girlfriend wants sex all the time" . . .

ADAM: Mark?

MARK IN MICHIGAN: Hi.

ADAM: You're sixteen.

MARK IN MICHIGAN: Yeah.

ADAM: Girlfriend's got a one-track mind, huh? And this upsets you?

MARK IN MICHIGAN: Uh-huh.

(*Pause.*)

ADAM: You gay?

MARK IN MICHIGAN: No.

ADAM: Hmm . . . Well, *I'm* tapped out. Drew, you got anything?

DR. DREW: I'm wondering if this is one of those "I'm sixteen and I'm having sex" calls.

ADAM: You mean a "someone is letting me climb on top of them" call. He's just calling to brag?

DR. DREW: Maybe.

ADAM: You're getting that vibe because why—he doesn't really have a question?

DR. DREW: That's part of it . . .

ADAM: What about that voice, though—he does *not* sound like he's having a very good time. Either that or he's stoned.

DR. DREW: Nah.

ADAM: Mark, are you stoned?

MARK IN MICHIGAN: No! I'm just—

ADAM: 'Cause you sound out of it, buddy.

MARK IN MICHIGAN: I'm upset.

DR. DREW: Yeah, he's not stoned. It's not that hesher voice, it's—

ADAM: He's just not having a good time. Okay. Well, why not? What's going on?

MARK IN MICHIGAN: I've been dating this girl since the summer started and we have sex, no problem, but it seems like that's all she cares about.

DR. DREW: Are you sure she's your girlfriend?

(*Long pause*)

ADAM: Ooh. Dr. Drew, everybody, dropping the Tough Love bomb!

MARK IN MICHIGAN: Like I say, she has sex with me—a lot—it's just the other stuff—like hanging out and just talking and going out in public. She never wants to go on a *date* date and the sex is always sort of crazy. So, I guess she's my girlfriend, only we just don't do any of that other stuff.

ADAM: The "other stuff" being the stuff that would mean she was your girlfriend.

DR. DREW: Mark. You two have a service agreement. But she's not your girlfriend.

MARK IN MICHIGAN: Yeah, but we're having sex.

DR. DREW: Right. We get that. You've made that clear.

ADAM: Crystal!

DR. DREW: But that's it, right? It's just sex. You say you don't talk about anything . . .

MARK IN MICHIGAN: Well, we do *some* stuff together. Only it's not normal.

DR. DREW: What kind of stuff?

MARK IN MICHIGAN: She likes to do stuff we shouldn't be doing. (*Whispering.*) Like, okay, one night we broke into this house . . .

ADAM: Whoa.

DR. DREW: To steal? Are you guys doing drugs?

MARK IN MICHIGAN: It wasn't to steal, it was just to . . . go in there and have sex there. For the excitement or whatever. No one even lives there. And no, I don't do drugs. Really. And I've never *seen* her do drugs . . .

ADAM: That's B and E, brother.

DR. DREW: Makes for a nice date.

ADAM: Personally, I usually save my criminal trespassing for anniversaries, birthdays. Yeah, I like to keep it special for my lady.

(*They laugh.*)

MARK IN MICHIGAN: Yeah, but, guys? The thing is, she's only interested in, like, doing it *after* we do something to get in trouble or almost get in trouble. It's like it gets her in the mood. It's not always something like breaking in somewhere, but it's still gotta be like on the beach or on a roof or . . . She went down on me at the movies— stuff like that.

ADAM: Well, gee, I thought you never did anything in public together. That's—

MARK IN MICHIGAN: I just mean like a normal date. We didn't even watch the movie.

DR. DREW: What happens if you try to have sex with her, say, in bed, with the door locked, in a house . . .

ADAM: That you *own.*

DR. DREW: Yes. Some place where it's not "danger sex"—where there's no prospect of getting busted or interrupted or caught. What happens then?

MARK IN MICHIGAN: Nothing happens. We don't do that. She says it's boring.

DR. DREW: She told you that?

MARK IN MICHIGAN: Basically.

ADAM: This chick is *sixteen*?

MARK IN MICHIGAN: I'm sixteen. She's seventeen.

ADAM: Well, hell, she's an older woman, Mark. How can you hope to relate when she's in a *totally* different place in her life like that? Sixteen and seventeen? Come on!

MARK IN MICHIGAN: Yeah, I know, but we're really only a few months apart.

ADAM: Nope. It'll never work! Never! It's that generation gap there, Mark.

MARK IN MICHIGAN: Yeah . . .

DR. DREW: I think Mark's got more of an irony gap.

ADAM: Those older women are crazy, man! Right, Drew?

DR. DREW: It's interesting: this is the sort of behavior we maybe fantasize about in a girlfriend, especially in adolescence, but that's the fantasy here, Mark. This is *not* an age issue, okay? Or really, it *is* sort of an age issue: she *shouldn't* be like this at this age and she has *issues*. At seventeen, if she requires this kind of extreme, *extreme* stimulation, just to not get "bored," there's something going on.

ADAM: Somebody monkeyed with her?

DR. DREW: Maybe. Or there's an addictive gene here. She's definitely got some energy.

ADAM: Well, she's a thrill-seeker, right? It's danger sex. Which is *like* a drug, maybe.

DR. DREW: Oh, very much so.

ADAM: Which is exciting and sexy in theory. In an adult woman . . .

DR. DREW: But a seventeen-year-old girl acting out like that, something's up.

ADAM: Right . . . Mark? Where's daddy?

MARK IN MICHIGAN: My daddy?

ADAM: The girl's daddy.

MARK IN MICHIGAN: Right this second, I'm not sure. He lives in a bunch of different places, I guess. He's here sometimes, but—

ADAM: Say no more. Dad-of-the-Year, it sounds like. Christ.

MARK IN MICHIGAN: No, really. He's okay. He's like a bigshot in Chicago. They're very well off.

ADAM: Oh, okay. As long as they're loaded.

DR. DREW: And by the way, a "bigshot" doesn't mean he's raising her right.

ADAM: Drew, let me ask you something. Have you ever met anyone you would describe as a "bigshot" who you would also turn around and describe as a "really nice guy"?

DR. DREW: Never. *You're* starting to become sort of a bigshot . . .

ADAM: Thank you. I rest my case. You wouldn't call me a "nice guy," would you?

DR. DREW: Oh no! Not at all. Mark? Any chance she's been abused in some way? Obviously, you're describing some possible abandonment, but does he physically punish her, maybe?

ADAM: You think the bigshot knocks her around, Drew?

MARK IN MICHIGAN: It's not like that. All I'm saying when I say "bigshot" is she doesn't live in a trailer or anything. They've got a big boat and—

ADAM: Oh that's good, a boat. So if he ever knocked her around, she'd just fall off the side, into the water. Nice.

DR. DREW: Much better situation.

ADAM: Well, it'd break her fall, see? A trailer, that's a whole different can of worms. You whale your kid through the side of your double-wide, that's at least a sixteenth-inch of corrugated aluminum siding and then a sheet of three-quarter particleboard she's got to go through. Maybe an asbestos firewall, too, if it's an older unit. That could do some damage. Worst of all, now you gotta go to Home Depot.

(*AUDIO DROP: PUNCH SFX.*)

ADAM: Let me ask Mark something. Mark. This chick: she's hot, right?

MARK IN MICHIGAN: *I* think so.

ADAM: I'm not talking "I think so" kind of hot, I'm looking for super-lava-hot. She's gotta be one real piece of ass, right?

MARK IN MICHIGAN: Pretty much.

ADAM: Pretty much. Thanks for backing me up on that, squirrelly. Jesus Christ. Such enthusiasm.

MARK IN MICHIGAN: No, no. I'm sorry. She is. She is very attractive.

ADAM: Like the kind of attractive where all your buddies see her as the local equivalent of Adrienne Barbeau—

MARK IN MICHIGAN: Who?

DR. DREW: Britney Spears.

ADAM: Go ahead and insert your own famous hot chick du jour there. What I'm driving at is everyone says "Oh we can't believe Mark is going out with this chick," right?

DR. DREW: Or more accurately, that *she's* going out with Mark.

ADAM: Exactly. She's so hot, you feel like she's doing you some kind of incredible favor. She gives you a handy, you send her a thank-you note. What I mean is, it feels, to you, like this chick got sentenced to community service and, luck of the draw, just happened to get assigned to your squirrelly ass. Right?

MARK IN MICHIGAN: You could say she's pretty much the hottest girl in town, yes. Like . . . okay, she was Miss Sumac Days? Like, two years in a row.

DR. DREW: What's that?

MARK IN MICHIGAN: The winner of the pageant? For Sumac Days?

ADAM: Aha! I knew it! Hold on a second, Mark.

(*The caller is put on hold.*)

ADAM: Drew.

DR. DREW: Yes, Adam?

ADAM: "Sumac Days": anything?

DR. DREW: Not a clue.

ADAM: Really? You mean you've *never* heard of Sumac Days? Shocking!

(*They laugh.*)

DR. DREW: Isn't that like a poisonous shrub or something?

ADAM: Drew. Do you get the idea that our callers are under the impression we ride around in a backpack slung over their shoulders all day long?

DR. DREW: All *life* long, more like.

ADAM: We're just back there the whole time, looking around, taking in the sights, peeking over the top of the backpack, jotting down notes . . .

DR. DREW: Like a papoose.

(*More laughter.*)

ADAM: Je-sus Christ. What goes *on!?* . . . (*Weary sigh.*) . . . Mark?

MARK IN MICHIGAN: Yeah?

ADAM: You listening to me, screwball?

MARK IN MICHIGAN: Uh-huh.

ADAM: Good. Now, look. You've got two choices with this crazy chaotic bitch: A, confront her . . . And by the way, the type of relationship you two have, confronting her would basically be like walking up to a stranger at a bar, some three-hundred-pound mongoloid, and saying, "Excuse me, sir, but can we discuss your drinking problem?"

DR. DREW: There might be some of that in her family background, actually.

ADAM: Mongoloidism?

DR. DREW: Alcoholism.

ADAM: Oh, right, right . . . Then there's B, which is run away screaming. No big explanation, just get out. Just say, "NO more! Do you hear me, woman?! No more will you be giving me BJs in the Bijou, bitch! Enough!" And then DO NOT see her anymore.

MARK IN MICHIGAN: This is a small town.

ADAM: You like that, Drew—BJs in the Bijou?

DR. DREW: Very nice alliteration. What's that, Mark?

MARK IN MICHIGAN: It's a small town, where we are. It'd be a little hard to pull off, avoiding her totally. We're both only here for the summer, so in the fall, no problem, but the town's so small—

ADAM: Hold the phone! *Really?* The town that Sumac Days put on the map, you're telling me that's a *small* town? Drew, you jotting this down?

DR. DREW: I'm stunned.

ADAM: Drew, didn't you *assume* it would take a booming *metropolis,* some sort of massive, teeming center of industry, to support a *world-renowned* event on the scope and magnitude of *Sumac Days?*

DR. DREW: Well, you couldn't hold it here in L.A.! Town's not big enough!

ADAM: Jesus Christ . . . Anyway, then there's plan C—and I think honestly, Drew, this is probably the choice for young Mark here, C being ride this ride till the carny pulls the brake handle. The carny with the grotesquely misshapen nose, the botched jailhouse tattoo and outstanding warrants in Florida and Georgia. By this I mean just go with the flow. Enjoy. Ignore the fact that she's probably screwed in the head and just enjoy until it ends. Abbondanza! But don't *extend* it, don't *compromise* yourself, don't beg for her to change or get in *any way* further wrapped up in her little web of manipulation and hot, hot danger sex!!! Now, Drew, I know you don't like this kind of advice, but in Mark's case, come on—he's not going to change this girl. He's sixteen, the summer's almost over . . .

DR. DREW: No, no. I agree. For Mark, right now, that's fine. Just don't get hurt, Mark.

ADAM: Keep your hand firmly on that car door button! I mean that metaphorically. They don't make those knobby type of car door buttons anymore.

DR. DREW: The door locks, you're talking about?

ADAM: Yeah. On the top.

DR. DREW: Not the handle, on the side.

ADAM: No, on *top* of the door. Drew, have you *been* in a car? Jesus. I know you don't even know how to change your oil, but you've been in one, right? Door locks! They're all recessed now. Flush with the door panel. So if you ever go over a bridge, you basically just drown scratching at the door.

(*AUDIO DROP:* "*Whooooooooooo . . . cares!*")

DR. DREW: Okay. Mark, those are your options. Got it?

ADAM: Right. Probably C is your best bet.

MARK IN MICHIGAN: Yeah, but . . . I really care about her.

ADAM: *Really?*

MARK IN MICHIGAN: Yeah . . . It's like . . . painful.

DR. DREW: Oh, Mark . . .

(*A pause.*)

ADAM: Hold on a sec . . .

DR. DREW: Oh, boy.

ADAM: I put Mark on hold.

DR. DREW: He's *in* this. You can tell.

ADAM: Yeah. He shouldn't be, but he is. Jesus . . . What're the chances, you think, he's going to be able to follow the game plan and just take it easy?

DR. DREW: "Ride the ride till the carny pulls the brake handle"?

ADAM: Yeah. Plan C.

DR. DREW: Honestly? Probably close to zero.

(*Caller is punched back in.*)

ADAM: Hey, Mark?

MARK IN MICHIGAN: I'm still here.

ADAM: Listen, buddy . . . maybe you oughta consider plans A or B . . .

52

FOR THE "FIRST DEBUT" of his sumac lemonade, Noah Yoder had a lot of big investors in for the weekend, at great expense, all of which would be itemized under the heading of business entertainment. Deery had found some lean-faced folkie down in Ann Arbor whom she hired to come up and play a song he'd written about the sumac being "on fire," which must have meant in bloom and was pretty and wistful and haunting and all but Noah couldn't help thinking the guy might have been convinced, thrown a few extra bucks, to add a line or two about how tasty the stuff was, at least. It was discouraging, sometimes, how he felt he had to do all the thinking. Didn't his people understand how much things were on the line now? He was taking a real chance here and they had to make it work.

Deery Lime made the presentation, speaking grandly from a new, more complicated piling of her applesauce hair. Noah said a few words and smiled and nodded his head in a sort of aw-shucks bow, accepting the smattering of noncommittal applause. They sampled the sumac lemonade.

Among them, there was an aging publisher who'd obviously made the trip to show off the four new breasts of his two companions. He begged off trying the drink because of his diabetes and his twin girl-friends sipped theirs with the expression of those used to commands, who spent their days ticking off a series of small chores that were not always particularly pleasant. There was a pizza baron who insisted on mixing his sample with gin and then complained that it was okay, but not "ginny" enough. Some teen beauty queen type Noah didn't recognize camped out on the chair in the shape of a hand with her boyfriend, who seemed to have the same last name. (Deery said they'd probably crashed with her dad's invitation. They didn't mix but whispered and giggled and then they were gone. No one saw them leave and later, no one could locate the hand chair.) Then the millionaire white rapper, the one of the bunch closest to his own age, who Noah really thought might get behind it, spent most of the gathering up on the roof, checking out the antiaircraft gun and doing who-knew-what with his posse. If an IRS agent had walked in, Noah would have been hard-pressed to convince him that this was a legitimate business expense and not just a gala bash for the decadent rich.

A few accepted a prototype case to take home. But he knew, down to the person, there wasn't one in the room who would invest. He knew this because of the way they made small talk. They asked him about living in this "funny little town" and about the house and what the architect Mishuki was really like—was it true he once designed a house made of cheese? They asked about the names of the lakes and the river and what types of fish they caught in these parts and what the weather was like and if he got to swim much and if he felt isolated up here and how the locals acted around him—did he require much security here? And was the dish really enough to survive without cable? And how did he get good bagels and coffee and essentials like that? They laughed about the gossipy things they'd heard on the charter connections up from Detroit or Chicago—local pilots with their puddle-jumpers: people were seeing lights in the sky? How absolutely darling! And there was some sort of civil unrest involving jet-skis?

Very little was said about the sumac lemonade. If the pitch had hooked anyone, they would have drawn him aside and said, "I'm in." That's the way these people operated. Big and from the gut. But as he watched the last of them leave, laughing and weaving toward the helipad, he caught a glimpse of the deputy sheriff out in the drive, on duty as security. She was leaning against her squad car, giving a wide smile and friendly goodbye to each departing group as if she herself were the hostess—and she was, in a way, in terms of the town. She was saying goodbye and being polite on the part of the town. And he remembered now that it was this very person who first told him about sumac lemonade and he was struck by the thought that the answer might be local. Start with local investors and a local customer base and branch out from there. Sure, they wouldn't have nearly the deep pockets as these blowhards, but if he could just round up enough people with medium-deep pockets . . . And who better to appreciate the potential of sumac lemonade than the people who had a whole festival around the plant?

He went back inside and found Deery and Tony sitting very close together on a couch and told them he wanted to try it again. "Whole new group," he said. "No outsiders this time."

53

VON KNEW FULL WELL that his son and new daughter-in-law had been driving out to visit Jack's great-great-aunt, Sadie vonBushberger, pretty regularly, because each time they returned, Marita made a point of informing him that Aunt Sadie had asked about him again, that she wanted to see him. Then, soon after Brenda announced she was engaged, she went to visit and took Miki along to meet her and when they came back, Brenda told him, "She's expecting you Wednesday at three o'clock."

Von noticed that none of the kids seemed to return with any signs of food on them. He wondered what made them so all-fired special. Perhaps Sadie wasn't well.

They had her set up at what was formerly—and what Von still thought of as—the Old Folks Asylum but Sadie insisted was a "senior community" and if you called it anything else, watch out. Completely overhauled, the place was now the Silver Maples, rechristianed by some idiot developer in a distant city, no doubt, who thought it elegant and distinguished and didn't know a silver maple was a frail, stinky weed tree better off slashed and burned. Sadie had one of the better setups there, the "independent living" option, which meant one of the tiny cottages that ringed the pond side of the property, outfitted with all the necessaries—emergency buttons and handrails anywhere you'd care to grab and monitors and attendants from the main building who checked in on the residents and did the housework and oversaw the cooking in their little kitchenettes. Von thought of it as "the stubborn wing," the place where they put the ones who just wouldn't give it up.

People like Sadie—if there really was anyone else like Sadie vonBush-berger, which he seriously doubted.

Sadie was his grandfather's younger sister, his great-aunt. And at ninety-one, just as opinionated and nutty as ever. The only thing keeping her out of the dementia wing was the fact that she'd always been that way, apparently as far back as a small girl, and anyone in the county would attest to that. "Mentally, Sadie—in the context of Sadie—" her doctor had recently explained, "is still in top shape."

She'd been a schoolteacher for years and never married, and those facts, in her day, her coming as she did from a farm family (an environment in which sons-in-law and future offspring were viewed as the primary labor force), might have caused pity or suspicion in the case of any other spinster—whispered wonderings about her sexuality. But with Sadie, that had never been the case. No one wondered *anything* about Sadie. She'd had boyfriends all her life, as recently as ten years ago, when she was a much spryer eighty—before she hurt her hip in an accident that could only be explained sexually (despite Von's many attempts to sell himself on any other plausible scenario). He wasn't entirely convinced she still didn't engage in some manner of courtship with the old goats at the "senior community"—the younger fellas in their seventies who could keep up with her or at least had substantial enough hearing left to know when she was so far out of line they should give her a crack in the mouth. The fact of her so-called maidenhood obviously never had anything to do with some secret orientation nor with a bad toss of the dice in terms of meeting Mr. Right; put simply, she was virtually impossible to get along with. The fact that she had worked, for several decades, in a position of absolute power over impressionable, helpless young people floored him every time he thought about it.

This kind of visit wasn't something Von had a lot of time for, so he took the shortcut from the parking lot to the rear of Sadie's unit. The back door was ajar, but he knocked as he entered through the little kitchenette, calling her name. He heard her grunt in acknowledgment over the blast of the AC as he stepped into the tiny front room. He knew to duck and did so, avoiding getting hit with what turned out to be, this time, a very old blueberry bagel, hard as a hockey puck. He picked it up and set it on the TV, which was vibrating from the AC. "Hello to you, too," he said. "Reason?"

"I said three," she explained. "It's three-ten."

The throwing things was pretty standard. She had a reputation, during her long career as a teacher at the old Weneshkeen Public, for throwing chalk erasers around the room to keep the children attentive. These days her ammo was usually food she saved till it was good and hard.

He gave her the regular kiss on the cheek, which she waved off, and then took a seat on the only option, the low hassock, and slid it a little farther away from the AC.

"Is it too cool for you?" she asked. "I enjoy the air-conditioning."

"I know you do, Aunt Sadie."

She frowned, sympathetically. "It's too cool for you, isn't it, dear?"

He knew better than to take her bait. She wasn't about to turn the AC down. "Well, you could say I'm overly aware of my nipples right now . . ."

She beamed. "What a delightful thing to be! Land, I remember a time I was constantly aware of my own nipples. For years! You could say I was entirely preoccupied with them. More entertaining, I tell you, than any dumb paddleball or yo-yo I ever got from Santy . . ."

It was his fault for being a smartass and starting it, but there was no way he wanted to sit here and listen to this excruciating nipple talk. Not if he was planning on eating again in the next month or so. Besides, he had to get back. "We're in the middle of the sweets, Sadie. Right in the middle of the run."

"Excuse me, Mr. Busy Bee. The Farmer's got to get back to the Dell, I imagine. The bigaroons are in!"

It felt odd hearing that term for bigarreaus, those white-pink cherries that always seemed so fragile to him, so fleshlike. The term was hardly used these days, but he remembered it now from his grandfather, the sound of the word taking him back to the original barn, watching the sorting from the loft. Every once and again, one of the migrants—a big brown man with one eye that didn't quite open, Paulo (he never knew his last name)—would lob a cherry up to Von in the loft, the only warning it was coming a quick low "Aquí!" or "Más?" It was their secret.

"Did you know," Aunt Sadie said, sliding right into her old teacher voice, "the name of the river over in town—the Ninny John—the real name, is something that means 'busy'?"

Of course he knew that, but he was trying to be patient with her. "I think I might have heard something about that, yes."

"Maybe you could change the name of the orchard to that—the word that means 'busy.'"

"Change the name of the orchard. Uh-huh."

"I mean, since you're in such a hurry all the time. Since it's become such a big production for you."

What the hell was she talking about? It had always been a big production, even before he was born. "You want me to change it from 'vonBushberger's.' Change all the signs, all the trucks."

"It'd give it a little more mystique. Folks are very het up about places and products with authentic Indian names these days. Some kind of reverse snobbery, I'd imagine."

"Just get rid of our family name." He was straining to be polite, but he knew now he was going to have to speak with her doctor again.

"You could get that man who taught the kids to swim at the new high school there to help you make sure it was spelled out exactly right. *He's* an Indian." She said it like she was being so damn helpful. Then again, you never knew with her when she was up to something.

"This was your big thing you needed to discuss? Wipe out a century of local name recognition?"

"Oh no," she said, "not this. This just popped into my head. But doesn't it make you stop and think—that the word *busy* got mixed up somehow with the word *ninny*?"

He looked at his watch, not bothering to hide it from her.

"Well," she said, "I know you're busy, but this may take a minute or two. I'm afraid I may be about to 'rock your world,' as they say."

"To *what*?"

She beamed. "Isn't that precious? I heard that on my shows the other day. Some crazy mixed-up family on the Jessie Jones. One girl says to the other girl she's about to 'rock her world'—I forget what unpleasantry the young lady eventually disclosed . . ."

"Right . . . And . . . ?" He could see now this was going to be something big and really had zero interest in trying to explain that the woman's name was *Jenny* Jones.

"Rock your world . . ." Her wrinkled brow knit with thought. ". . . Rock *your* world . . . Isn't that interesting? As if you and I live in separate worlds, not in the very same."

Jesus god. He closed his eyes, waiting for it. "Okay, Sadie. What is it?"

"I think words are so interesting sometimes, the way folks use them, twist them around, connect things with them. Like *busy* and *ninny*." There was a canvas bag on her lap, he noticed now. Certainly it could contain knitting, but the chances were good it contained more ammo. So he said nothing. She said, "I'm going to tell you something that you'll probably find hard to believe."

"Is it about the lights?" He was kidding—he *hoped* she wasn't one of those people who were supposedly seeing lights around the area.

"It's about you. It's about your family." She pulled from the bag a cracked brown photo he recognized in an ornate frame. It was Karl vonBushberger and his then fiancée, Dor Sorensen—his grandparents— standing on the running board of the old Model TT truck, and she had a ring of blossoms in her hair. This would have been sometime in the twenties.

Sadie confirmed this, saying this was the summer she wanted to tell him about—1926. His grandfather, she said, was getting "flippy-floppy" after the initial bliss of the courting and after all the engagement fuss wore off. "It was unusually warm that spring and he was feeling his oats. Maybe you don't want to hear that. Sorry, but he was. And this was after them two'd spent the winter bundling. You know what that was? Bundling?"

He had some vague idea what she was talking about, that Old World courtship ritual, still in practice in rural America in the early part of the twentieth century. As a gesture of faith accorded a suitor who showed a proper degree of serious commitment and respect in his pursuit of a young lady, he was sometimes actually allowed to sleep over. In the same bed. The idea, even to Von today, seemed asinine. The only precaution against premarital monkey business was the "bundling"—the future in-laws themselves wrapped the boy very tightly in sheets and blankets—essentially, making the bed with him already in it. A whole-body condom or chastity suit, is what it was, the idea being that he wouldn't be able to move much without a significant ruckus. Except it was nonsense: who couldn't get out of a bed? And with the girl lying free right there beside him, on top of the sheets, couldn't she lend a hand? If he hadn't seen the thing in practice once, in a movie Carol rented one night about the Revolutionary War (last winter, it had to be, the only time of year he allowed himself to stay up late and watch TV), he wouldn't have believed it. Granted, there was some small degree of practical reasoning behind it—traveling to court a girl across great distances, one farm to the next, especially on a sleigh or wagon, it was just impractical not to allow the kid to spend the night. And the boy would not only be bound physically but also, back then, ethically—he was bound to her by getting her pregnant (which was probably the unspoken plan all along). Or even bound by just the simple act of compromising her good name. Back then, that would be enough. It was a wink-wink situation, with no legitimate expectation that they would remain virtuous. Had to be. And really, who was the one being taken advantage of—literally tied up?

"There used to be a phrase," Aunt Sadie said. "'Leading her down the primrose path'—are you familiar with that concept? I was young, sixteen, but I wasn't a fool. I knew what my brother was up to. Karl was seeing some Indian girl down around Government Lake. And his best friend at the time, Warner Stroebel—who later married *my* best friend, Binnie—he told her years later they both went to the whores up around Camp Grayling that summer. And hell, Karl was *seen* by half the town carting around one or two evenings with Flanna McConkey, who was a whore through-and-through, only difference was she never charged!"

Von remembered a Flanna McConkey but had a hard time thinking of her as anything remotely like a whore. The Miss McConkey he remembered used to run the mitten-and-sock tree for charity every Christmas. She wore those black net-veiled pillboxes in church, right along with the widows. An old maid with long, stretched-out earlobes and bad costume jewelry strung around a wrinkly neck. He decided this had to be someone else. Either that, or Aunt Sadie was making it up, which was entirely possible.

"So your grandmother, Dor, who really was always very sweet to me, was, as the kids say today, really getting dicked around."

Von was horrified. "What kids today? Who says that? Around you they say that?" Jesus god.

She hurled something at him that turned out to be an Oreo, but otherwise ignored his interruption. "So she really had no business not saying yes when she was asked out by this very well-mannered summer person named Mr. Al Brown. From Chicago." She waited, then added, "Staying out at the bootlegger's place?" That twinkle came into her eye like she was either palming a hardboiled egg in the bag or about to lead into something real juicy. He waited, but she wasn't forthcoming. "*Al* Brown?" she repeated, like *he* was the nitwit. If they were back in her classroom, she would've called on another student by now. But really, how could she expect that plain a name to ring bells when he was still kind of iffy on truly memorable names like Flanna McConkey?

"I'm supposed to know who that is?" he asked finally. "Some guy my grandmother dated before she got married a million years ago?"

He looked away in disgust, out at the pond, for just a *second,* and something very heavy hit him square in the chest and landed in his lap. It was a black banana, frozen hard. "You *froze* this? Just to throw it?"

"What—you'd have me making a mess, slinging a rotten banana around?" She threw up her hands like he was hopeless and said, "Al *Capone,* dimwit! Of course, she didn't realize it was him, not until your daddy was about five and she saw his face on a newsreel. Al Capone's face, I mean, not your daddy's. Though in a way . . ."

The banana fell from his lap with a thud and he didn't really care. "What are you talking about?" He was sure now she was on some new meds. Or needed to be.

"And there's a reason why he was here. It all sort of clicked, made more sense to me years later, when I read a book that explained it. It seems some of his bunch accidentally killed an assistant district attorney in Chicago earlier that year and so were laying low in Michigan the whole summer. I guess he visited these parts normally, lots of times, even when he wasn't evading the law. Had a grand farm down south a ways, more toward Benton Harbor and that. And two cottages up north of here somewhere. But that year, '26, this was for the whole summer he stayed up here. And no one was to know who he was. So he used this alias he used all the time. Same name as your grandmother's summer beau—Al Brown."

Von started to get up. "I can't believe you dragged me out here for this lame move."

"Fine and dandy," she said, employing that tone he remembered from the one year he actually had the misfortune of being her student. "We'll go through it then, step by step. For the slower children . . . What was your father's name?"

"Fred."

"Incorrect. Alfred. Born 1927. Alfred Karl vonBushberger. Remember?"

Of course he remembered. Hadn't he had to deal with the man's headstone just a year previous? This was idiotic, but he continued to play along. "Capone's name," he said, "was Al*phonse*. Not Alfred. So please."

Aunt Sadie made a very wet raspberry. "So she's going to call the baby 'Al Capone vonBushberger'? What are you—simple? Don't be such a dunderhead!"

This is why he drove out here—the insults, the browbeating? "So," he said, sighing, "my dad was actually the son of the world's most notorious gangster. And nobody objected. Got it. Anything else?"

She eyed him levelly. "Of course no one knew. No one caught on. Everyone said of your daddy that he was the most vonBushberger of the bunch. They'd say, 'Boy, he sure is a vonBushberger, that Fred.' The point is, what matters is who you are and what you do. It's not whose juices you come out of."

The word *juices* made him wince.

"Look, Karl was my brother, sure, but Dor and I got real close. We were friends. I know what I'm talking about. The fact is, me and you, we're not even really related. Not by blood. You want to talk about the last living members of the bloodline, who's a true vonBushberger, there's me and there's your two aunts, Fred's younger sisters. Those girls were legitimately Karl's, that was obvious. Hell, I think I even witnessed the conception of them—heard it, I mean. It was hot that summer and we had all the windows thrown open and you could hear noises down in the little house from the main house. You're probably familiar with that phenomenon yourself, everyone so huddled up close together out there like circling the wagon train. You got to stopper up your ears sometimes."

He took a deep breath before speaking. He wanted so much to sound calm—as impossible as that now seemed. "If this is to make me ease up on the kids, Aunt Sadie, and be all *accepting,* you're wasting your breath. I already decided not to make a big huge stink about everything. So thanks. Now I have to walk around with this lead balloon over my head. Just on account of you like to tell wild stories."

"Well," she said, "tough titty, as they say. Maybe I should've kept my trap shut, I don't know. But too bad, honey. The truth is the truth, it is what it is, and things are the way they are."

"Anything else?"

"Just that I love you. And I accept you. Always have, no question."

He took this as his chance to exit, heaved a sigh and rose to kiss her on the cheek.

"Just—could you be a dear," she said, "and go out through the front there and around? I can't watch you if you leave through the kitchen and you might pocket my silver."

He just gaped at her: *pocket her silver?*

She winked. "You do have some criminal in you, you know."

He wasn't going to dignify this. He turned toward the kitchenette, ignoring her foolishness about the silverware and felt something hard and wet hit him in the back of the ear.

"*Ow!* Damn it, Aunt Sadie!" He looked to see what it was at his feet: she'd walloped him with a section of gnawed cantaloupe rind.

She always did have a good arm.

BRENDA WAS STANDING OUT in the turnaround to meet him as he pulled in. She had her arms folded across her chest and a frown creasing her brow dark as a charcoal smudge. Behind her, Miki stood, almost as if at attention, at the bottom step of the front porch. She kept coming, walking straight up to the truck in this peculiar folded arm way. "It's Marita," she said, before he could even get out. "They're all at the hospital."

He didn't understand. "She's having the baby?" Even a contrary little squirt like Marita wouldn't be contrary enough to have the thing this prematurely. It wasn't due till September or October or something.

Brenda shook her head sorrowfully. "I don't think so, Dad. There was an accident. I think you should go to the hospital. *Calmly.*"

It was only as he was turning the truck around to head back out that he caught sight of the smaller of the two roadside stands—what was left of it. It was stove in on one side, the roof tipped, like something heavy had landed on it and flattened it. The sides were all wrong, too—no longer lined up square with 31 but shoved aside, catawampus from the road. And there were tire marks, deep in the dirt, right in line with the new angle of the demolished stand.

He was starting to see it now. It wasn't something he wanted to see but he could see it now, all the elements coming together like a picture.

MARITA'S COMA was the biggest thing going on at the county hospital that evening, so the head nurse assured Von and his family they weren't going to make a stink about visiting hours. They could all stay as long as they wanted. Come and go. But after several hours of standing around and not knowing what to say to his son, who'd been rendered a zombie, sitting there like some piece of unexplained medical equipment that came with the room, or to Carol, whose response to the situation seemed to consist of walking around rubbing everybody's arms—stroking them like pets, like they had something on their sleeve or had poor blood circulation—Von couldn't take it anymore. He had to get out of the hospital.

At first, he didn't know where he was heading. He just wanted to get out in the air where he could breathe and not feel so closed in and surrounded by family and dependents and employees and the medical staff and everybody coming at him with panic and fear and anger. Back out on 31, as he approached the orchard, he saw the darkened shape of the smashed-up fruit stand and felt like he could see it happening all over again. The deputy at the hospital, Janey Struska, had said it was a Fudgie talking on his cell phone and in a hurry somewhere, worried he was lost. Von kept going, passing his own driveway, and he realized now he was heading into town, to the Oh-John and the marina.

He took Don Vanderhoof's fishing boat, *The Wet Debt*. Don had always said he could use it anytime, though Von had never before taken him up on the offer, never having had time to relax. He rumbled it back out of the slip and wound his way out the river, trying to keep it slow, no wake, but itching to go, and then he was cutting into the big lake, out past the lighthouse and opening it up, full bore, in the general direction of Chicago. And in the spray and roar, the crying began. He would run the fucker till he ran out of gas and then he would raid the fridge, splay-legged on the lolling deck, under the cold starlight, and drink every single one of the Bell's Ambers and Bell's Pale Ales and whatever else skunky beer Don had stowed away in there. He felt it was the best plan he'd had in a very long time: go and go till the big beast sputtered and died, then drift, powerless, and get drunk and cry and cry until there was nothing left to do but fire up the radio and call for help.

54

OF ALL THE AWFUL sites he kept returning to, the thing that Gene found so infuriating about this Ultrateen.com in particular was the fact that it was updated daily. Each day it grew closer to feeling something akin to a physical addiction, and he railed against it, but curiosity kept driving him back with a desire to just peek in and see what was new. And it loaded so fast, the tiny pictures—thumbnails, they were called—popping up in rows and columns like a tempting box of candy, each little square demanding his perusal.

The degree of volition was what was so blurred for him. Because how much interaction or effort was required here? To simply lay that little white pointer over the picture and hit the button marked *Enter*—was that anything at all comparable to sneaking into a peep show, wearing a raincoat and dark glasses, driving to another city to see an actual movie—to pay your money and get a ticket and find a seat? Was it anything comparable to renting a video, pushing through those swinging doors in back of the Video Vault that seemed so oddly Old West, like entering a saloon? It was nothing like being a Peeping Tom, sniffing panties on a laundry line. (He remembered years ago, there being a problem with a sad, mixed-up man named Lem who did just that—the former sheriff, Sloff, did something unofficial with him, put him on a bus or something.) This was certainly nothing like grabbing a young lady, "copping a feel," as his friends had called it when they were young. It was nothing like lurking around a playground, being a molester or a rapist. It was nothing like visiting a lady of the evening. There was more volition and intent, he decided, in calling one of those phone sex numbers. There was the intent of dialing and the consequence of cost and the humanity of the live woman on the other end. This was more like thumbing through the magazines at the barbershop. This was idle perusal.

He could hear the voice of his old adviser from seminary, Dr. Getner, rumbling the word *semantics*.

And it wasn't really kiddie porn—he was fairly confident of that. It seemed to him he'd heard enough about the FBI in the news to understand that those busts they made were big events. Truly illegal pornography was now therefore a pretty rare duck. In this context, the "teen" moniker was merely a marketing device to connote youth and beauty and a devil-may-care sense of sexual adventure. They weren't actually minors. Which was fine. He didn't want to see that sort of thing.

Actually, he didn't truly want to look at *this* sort of thing either, but he was starting to feel as though he couldn't help himself. There really was something about the idea of oral contact, the lively passion of it, the pure illicitness, that triggered his libido in a way that he had not felt in years. He could look at those pictures and imagine the heat of their breath.

Today's selection was mostly outdoor shots, girls on the edge of chaise lounges, their summer reading set aside, splayed on the binding beside them, as if they'd been engrossed in a good book and looked up and said, "Oh! A penis!" as if they'd spotted a robin. Some were poolside or in the water, some kneeling in hiking boots along desert mountain nature trails. California sunshine washed across their skin with the candlepower of a prison searchlight. Some wore sunglasses, and these pictures, to his amazement, were paired with follow-ups with the sunglasses soiled, the white seed glopped onto the plastic lens and in the hair. It was too much, really, but he looked on, opening the next and the next.

There was a stirring and the rubbing began through his trousers, noncommittally. I'll stop this right now, he told himself, and then scrolled down to find there was an entire additional, unopened block of thumbnails, more arousing than the first batch. He liked the grins in particular, appreciated the fact that they didn't look walleyed or drugged or under duress. The eye contact, he decided, was acutely enticing, the way they seemed to be holding his gaze, as if looking up at him, not the camera or the man who remained unseen but for his most primary part.

Gene unzipped and began stroking in earnest.

Then there was one that made him sit forward in his desk chair: a girl—dark hair, the set smile, her teeth and lips white with semen as she blew a bubble.

It looked like the girl. It looked like Kimberly.

He let go of his member. But he couldn't stop studying the photo. Okay, maybe it wasn't *exactly* like her—this girl had two studs in her ear and he was pretty certain Kimberly's only piercing was in her navel. But still, there was a rather striking similarity. Close enough that one could look at this and easily pretend it was her. The more he looked at it, the more it seemed to become her. And she had the eye contact, that straight-on gaze, almost taunting the camera. And her lip curled into a smile, as if about to burst into laughter, amused at the bubble she'd made with the man's juices. It was an image that made his breath catch, made him cough and the whole plane of the room shift and shimmy, like a visit to that childhood haunt the Mystery Spot, down in the tourist trap Irish Hills, hitting him with a slight but sudden dose of vertigo. It was a powerful image and he realized, with dismay, that he was harder than before.

No, he told himself, *I will not pleasure myself to this image,* and he moved on, opening the rest of the day's thumbnails. They were okay; acceptable; perfectly arousing; adequately obscene—the sort of thing that would have caused him, as a teenager, to walk into traffic in a daze if he were to so much as get a momentary glimpse. But now they didn't seem to be doing the trick. He flip-flopped from one to the other and back, but he just couldn't finish. Finally, when he felt his urethra starting to burn and heard the Westminster chimes from the living room clock, announcing it was already four in the afternoon, he relented and opened the off-limits one, the one that looked like the girl, the bubble perched on her playful smirking lips, and Lord forgive him, it offered something more; it was enough to complete the task.

The hard part was after. Moments after. It hurt, for one thing, his member sore from the lengthy rubbing. He mopped up the mess with a few sheets of used paper from the wastebasket but knew the carpet would be hard and crusty right in that spot and if he ever stepped on it with his bare feet, he'd feel the difference in the texture there and remember the shameful thing he'd done. And the worst thing was, since he needed to get up and wash his hands, he couldn't close out of the site yet and so the picture remained frozen on the screen, staring accusingly back at him, the dirty old man.

Later, he took a shower and cried and then prayed about it and went for a walk down along the Oh-John. There was a wind coming in from Lake Michigan, cutting the day's heat nicely, and the gulls arced overhead, squawking about something trivial, and he felt a little better, breathing in the clear breeze and watching the boats work their way through the narrow river, but even so, he knew this wasn't over. It was only going to get worse.

A few members of his former flock stopped to exchange a few words or called out hello or, if they were walking on the other side of the river, waved. One, Reenie Huff, down below in her fancy one-man rowing contraption, even called up, "How *are* you, Reverend?" with that emphasis given the grieving, as if she truly wanted an answer and was not merely being rhetorical. People had been saying it that way since the fall, when it was clear Mary was dying, and then continued through the funeral and extended it, like renewing a library book, after he announced his retirement. He wondered if he would live to see a time when they would drop that emphasis and go back to the less-inquisitive "How are ya?" that served only as a greeting.

He had an urge to confess, *I'm becoming a dirty old man, that's how I am,* but he just told them, "Fine, fine! Starting all kinds of new hobbies . . . !" and smiled like a goon, squinting up at the gulls, grateful that they were there to drown him out.

55

"YOU HAVE ALL BEEN A GREAT DISAPPOINTMENT," Roger Drinkwater muttered to himself as he scrubbed the base of the statue of Chief Joseph One-Song. *Nimaanaadendam Gaa Zhi Binaadkamgiziik*—they should inscribe that right on there, he thought. Get the tribal council to kick in some of that casino money toward altering it, like they did the sign for the river.

It fell to him every year at this time to go down to Scudder Park and "spruce up the Chief," as the Sumac Days committee liked to call it. Remove the lichen, birdshit and teen Fudgie cigarette butts, was what it came down to. And though Roger had little use for the ridiculous event, he had enough respect for his childhood hero Bezhik-Nagamoon to make the effort.

Somewhere along the way, Sumac Days had appropriated—idiotically, Roger felt—this great chief who told off Congress.

There was no birthdate on the marker, just the year of his death, 1837—the exact date being the same as both that of the speech and the state's admission to the union—but the legend Roger Drinkwater had heard all his life was that Chief Joseph One-Song had been a small boy when that first outsider stumbled in, that Greek deserter; that he might have been old enough to form words, to join in the puzzled grilling of *"Wenesh kiin? Wenesh kiin?"*—"Who *are* you? Who *are* you?"

But Roger knew that part was a load of crap: just look at the dates, do the math. Even a healthy man, pre-pollution, pre-smallpox—even a blessed man, in the grace of the Great Manitou, privy to all the herbs and nutrition of all the surrounding bounty of what once was at least *his* idea of at least *relative* paradise—could not live to be almost two hundred years old, to span the time between the first outsider and his death in D.C. So surely that part was a myth. He wasn't a naked papoose, staring wide-eyed at Argus (or Anastasius) Mulopulos. Didn't happen.

Maybe it was because the Chief's statue stood in a good shaded area where all parades congregated beforehand that people just started associating him with all heritage events and sumac and with Mulopulos as well. Maybe it made him more palatable to them. Adorable. Safe.

Besides that part of the legend, the statue itself was a lie, too. If you looked up an oil painting of Chief Joseph in a book and held it up to the statue, anyone could see they didn't match. In the statue, he was dressed in a full suit and high collar, the complicated necktie of the time, with a beaverskin hat in one hand and the Holy Bible in the other. He looked like a priest or Mafia don, his hair pomaded, slicked back, his nose noble, Roman, even. In the painting, he was more of a blob, like an apple granny doll, with features flattened, squished. Roger had heard the man in the statue was actually the sculptor's assistant or lover, a marble worker from Tuscany who came to North America to learn bronze work. Maybe so. All he knew was the greatest and only similarity between the statue's subject and its life model was that probably neither one could speak much English.

It was possible, however, that the Chief heard firsthand the tale of that first outsider—the "bloodless man" whom earlier generations tricked into drinking that crappy sumac concoction. Joseph One-Song's own father or grandfather or uncle could have been one of those wide-eyed kids and maybe he himself was present when the *next* outsider visited—the official "discovery" by Marquette and the crucifix-wielding Jesuits, the "Black Robes" or *Wemitigoji* ("Wavers of Wooden Sticks"). That would work, mathematically. Chief Joseph certainly witnessed subsequent *similar* encounters—the trappers, the redcoats, the wicked marauders of all those distant bands and countries during the French and Indian Wars who made the woods a terror for many lifetimes and left it, when the redcoats finally won, and then the Americans after them—everyone winning and losing, one side and then the other, in the manner of a canoe being paddled—with all the screams that traveled along the water gone, but not the fear. The fear, along with a sadness, remained after they departed, like the smell of bad meat. And to each of these outsiders Joseph One-Song and his people continued to ask, growing only more befuddled with each visit, "Who *are* you?"

Roger wondered, as he refilled his bucket, who would do this if he wasn't here.

56

IT HAD BEEN DAYS and Jack was still a zombie. Von knew his son would benefit from some air, a walk down the halls at least, maybe get him into the snack room and get some food into him. But when he put his hand on Jack's arms and tried to pull him to his feet, his son resisted, twisting out of his grasp. So Von backed off and watched as the boy lolled his head, like deadweight, against the foot of Marita's hospital bed. His eyes were closed, as if in pain, and then they opened slightly and it seemed for a moment that he was aware of Von's presence. "Leave me alone," he said and the eyes closed again.

Von kept standing there, watching, keeping his distance as if these two young kids carried some sort of dangerous electrical current. Eyes closed, slack-jawed—they appeared merely asleep; like two toddlers, exhausted from a day of shrieking play, who'd passed out in the backseat and now must be carried into the house and upstairs to bed. Carol had photos like this, taken when Jack and Brenda were young and innocent and sleeping like lambs in the Bible.

But neither Jack nor Marita were sleeping. It just looked that way. After a long while, without opening his eyes, Jack said, "Why are you even here?"

Von stepped closer and laid his hand, just for a instant, on his son's back where the sweat clung to his shirt, but he didn't answer the question. It was a good question, he decided. Then he turned quietly from the room and followed the signs downstairs, to the basement, to the little hospital's morgue—smaller than the laundry room he first passed—and asked the attendant in charge, a kid who looked younger and less worldly than even his son, whom he would talk to about releasing the baby's body.

"VonBushberger, right?" The kid got this just from glancing up at him, which struck Von as a little weird, on account of he'd never seen this morgue kid in his life and he wondered where he'd come from, whose family he belonged to.

"Jack, not Von, though. It's my son's, the husband of the girl in—"

"You understand it was stillborn, right?" The kid had papers and forms on clipboards but didn't bother checking them, and Von understood now. This wasn't exactly Gary, Indiana. The kid didn't see a lot of action down here in the basement. It was probably the only one currently on ice. "It was never actually breathing. And in this case, the degree of premature and all, we are set up to handle disposal ourselves."

While the kid explained there would be no additional charge for this, Von spotted the large metal bins behind him, tagged with little international sign stickers: BIOHAZARD and MEDICAL WASTE. Von waited for the guy to use the term *medical waste,* curious to see how he himself would react to such a phrase in connection to this baby. Would he pop the guy in the nose or would he really care? Hard to tell. But the guy didn't say "medical waste"—which meant he might have had more training or at least more common sense than he initially appeared to.

"The mother's Catholic," Von said, "so we'll need to bury it proper. And stop saying 'it.'"

"Excuse me?" the kid said. Apparently, he hadn't heard himself.

"You keep calling my grandson 'it.'"

The kid studied him for a long moment. "Right. My apologies." He started to turn his clipboard Von's way, perhaps to have something signed, but quickly withdrew it, frowning. "You understand that we do not provide a container."

At first the word *container* made Von recoil. But then the word choice prodded him in the direction of a rather obvious solution. He went out to the parking lot and rummaged through the fruit baskets he had with him in the bed of the truck. Most were old, banged-up bushels, but there was one cute little red-and-green peck basket he thought would do.

Back inside, passing a linen cart, he snatched up a few items that he discovered, in the elevator, were pillowcases. Riding down to the morgue, he pressed the linen to his face. It was cool and smooth and smelled, in a good way, like his grandmother. The memory reminded him of his visit to Aunt Sadie the day of the accident, that cock-and-bull story about his grandmother stepping out; about his not really being a vonBushberger. What a load that was. It was weird now how it seemed like forever ago since he was sitting in her small chilly room, being pelted with compost and lied to.

The morgue guy frowned when he saw the red half-peck basket. "Relax," Von said, arranging a pillowcase down inside it. "I'll line it with this, and then put another one on top."

The attendant sighed and went to get the body. Von signed the forms on the clipboard, and the attendant, still sighing his disapproval, placed the tiny body into the fruit basket. Von took a moment to study the tiny purple face. No, he did not look anything like a gangster. He laid the second pillowcase on top and used both hands to carefully carry the basket back upstairs to take it home.

HE HAD A CRATE IN MIND that he'd been saving for a few years, thinking it would make a special cradle or something if the right kid came along. It was one of the really old shipping crates with the first vonBushberger label, from back in the 1910s. He had only a few of them left. He wouldn't just use the crate as it was, of course, but it would be the base.

He went into the main house and located the crate, up in the top of his closet, where he'd stashed it, and dug around in Carol's sewing stuff for some nice bright red sateen kind of material—*Cheery,* he thought—and went out to the tractor barn to use the workshop. While he worked on the crate, he had Brenda call the monument place they'd used just last year, for his dad. He knew they'd have to erect it after the fact, but he knew by now how this worked, how they'd have to order the stone so it all matched, and he wanted to get the arrangements under way. Brenda came back in and asked about the name, that they needed something for the estimate, just for a tentative character count, and he told her, "Santiago vonBushberger." He'd been thinking about it and that seemed acceptable.

"With a hyphen or is that a first name or . . ."

"Either way." Jack could decide what he wanted when he was less of a zombie, but for right now, that sounded about right.

STRICTLY SPEAKING, he knew they weren't supposed to be using the old family plot in the beech grove anymore. There were county ordinances. No new graves on private property. They'd broken the rule last year, when they buried his dad up there, but Don Sloff was still the sheriff and he arranged for a "special dispensation," which probably meant Don had actually passed along to the county coroner the warning Fred vonBushberger had made the last time they all went fishing, before he got too sick: that he'd come back and haunt any pencil pusher or county toady who kept him from getting buried with his family.

While Von dug the hole, he considered calling Reverend Gene and seeing if he could come by and say a few words. But the guy's wife had just passed and maybe he wasn't up for it. Maybe it would be a little insensitive to drag him out to another gravesite just a few months after. Besides, he was retired now and maybe they weren't supposed to bother him with such things. Then, too, there was the whole Catholic issue. If they got somebody official, Presbyterian was probably not the best thing. Marita probably would want it to be Catholic or nothing.

In a way, the whole thing *felt* pretty Catholic—this baby would probably be the first stillborn in the beech grove to rate a headstone and any sort of ceremony. He knew there had to be others out there behind the low rusty fence—the unnamed vonBushbergers who didn't make it. But things were different in those days and he knew those kinds of personal losses weren't discussed as much. They were different people back then, with different views, and strong opinions on how things should be done.

When everything was ready, he walked back down to the house and told Brenda to put on a dress or something and then he drove back to the county hospital to retrieve his wife and son. And round up Santi, whether he was with his crew or, understandably, at the hospital.

THE NEW INTERIM SHERIFF did show up. They could see the patrol car approaching, from the high ground of the family plot, as he pulled off 31 down by the main house and then bobbed along the gravelly tractor ruts and kept coming, the big Crown Vic gunning as he climbed the rise and put it in park in the high weeds just a foot from the old rusted gate. And then he got out, the radio squawking behind him, and sighed deeply, like he was very disappointed. He did take off his hat. Von had to give him that. But then he got all official, telling them he was sorry, but they'd have to cease and desist. They couldn't bury on private property.

Von wondered if it was the morgue kid at the hospital or someone at the monument place who finked. Or maybe this Hatchert guy was just particularly snoopy. Von stepped forward so he stood between the new hole and the new sheriff. "He's a vonBushberger, Sheriff. This is where he belongs."

"Maybe a hundred years ago, fine, but not anymore. There's zoning."

"Zoning?" Jack said. "Screw that." It was the most lively thing out of his mouth since the accident.

"Look," Von said, "my fruit stand isn't zoned as a public highway, either, but that didn't stop that dumbass kid driving through it."

The sheriff stood resolute. "You can't do this." He shook his head and removed his sunglasses, folding them and slipping them into his breast pocket. "Not that I don't understand your grief, sir."

How could he? Von himself hardly understood it. The radio in the sheriff's patrol car crackled and he leaned back into the open window and scooped up the handmike. "Yeah! Hatchert here."

Von could hear Janey Struska on the other end. "Down at the bootlegger's place," she said. "Possible break-in. Probably just kids, but maybe you ought to—"

"Hang tight," Hatchert said into the mike. "I'll handle this. Call the real estate guy, whoever's got the listing, tell him to meet me there. Do *not* enter."

"Right," she said.

Hatchert threw the radio mike back through the window, swung the door wide and slid in behind the wheel. Before he pulled out, he jabbed his finger toward them. "You people just sit tight, please. I know this is a very difficult time for you, but there's a right way and a wrong way. I'll try to send someone over to . . . retrieve the body." He roared out of there, the cruiser bouncing back down the rutted road. They watched him go, the plume of dust as he rocked back up onto the paved road, the lights and siren wailing into the distance as he roared south on 31.

"Okay," Carol said. "Keep going."

Von wasn't sure how to proceed. He felt like he was underwater, every movement an effort. Maybe they shouldn't be doing this. He just wanted to lie down in the tall grass and take a breather. He looked at Santi, Santi looked back. And then they heard, again, the crunch of gravel.

At first, he thought the sheriff was back, the unlit light bar of the cruiser bobbling along above the line of tall grass, heading back up the dirt path toward them. But when the car rounded the last turn and pulled up close, he saw now it was just Janey.

"Probably ought to keep it short and simple, Mr. vonBushberger." She was staring past him, at the crate with the baby. "It'll take him twenty minutes to get down there, five to figure out nothing's shaking, maybe ten to speed back pissed off. So you probably want to get it all done in a half an hour, if you could."

He understood now what she had done, calling in a false report in order to divert her boss. Pretty risky behavior. She could easily lose her job, and for what? She hardly knew the family. He thought maybe Brenda knew her slightly when they were kids, but that was it. No special connection—just someone who understood the place, the people. He said, "Thanks, Janey."

She nodded, waved off his thanks like it was nothing, gave a sad little smile, and put the cruiser back in gear. He wanted to tell her he'd help back her if she decided to run during the next election, that he knew several other prominent local men who would support her campaign, but this wasn't the time to talk about that. He had a grandkid to bury.

57

HATCHERT BARRELED TOWARD HER from the opposite direction, flashing his lights for Janey to stop, and they pulled alongside, window to window, blocking traffic on the main drag, right in front of T.G.I.Fudge. The power windows, she could tell from his grimace, weren't moving fast enough for his liking. But he didn't speak until they were all the way down, probably because he wanted to point his finger at her, jabbing it so close it crossed into the window of her own cruiser. For a long moment, he said nothing, just jabbed and set his jaw.

"We're issued sidearms, you know, Hatchert. You don't have to make one with your finger and go 'Peeoww! Peeoww!'"

"Your resignation. My desk. First thing in the A.M."

"Sorry," she said. "Not going to happen."

Hatchert pulled the finger back a little but kept pointing. "You want to challenge me, Struska?"

"What do you think I've *been* doing?" She thought about that, reconsidered. "No, that's not exactly true. I haven't been doing it nearly as much as I should."

"Fine," he said. "Then we go in front of the council and the whole thing gets ugly."

"I don't think so. I don't think you want to do *that*." Reenie Huff and her grandson were crossing on matching razor scooters in front of her cruiser, squinting in at her, and Janey smiled and waved. She didn't do it to illustrate what she was about to say to Hatchert, but because that's just what she did. It was part of her job, really. Wave to people and say hello and show them everything's the way they think it is. The grandkid lagged behind, not as adept as Reenie, and so Janey gave him his own separate wave, as encouragement, before turning to face her boss again. "You really want to do that? Put it in the hands of people who've known me all my life, people I went to high school with? People who know Von, went to high school with *him*, or with his kids—remember: the father of that baby you're so riled up about? These are people who come to Von every year for good fruit and pies. You think you stand a chance in that arena? Really? What element of this equation are you missing—you never had one of his pies? That it?"

There was a deerfly buzzing around in the cruiser now. This is what happened when you let the hot air in, damn it. She lifted her trooper hat off the shotgun seat and shooed the fly out the window, hoping it would cross over into Hatchert's vehicle.

He was silent, picking his words, and they were still blocking traffic, but she told herself it was time to keep her mouth shut and wait the other person out. Let the silence do the negotiating. She'd said enough. It was out there. Let it sit there. She did that, biting her tongue. And she wondered if this was something she'd picked up by hanging around Roger Drinkwater lately. Of course, for his part, Roger was more chatty and sarcastic than she'd thought him to be, back when he was her coach, so maybe it was a fair trade. Maybe they were rubbing off on each other some.

Meanwhile, Hatchert was starting to squirm against the vinyl, gripping and ungripping his steering wheel. "Look," he said, and in that one word she heard him start to backpedal, hedge the thing, turn Mr. Politician, "forget about the resigning, okay? Fine. But just—in the future—you're really going to have to learn to do things my way."

She laughed. "I don't think so. I don't think I am. I thought for a while I might have to, but I really don't think so now. Not so much. Look, I'm *from* here, okay? I'm a local. I'm not going anywhere. You, on the other hand . . . I don't know how long you'll be visiting, but you're just passing through." With that, she put it in first, out of there.

JULY INTO AUGUST

58

AFTER THE FUNERAL, Von spent most of his time at the county hospital. It felt as if he could describe every piece of junk food in the vending machine by heart. Not just the brand names, but the exact wrinkles of each package, the tiny and alarming "sell by" dates just visible on some. There was that one sun-faded Zagnut in particular that he felt he'd known all his life.

He wasn't sure what he should do there. Marita was handling the being-in-a-coma part, and his son was handling the watching-Marita-being-in-a-coma part. Carol's duties worked out to be mostly as liaison officer: she went for coffee and did the crossword puzzle and tried to make Jack more comfortable when he fell asleep with his head on Marita's bed, the rest of him half on a chair, half on the floor. It also seemed to Von, judging by Carol's breath, that part of her job might also be to sneak back on the cigarettes, but he didn't think this was the time to chide her about that.

The doctor, though not making any promises, seemed fairly convinced Marita's chances were good. Her nonbrain injuries were under control, and he'd been consulting with a neurologist down in Ann Arbor who thought it fairly likely that she would eventually come out of the coma.

Even Marita's own father was practical enough to force himself not to abandon his crew and his responsibilities back at the orchard. He came in for a couple hours every evening; if no one was heading back to the hospital at the time, he would drive himself, illegally, on the old International Farmall with the sprayer still hitched to it on account of it was such a hairy bitch to monkey with, getting it on and off—putt-putting along at twenty miles an hour, tops, way over on the shoulder. Von knew, after several days of this, that someone at the sheriff's office must have gotten wind of this road hazard by now but was turning a blind eye. He expected he had Janey Struska to thank for that, too.

On the fifth day, Carol told him to go home. Then, when that failed, to get the hell home, and finally, quietly, to get the fuck home. "Listen," she said, doing that thing she did on occasion to ensure she had his full attention—standing very close, looking up into his eyes and literally grabbing his balls, squeezing him through his pants, not painfully but not exactly lovingly either—"Are you listening to me, Hubert von-Bushberger?"

"Yes."

"Good: like *HELL* if you think I'm going to stand out in the snow watching the bank auction off the place because you decided to have some sort of 'inner turmoil' at the height of the season. Think again if that's your plan." She kept her voice low, level, but it was clear it was time to go home and check on things there.

"Well," he said, trying to save a little face. "I guess I could use a shave and a shower . . ."

TO HIS SURPRISE, everything was in fairly good shape back home, considering. The small stand had been repaired, repainted, and dragged back into its original position, in line with the road. As a precaution to any future idiots who might plow into the shoulder at seventy miles an hour, someone had laid out an arrangement of old tires, painted a bright orange, as homemade traffic cones. They wouldn't physically stop cars, of course, but they would at least serve as warning that you were about to hit something significant. Brenda told him that Miki had done it personally: "He's way behind on his slides, on his research, but he wants to help."

"Well," Von said, "I appreciate the pitching in." He figured she could interpret that as both of them pitching in, if she wanted to relay his thanks to the guy that way. Or not. She told him the bug count was holding, still low for that time of year, so she'd instructed the spray crew to hold off that week. Von grunted, only vaguely aware what she was telling him. To a certain extent, it still just all sounded like a muted noise in his ear, like distant traffic. "Sounds fine," he said. "Whatever you decide . . ."

She walked him over to the porch to show him the books for the week, a thing they normally did at the kitchen table, facing each other, like they were two regular business associates with appointments and contracts. She explained the table was too cluttered and so sat him down on the porch swing, and then plunked herself down, right up against him. It felt nice. It seemed like he hadn't touched another person all week, though he certainly must have—he must have hugged Carol and Jack back at the hospital. Brenda showed him in her binder the expense line and the gross profit line on the two road stands, the shipped product and the local, and the projected line for the net and the following week. It all seemed about average. If he hadn't known there'd been an accident, if he was just skimming through the accounts, he probably wouldn't be able to tell anything had happened here, just from the numbers.

"I suppose," he said, sighing, "I ought to go out to the back fields with Santi tomorrow, see if it's time to shake the last of those Royal Anns."

Brenda shook her head. "Actually, we went ahead and sent in the shaker trucks yesterday." She bit her lip. "I know, I know— It's not my call to make. But I had Miki look at them, too, and some of Santi's senior guys, and they all thought I was right, and well, we just thought we should make a decision and not bug you."

This was surprising as hell—she'd never before made a decision that held that much financial significance. Not on her own. And it wasn't that she wasn't qualified—hell, how qualified was *he*? He'd never had a fraction of the horticultural education of those two, Brenda and her blossom boy. It was just that she'd never shown any inclination to make decisions like that. She maintained the books and kept it all organized, charted patterns and offered suggestions, but she never made actual decisions. Let alone handing out orders to an entire crew.

To show her it was fine, she'd done good, he pulled her closer, patting her arm, and kissed her forehead. He asked if she smelled fish.

"That's Miki," she said. "He's cooking dinner."

When they went inside, he found dinner was something that looked like a lot of little cocktail hors d'oeuvres, only maybe less appetizing. Miki was still bustling around, laying out the finishing touches. With his glasses and white apron, he looked like he was working in his lab. Brenda explained it was sushi, which was a little surprising, given that she'd just said he was *cooking*. But he didn't object. He sat down with his daughter and her fiancé and they held hands and said grace, during which he mentioned, by name, his son and his son's wife and there was a little pause at the end, right before he said amen, where he asked—not out loud, just in his head—for a blessing on the little grandkid who hadn't quite made it.

Miki began serving and explaining what each item was. After about the third description, Von held up his hand and said, "Okay, that's okay. I think maybe they'll slide down better unexplained . . ."

It all seemed very quiet, like half the house had blown away in a big windstorm. Because there were only three of them, he wasn't in his usual chair at the head of the table, but in the middle, where they sat bunched up. From this unfortunate position he could see the phone, hanging on the wall in the kitchen, and he kept thinking it was going to ring. Brenda said, so low she was almost whispering, "Please eat, Daddy." She hadn't called him that in maybe a billion years, way back sometime when he wore his hair long, just over his ears so it poked out of his cap like a fringe, and she used to ride around on his shoulders wherever she could. Any chore he had to do around the place, anything that didn't involve stooping down a lot, he'd scoop her up and perch her up there and he'd feel her little fingers hanging on to that dopey hair he had, like the handles on the little plastic wheeled pony she rode around the cement slab in the big barn—the only substitute they had for a sidewalk around the place—and she'd say, "I steer you, Daddy," tugging on those hair-handles, and he'd say, "Yes, you do, pumpkin. You sure do."

He looked at her now and he understood what she was saying—the words at least—tapping his plate with her fork, and he looked down at the food spread out before him. It was sort of pretty, he had to admit—the colors and the precision of it. Very orderly and artistic, he had to give it that. And if nothing else, a real nice gesture on the boy's part. "Thank you," he said. "Thank you for doing all this, Miki."

Miki smiled and raised his index finger.

Oh Christ, Von thought. *Guy's going to make another goddamn toast.* It'd be that night they announced their engagement, all over again. But he was just reciting some quotation, probably some ancient Oriental: "Every family has bad memories."

After letting it sink in, Von said, "True enough," because it actually was. It helped a little to think of it from that perspective. This was all

weather. Bad weather, but still, the kind of thing that had visited families as far back as centuries before Christ, even way on the other side of
the world, where some wise man, probably with the one long gray chin
whisker, cooked up this saying. That's how families worked, everywhere, all the time. No one was exempt.

"*The Godfather III*," Miki said. "Michael Corleone says it."

Okay, so it was Mario Puzo, not Confucius. Von ate the sushi. He
cleared his plate and tried to smile about it. The guy had put some time
into the meal, so why criticize? Granted, it wasn't like he'd been slaving
over a hot stove, but he imagined there must have been *some* time put
into it. Some of the doodads were rolled up and stuff. A tiny sliver of
carrot was on top of one of them—that had to take at least a couple
minutes, just that alone.

After dinner, after pie and the dishes, after he convinced the two of
them they didn't have to keep him company, that he was fine, the kids
finally retired to Miki's camper. Von sat on the porch, rocking for a
while, then went inside and took down the old family albums his wife
kept stacked up on the player piano that never worked. Several albums
down, he found the ones that covered his own childhood and he looked
closely at the shots of his dad as a man in his twenties and thirties. Von
clicked on the piano light for better inspection, trying to recall, in his
mind, all the photos he'd ever seen of Al Capone.

He closed the albums and squeezed them back into the pile, right
where Carol had left them, then dug out the earlier ones, the ones with
baby pictures of his dad, and shots of his grandfather and grandmother, Karl and Dor, courting and in wedding garb and posed in front
of a toboggan, looking young and fun and full of fire.

In the professional studio baby photos of his dad, Fred, his lips
seemed full and bee-stung, his cheeks jowly, but come on—all babies
looked a little like Al Capone, didn't they? More accurately, wasn't it
more a matter of Al Capone looking like a baby?

There were candids of his dad with his grandparents, a blobby bundle in the arms of Grandpa Karl, sitting out on the well cover that was
still there, straight out the back of the house. There was nothing defin-
itive to be found in these albums—frankly, Von didn't feel like he
looked like either one of them—and he knew for sure he was related to
that baby, his dad, by blood. Unless, of course, there was some big

secret he didn't know about *his* mom as well. Like maybe she'd slept with an Eskimo behind *his* dad's back.

He decided this had probably been a bad idea, looking at these pictures. Rather than making him more sure of himself, looking at them made it all cloudier. He got out the first one again and flipped to the school shots of himself and his siblings: there they were, lined up in a row, him (fourth grade), his sister Harriet (second grade), his sister Francy (first grade), and his brother, Emil (kindergarten), who died of pneumonia about two years later, probably from swimming in the pit vat, which they weren't supposed to do. He looked at all the eyes. Then at all the noses. Then at all the mouths.

Jesus god . . . Francy looked kind of Spanish, Emil a little Chinese . . .

He told himself that nobody thinks they look like their family. Everyone thinks they don't fit in, they're the oddball, that these people around me are strangers, not my responsibility, not my own, I have no connection or relation to these people.

Still . . .

59

BY NOW, HE WAS DREAMING OF MOUTHS, ripe and yawning; dreaming of oral sex, his nights a feverish slide show of the images he'd wasted most of his days viewing.

But if it was simply some corporeal rutting he required, some hedonistic reduction of the human experience to a swapping of parts and spittle, wouldn't he just take a little trip down to one of the cities, check in to a hotel, call one of those escort services? Granted it would be a degradation, a shameful hell, but that wasn't what kept him from doing it (for wasn't the degree to which these thoughts were now in his mind, wasn't that sin enough, hell enough, to count himself among those needing salvation?). No, he wasn't pursuing any of that because deep down, a true physical coupling wasn't at the heart of his impulse.

More and more, Gene lay in bed into the small hours, unable to sleep. And it was on one of these nights that he thought he discovered the crux of it.

He'd turned on the small black-and-white in his bedroom. They'd never kept a TV in there while Mary was alive, but he'd rescued this one from the basement rec room after she passed—a poor substitute for a fabulous wife, but at least it made noise on empty nights like this one.

There was an old Bela Lugosi movie on, as corny as vaudeville—the vampire bug-eyed and drooling over his swooning, boneless victim, her head flopped back as if her neck had been wrung, her tender skin exposed in a long, titillating expanse of white like the neck of a swan, the whole thing so lascivious, as if it were her privates he was about to bite.

And it hit him—this is what he was: a vampire.

Not really. Not a guy in a cape with a bad accent harping on about *"thee cheeeeeeldren of thee niiiiiight . . ."* He didn't imagine he was a bat, though undoubtedly, he was batty and getting more so every day. But this was close to what he was feeling, with the images on the Internet, with the images in his head at night. With his thoughts of the girl.

He just wanted to connect with *youth,* get inside it, feel, for even a short, shuddering moment, as though he might regain it somehow—all that hope and excitement and wonder.

Lord help me, he thought. I am such a creep.

And some nights, nights like this, he thought he might bust an artery from crying, from sobbing at the thought of what he had become.

60

KURT LASCO BROUGHT HIS OWN MOWER. John Schank, the one who'd hired him to go over and mow the parsonage, told him there was an old Toro in the parsonage garage, the one Reecher the Preacher used whenever he got around to it—which wasn't often enough, according to Schank. Kurt listened to the instructions, but he knew he was going to just take his own mower. He always did and it was just easier.

He unloaded in the driveway, did the short front piece, then came around the hedge to do the main part, the parsonage lawn that ran from the back patio of the house over to the line of arbs along the church and straight out to the river. That river edge was pretty abrupt, as he remembered, a sheer high bank, and he could see why the old guy might be a little leery about doing it.

As he came around the side, moving toward the patio to edge the flagstones, he saw there was someone in the chaise lounge that faced away, out to the river, and he thought, with slight annoyance, that he'd have to jam the thing into idle and go over and say hi to the Reverend, be diplomatic about why he was mowing the lawn and not leaving it up to him. But then he saw the feet, the painted toenails, and knew it was a girl and then she raised up, slipping her headphones away and twisting to see what the disturbance was and he saw the hair clip and the hair and the face. And the outfit, the skin. And everything stopped.

She was squinting at him, saying *Dad,* and the sound seemed to be receding, the roar growing dull as her words got louder, less inquisitive, more urgent: "Dad? Dad. Dad!" And then he heard the sudden short gunning sound, the sound the mower makes when you tip it up to clear a root or pivot, the blades roaring in the air, and heard the splash and turned to look down the long pale trail of mowed grass leading straight out to the Oh-John-Ninny.

She held her book up in front of her chest and pulled her legs up close, defensive, as if he'd caught her lying out nude. She wasn't, of course, and he'd seen her in such skimpy outfits before. But that was back at his house, not out in public. Not at the church parsonage. Worse, the Oh-John was right there, with those pilot-boys going by all day, ogling his daughter. Never mind the fact that the whole town would see.

He needed to explain all this to her. He took a seat, practically collapsing into the other lounge chair, weary now from the sun and the strain of everything that had just happened in the last thirty seconds. He tried to lay out all the things that were just not right about the way she was behaving, but she didn't seem to get it. He wasn't going to yell at her—things were too shaky between them right now to do much other than try to gently persuade—but what she was doing here just didn't seem right. If it wasn't exactly wrong, it just didn't seem appropriate.

He got up a few times while they talked and peered in the back window, hoping to catch a glimpse of Reecher and apologize for his intrusive daughter, but she insisted he was out at the hospital for the afternoon, visiting, and Kurt decided this was probably true because John Schank had been real specific about what time he should come over and mow. Finally, he sat down and tried to hear her version of things, but he did wish the Reverend was around to double-check the facts as she was spinning them.

She claimed—spitting it out almost reluctantly, like she couldn't think of anything better—that she was "working" for the man. At first she wouldn't get specific, but he kept pushing. "I tutor him on the computer," she said, "and I help him with the housekeeping. And we hang out. We're friends."

"You're friends," he repeated, hoping it sounded as idiotic to her as it sounded to him. "He's the minister. He's friends with everyone. You're taking advantage. It's not appropriate."

She rolled her eyes at this. "Oh right. Being friends with someone is very inappropriate. I forgot your commandment: hate thy neighbor."

Kurt chose to ignore this. He was beginning to have new respect for his ex-wife; having to deal with this sort of thinking nine months out of the year must be damned exhausting. "Tutoring him is fine, housekeeping is fine—maybe—but you can't embarrass the man, lying out here in your bathing suit."

She snorted, and she sounded awfully like his ex. Lisa used to make the same noises, especially near the end. "This is *so* not a bathing suit! It's shorts and a top."

He knew better than to debate the particulars of fashion—not his field, by a long shot. Instead he pointed out that they had a perfectly good yard back at the house. He tried to keep his voice low, like it was a thought that had just arrived: couldn't she lie out at home?

Kimmy looked away, down at the high grass, and shrugged. "I'd feel . . . uncomfortable lying out in our yard. Talk about embarrassed . . ."

He decided she was probably thinking of the neighbor boy, Starkey's kid. He'd read something about this: teenage girls were sensitive about that kind of thing, worried that their peers would judge them or stare. She probably thought that Mark Starkey would peep from his bedroom and beat off. And she was probably right. Of course, he could probably peep at her here anyway, going by on the river all day, but with that he could only stare, being at work and all.

There was disappointment in her voice, and he wondered if perhaps she'd prefer to spend more time at his house but maybe she felt he'd let her down in not providing a better home and not defending it better from the stupid neighbors. It was almost like she was irritated with him.

He lingered a little while longer, sitting on the edge of the lounge chair beside her, halfheartedly still trying to get her to budge, to gather up her stuff and come home, maybe even quit the tutoring and the housecleaning, but he knew even as he said the words that he held little sway over her. He thought of the life she had most of the year, down in Ferndale, over which he had no say, no input, and this apparent secret life she was leading in his town that was also far beyond his reach, and the weight of it was great, this feeling of irrelevance. It took him a while to gather up the energy to get up, to give up, to go into the garage and wrestle the parsonage's mower and finish up.

When he rose, he felt like a defeated man. And it must have shown because she said, with sympathy in her voice, "Dad? Hey, I'm sorry about the mower."

WHEN HE GOT BACK HOME, stepping around back to the rear of the truck out of habit, before remembering the bed was empty and the mower was gone, he thought he could still smell the gas from the mower. He actually did smell gas, he decided, as he came around the side of the house: it was wafting over from Starkey's deck. They were cooking on the grill. He stood and stared. Starkey looked up from the grill and stared back. It struck Kurt that the trees he'd removed would have blocked this staring contest. He went inside and closed the patio door so he wouldn't have to smell the cookout.

He had a lot on his mind—like what the hell his daughter was doing hiding out at the church, and whether he could claim the mower on his insurance—so it wasn't until a few hours later, when he thought he heard sirens, that he realized there was some sort of commotion over at Starkey's.

Back out on the deck, it was twilight now. Two sheriff's cars were pulled in at rakish angles next door, lights still flashing, and then there was a louder rumble and the trees swayed and there were lights overhead. His first thought was that the rumors were true: there was something in the sky. But it was a helicopter, the county medevac unit, landing in the clearing between their two houses—a landing, he couldn't help but notice, that would have been much trickier if he hadn't cut down that stand of poplars, thank you very much. He watched as they hustled someone out on a stretcher and then dark figures hopped aboard—he thought it was Starkey—and the helicopter lifted up and away and one of the patrol cars pulled out and bounced away down the road, probably going to meet them at the hospital.

The one who'd left was Hatchert, the interim sheriff, because when he walked out to the property line, he found Janey Struska still there, putting down her radio mike and getting into her car. Not wanting to cross the property line, he called out to her and asked what was going on.

"Oh, hey, Kurt," she said. "It's the wife. Went into anaphylactic shock. Ingested some nuts by mistake, they think. Looks like it was from Don Sloff's brauts. No one seems real clear why she bought the kind with nuts."

"Wow," Kurt said.

"Yeah. Gotta read the labels, folks."

"I guess," he said. "Boy! So is she . . ."

"Yeah, she should be okay. They had her stabilized in the kitchen, on the floor, but they'll need to monitor her for a day, probably, to be safe. The paramedics saw right off what was going on and did everything by the book." Janey was chuckling now. "Can't get over the fact they were Don's links! Man, if he was still on the job and took the call . . . You think he would've hid the evidence? Just chucked the brauts in the lake?"

He tried to smile along with her, but it bothered him, the way she was shrugging the whole thing off. He liked Janey a lot—would probably vote for her if she ran against this temporary guy, Hatchert—and he guessed it was because of her easygoing attitude. She wasn't a hard-on like Hatchert seemed to be. She was more like a female Don Sloff, opting to settle problems with a funny story or a cup of coffee when possible. But still, he thought she was being a little inappropriate here. After all, the woman had almost died.

And he had had something to do with it. Actually, he had had a lot to do with it. Maybe everything to do with it, with his grocery-swapping high jinks at the Spartan.

He'd really screwed up. Jesus, he thought. How old am I supposed to be now? Thirty-six? Jesus Christ.

And if his daughter wasn't hiding from him already, she certainly would be now. If I were Kimmy, he thought, I might spend all my time as far from me as possible, too.

61

DESPITE ALL THAT FUSS about getting him back to the orchard, it was clear things were running fine without him. Or close enough to fine. It was funny, but he'd always thought, if anybody would take over down the line, it would be his son. With Brenda's guidance, of course, whispering Kissinger-like in the background. But Brenda was not doing so bad with the actual bossing. He and Santi mustered their perfunctory supervisory commands, but the hands-on of it was pretty much covered now by Brenda and Miki, aided by a new surge in conscientious behavior on the part of the crews—no late-night hoopla down in the migrant shacks, Santi reported, stunned by this himself. He pointed to his head: "Not so loco down there no more." Von wasn't sure if the workers were cowed into docility by the accident or if they believed, in some superstitious or penitent way, that if they toed the line and dug in and did the best they could, they would be rewarded by Marita's recovery. Workers Von had never said boo to would approach him with some meager offering—sneezeweeds, horn poppy, devil's paintbrush, even trillium, though endangered and protected by law, wrapped in wet paper towels; peach blossoms floating in a baby food jar; praying hands carved from a peach pit; little crosses made of woven grass—"to take to Marita," they said. Von would thank them and get their names from Santi after they left, writing them down so he could remember later.

Whatever the reason, the season was proceeding with very little meddling necessary on his part. Which was fine, because, though he needed to stay busy, he had a few projects he'd rather be doing. They were still forming in his head, vague schemes and impulses, half-witted gestures, and he thought he knew what drove those people to come to him with their wilted flowers and trinkets to take to the hospital, because all his own plans right now had something to do with that girl waking up and coming home. The things he planned were dumb, he knew, and probably pointless now, but he still had to try them. All he knew is he wanted to see Marita round and happy again.

VON DROVE THE TRUCK INTO TOWN and talked to Don Vanderhoof at the feed store about trying to rush-order some mature pepper plants. "Not green peppers," he said. "I'm talking about the hot kind."

"Cayenne peppers."

Von wasn't sure. "I mean the kind you hang up to dry."

"Them Mexican shits, maybe—jalapeños?" Don seemed puzzled. "Maybe *anchos*?"

"Yeah . . . or at least some sort of red peppers, anyway."

Don started flipping through his distributor book, leaning over his counter and sighing like this task was a backbreaker. "How mature are we talking about?"

Von shrugged. "Mature. Fairly ready to go. Like, I don't know, as far along as they'd be if I'd planted them when I was supposed to plant them."

"You're not really *supposed* to plant them," Don said. "Not around here. I could get some. Probably. But I don't think they're going to take, Von. Not unless you put them in a greenhouse or something."

Von told him he wasn't going to worry about that right now, he just wanted to know could he get them? Don said, probably, but it might take a while.

"Forget it," Von said. "I'll call around, find someone who can do this for me." Clearly, Don was operating under the illusion that this was a normal transaction in which the expense and practicality were being weighed. Hell, he'd drive down to Lansing or Chicago if need be. Someone would be able to accommodate him, even if it was an impractical request.

"Now hold on, Von," Don said. "Let me call some distributors, see what kind of rush they'd be willing to put on a crazy thing like that."

Von told him he wasn't expecting it to be cheap, but he did need them in the next couple days.

"Let me see what I can do," Don said. He didn't look too hopeful.

Nodding, Von turned to leave, then stepped back for a further word. "Look, call me if you can't get them or when they arrive, but don't bother waiting to clear the price with me. Whatever it costs, that's fine. I don't want to hold it up quibbling over the cost. Okay?"

"Sure thing," Don said. He looked now like he finally saw how important this was. Von left the feed store, grabbed the little can of tractor paint out of the back of his truck and crossed the street to McCreery Hardware, heading straight back to the paint section. Dinging the hotel bell on the little counter produced Roy Kunk, McCreery's load of a brother-in-law, who sidled up from behind, breathing on him. Von slapped the can of tractor paint down on the counter.

"Roy," he said, "can you match this in a housepaint?"

"Oil or outdoor latex?"

"Better make it latex," he decided, thinking he might not have that much time. She could come out of her coma anytime now. "Five . . . no, six gallons, let's say."

Wheezing through his nose a little like he was exerting himself, Roy shuffled over to the rack of color samples and squinted at the chart. "Must be one mutha of a tractor."

"Did I say match it in a housepaint, Roy? Wouldn't that indicate to you that it was for something other than a damn tractor? Perhaps a structure of some kind?" He'd had little patience for Roy Kunk ever since he had to grab Roy by the throat when Roy latched on to Carol's ass at a costume barn dance they'd hosted out at the orchard a few Oktoberfests back. Granted, her ass looked especially spectacular in that old-timey dress she wore that day, and Carol could never be accused of not being able to fend for herself—and it turned out the cherry cider they were serving, which Roy, who was on the wagon, was guzzling like a man in a desert, had turned hard and was probably about eighty proof, by most estimates. So Roy was hammered as an anvil and had no understanding why. Still, excuses aside, Von didn't really like the guy.

Roy was holding up the little paper slips of color samples. "Jeezo . . . On-the-nose match it or just hand grenade close?"

"Hand grenade. It just needs to be cheery."

Roy looked up when he said the word *cheery,* made a little frowny face, almost a pout. It was weird seeing such pity on a person like Roy Kunk and it made Von even more uncomfortable. "Sorry to hear about all the bad luck you've been having out there, Von," Roy said. "Things any better?"

"Getting there," Von said and tugged down his feed store cap. Goddamn it, he was going to *make* things better if he had to.

NEXT HE COLLARED MIKI and took him around back of the main house to the family garden. "You like to use a lot of vegetables in your cooking," Von said. "If there was one item in here that you could choose that I could rip out right now and you could make something out of it, so it wouldn't go to waste, what would it be?"

Miki jutted out his lip and frowned, studying the situation like he'd been asked to perform some elaborate algebraic equation. Finally, he said, "With the cabbages, perhaps I could make something."

"That we can use all at once?" Von imagined vats of uneaten coleslaw, a horrifying thought. "I don't want to waste anything."

"There would be no waste. What I'm proposing is a pickled cabbage dish, very spicy. You will be able to store it safely for a long, long time. One year or more."

Von didn't like the sound of this. "You talking about kimchee?"

"Kim-chee. Yes."

Von asked him but wasn't that Korean—kimchee? Miki said sure, but just because he was Japanese didn't mean he didn't know how to make it. Von wasn't about to argue the point. The two of them set to yanking up the cabbages, loading them on the wheelbarrow. Pretty soon, they'd cleared away about twenty square feet of crop.

"It certainly is a large area of space that is left denuded now," Miki said. "I have an idea. I would have to take a soil sample, of course, to determine if it is properly . . . uh, do you say *aroused*?"

"No, you don't say that. Not at farms around here, not if you don't want to get slugged. Or worse, get them thinking you're sneaking out at night, sticking your pecker in the earth. *Aroused*? Jesus god. Try *fertile* maybe?"

"*Fertile*. Pardon. But here is my idea: it is perhaps too late in the growing season to do so, but perhaps this space could be used, if it is *fertile*, to grow some *tomorokoshi, horenso, azuki* . . . maybe *mitsubu*, Japanese parsley?"

Von told him, "Relax, son. We'll make room for *your* vegetables next summer. This here's for Marita, for when she comes back home. Now go on ahead. Go start pickling that crap there, get the house all stunk up and farty . . ."

Miki started off with his overburdened wheelbarrow. Von thought better of his gruffness and called to him to hold up. Miki stopped pushing the wheelbarrow, looking up as if awaiting his next command. Von had to admit the guy was an agreeable son of a bitch. Not a lot of back-talk and contrariness, he had to give him that.

Gesturing along the strip of lawn where Miki stood on the other side of the fence, Von said, "We'll rototill all that out the west side there, bring it out another twenty, thirty feet. Next year. I just don't see the point doing it now, do you? You figure you can squeeze what you like in that space next year?"

Miki grinned. "Yes, sir, Vonison! More than enough space! Thank you! Very nice!"

"Very good then," Von said. "We'll make room, don't worry."

"I will be looking forward to it, Vonison!"

He'd been planning to ask him to knock that off, next time he did it—it sounded way too much like deer meat. But now that he'd done it again, he decided to let it pass. The guy just looked too pleased to spoil it for him.

AT THIS TIME, SANTI'S CREW would normally head north to help pick the last of the tarts up at Bridgman's near Petoskey (where the difference in latitude always put them a week behind Von), then return in a week for the start of peaches. Santi was clearly torn. He said he really needed to go with them, but the thought of leaving his daughter, Von could see on the man's hard face, was breaking his heart.

"We'll keep in touch with you up there," Von assured him. "I know Hans Bridgman. He'll put you on a phone if we need to get ahold of you. I know it's a couple hours away, but I swear, if there're any problems or *anything*, hell, one of us'll drive up and get you, if need be. And you'll be back down here in just a week, right? To start on the red havens?"

Santi looked like he was in pain. They were standing on the porch, looking out at the sunset playing across the faded sides of the little house, turning it almost pink.

"I promise her mother, *que en paz descanse,* I look after her," he said. "Is why she's always by my side."

Von touched the man on the shoulder. His shirt was soaked with sweat. "I know how you feel," he said. "But you need to keep going."

"Why?" Santi said, and the truth was, Von really didn't have an answer.

"Let's see if maybe we can come up with a plan," he said. With that, he stepped off the porch, walking off, away from the buzz and clatter of his home.

"HERE'S THE DEAL." He was addressing Santi's crew the next morning, standing on the front porch of the empty little house, right in front of Marita's half-red door. "You stay on the next week, full wages, and until we start with the red havens, you help me get this house painted." He squinted out at the gathering and this one glance told him they understood and liked the idea. "If you're a crappy painter, you scrape, clean brushes, tape windows, fix lunch, whatever—we'll find something for you to do." He explained about the scaffolding, the tarps, the regrouting. "Take your time, do not fall off the scaffolding, do not get hurt. You all know how picky Marita is, so do a good job."

They all laughed and moved in to select a job for themselves. One of them—the almost Indian-looking older man who'd carved the peach pit, clamped his hand on Von's shoulder and said, "Gracias, Don Von. Too many Fudgies up there in Petoskey, anyway. They look at us funny, the Fudgies. This is much better."

He wondered if this was how Capone felt when he set up the soup kitchens.

Later that day, Don Vanderhoof showed up, unannounced, with a flatbed of three-foot-high pepper plants, and Miki hopped up to help unload. It was Miki, too, who was prepared for the plants, who stopped them both from touching the buds. He ran back into his camper and returned with a box of disposable rubber gloves.

"The spicy hotness," he explained. "You can get it in your skin, in your eyes . . ."

"How about that," Don marveled. "Handy guy to have around, this guy."

Von said, "What—you don't have your own resident botanist? Must be rough."

Don hung around long enough to kibitz over the initial planning. He still shook his head at the whole idea, marveling at this fool move on Von's part but chuckling about it now. He also said he liked the new look of the half-painted house. "You realize," he observed, "now you've got yourself a house that's the exact color of your sweet cherries? Talk about your subliminal advertising. That can't be an accident."

Von denied it was an accident, though he'd honestly never really made the connection and he wondered if the girl had.

"Smart," Don concluded. "Folks'll be salivating, thinking about cherries a mile away. Won't even know why."

Later, before they closed up the cans of red paint for the day, Von took an old shingle and a garden stake and painted a nice little sign.

62

THE HOSPITAL'S BIMONTHLY SEPTIC TANK CLEANOUT wasn't
scheduled for another week, but Kurt Lasco ran it early. His contract
with the hospital allowed him some leeway so he could juggle other
jobs, emergencies being a major component to his line of work, but
that wasn't the reason he was doing it early. This business with
Starkey's wife had been bugging him and he kind of wanted to get the
straight scoop on her condition. It wasn't like he wanted to visit her at
the hospital, but if he happened to be out there, he might ask around a
little, make sure she was okay.

And what the hell—since he was passing vonBushberger's orchard
on the way out there, why not pull in at the stand and buy one of those
fresh wildflower bouquets they sold? They were cheap enough and he
wouldn't be paying for some unnecessary add-on like delivery. And he
wouldn't have to give them to her in person—he could just drop them
off anonymously. No doubt if Starkey knew he'd brought flowers, he'd
take it as some sort of apology, like he was wrong about the trees,
which was not how he meant it at all. After all, he might have screwed
up with the sausage gag, but that didn't make him wrong in general,
did it?

He took care of the tanks first, then cleaned himself up in the jani-
tor's room and stopped in at the nurse's station. He'd hidden the flowers in a length of PVC drainage pipe—a clean sample scrap he kept
in the back of the rig—and was waiting for a moment Jilly, the nurse
on duty, stepped away so he could leave it anonymously for Marcie
Starkey, when he noticed the visitors book and was curious to see how
many folks had stopped by. He slid it over and glanced through it,
casually, like he was bored or waiting for someone to show up to
authorize his job invoice.

The thing listed the time of the visit, beginning and end, the name of
the visitor and the name of the patient. She'd only been there a short
time, but still, there were more entries than he would have thought. For

a summer person, she must be more of a joiner. There were at least a half a dozen names there. One name leapt out at him: *DeWalt*. His ex-wife Lisa's maiden name. And not Walt DeWalt, her distant cousin of some sort who supervised the river boys. *K. DeWalt*.

It floored him. Not only was Kimmy visiting the enemy, she was going by DeWalt now? Since when, he wondered? Lasco was still her legal name.

Why does she hate me? She must hate me, he thought, and he thought about little else the whole rest of the afternoon.

KIMBERLY WAS IN HER DAD'S OFFICE, checking her e-mail. There was one from the nurse at the hospital, Jilly, warning her that her dad had been by that afternoon. Kimberly was pretty sure she was in deep shit. But she tried to remember what Reverend Gene had said about having to do what she knew was right and not worry so much about her dad being right. So maybe he'd be pissed—what would he do about it? Send her home early? Maybe. More likely, he'd just rethink having her up next year.

Well, whatever . . . Still: *make my own relationships with the world* . . . She closed her e-mail, moving ahead, logging on to Amazon to do a few searches for a possible birthday present for Reverend Gene. She had the cookbooks out, too, thinking maybe that was a way to go, because really, did she really know enough about him to figure out what he would really like? Probably not. The guy's record collection was huge and besides, baking something would be easier.

It struck her, with a small pang of guilt, that she wasn't sure she knew her own dad's birthday—March something, maybe? But then again, it wasn't part of his e-mail address like it was for Gene. *Reverend* Gene.

She had her Walkman on and was listening to one of his things she'd found at the library on CD, Mary Lou Williams playing "You're the Cream in My Coffee." Dusk had started to settle. She hadn't noticed till she got up to pee, heading for the little half-bath jammed in between the office and the kitchen. No lights were on yet. Just then, her dad stepped into the kitchen and picked up the cordless. He had a scrap of paper in his hand and referred to it as he punched in the numbers. He didn't seem to notice her as he moved into the living room.

It was the first she knew he was home. The time had gotten away from her and she hadn't heard him pull in thanks to her Walkman. She turned it off now and stood motionless in the shadows, listening.

Leaning flat against the wall, she watched as he settled down into the creaky leather easy chair, his back to her. He let out a deep, uneasy sigh and waited while it rang. Kimberly waited, too, wondering if maybe he was calling her mom. But no—certainly he knew their number by heart. It had to be something else.

And then her dad spoke. "Scott? Did I wake you? . . . It's Kurt Lasco. Listen, I know you've got a lot bigger stuff going on over there now, but this business with the trees— Look, you don't need to drag me into court. It's not necessary. I'll get some new ones in, no problem . . . No, really. Could you give me maybe a week—is that gonna be soon enough . . . ?"

She crept closer, sliding her socks along the linoleum till she was standing in the dark kitchen, just a few feet away.

"Now, also? The wood? That's really yours, if you want it. It really ought to dry for another year before you try to burn it, but . . . Well, think about it. Like I say, it needs to sit and dry anyway . . . Yeah . . . Okay . . . Yeah, that would be good. We should do that. Kimmy's gonna be here a little while longer—let's plan on that . . . Listen, how's your wife doing anyway? . . . Oh, that's great, that's really good. We were wondering about that . . ."

After he said goodbye and hung up, he sat there with his hand still on the phone, exhaling a big puff of air. He looked a little scared. Even from that angle, just the back of his head and a little of the side, she thought she could tell. She'd never seen him like this. It had been a whole summer of seeing him in ways she never had before, but at least for this moment, she felt proud of him.

I could tiptoe away, she thought. We can just keep everything the way it is. He doesn't have to know I'm here.

But I am here, she thought, and she decided to show herself, stepping out into the doorway, into the light. He looked up, distracted, and it was clear he was surprised to see her. He just sat there, childlike in the oversized chair, staring back at her silently. He looked like he'd been shot or something, like he was paralyzed. She stepped over to the edge of his chair and leaned in to half-hug him, sliding her arm along his shoulder in an awkward little pat. "How much is all this going to cost?"

"It'll cost what it'll cost," he said, not annoyed, just matter-of-fact. Then he caught her eye and put on a smile that looked only a little manufactured and pulled her closer, nuzzling into her shoulder, kissing her on the material of her shirt, the gray lightweight plaid one she'd lifted from Reverend Gene. "Don't worry," he said. "Just means I'll need to clean out that many more tanks. And that's one good thing about this business. It's like being an undertaker, a CPA, anything like that. There is no end to the amount of shit in life."

She leaned against him more, till she was half-sitting on his leg. She put her head in the crook of his neck and smelled that old dad smell that was always there. They stayed like that for a long while, staring out into the blank descent of night, the featureless view through the row of open windows, and she didn't want to let go.

63

IT WAS GENE'S TURN to stand in that Sunday. When Mrs. Hiram Henderhoch called him to ask for the title of his sermon, so she could put it in the program and on the message sign out front of the church, he told her "The Devil in the Box."

There was a pause. "Sounds a little Baptist." He could hear her frowning. "The Devil and all . . ."

"Not really," he said. "It's a message for everybody." He didn't tell her it was about censorship, pornography and the like. He didn't tell her, *Just put down "Internet Porn."*

That Sunday, when he took to the pulpit, he eased into it, first spending about ten minutes laying out what constituted "the box"—

the various modern-day media—and then danced, lightly, around the implications of what deviltries could be uncovered there, and cited law-suits and news stories where the evil influence of these media were declared the cause of trouble, the thing to blame.

From there, he knew what they were expecting. Some sort of Pandora's box paradigm, chagrined bemoaning, a *what hath man wrought?* plea for the simpler things of a simpler time. But that was not where he was heading.

"The fact is," he admitted, "there is no 'Devil in the box.' It only contains those things that we put there ourselves. If we can find it on the Internet, on TV, in movies, on the cable, in music, it's because we put it there. Look to yourself, not to the Devil."

Maybe that much would have been acceptable—wrapping it up, going to the prayer, stopping it there. Only he didn't stop there. Con-crete examples were always the stock of his sermons—Dr. Getner had taught him that, decades ago. Examples were what kept an audience. Examples made the snoozers stay focused; pay attention; stop thinking about the television ballgame later that afternoon; stop studying the curls at the nape of the neck of their neighbor's wife, seated in front of them; stop wondering if they were having ham for dinner. And the more memorable the example, the better. And so he asked the congre-gation to take up their Bibles and look at Ezekiel, chapter twenty-three, verses seventeen through twenty-one.

Perhaps it was ill-conceived. After all, he wasn't really at the top of his game anymore. He needed practice. He missed his wife. He'd pos-sibly lost a part of his mind when he lost her. He wasn't supposed to be counted on for this sort of thing anymore. He was supposed to be free.

"'For she lusted for her paramours,'" he read, "'whose flesh is like the flesh of donkeys, and whose issue is like the issue of horses. Thus you called to remembrance the lewdness of your youth, when the Egyptians pressed your bosom because of your youthful bosom.'" He closed his Bible, smiled out at his flock. The ones who seemed to be paying attention looked a little perplexed now, as if he'd derailed, jumped from one sermon to another; as if he were showing signs of dementia. The rest looked blank-faced, still probably thinking about those issues of televised sports and ham and not understanding that he'd made an apparent hard left turn.

"'*Whose flesh is like the flesh of donkeys,*'" he repeated. "Which means, essentially, 'donkey dick.'"

Now they were paying attention.

"I don't mean to shock, but that's what it means. Examine it again and you'll see that there's really no other way to interpret it."

The sanctuary crackled with the sound of pages turning—voices murmuring in the pews with whispered requests for the chapter and verse again—as they snatched up the Bibles they'd just put away and thumbed their way back to the quotation.

"Of course, that's only one example. Many of you know of others. The point is: even in the Bible, you'll find some pretty hot stuff. Does that make the Bible bad? Of course not. But some of the Bible, you may say, is perhaps not appropriate for all readers. So . . . should we petition the government to install some sort of microchip in every copy of the Bible that would restrict the reading of Ezekiel 23? Maybe we should, because the minor or child or even an adult—some unprepared, simple soul for whom that passage is 'inappropriate'—might react negatively. It might stir them up. Do we blame the Bible if at some time, somewhere, an individual may find himself or herself fixated on the sex organs of livestock? Is that the fault of the Bible—or even of Ezekiel? Do we say then that there is a Devil in the Bible? Of course not."

As surprised as he knew they were by this sermon, it couldn't compare to how strange he felt; what it felt like to stand in the pulpit saying these things. It felt like a completely different event than the approximately sixteen hundred sermons he'd delivered there in the past. Past sermons now all seemed like something closer to reciting an English thesis back in high school or wasting his time on the debating team. Comparing them to this thing that was coming out of him today was like comparing a medical chart of the eyeball and the tear ducts to the act of crying yourself to sleep. Or the legal terms of a marriage contract compared to that semi-conscious lovemaking that occurs only after years of spooning; when you wake, gasping, amazed, to realize you're joined.

"These things," he went on, "—these 'unsavory elements,' if you will—are included because they are part of life. They come along as a package deal. Gratis. No extra charge. And if we attempt to exclude these things, weed them out, sanitize content, hide from what we find troubling and possibly affecting (which is even more troubling, oftentimes), then we are denying part of life. And so we include it all and we must face it all and not blame and point fingers or we are blaming life. It *is* the message, not the medium. Not the box it came in. We must take responsibility for how we feel when we come across pornography on the computer and when our toe starts tapping to that rapper's string of vulgarities and even when Ezekiel starts talking about donkey dick . . . Let us pray."

Not an hour later, during the Coffee Chat—that time Mary herself had instituted years ago, during which the congregation was encouraged to linger and mingle in the social hall and talk in a more casual forum—the board of trustees snuck into the kitchen and closed the bifold shutters along the serving windows for a hastily assembled confab.

His help with the interim sermons, he was informed the next day, would no longer be required.

THAT NIGHT, HE WENT ONLINE and checked the First Pres Web site. There was no mention of the sermon he'd delivered that morning, nor was there any announcement that the hiring committee had filled the position. But there was one obvious change: the entire *VOTE* section had been removed and there was no explanation.

He wasn't sure what it meant, but the church, at least at present, appeared no longer interested in opinions on what to do with the parsonage. Either they'd already come to a decision, or there was something in that section they no longer wanted to flaunt, some shady aspect perhaps. Or maybe he'd imagined the thing.

Either way, it was troubling and he stared at the screen, the half-tone photo of the church steeple and the veterans memorial maple fanned out behind it, and he wondered how he could make it come back the way it was. There had to be a way.

64

THE GIRL WAS IN THE DEN WITH HIM, taking command of his computer. She was trying to help him find the earlier version of the church Web site. She wasn't sure it was possible. "Did you bookmark it? Did you save it?"

He wasn't sure if he'd saved it. He wasn't sure he remembered that lesson or if they'd even covered that.

"There's a chance it's still in your history . . ."

He hadn't even known he had a "history" or what it was. He was somewhat preoccupied, wondering if she'd gotten wind of his "donkey dick" sermon. He couldn't imagine it had escaped her, working at the fudge shop.

Leaning closer to the screen, she said, "Let's see what you've got here . . ." and began scrolling down, squinting at it. Gene squinted, too, and saw, finally, what was there.

He couldn't breathe. There, on the left side of the screen, was a whole list of Web sites and, immediately, several whose names he'd never noticed initially, popped out at him as if in neon—things like *amateurteen.com, facialgirls09.jpg, hotcmsk27.mpg, jizz4u13.jpg, nas-t.com, teenguzzlers05jpg, cumonher18.mpg, cummylips80.jpg.* He clenched his jaw, afraid his lip might quiver, a whimper might erupt from deep inside him, from his heart. Lord forgive me, he prayed, silently. This young woman may not.

He held his seat, waiting for it, expecting her to snarl at him, call him a disgusting pig, scream, *Don't ever talk to me again!* or at least wrinkle up her nose with an *ewwww, grooooss.* At least quietly gather her books and announce, muttering toward the floor, unable to look at him anymore, *I gotta go . . .* Either way, make a dash for the door.

But no dashes were made. She stopped scrolling. Her eyes flicked down the column. If she moved at all, it was a slight tucking in of her lip, folding the bottom corner under her overbite—an expression of concentration he'd seen her make many times before. Then her finger was back at the down arrow, moving on. Casually, she said, "It's always awful how you get swamped with all this junk you don't even want to look at . . . You must hate it . . . Stuff arrives in attachments, you don't even know it's there . . ."

He could tell she didn't believe that. Not for a minute. She was being so lovely about it. He couldn't get over the degree of poise. *Class,* they used to call it—a word that failed these days, that created the opposite impression the instant you used it. She had a soul that had nothing to do with her age and he thought, Why did she have to come along now, at my age, at her age?

He wouldn't have had such composure when he was that young. He tried to imagine the situation reversed, the sixteen-year-old Eugenie Reecher in 1949 Tecumseh, Michigan, helping the Widow McDonough with some work around her house. Maybe painting her bedroom, finding a device even, something as innocuous as a vibrator—a "marital aid" for someone no longer married. No, he would've flown out of there before the screen door slammed. The stepladder would topple, the cans would remain open, the paint ruined, growing a layer of skin. And he'd tell. Boy, would he tell. He'd regale his friends with horror tales of the sick old lady and her deviant doodads. He would be struck by a serious, perhaps lifelong-debilitating case of the heebie-jeebies. Very possibly, it would affect him for life.

No, he wouldn't have had an ounce of the self-possession this girl had. Perhaps, he thought, I still don't. When she spoke again, it was just as friendly as ever. "I'll have to show you how to save important sites . . . My fault, really . . ." Watching her tap her way down the towering column of suspicious-sounding jpegs, showing not even a flicker of disdain, he realized, *It's not only our ages that's the barrier between us. The barrier is that she's far too good a person for me.*

THREE DAYS LATER, IT WAS HIS BIRTHDAY. Other than two phone calls—a screaming serenade over the speakerphone from Ben and the kids and another aborted attempt at "Happy Birthday" half-sung by his daughter, drowned out by her accompanying dogs—it was like any other day. No cards arrived in the mail—which was expected: both Ben and Abbey admitted they had a slow start this year, that they might be a few days late. And he was okay with this. There didn't seem to be much point in it this year. It was just Thursday, really, a plain old Thursday, and so, as the merest self-indulgence as the birthday boy, he put on his favorite old Abbey Lincoln record and moved the needle to "Thursday's Child."

And then the girl arrived, balancing a large Tupperware cake box. She was beaming as she flicked off the hi-fi, practically bouncing through to the kitchen, and referred to him excitedly as "Birthday Boy."

He was stunned. And *positive* he hadn't even mentioned it.

"That site you showed me," she said. "The church's Web site? You look under the congregation directory and it lists everyone's birthday. It's all there. At first, I thought they had it wrong, 'cause I always thought the numbers in your e-mail address were your birthdate."

"No," he said. "That's something else . . ." He couldn't tell her it was the date he'd first made love to Mary. It was coming up, actually— the anniversary of that crazy night on the beach.

And he thought that, if this was true about the church Web site, then it was sort of surprising to him that none of those busybodies had used the excuse to come by today. Of course, he reasoned, they'd already poked around not too long ago. Still, he had to wonder if they were staying away because they were up to something; had something in the works—plans for the parsonage and plans for getting him out. Or maybe they were afraid of him now, since his last sermon.

But none of that mattered today because it was his birthday and here, just when he thought this would be the first birthday since Ike was in office that he didn't celebrate with a beautiful woman, with Mary, here was this lovely girl who smelled like a fudge shop, arriving with Tupperware and baked goods and a sugar-induced grin.

Tupperware had become a common sight on his counter. He'd seen too many of those cake boxes since Mary passed. Only this one did not contain a rubbery lasagna or apricot bread pudding, but a dozen cupcakes with white frosting and those little shiny silver balls. "My goodness," he said. "You need to tell me when *your* birthday is . . ." But it was overwhelming and he wasn't sure he could ever give her anything that would top this.

She poked two little candles in two of the cupcakes, lit them and serenaded him with a shy "Happy Birthday," speeding up with each new line, racing for the finish. He blew them out with one puff. She clapped and patted him on the back and removed the smoking candles. As she handed him a cupcake on a paper napkin printed with Mrs. Hersha's T.G.I.Fudge logo, she asked if he'd made a wish.

"Oh," he said, "I never really do that. I just blow out the candles."

"In my family," she said, "you get a birthday kiss."

They ate their cupcakes, standing over the cake box, and he found himself watching her eat, her tongue darting out to clean her lips of the frosting. Inside his head, he screamed, *What did she say?*

She announced she was having seconds and pressed another to her mouth. His hand came up to his stomach and he made himself wince. It was time to fake a stomachache and get the hell out of there and think. Excusing himself, he retreated to the hall bathroom, locked the door and examined himself in the mirror, making his mouth silently form the words from James 1:12: *Blessed is the man who endures temptation; for when he has been approved, he will receive the crown of life which the Lord has promised to those who love him . . .*

She's just talking, he told himself. Just telling you about her family, her traditions. That's all. Maybe wanting to open up about her feelings about the divorce.

No, he decided. That wasn't even it. She's not trying to talk about her family situation. But neither was she asking to be kissed. No sir. It was just conversation, small talk.

I have too much time on my hands, he concluded. I need my job back. I need my wife. A single yelp slipped out of him. He was afraid he might launch into sobbing. He pulled one of the guest hand towels off the rack and bit the corner of it, not wanting her to hear. He would just stay in there as long as it took to control himself.

The towel smelled differently than he remembered. She was using a different brand of detergent than Mary used to use.

It was taking him more time to get himself together than he would have preferred, because eventually there was a tentative knock.

"Are you okay?"

Taking a deep breath, he unlocked the door. He waited a moment, then stepped out.

"Listen," she said, "if I upset you, I'm really sorry. But just tell me. Did I embarrass you or do something wrong or . . . ?"

"No! Hon! Child! No!" And then the tears came, his vision wobbled from the welling up and she looked even more concerned at the sight. This was not going well at all. "The cupcakes were wonderful. I just . . . I guess I must be allergic to the little metal balls or something . . ." He smiled and choked out a laugh and wiped at his eyes, wishing he wasn't such a foolish clod.

She reached out and touched his arm, stroked it, smiling and frowning at the same time, so sympathetic and adorable. "I'm so sorry," she said. "I just wanted to give you something. I should have thought it out better. I just put those on there 'cause of the thing you said—you know . . ." She pointed to her belly.

He didn't get it. She flipped up her blouse a matter of inches, revealing her belly button and that little silver ball.

At that moment, he told the Lord he would do nothing to harm this girl. Even if it meant putting himself in jeopardy. He vowed he would rather die or go to jail than harm her just because he was starving for some kind of connection.

65

JANEY WAS OUT OF UNIFORM, raising eyebrows throughout the sumac pop gathering at Noah's Ark. Even Roger, her date for the evening, had commented. "Never seen you like this, Struska. Man." Coming from the Coach, it was as close to *You're gorgeous* as she could imagine, though she wasn't sure she warranted even his meager compliment.

It was a supposedly simple summer dress, white with tiny holes along the hem. Both Della and Stella at Togs N' Clogs had assured her it looked "elegant" and "lovely" and "just dear" on her, but she had to question their sincerity, considering they carried only two other options in her size. But what did she know? She never bought dresses. In fact, it was such an odd purchase for her, she knew for a fact that news of it must have traveled around town—farther, even: as far as the

Silver Maples retirement community outside town, because two days after she bought it, Brenda vonBushberger pulled up in front of the sheriff's office in a sprayer truck and ran in with a handknit shawl to match, a thank-you gift, she said, from her Aunt Sadie, for helping with the burial problem.

The whole thing was just so awfully femmy. She wasn't used to this drape-y feeling. It felt like they were going to come in and paint and they'd covered her along with the furniture. "It feels huge," she muttered in response to the compliment, readjusting the strange open neck along her shoulders and trying to hide more under the shawl. "It feels like someone's going to yank it away with a 'Ta-daaah!' and there will magically be a full place setting of silverware remaining on me."

They were down on Noah Yoder's private beach, walking along the crush of waves as the sun made its last tangerine glimmers somewhere over the unseeable Wisconsin. She had her new white sandals in her hand. It seemed dumb that they'd called them sandals back at the store, because now, faced with actual sand, they seemed about as functional as paper shower caps.

As much as she wanted to be up at the house when—or *if*—David Letterman made his rumored appearance, she'd relented and slipped away with the Coach to investigate the billionaire's beach. Logically, she knew that there'd be such a hubbub when Letterman arrived, they'd certainly hear it down on the beach and know to return to the house. Plus, she was reluctant to admit why she'd insisted they attend such an event. And on their first sort-of date. But then he asked, directly, actually touching her, reaching out and touching her arm where it felt so exposed in this girly getup. "Hey," he said. "Want to tell me what we're doing here?"

At first, she didn't understand what he was asking. It sounded like he wanted her to state her intentions with him or something; put a nametag on their socializing. "Well, I thought we were just . . . hanging out . . . I mean, I always thought you were cool, way back and all . . ."

He smiled that rare smile and it felt like a generous gesture. "I don't mean you and me. I mean the location. We were having such a great time at dinner . . ."

It was true. They'd rushed away from a great table out at the Log Jam, where they'd wolfed down a delicious buffalo meatloaf and she'd barely finished her Cosmo—she'd thought it would be sophisticated but found it alarmingly pink—and he'd been telling her an actual personal story, opening up: something about the Korean-made motorbikes in Nam.

So she told him the whole thing: the rumors about Letterman summering in the area; her secret attempts to locate him; her long-standing dream of writing comedy for him; how she hoped to somehow connect with him, get him laughing and how *boom!* he'd offer her a job.

"So you'd leave? Move to New York?"

It was surprising that this was his first reaction, rather than focusing on the issue of her being kind of nuts and stalky, chasing a phantom talk show host all summer, with nothing more to go on than hearsay. Instead, Roger just seemed interested in the logistics.

"I know it's great here and all . . ." she said. "Weneshkeen's great . . ."

"Great?" He chuckled. "I wouldn't go that far."

"But . . . don't you ever wish things would change a little? At least some of it?"

"Never," he said. "None of it. And plenty of it *is* changing." He raised his hand, gesturing toward the world behind her left shoulder, which she took to mean Noah's Ark back behind her up on the ridge.

She said, "I guess we're opposites, you and me."

"No we're not. You're just . . . looking at things lately. Making decisions, not just taking it as it comes. That's good. That's healthy. But David Letterman . . . ?"

"It's dumb, I know. He'd never in a million years . . ."

"Well, have you seen him around?"

She bit her lip. "That doesn't mean anything. I've been hearing things. A lot of things. He's just a very private person. Anyway . . ."

There was a long pause between them, injected by a burst of chatter from up at the house. Roy Kunk, she bet—she'd heard him drunk enough times to know that voice.

"So," she said finally, ". . . what do you think of all that, what I just said?"

He didn't answer but stepped away, facing the darkening lake. "That depends. You want my response as your friend and former coach or as someone maybe trying to get in your pants?"

She couldn't believe he'd just said that. She had to bite her lip again to keep from grinning. "The former." There was a flicker of something on his face—disappointment, maybe—so she added, "Which is probably an easier way to get in my pants—being straight with me."

He took a deep breath. "Let me ask you this first: who's the best swimmer you know around here?"

"Well, you definitely would be one of them. Obviously."

"Okay. Did I tell you I'm thinking about training for the next Olympics, going to the tryouts?"

"How old are you?"

He didn't answer. "See what I'm saying? I don't like being the bubble-burster here, Janey, but . . ." He didn't finish the sentence, but he didn't have to. She was pretty sure she knew what he meant: sure, she was funny, but moving-to-New-York funny, that was a whole different level of funny. And you had to be a kid, a fetus, to write for TV. That's what he was saying.

"Besides," he said, "the fact is, Janey Struska, you would be a great disappointment to this town if you left. You would."

"Yeah, yeah," she said. "I serve the community . . ."

He sounded a little impatient. "Yeah. You do. In ways that Hatchet-face doesn't begin to understand. And if you want to write or be funny, great—tell Glenn Meeker you want to do a humor column or something."

The second he said it, she knew it wasn't a bad idea. Glenn would welcome having a little less space to fill in the *Identifier* every week.

"You get in there . . . you hone your skills . . ." He sounded like the coach again, preaching practice, practice, practice and doing it the hard-earned way. "Only, be sure he runs your picture next to your byline. That's key."

"Why is *that* key?" She was starting to giggle—with the excitement of the idea; at her old swim coach using the term *byline* like he was Jimmy Olsen, cub reporter.

She could hear in his voice the sly smile he was now fighting to contain. "Free publicity, Struska. For the next election, maybe?"

It really made sense. It would certainly make for an amusing hobby for a while—she could have a ball poking fun at whatever local issues were bugging her, maybe even give her boss Hatchert a gentle crack in the ass every once in a while . . . And then she would have more options, too: she'd gain a little real-world experience writing humor, at least semi-professionally, and if she then decided not to pursue that any further, if she decided to run against him, she'd have a public forum in the paper on a regular basis. Who'd stand a chance against that?

Roger kept checking his watch and squinting out at the darkness over the lake. "People here know you, Janey, and they like you."

"Well," she said. "That's definitely a lot to think about." Which it was, but she wanted to put it aside and think about it later. It was a lot of tough love and straight-shooting and coachlike mentoring and she would much rather get back to the part about his maybe trying to get in her pants.

66

HE TOOK HER TO DINNER out at the Log Jam and wore a blazer he didn't recall owning—a telltale sign, he thought, that this was now officially a date. Then they went to this thing she'd been invited to out at Noah's Ark—some sort of presentation and tasting party for potential investors in a new soft drink. The house and the people were horrible, but it was kind of interesting—he couldn't imagine ever having another reason to set foot in the place. Plus, it gave him a crowd of witnesses to his alibi. But as soon as it was clear that some person Janey was looking for wasn't showing, she seemed less interested in the whole thing and suggested they go for a walk down along the billionaire's beach. Roger was glad enough to get out of there but it made him a little nervous, abandoning all these witnesses.

He watched as she slipped off her dressy white sandals to negotiate the winding stairway—not a very well-practiced maneuver, it seemed, but it was still nice to see her attempting something so feminine. He didn't think he'd ever seen her so dolled up. She looked great. He wasn't sure he made that clear, but she did. Womanly. Not like a little breakable girl, like you saw on TV, but strong and soft, like the women he'd known growing up on his side of the lake.

It made it a tough balance: he wanted to be focused and connect with her, but he also had to keep his wits about him; stay aware of the other thing that was happening that night.

He decided that maybe this beach stroll hadn't been such a bad move. It would firmly establish his presence on Lake Michigan, which was clearly not Meenigeesis. In the company of a member of the police force who would vouch for him. Still, it would have been better to be either inside, up at the party, or back at the Log Jam, surrounded by diners.

She was barefoot now, walking beside him in the sand. It felt odd, strolling along the beach with no real purpose, but he supposed this kind of thing was expected, in order for their evening to qualify as a date. Besides, he still had another hour to kill, just to be safe.

The key, he thought, is the leisurely shuffle. He really didn't have that hands-in-the-pockets shuffle down. Which is maybe why he didn't normally go on a lot of dates.

He checked his dive watch—2230. Ten-thirty. If it was going down, it was going down soon. He wished he could be there for that one, but he would have to settle for imagining it: the initial weirdness of the wind, then the *chocka-chocka*, the treetops dancing, the spot cutting on suddenly, a beam of light from on high as they drop the harness and one man rappels and secures the grab, cinches the harness, and then the pull-away, the slight reluctant give of the rope, the chopper straining slightly but pulling, and the lake releasing it finally, the jetski up and streaming water, spinning slowly in the white light like a goddamn disco ball. Probably by then, the owners would be up and outside, deck doors thrown wide, hands held against the blinding light, squinting as it all goes bye-bye. Probably, they'd swear it was a UFO.

He tried to act normal, do the date talk. When he asked why this party, she told him this whole spiel about some crazy idea she had that David Letterman was in town and how she wanted to run off to New

York and become some sort of literary wit or maybe more like Sally Rogers from *The Dick Van Dyke Show* and let the new guy, the interim sheriff, just do whatever the hell he wanted. He tried to give her his honest reaction to all that and he let something crude slip about wanting to jump her bones or something. *That* seemed really inappropriate, plus he felt like he was picking on her a little, and so he changed the subject, pointing out at the now dark horizon of Lake Michigan, in the safe direction, to the southwest, the compass point that would not include the flight path of Colonel Landry's boys. "Hey," he said, "was that a meteor?"

"Now *you're* seeing lights in the sky?" she teased, but looked and then he looked again, higher, tipping his head back further. It seemed so empty up there and yet so full at the same time and he wondered if he had in fact seen something. Maybe there was something to see if he just let down his guard a little.

He thought of his old girlfriend Crystal again and resisted the urge to slide his hand up and protect his jugular. "Hey," he said. "Your turn to pick me apart: honestly, is *crusted* a word you'd use to describe me?" He felt genuine surprise at the dumb words gushing forth. He really was awfully poor at this whole social conversation thing.

She tipped her head down suddenly, as if shy, and pulled at something in her hair. "You're not that crusty. No. You're really holding up for— I mean, you're not *that* old. Jeez. Come on."

It wasn't what he meant. He meant *hardened,* not *old.* But he let it lie there. Her version suited things better. Did he really want to get into a whole discussion of vulnerability with Janey Struska, for Christ's sake? She punched him lightly on the shoulder, palsy, recovering from some stumble he didn't quite understand, and turned as if to continue.

He stepped forward to follow and, somehow, they were kissing. It just happened. He'd thought they were moving on, but she'd stopped to add something, turning, and he tasted her black hair as it brushed across his lips and they were kissing. As soon as he realized what was happening, he stopped.

"Coach . . ." she said, still very close, a muttering against his mouth, and kissed him again.

They stood there kissing, very gently, his fingers tentative at her sides, cautious, as he listened for sounds in the distance. Maybe he was imagining it, but he thought he heard some kind of *whumpa-whumpa-whumpa* over to the east, toward the other lake. It had to be to the east, inland. It couldn't possibly be his pulse, his heartbeat. Not him.

67

THE "SECOND DEBUT" of Noah's new soft drink was equally disappointing yet came with its own special flavor of disappointment. Whereas last time, his guests seemed to be ignoring the purpose of the gathering, acting as if less was going on than announced, that it was just a friendly party, this time, his guests seemed to be waiting for something more to happen. He couldn't help but notice the way several of them glanced up expectantly at the clang of the spiral staircase whenever one of the girls from the caterer appeared on it with a replenished tray of "aps," which they took and ate looking disappointed.

At one point, things turned ugly. The hardware store guy—Roy Kunk, he later found out the guy's name was, not even the one he'd invited, the owner of McCreery's, but the guy's brother-in-law in his stead—seemed at first to be hitting on Deery Lime, leaning against the wall next to her, trying to monopolize her, and Noah did notice the way Tony squinted and scowled and moved serpentine through the crowd, trying to get to her. Deery was more than capable, of course, and must have inserted something to set the conversation back on track, toward the subject of investment, because Kunk pulled back dramatically, shaking his head, mouth open as if slapped, grinning pumpkinishly, and it was clear now that he was pretty drunk. "You want *us* to give *him* money for this stuff? Really? You got some balls, lady. What's so wrong with the kid billionaire's money, he needs ours? You gotta be shitting me, Dolly or whatever the hell your name is . . ." And the room seemed to darken and those around him turned in annoyance and it felt to

Noah as if they weren't just annoyed with the drunk but maybe with the matter he had bellowed. And he wondered if maybe this evening wasn't one more horrible mistake in an ever-spiraling string.

By now, his financial adviser had reached the man and had a hand on his elbow. Deery turned immediately, beaming, to the nearest guest on her other side, clearly relieved. Kunk yanked back, starting to leave but resistant to being led. Tony tailed him as he reeled toward the nearest open glass door. Noah glanced around for the deputy sheriff, but she must have been outside or something. Perhaps she'd left already. She seemed to be on a date. He'd only put her on the list as a nice gesture because he'd first heard of sumac lemonade from her, not because she would have any money to invest, and she'd dragged someone else along to mooch up the snacks.

Here this was supposed to be for people who would invest and it had turned instead into a spectacle to be crashed, into Sodapoplooza, with all the wrong people attending, invitations being borrowed or ignored or passed around. Last time, his guests made him feel like they were just there to see him, that they didn't care about the pop. Now they made him feel like they didn't even care if *he* was there.

As Kunk passed the bar, almost to the door, he either accidentally or intentionally—it wasn't clear from where Noah stood, Gatsby-like, midway up the nearest spiral staircase—knocked over the photo of David Letterman displayed on the bar, and the glass frame broke on the floor.

After that, the crowd pretty much thinned out.

As soon as the last guest left, Deery pawed through the response cards, separating them into two stacks. Where it said *Would you be interested in investing in Sumac Lemonade?* half the cards had the No box checked, but they'd scrawled in an addendum: *No thank you, but it was very nice,* and the other half wrote *No thank you, but we'd love to have you over to our place sometime for something out on the grill. Don't be a stranger.* Nobody marked yes.

"I don't get it," he said. "This is the local drink." He knew it wasn't truly the local drink—it was merely a traditional novelty, tolerated once a year—but still. "Don't they have any civic pride? What the hell's wrong with them?"

"Do you know what circus people call local townspeople?" Tony asked. He sounded a little drunk. "*Clems*. Like they're all named Clem."

Deery glanced at Tony before speaking. She looked like someone trying to get her story straight. "They were mostly very polite on the cards, but frankly, I think a lot of them were kind of irked that *he* wasn't here? Maybe even came just to meet him."

"What? *Who* him?"

"Letterman."

Oh God, he thought. "*David* Letterman? They thought he was going to be *here* here? At my house?"

Tony jerked his thumb in an easterly direction. "That Mrs. Self told me in the driveway just now. Very disappointed. Said she even had a stupid pet trick she wanted to show him. Something with an enlarged sinus cavity or something. I did *not* pursue."

"Did you *tell* them David Letterman would be here?"

"Absolutely not. They didn't hear it from me." Tony was prying off his shoes, getting comfortable on the couch across from the bar, a solid chrome couch in the shape of a bear, padded with only small paw-shaped pillows in a few key spots, made of actual grizzly bear fur. It cost, if he remembered right, probably ten times the cost of an actual live bear. "But there's been stuff going around. People say he's buying some big place out here, so I guess it made sense. Hell, I even heard something myself. About him attending, I mean."

"*You* thought David Letterman was going to be here." Even as Noah said it, a small part of him had to admit he'd seen this glitch as a possibility and knew he himself was to blame. "Here tonight. That he was interested in investing in sumac lemonade?"

Tony shrugged. "I thought maybe you had something last-minute up your sleeve. A surprise, maybe." He shrugged again, as if to say, *Don't look at me like I'm a moron,* and said, "I heard rumors. I didn't start them, I just—" With his shoe, he gestured toward the bar. Specifically, the smashed Letterman photo, now lying flat in a pinkish puddle—probably the prototype pop. "You have an autographed photo of the guy, Yo. It's out where everyone can see! Come on!"

Still . . . Noah thought. Couldn't people ever get anything right? The Letterman rumor was meant, of course, to help him possibly sell the *house,* not the sumac lemonade. Idiots! What was the point of bothering trying to deceive the public when they didn't even listen?

"It wasn't just Letterman not being here," Deery said quietly, clearing her throat, raising her chin. "I picked up another vibe from the guests? There seems to be a pre-existing resentment toward you and your wealth and this house, building it here? Yes? Well, the sense I got, the talk I overheard, for *some,* that resentment was somewhat exacerbated tonight. There was a perception that you were rubbing your wealth in their faces—'flaunting' it, was the word I heard—and then asking them to help finance your new product. And then also, not producing Letterman. That didn't help. For *some,* this was the takeway— the wealth-flaunting thing. I don't know how the numbers break down. But that angry drunk asshole who called me Dolly? He wasn't exactly alone."

This was terrible. After he spent all this money on entertaining, he'd at least expected it would raise his standing with the locals; spread the goodwill. "They hate me even more now."

"We don't really have hard data on that yet," she said, moving over to join Tony and sitting on the edge of the bear couch.

"So this whole get-together—pretty much the opposite of the desired result, you're telling me?"

Tony shrugged. "You're disappointed, sure, but—"

"More like I'm *nervous.* Worried. Shouldn't I be?"

"But this isn't really your kind of thing anyway, is it? This pop thing, scraping up backers . . ." Tony said it like he was talking about losing one small softball game; like a guy who had other things on his mind that night, like getting laid.

"*Some*thing's got to be my thing again, *soon,* or . . ." He didn't need to spell it out. Tony knew more about that fact than he did. This wasn't some whim he'd tried just for kicks but didn't have a knack for. This wasn't Malcolm Forbes fiddling with Harleys and hot air balloons. He was in a goddamn financial tailspin here.

"It's just this economy," Tony said. "Things have got to bounce back, Yo. You watch: fourth quarter of 2001's gonna be great. We'll just have to ride it out." Tony was shifting lengthwise, actually getting comfortable, his stockinged feet pressing, playfully, against Deery's hip.

They both seemed so relaxed, like they genuinely enjoyed lounging on that awkward piece of furniture.

Earlier that evening, though the room had been packed, no one sat on the bear couch; they stood around it, commenting on it and studying it from all angles, as if it were sculpture. He wished now he'd never bought it. He wondered what he'd paid for it exactly and why. Was Tony with him at the time? Maybe Tony had talked him into it, or at least agreed it was a nice couch. He wondered what kind of couches the people tonight had in their homes—the kind you get at the Salvation Army for fifty dollars or from some dead aunt and there's a small dog bite or stain, but you cover it with a well-placed afghan and it never gets thrown away, just demoted, down to the rec room, out to the garage, off to the frat house. The kind of couch you can collapse on when things are bad and doze off and forget all your problems for a time. He'd give a lot to have one of those fifty-dollar dog-bitten couches—and the kind of frank, honest, nonsycophantic conversations people used to have with him on such couches—and he had a strong feeling he soon would.

He left Tony and his marketing genius alone now to do, on his ridiculously impractical couch, whatever it was they were starting up or covering up—if they could get it on on that thing, more power to them—and he took the spiral stairs up to the tower and looked out at the last little lights down in the village, the bars still open and buzzing as if it were a tiny Fisher-Price town, a toy town. And he decided he should start going to those bars. Not for any great financial scheme, not to schmooze and get backing for sumac lemonade, just to hang out with the locals. If he was going to be a pauper, go bankrupt, he might as well do it in a cheerier setting, surrounded by people, normal folk like the one he was about to become. One of the regulars. Tomorrow night he'd start. He probably couldn't blend in or meet anyone—probably no one would even talk to him—but he'd at least give it an honest try.

68

THIS TIME, SEVERAL WITNESSES CAME FORWARD. They'd seen lights in the sky and heard a whirring sound. This was right over Meenigeesis. People came out of their cottages. Dogs were barking. Treetops shimmied. They saw the water ripple, it came down so low. And a beam of light shafted down, near the old Willoughby place, right at the end of the dock and—here was the part they *insisted* was true—it lifted up the jet-ski there. Up into the *sky*. And then the big white light was gone, as if it had been switched off, leaving just the tiny blinking lights, and the sound faded away along with those little lights—like running lights of some kind—and it banked to the north and disappeared.

The sheriff insisted it was a helicopter. What he wanted to know, from each witness, was if they saw the craft itself, or did they just see lights. Unfortunately, everyone agreed that it was too hard to see much of anything with that blinding beam of light shafting down like a ray gun. The one witness who remembered getting a glimpse of the dark shape behind the lights was pretty certain it wasn't a helicopter: "Helicopters are squat and round and bubbly, right? This seemed long and cigar-shaped, what I saw."

The younger witnesses seemed to really want it to be a UFO. Hatchert just fixed these kids with a severe look. "You think some superior life-form wants to study our jet-skis now? That it? They've moved on from Florida fishermen and Montana cattle?"

All this was being reported to Roger by Janey, back in uniform and leaning against her cruiser in front of his house, shaded from the noon-hour sun by Grandma Oshka's beech tree. She wasn't asking him any questions, he noticed, just smirking a little, telling him of the progress her boss was making—or *not* making—with his neighbors. Roger had been watching him all morning, working his way around the lake, and even from a distance, through his field glasses, the guy's ever-reddening face made it clear his investigation was getting nowhere. He had nothing on him.

"Maybe it *was* a UFO," Roger said. "Maybe they're going to give it an anal probe. I know *I* would. Seems like the best thing you could do to a jet-ski."

The other cruiser pulled in, separating them with a cloud of dust that rose between them. It was the sheriff, leaning out his window with his mirrored shades. "You. Chief Water Moccasin. You're going to need to come in for a talk."

"Oh? About my lawsuit for that racial slur you just made? You have some official complaint forms I need to fill out or something?"

"I'm sorry. *Mr.* Water Moccasin. *Coach.*" Saying it like the only wrong part was *chief*.

Roger glanced at Janey over the top of the cruiser. "Could he really honestly think that's my name? Is he actually that dumb?"

Janey shrugged, like *Anything's possible*—that big wide smile—and he thought, God, I like seeing that, and he knew he was smiling, too, like a dope, thinking about kissing her last night.

Hatchert jerked his head toward the backseat. "Go ahead. Get in. Let's do this official. Have a nice long sit-down, by the book."

Janey bent down and told him through the window, "Forget it, Jon. Not our guy. I can vouch for the Coach's whereabouts at the time."

"Oh really?" Hatchert said, snidely. "Interesting. All night?"

"From around seven P.M. to around midnight . . ." she said, then added, with no apparent rancor, ". . . you jackass."

Roger said, "The neighbors all tell me this happened at ten-thirty. Twenty-two-thirty. Right on the money. That true?"

Hatchert turned his head from one to the other, then back again, sizing them both up, acting like he had their numbers. "Cute," he said. "Real cute." He put it in gear and pulled out of there, rooster-tailing road dust.

Janey sidled over to her cruiser and eased in. She leaned out her open window and waved him over. Roger obeyed, crossing the short distance to join her. "Next time you use me for an alibi," she said, cool as Clint behind her mirrored shades, "I expect to get further than first base."

He leaned in the window, not sure, till he did it, if it was against regulations for her to kiss while on duty.

69

THE POLAROID Von taped to Marita's bedside lamp at the hospital was one he had Miki take, with him and Santi, arms linked awkwardly, standing in the garden right behind the sign. It was the best shot of the bunch, he decided, with both of them smiling and the pepper plants just showing down at the bottom and the sign clearly legible:

¡Peligro! Danger!
El Jardín de Marita
Marita's Garden
No moleste.

He knew it wasn't going to bring her out of her coma, but it did make his son stand up and embrace him and even smile a little, which was a start. "I'll check back in on you two in a little bit," Von said, feeling awkward with all this sudden touching. "I need to go talk to your mom now."

He had the older photo album with him, the one he'd been studying, as well as the family Bible with the family tree written in the front. He brought these things along in case he needed visual aids.

He found his wife out at the picnic tables in a little patch of green in back of the waiting room. He wondered again if she was sneaking cigarettes out there but he had more important things to discuss. He opened the album to the picture of his grandparents, the same one Aunt Sadie had shown him the day of the accident, and he opened the Bible to the family tree and then he told her the crazy Al Capone malarkey Sadie was now claiming. After he'd told it all, he said, "The woman's nutty as a pecan log, of course, but I thought you should know what she said."

Carol seemed to be taking this in for a moment, squinting out at the shimmering stand of birch and the black pool of parking lot beyond. "You could get a DNA test. See if you match."

"Please," Von said. "I'm not digging anybody up for some stupid test." He thought of that new sheriff and the holy hairy bitch it had been just putting someone *in* the ground.

A tired smile flickered across his wife's gorgeous mouth. "What I meant, of course, was a sample from you and a sample from Sadie. Or you and one of your dad's sisters. See if it matches. If you really think all that's necessary." It sounded like she didn't think it was. She studied him for a moment, as if trying to figure something out. "I seriously doubt this would affect us getting the Centennial Farm status," she said finally.

"I know," he said, though he wasn't positive.

"If that's what you're concerned about."

"It isn't."

She sat looking at him, waiting, alert. Sometimes, like this, it felt as though they spoke two different languages and she would look at him like this as if he were Lassie, trying to explain that the barn was on fire.

"It doesn't bother you that I may not—*may,* okay?—*may* not—be a vonBushberger?"

She snorted. "I'm not even going to waste my time answering that." As if changing the subject, she flipped ahead in the album, to the photos of Von as a little boy. There was one of him riding the sprayer like a pony with that migrant, Paulo, grinning alongside, keeping him steady, and it made Carol grin, too, looking at it, and he watched her touch the nail of her thumb to her lips. And then there were photos of Von as a teenager, standing proudly on the tractor seat and then in his baseball uniform, posed on one knee, for the Weneshkeen High Whos, and the two of them, Von and Carol, preposterous in Easter egg colors and mounds of hair, standing stiffly on the front porch, right before the prom. Just looking at that picture, he could feel the pumping of his heart that night, that feeling of *What the hell is going to happen next?* and that was the last photo in the album. It was all continued in the next one.

They lingered over this last page. Carol touched the plastic over the prom photo, smiling, then closed the album and slid it back to him. "Okay," she said. "Anything else, or is this family meeting adjourned?"

It sounded familiar, a phrase he'd heard recently, and he felt he sounded a little like Aunt Sadie being sassy when he blurted out, un-planned, "Yeah. If you're smoking again, knock it off. I don't like being a permanent fixture at this place."

"So noted," she said, and they got up from the table and went back inside and she wrapped herself around him, leaning into the crook of his arm as they walked down the hall. "You always did like Italian," she murmured, meaning the food. "Hey, maybe this means I secretly had a mysterious Italian lover all these years. Mama mia . . ."

"Quit," he said, though it did make him smile.

He thought there was something different about the light or the air, something palpable, as they neared Marita's room. There were voices, for one thing, but there were always voices, hushed churchly voices. A large nurse he didn't recognize strode out as they entered and he saw now there were more staff in there than usual, several nurses surround-ing the bed. He pushed his way in, demanding, "What's going on? Did anybody call the—?"

He saw Jack's face first, smiling, then Marita's, eyes drowsy but open. The two of them, with their heads tipped together on the pillow, looked oddly like a couple who had just had a healthy baby, the wife exhausted, the husband beaming. The thought of this, the little joke played on him by his own brain in that moment, made Von's cheek twitch. But still, she was awake. And Jack looked alive.

Marita saw them now and tried lamely to reach for the Polaroid taped to the lamp. "I like . . . my garden . . ." she said, faintly, like it was laryngitis she was recovering from or she had just been pulled from a mine shaft where the air was thin.

"There's another surprise for you, too," Von told her, "but you have to come home to see it." He'd cautioned them all not to say a word about the new paint job.

The large woman he didn't recognize was back at their side. "I'm sorry," she said, starting to herd them to the door. "The doctor's going to need to run some tests before she can have visitors, but he's on his way and—"

"Hey." Von moved out of her grasp. "Relax. It's okay. Really. We're family. Immediate family." He shifted with Carol out of the way, but like hell if he was leaving the room.

70

TWO DAYS AFTER the big jet-ski abduction on Lake Meenigeesis, Roger Drinkwater got a call from Colonel Glenn Landry, up at Camp Grayling: "You heard I got a new toy?"

Roger said, "I heard there's a new toy up on Neptune or someplace, is the way I heard it."

Landry chortled. "Neptune, nothing! I'm having too much fun with this puppy to let any aliens get hold of it."

"Just don't play with it down in my county, all right? That's the deal."

"I know, I know . . ." Even though he was now going to ride a jet-ski, Landry wasn't a bad guy, really. Compared to the regular type of loser drawing pay as brass in the Reserves. Normally, it was a bunch of fuck-ups who couldn't quite cut it, but Landry was better than that. He probably would've done fine staying in as a career man in the regular service if only he didn't have a such a fondness for bluegill. But the fact that Camp Grayling was only few minutes from the Au Sable—one of the finest fly-fishing and canoeing rivers in the country—was far too tempting. "I'm going to have to time-share the thing with this sergeant. But don't worry, he's cool."

"He the one did the rappel?"

"No rappel, man. We grappled the fucker."

"You are kidding me." Roger would've liked to have seen that. He'd just assumed they dropped a man into the water on a harness line. Someone to tie the cargo line to the jet-ski before they yanked it up.

"Yeah, no one even got wet. We just hooked it. Can you believe that? Not the whole ride back, of course. Jeez, can you imagine: the grappling hook slips, we drop it through some Fudgie's two-million-dollar A-frame?"

"Bad times," Roger agreed.

"Yeah, so we set it down in a field once we got over the rise a couple clicks and secured it better. But initially? That was fly-fishing, my friend. Like working the claw game at the Chuck E. Cheese."

"So it wasn't exactly by-the-book, huh?"

Landry snorted. "You think there's a book covers what we did?"

They chuckled together some more for a moment and he knew it was merely the preliminary niceties, the lead-up to getting down to business, but that was okay. He'd agreed to the deal and now he had to pay up. And already he was feeling a little like his old self anyway, his younger self, with all this hoo-rah commando talk. He could do this.

Landry told him then that the demo class he wanted Roger to teach wouldn't start till late September sometime, but he wanted to make the "shack," meaning the ordnance depot, available to him beforehand, so that Roger could reacquaint himself with anything he might need. "I know you've got some . . . issues . . . with the blasts and all, so I thought I'd give you a free hand to practice a little, so it's not so . . . *whatever* . . . for you."

"So I don't wince and cringe in front of the men?"

"Exactly," the colonel said, giving it right back, "so you don't piss in your pants and cry like a girl."

And with that, he was right back in it. Back in the ranks, it felt like. Time to suck it up. Drop your cocks and grab your socks, as they used to say. And surprisingly, he felt okay with it. No panic. This was something he'd agreed to do and he would do it, no problem.

71

COURTNEY'S ARMS were folded across her chest and she was staring out toward Sumac Point like if you made a list of things she found interesting around her, Mark would be maybe number thirty-seven. If he was lucky. She didn't even look at him when she said, "Maybe we should just forget the whole thing. If you're going to be this huge pain and all."

"No, no, no," he said. "I won't be a pain." Was she breaking up with him? They'd said on *Loveline* she probably wasn't really his girlfriend, but this sure sounded like she was breaking up with him and it was maybe the most horrible sound he'd ever heard. "Really," he said. "Don't— Please."

Now she turned and pouted at him for a while, considering. "We're only in town for like . . . not that much longer, really, so I want to spend my time wisely. My stepbrother's here, and then there's the Sumac Days Court . . . I just don't want to waste my time doing stuff that isn't really, really fun."

He told her he understood. He told her he could be really, really fun. No problem. Don't worry.

THERE WASN'T A PLACE MORE OFF-LIMITS than inside the Sumac Point lighthouse. If it were any other girl, he never would even think of going near it. But this was Courtney Banes. And he had to come up with something.

It would be all boarded up. But he remembered the crowbar in the toolbox Walt kept in the main pilothouse. After the difficulties at the bootlegger's place, he knew to go prepared this time.

COURTNEY WAS ON TOP OF HIM, riding him like he was a horse, and though it had started out as seeming sort of wild—he'd seen movies, of course, knew grown-ups did it that way a lot—it was starting to feel a little weird. Not just the damp stone floor against his back or the wind blowing through the smashed-out windows and up the metal spiral staircase from below or the clicking sounds that might be bats. Weird in a way that had nothing to do with them being up in a lighthouse. He'd never done it quite like this—not that he was about to admit this to Courtney and risk looking like a kid, someone she wouldn't want to bother with. It was real obvious she had done it this way plenty. And what was kind of not so hot about it, after a couple minutes of this, was the way he started to feel like he wasn't even there. She was moving like she was hooked up to something, some gizmo she thought she'd try out on her junk because she was bored. He imagined, the way she got going back and forth so fast—Jeez, no way could he move his pelvis that fast, not on a bet!—that she'd practiced this move many,

many times before. Maybe not with a guy, but on something—the edge
of a couch maybe, the armrest of a big easy chair. He'd heard of girls
doing that, beating off that way, straddling something. They talked
about it on the radio, on *Loveline*. That's really what that show was:
kids called up and explained their favorite way to beat off and the doctor told them what they ought to do instead. It was a good show for
that sort of information, but they hadn't scored high points with him
with that sucky advice about Courtney; about walking away. That was
easier said than done, that kind of advice.

She just kept doing it, faster and faster, grinding her hard bony pelvis
against him like that, little bunny moves, and he was starting to feel
like *Hello! I'm here! Remember me?* Like *he* was a goddamn armrest
or something. And she kept saying, "Come on," over and over. But real
low, like it wasn't even meant for him to hear, which was another slap
in the face: "Come on, come on, come on . . ." Like that.

He tried getting her attention. Not stopping and saying, *Hold on a
second, you crazy chick,* but just by sitting up slightly. It was hard to do
with her straddled on his junk, pressing down, but he managed to sit
up enough to almost kiss her. It was clear she was going to have to help,
to span the distance, and he whispered, "Come here . . ."

"Don't," she said, wincing, possibly annoyed. Which was crazy because he just wanted to kiss her. She pushed him back down and kept
him there, pressing with her palms against his chest, holding him flat
and sort of using his nipples as handholds as she increased the fre-
quency of her wiggle. "Don't move, okay? Just . . . yeah . . . yeah . . ."

She was talking to herself again. It was the kind of thing he knew if
he'd tell it to his buddies back home, they'd say, *Shit, man, what is your
problem? That sounds hot as shit!* And he liked her talking, saying
those things. It was just he wanted to feel she was saying them *to* him.
Not like he was eavesdropping on her, intruding. He reached up tenta-
tively, to hold her little breasts. "Can I . . . ?"

"Fine, yeah." Just a mini lip snarl, no actual frown or wince: an
improvement. But this didn't feel like a connection either. He felt like
she was lending them to him, like they weren't attached. He wanted to
touch her hair, her face. He reached up, brushing it from where it hung
down, swinging. "Can I at least—"

"Dude! Jesus! I'm close, okay?"

He pulled his hands away and lay there, afraid to move. He didn't want to do anything wrong again and risk getting scolded. Better to let her handle it, he decided, or she might get pissed off or bored and climb off and leave him, and the idea of her running off again was too much.

But Jesus, he just wanted to touch her hair, hold her face in his hands. Weren't girls supposed to like a guy who wanted to do that sort of thing? Normal girls, at least? From what he heard on *Loveline,* it seemed like half the guys his age were trying to put their fingers in their girlfriend's butthole. It's not like he was trying to do that. He had no interest in her butthole. Zero.

She was really moving now and it felt like she was shaking his entire body, sliding him back and forth against the stone floor. His skin would be raw tomorrow, he was sure. He'd have to stay covered up, in long sleeves and jeans, or his mom might ask about it. She'd ask if he was in a fight, maybe, but she'd probably have her suspicions.

But no, wait, the floor was moving.

He laid his palm flat on the floor beside him, felt the tremor, the sprinkling of something coming down on them—dust? Crumbs? They were shaking the whole place.

"Wait. Wait!" He tried to sit up again, tried to tell her. It was all in her hair, glowing.

She shoved him back down, growling this time, saying, "Goddamn it—can't you even—" There wasn't even time for her to open her eyes.

72

WHAT WOULD IT HURT, Janey Struska decided, to give the Letterman thing one last solid try? Everything Roger had said the other night, right before he kissed her, the night of the sketchy goings-on over on the other lake—all that still made a load of sense and the thought of pursuing this further, or of Roger catching wind of it, made her feel a little silly, even deluded and stalky, but she did have this one good hunch and the night was clear and fair and that dickwad Hatchert was off-duty, settled in, no doubt, for an evening of watching midget leather bondage porn, so who would know?

There was a big sailboat, a three-master, that had been seen anchored out past Sumac Point for two days. It was the sort of charter boat only someone very wealthy could swing. And the distance from shore seemed to indicate privacy was preferred. If the rumors were true, he had to be out there. The police boat could cut the distance in no time and it was sort of within her charge, wasn't it, to make polite inquiry? She took along a small foam cooler with a couple frozen packs of Don Sloff's sausages, thinking it would be a nice gesture, a welcome-wagon gift from her and the village. Really, it would just be an excuse to get the conversation started. He'd invite her aboard, of course—the big brown star on the hull of the boat would ensure that. Not that he had to legally—she wasn't the Coast Guard—but she felt confident the boat and the uniform would be enough for him to come out on deck and say hello.

She would tell him she just came out to make sure he wasn't being bothered and to offer the services of the sheriff's department during his stay. He'd have to act grateful, even though she was sure he got that kind of thing all the time from people who just wanted to tell their kids they met David Letterman.

Maybe she'd do it in phases. Get in and out tonight, give him the SloffBrauts, make him laugh, and get the hell off his boat. Then come back in a few days, earlier in the day, and stay a little longer—bring some brochures or something . . . *fudge*. Tell him facts about the area. Only, tell him in a funny way, demonstrate the wit. Maybe hint at the fact that sheriffing may not be the thing for her anymore.

The third visit—*that* would be the time to admit that she'd like to write comedy. Tell him how Weneshkeen was getting too small for her, how she needed to reinvent herself, how life had bigger plans for her, she just knew it. Impress him with her spunk, that she was a "spunky gal," because wasn't it a well-known fact he admired spunky gals?

Well, it was an idea, anyway. At the least, she thought she'd determine if he was actually on board. At least give him Don's sausages.

But she never got that far. She didn't even get past the lighthouse, really, because as she was bringing the patrol boat gently to starboard, coming alongside Sumac Point, thinking she was just seconds away from opening her up full throttle, hearing those big twin 200s roar to life and feeling the spray in her hair, it dawned on her, suddenly, that something was wrong. Yes, there was a familiar glow in her periphery, off the port side, but it wasn't tall. It was horizontal, sort of. The whole base of the lighthouse was glowing, the whole tip of Sumac Point. She cut the engine and really looked now and saw a flash of white movement—a windbreaker or piece of clothing—and the glowing was all jumbled along the rocks, phosphorescent rubble, some of it underwater, just off the port-side rail, emanating up through the lapping waves.

She snatched at the spot, swiveling it around and clicked it on. The lighthouse had collapsed all right, and there were people in there—two at least. "Hey!" she yelled. "You okay? I'm Deputy Struska of the sheriff's department."

The way they lurched and tried to scramble out from under the rubble, despite being hurt, at the mention of her official status, told her they were just kids. Adults wouldn't be thinking they could be in any more trouble than being trapped on the edge of Lake Michigan under a bunch of possibly radioactive rubble. Adults would be demanding service, not trying to evade the police.

"Relax!" she commanded. "I'm just here to get you out of this. Boy, what a mess, huh?" She could see them moving now, crawling. One was a girl, long blond hair hanging down, clotted with blood. She couldn't tell about the other. "Don't move! You might be hurt." The one who was definitely a girl gave her the finger. She couldn't quite stand, her foot or something snagged in the rubble, and she fell back with the effort of flipping the bird. Well! Janey thought, I guess I know which one I'm rescuing first.

But the truth was, she really couldn't just hop over the boat rail and scoop up either one of them. There was no dock or way to get up close to the tip of Sumac Point normally, and now, with jagged chunks of concrete and rebar sticking out, she'd certainly tear a hole in the hull if she pulled in any closer. And it would be irresponsible to try to get them to swim out to her. They might have concussions or just not be up to it and drown in the short span of a couple yards.

She really didn't want to call for backup on this one. The Coast Guard station was too far off and if she called Hatchert, he would probably first demand a lot of information about why she had the patrol boat out in the first place.

And she was already here. She could do this.

Then she figured it out. Shining the searchlight around, she could see now that, there on the other side of the narrow pile of rocks, sticking out more toward Lake Michigan than inland, there was a good solid section of the tower that had fallen more or less intact—a section maybe twenty feet long that had retained, mostly, its columnar shape. It looked sort of like a giant stepped-on paper towel tube, but at least it wasn't rubble. "Sit tight!" she yelled, then eased the throttle up and slowly skirted around to the western side, dropped anchor and stepped down on the makeshift dock.

They were both naked as monkeys. She wrapped them up in the first-aid blankets that were stowed in the hold. It was hard to tell, even once she got them in the boat, if they were any worse than just badly banged up. The boy, she could tell, had taken the brunt of it, though you wouldn't have guessed that from the girl's histrionics. They were both covered with cuts and bruises, though she didn't see any spurting arteries or anything that needed a tourniquet. Janey knelt in front of them and gave them each a quick, rough once-over, giving everything a wiggle and tug. No bloodcurdling shrieks, though glares from the girl and a homophobic "I'm not *like* that, okay? You try anything and you are *so* sued!"

The boy spoke for the first time, a slurred garble, but clear enough. "Pie . . . hole . . ." he told the girl. "Just . . . shut it . . ."

They seemed to be able to move their arms and legs, though she wasn't sure yet about parts of the boy—his ankles and wrists and neck seemed real tender to the touch. She wouldn't be surprised if he would end up needing a cast or two for sprains that he was either currently too much in shock to notice or too cowed by his pit bull of a girlfriend to mention.

The girl complained that her blanket was scratchy. And that it smelled like fish. Janey gunned the engines, heading for the hospital. Time was of the essence: the longer this took, the more she'd be tempted to toss this bratty little stick-bitch back in the drink.

73

THE FIRST SHERIFF HATCHERT LEARNED of the lighthouse collapse was on the goddamn CNN. He was at home, in his lounge pants, and he wouldn't have known anything if he hadn't realized he'd already seen that particular episode of *Cheers* at least twenty times and so he started surfing and, though he rarely watched CNN, he was stopped by the familiar shape of a green mitten. They had a hasty cartoon map of Michigan up on the screen and a red star right around Weneshkeen, with the words SUMAC POINT floating in the blue of Lake Michigan. And the voice, over a phone line, was so everyday familiar to him, that at first he couldn't place it. But it was, of course, Jane Struska.

He couldn't believe he hadn't been notified, that Struska took the call and did not check in and had violated at least a dozen different regs and procedures, just thinking off the top of his head, which meant probably at least twice as many if he got the book out and dug a little. Here now was the perfect excuse to get rid of her. There could hardly be any PC wrangling over her being a gal or any more of this "I'm a local" nonsense—he'd have whole sections and subsections of the manual he could cite. Hell, it was so cut-and-dried, he could even allow himself the luxury of acting all forlorn about it, shake his head like he hated to do it, but here it was, in black-and-white. Can't argue with regulations.

But then the coverage continued. He wasn't there to see the story evolve and balloon—he'd already dressed and headed off to the station, then up to the county hospital, the lights there much brighter than normal as he approached and saw the media was in full frenzy.

He pushed his way through the milling crowd and the various reporters, each with their own little island of technology, doing their stand-ups, reading from notes and forming serious faces for the camera, gesturing to the little hospital behind them. It was an odd sight, this much press in the parking lot, since there wasn't a local TV station for several counties. Everyone here must have driven in from pretty far off. He wondered how fast they'd driven to get here. Lots of speed violations, he imagined.

He scanned the parking lot. Twice he tripped on their stupid cables and several times someone bumped into him or jostled him. No one asked him any questions, which he found surprising, since he was in charge here. Then he pushed on, through the sliding emergency room doors. It was like arriving late to a party and not recognizing anyone. What was weird was, Struska wasn't anywhere around. He didn't get it, because there she was, up on the waiting room TV, talking in a split screen with that Natalie-what's-her-name at CNN. No way was Struska down in Atlanta or wherever and there was no TV station for miles and miles. He turned on his heel and marched back out to the parking lot.

The most likely source was the rather obvious white panel van, larger than the rest, with the extended antenna cranked up at least two stories out of the back like a space-age hook-and-ladder. There were no windows, just call letters and a phone number for the action news in Grand Rapids in a bold blue flash that ran the length. He thumped on the side of the vehicle and a woman in a black windbreaker popped out of the front, asking in a patently lowered voice if she could be of assistance and walking him deliberately away from the van. He took this to mean his hunch was right: they were interviewing Struska inside the vehicle and broadcasting it live somehow.

"You're with CNN?" He identified himself with his badge and asked if she had any questions for him. She said she herself wasn't *with* CNN, they'd just been called to freelance a live remote feed for CNN, since her team had to race up there anyway to get some footage for their own local eyewitness news.

He offered to let her interview him once they were done interviewing his deputy. She appeared confused, then stated that she and her crew weren't actually interviewing the deputy, just providing the feed. "She's talking to Natalie Allen right now. It's been a slow news cycle."

"What about you guys—the local news in Grand Rapids? Would you like to interview me for that?"

"Oh, you have some additional information? We haven't been expecting any updates . . . Are the kids still stable?"

Information, he thought. He'd only heard about this whole thing maybe a half-hour ago. He wasn't even clear what had happened, never mind what the hell kids she was talking about. He straightened; set his jaw. "I'm the sheriff."

The woman smiled. "Yes. I know. I think we're all set, though."

"You're all set?"

"For the late local, yes. We're all set. We're not going to break back on the air unless there's . . . But thanks."

This was not happening. No way could they be all set. They didn't want to talk to the top command? He looked past her, at the white van she now seemed to be guarding. What the hell could they be in there talking to Struska about for so damn long? Man, they *must* be starved for news these days. "Maybe . . . maybe CNN'd like me to add a few words?"

He thought he caught her glancing down at his holster. She smiled that curt little smile again and pulled out her cellphone and hit redial or something. She held up her finger for him to hold on, then stepped away, wandering over toward the van. She returned, clutching the phone to her chest. "I'm on with Atlanta. Producer says they're pretty much set."

"I see. They're set, too. Everybody's all set."

"Yes. Unless you'd like to say a few words about Deputy Struska in general, give us some background . . ."

He stared at the phone she had buried in the baggy front of her sweatshirt, considering. He could get on camera, but he'd be on camera praising his deputy. And maybe they'd ask questions about the specifics of the rescue, answers to which he had none. Either situation would not be politic.

He waved her off, tried to beam a smile, clapped his hands together like a leader in full command, addressing all those gathered in the parking lot. "Okay! Sounds like you people are all set . . . Very good!" He turned and strode back across the empty asphalt, trying to think of something to whistle, to show he was perfectly cool, just doing his job, just another day as sheriff; trying not to think about the fact that he would probably never again get a chance to sit in a little van like that with a blue curtain behind him and talk to someone on CNN. That Warbucks guy had promised fifteen minutes, but it was people like these who'd managed to whittle it down to mere seconds.

He thought if he got in the cruiser and drove home slowly, it might all be off the air by the time he got back. And maybe that would be better. But no, he was a glutton for punishment. He'd have to watch. Besides, it was better to know what he was up against. He headed back in though the electric-eye doors of the emergency entrance and flopped down in a row of empty plastic seats in front of the TV.

It was a nightmare.

They had footage now of the lighthouse, circled from above, a helicopter shot. The whitecaps were really picking up now, breaking against the rocks, which only made it look more dangerous; anyone who ventured in there, heroic as Audie Murphy. The way they had it framed, too, you would've thought it was miles offshore, unreachable, rather than a lousy quarter-mile away from a row of fudge shops. Hell, he'd seen old-timey sepia-tone photos of kids in sailor suits, a long time ago, before the rotten paint, when an actual keeper lived out there with his family and the kids in the picture were playing with their toy boats out there, off the rocks, one calm and sunny day. They didn't show that picture, now did they?

And there was footage of his deputy, shot in the van, he guessed, but it didn't look like the inside of a van behind her. It was very professional. Someone had even spruced her up, he thought, gave her a little makeup and maybe primped her hair.

And that bitch Natalie Allen loved her.

He knew right then, even before the hard plastic seat started cutting into his ass, that he wasn't going to be able to fire her for this. Forget firing, he thought. When the election rolled around, if she ran against him, he probably wouldn't stand a chance. You can't win against someone who's been on CNN.

74

BARRY SELF, real estate broker and part-owner of the Riverview Bed & Breakfast, wished he was alone. He'd really hoped his wife wouldn't join him this evening walking their high-maintenance dog down to the beach. It was one of the evenings he was supposed to "casually" meet up with John Schank, his secret partner, down along the Lake Michigan side of the point. They would go over the latest version of their business prospectus for "Sumac Estates," sit on a bench or a driftwood log and discuss what they needed to do next. They were still working out the details—nailing down the location, agreeing on a major investor to approach, tweaking it constantly—but already he was confident they were going to make a bundle. It would be the biggest real estate development to ever hit Weneshkeen. Granted, the business proposal was still evolving, but between Schank's juice at the savings and loan and his own real estate expertise, it couldn't possibly go south now.

They'd agreed to hold off telling their wives. No sense, they figured, taking a chance of gossip getting around and foiling their plans, raising people's hackles or driving up the asking price of land, or stirring up gripers who would rail against two relative outsiders significantly altering the local landscape and tax base. No sense giving people time to throw up more roadblocks. Not until it was all-systems-go.

But tonight, his wife, Kathy, had tagged along and he needed to figure out a way to ditch her. Despite the several stops for Oodles to unload, they'd managed to make it down to the water's edge before dark. They hadn't missed the sunset. He stood close behind his wife, the dog noodling around at their feet with something dead and fishy, and they were looking straight out at the last orangey glimpse, like the slit eye of a sleepy wink, of the sun setting somewhere over the theoretical Wisconsin. And then it was purply-gray, twilight. He rubbed with rapid friction on his wife's arms and asked her if she wasn't cold; if maybe she wanted to go back without him and he'd finish up with the dog alone, prodding its congested anal glands with a Q-tip. John Schank was either about to appear or was waiting in the shadows, holding back till he got rid of Kathy.

"Sweetie," she said. "You can keep me warm . . ." She leaned into him, tipping her head back lazily, starting to turn, to be kissed, when a bright light appeared over the lake and they both froze, watching it. It seemed to drop straight down with the coming darkness that was descending from the east at their backs. Maybe it came from behind them, from inland, a bottle rocket lobbed from the village, over the trees, over their heads . . . but no, it wasn't a bottle rocket. It didn't continue into the water but hovered, then seemed to flare, coming toward them, back to shore, then zigged sideways, heading north in the direction of the tip of Sumac Point, where the ruined lighthouse no longer stood, but then reversed, another change of plans, back the other way, past them again, laterally, moving south. They stood, watching it disappear down the coastline, and then they both breathed out at once and he saw that Kathy was patting herself down, searching her pockets for her cellphone.

"Oh, fudge, oh fudge, oh fudge!" she said. "I left the phone back at the house!" She turned away from the lake so suddenly she kicked sand on his shoes.

"No," he said. "Wait! Hold on. Don't." He gripped her arm, afraid she was about to run back up the path, to the road, maybe flag somebody down or get to the pay phone in the park, maybe sprint all the way back to the house. He was thinking of the project, Sumac Estates. This "lights in the sky" nonsense that had been going around this summer didn't need any further confirmation or flame-fanning—not from them. It was exactly the kind of tacky, low-rent Ripley's Believe-It-or-Not, Irish Hills, Mystery Spot tourist-trap three-ring-circus vibe that they absolutely did *not* need attached to this great thing he was cooking up with Schank. These units were going to have *white* gravel driveways. Pure white. They were supposed to be *high-end;* classy. Twenty-four-hour security monitors, built-in sprinklers, heated roofs, three-car garages.

And he'd seen this happen before, back when he was a teenager. He'd grown up just outside Ann Arbor and remembered well the hubbub of their own UFO scare, back in 1966. *Time* or somebody dubbed it "Saucer City USA" and he reminded his wife of this now—how that Project Blue Book egghead Dr. Hynek blew into town with his goatee and lame explanation of "swamp gas," which became a national punch line, with all of Washtenaw County feeling like the butt of the joke.

"But Barry," she said, "wouldn't it be great for business? I know we're usually pretty booked up in season, but still—think of the draw that would bring."

"But what would it draw—kooks? Crackpots?"

"It wouldn't just be kooks, silly. Normal people'd get a kick out of it, too, visiting the new 'Saucer City.' Probably off-season, even—year-round. Wouldn't that be a super-fun weekend getaway, Barry—'Come see the saucers'? It'd be a real novelty! We could double the room rate, I bet! Seriously, we could lend the guests binoculars, open the old widow's walk for an observatory—"

"We were the *laughingstock,* Kathy! That 'Saucer City' crap. The whole area. For years after, when I said where I was from, going off to school, people brought that up—'swamp gas,' 'Saucer City.' We looked like fools, Kathy. It wasn't a great Chamber of Commerce moment in the local history, I promise you."

He knew she was right about the B&B. The lights in the sky would certainly appeal to tourists, to people just passing through, with nothing invested, and it would be easy enough to capitalize on that—people wanting a souvenir T-shirt with maybe an antennaed Martian on it. The sort of gawker-appeal of Area 51. But in terms of the *other* project, the one he couldn't tell her about yet, it would have the opposite effect. Because *living* in a wacky little town was a completely different prospect from just visiting it.

She hooked her arm in his; leaned her face in close against him, flirting. "Come *on,*" she said. "Let's *tell.* Let's call somebody and report it."

He couldn't explain to her yet that he had a bigger plan, one ultimately much more important than her little B&B. "The whole country snickered," he said. "No. We're not telling *anyone.* We didn't see anything. End of discussion." He said it in a way he knew would resound with finality, finally shut her up on this nonsense, and then he bent down and lifted Oodles's tail and told Kathy to please hold the flashlight. It had grown very dark and he still needed to check the dog's ass.

75

MARK WAS SURPRISED he had to stay in the hospital. He knew he'd been banged up pretty badly, but the way Courtney had been carrying on, yelling at him like he'd done something, like it was his fault the lighthouse was unstable and couldn't take her crazy nympho gyrations, made him think, in the police boat, that he could probably shake it off, put some ice on it. Otherwise, why, if he was really hurt, would she be such a jerk to him?

But he'd managed to crack three ribs, sprain both wrists, fracture his ankle and break the big toe on the opposite foot. Apparently, he'd not only had the weight of the tower crashing down, he also bore the weight of Courtney. Just a little slip of a girl, sure, but when there's a whole lighthouse falling with you, there's some momentum. Despite the severity, he still wanted to leave. The whole thing was so embarrassing, especially since it was being reported on the news that they were boyfriend and girlfriend and, actually, Courtney wasn't even speaking to him. She wasn't even there. Her parents had flown their family doctor in late that first night and he'd recommended a plastic surgeon back home in Chicago and she was there now, having her nose reconstructed.

His own dad was being particularly cool about this, he thought. He'd even assured him that, despite Courtney's ranting about suing in the police boat, he shouldn't worry—"She's not going to sue anyone, buddy. I don't care who those people are. Or who they think they are." He was being so great, really—the guy's wife finally checks out of this place, and now his troublemaker son has to check in . . . ? Man. They were both pretty cool, when he really thought about it. And he didn't seem to be fooling either one of them about the true cause of the accident. The doctors seemed to know, too. Though, when they mentioned it on TV, the deputy lady was telling it kind of differently, claiming they were swimming, racing from the shore to the lighthouse on a dare, that the thing finally just collapsed in the wind. Unfortunately it just happened to do this at the *exact* moment they arrived at the point. He wasn't sure why she was telling it that way but it was okay with him. A hell of a lot better than being known as the guy and the girl who fucked the local landmark to bits.

They also said they wanted to keep him for "observation"—whatever that was. Something about a concussion and the possibility of internal bleeding. He seriously hoped it didn't mean they were going to gather around him in one of those operating theaters and just stare at him the whole time he was there. He wasn't sure he could take that kind of scrutiny right now.

Some nurse brought him the Weneshkeen *Identifier* and there was a big story across the front. Several stories actually, with different angles on the accident. But the thing that stuck out, really, was the photo of Courtney. It was her official portrait for the Sumac Days Court. They were running it early, as part of one of the articles about the accident. They said that her position would be filled by the remaining girls in the court—and so to fill it out, they were adding another girl, Kimberly Lasco (photo unavailable). It dawned on him that he had no other photos of Courtney and he probably wouldn't be getting any in the future. In this one, she smiled the small smirk of someone who knows they're going to be the big winner, and the pearls she wore over the open neck of her gown he recognized as his mom's. They'd taken the court photos that Friday after he'd borrowed them for her.

He was trying to remember if she'd given them back, when Walt and Keith appeared. The medication was making him groggy, but their appearance woke him right up.

"He look dead to you?" Walt asked.

"No more than usual," Keith said. "Not dead, just not paying attention." He pounced on the footboard and gave Mark's bed a solid shake, which hurt a little, but Mark didn't care. It was almost shocking, seeing them there, especially since they came together, in an organized, cooperative way, not just swinging by individually, on a whim. He wondered if they'd closed up the pilothouses early that day. Beyond them, nurses were passing in the hall, looking in and shaking their heads but smiling. Everyone knew the two veteran riverboys. It felt, oddly, like he'd had some sort of sports injury and his teammates had shown up to cause a ruckus. It was nice.

Keith announced he had a present and produced, from under his shirt, a skin magazine called *Hometown Honeys*. It was still sticky with sweat.

"Lovely gift," Walt grumbled.

"Hey," Keith said. "It's not like they sell even *Playboy* anywhere in this whole damn county. You gotta drive up to Traverse, you wanna see a lousy frigging bare breast. So please—this here is thoughtful as shit." Keith scanned the semiprivate room, with the plate glass windows and the big wide door fully open, hooked in place to the wall. "Not that the kid's going to have much opportunity to whack it in here . . . Jeezo. What is this—the *Big Brother* ward?"

They sat for a while and talked about his injuries, and about a bad scrape one of the other under-boys had caused the other day, getting caught up against the drawbridge pylons and "banging the bejeezus out of *The Podunk Finn*." Then Keith said, loudly, like a declaration, "Just so you know, everyone I talk to—on the river?—no one blames you or is pissed at you or anything like that."

"'Course not. The thing should've fallen over years ago," Walt agreed.

But Mark did not. "Courtney sure blames me. And her dad. Before they left, they were screaming about suing. My dad's a lawyer and all, and he says not to worry, but Mr. Banes . . . you know—he's a big-shot."

"Listen to your dad," Walt said. "The Baneses won't do anything."

Keith was bouncing on his heels, worked up. "They do, and they'll come back next summer to find *The Courtney* has spent the winter at the bottom of the marina. And they know it, I'm sure. A harbor town like Weneshkeen, *we're* the goddamn bigshots and don't you forget it! No one fucks with *us,* my friend. We are the goddamn Cosa Nostra around here and you, you're almost like a 'made man' yourself."

Walt rolled his eyes at Keith. "Worse thing in the world, the day this guy got satellite TV." He rested his big meaty hand on Mark's arm, near the IV tape. "Now first of all, the lighthouse? That thing was a nuisance and an eyesore. A major hazard. Everyone knew it."

"No shit," Keith piped in. "And second of all, anyone with half a brain knows it was that Banes chick put you up to it. It's that outsider bullshit all over again. Always something with them, coming in here.

You gotta steer clear of those people, Mark. And I don't just mean the Baneses, neither. It's those summer people in general. Those boat people and Fudgies and all. Next year, you get yourself a nice local girlfriend." He nodded, as if agreeing with his own brilliance. "I can help you with that."

Walt tipped his head, reflectively. "I got a niece about your age."

"Or . . ." Keith said, ". . . there's also some *good*-looking girls in town . . ."

Walt backhanded him.

"Hey!" Keith said. "Besides, Ass Boy don't need any help finding a girl. Kid's an under-boy, jack. That still carries some weight in this town, I'll tell you."

Before they left, Keith became interested in trying to pull back his bedsheets and find out what he had on. Despite feeling weak, Mark, shrieking with laughter, struggled to keep the sheets clamped around him until the older man intervened and pulled Keith off him. "What the hell's wrong with you?" Walt said. "You trying to put him in a worse condition, get his stay extended, jack up the kid's hospital bill? That it?"

"No, I'm just thinking: if it's one of those breezy, open-backed robes, maybe he could make a couple strolls down the hallway when he's up to it, flash that hottie-winning keister of his past a candy striper or two. Get the ball rolling on the whole new-girlfriend front."

Walt swatted him again and Keith yelped and laughed and Mark wondered now if they'd stopped by Carrigan's first for a few drinks. Then they were patting him on the arm, and telling him to get better real soon, that they'd be by to check on him again. After they were gone, the nurse came in and gave him a sedative for the evening and despite this, he did not nod off but lay there watching the muted *Simpsons* and thinking how peculiar this summer had been and how strange these two men were: he'd never said he was going to do this job again. And if he did want it, he would have had no business just assuming he could have it again next year. It was too popular a position. And wasn't he himself one of those same summer people they were telling him to steer clear of? And when had Keith Nuttle ever called him *Mark*?

He thumbed through the magazine for a time, then he did start to feel himself nodding off, whether it was from the drugs or from Keith wearing him out, and he loved the heat of the sun coming in through the window and sensed, in that heavy, underwater feeling, half-asleep, that someone was in the room. A girl maybe, standing in the door, then by the bed, and when he finally won the struggle to wake, and focus, there was something on the rolly tray thing that they swiveled over his bed. He reached out and pulled it closer so he could inspect it. There was a box of fudge and a card, which he opened:

Mark—
Sorry you got hurt & all. ☹
This isn't just from me but from my dad & I both, so don't think it's all weird of me or whatever. It's no biggie or anything, just to say get well soon & all.
Your neighbor,
Kimberly Lasco (& her dad)
P.S.
NO peanuts, in case your mom wants to try some. ☺

He wondered if she'd noticed the porno Keith gave him. Raising himself up a little, in a sort of inching, side-to-side roll that made moving only slightly less painful, he peered out at the parking lot, hoping to see her, and just then she walked past his window, the wind in her dark hair. She was turned away, looking out toward the sliver of blue beyond and to the west that was the beginning of Lake Michigan, the white snaky breakers of whitecaps that meant the big winds were coming and the rain and then what was that called—photosynthesis?— with the leaves and of course, the end of summer. It looked chilly out there, though it was still boiling out, the heat bugs humming. Still, it looked like a bad place to end up, late at night, heartbroken, crashing around in that surf out there.

He watched her start for the bike rack, then go past it, around it, to the weedy marshy area that was some sort of preserved wetland spot. It looked like she wanted to pick something over there, that red weedy-looking plant, the whatayacallit—sumac.

He timed her. She stood there for four whole minutes, just looking at it, like it was the most interesting thing in the world.

76

JANEY PULLED UP in front of his cottage while he was loading the pickup with boxes of his jerky. He had the temporary magnet signs with his brand name, Schmatzna-Gaskiwag®, slapped on the doors. It was time to make a few store deliveries. He'd sort of let orders slip in the past weeks, distracted by his war with the jet-skis. They were still out there, a few of them, buzzing around behind him in the white heat shafting off the lake, but he had other things he needed to focus on, too: the jerky business, this promise he had to fulfill up in Grayling, the fact that he might actually have the beginnings of a girlfriend . . .

"Can I get your autograph?" he called as she approached. She slapped him on the ass as she stepped up on the tailgate to give him a hand. He liked that she was the roll-up-your-sleeves type, pitching in. "Hey." He grabbed her arm and yanked her down to his level for a second. "Big kiss for the local hero," he said and gave her one. He began lifting the cardboard boxes to the tailgate and she slid each one forward, securing it against the cab. "So. Media darling? I see where the official report you filed claims that the two of them were just swimming? On a dare, from the shore to the point?"

"You don't have a TV," she said, concentrating on the boxes.

"The special edition the *Identifier* put out?"

"All Glenn Meeker. I just answered a few questions and gave him a copy of my official report."

"Uh-huh."

"I did speak to him, though, as you suggested. About maybe writing a humor column."

"Good. So the lighthouse just *happened* to collapse in the winds when they reached the point?"

She only grunted, rearranging the boxes.

"That was a cute little tale, I thought. Some of your creative writing?"

She looked up now, frowning. "I don't get your meaning. I just reported what happened."

"Really. So it just fell on them. They weren't up inside it, shaking it down." It was hard not to smile—something he had been doing a lot of lately. "Please. Who are you kidding?"

She shrugged. "I figure, I've got to live here, you know? Get along with everyone. Even the summer people. That's my job."

He didn't say so, but he was glad to hear it. She sounded much more focused than the other night when she spoke of David Letterman and running off to New York.

Then she changed the subject: "You think it means anything, two important men in my life both sell homemade meat?"

She was of course speaking of old Don, his SloffBrauts. He knew they were close, like father-daughter almost, and he was kind of surprised to be lumped in with such company. It wasn't bad, it just took a moment to sink in. *Important,* huh? He should be flattered. He came around to the side and tossed the tie-down to her. She straightened the boxes and secured the line and he cinched it tight. "Things don't always mean something," he said. "You see much of him lately?"

"He wants me to run. Next time, the regular election."

"Good." All in all, Sloff hadn't been a bad sheriff, for a white man.

"Said he'll support me. Advise me and stuff."

Roger could picture the campaign slogans now, if Sloff advised: *Try Not To Be A Jackass. Vote for STRUSKA.*

That was all of the boxes. As she started to hop off, he reached up and helped her down, even though she clearly didn't need it. "What's '*shmatzna*' mean again?" she asked.

Roger had always thought she also was part Polish. "Delicious." He kissed her quick, a wet smack, as if to help with the definition.

"Oh, right." She seemed to be remembering. "*Schmatzna.*" They slammed the tailgate shut together and then she turned and punched him lightly, playfully, just under the ribs. "Hey. All this hubbub over the lighthouse collapse—you make fun, but notice how it sort of overshadowed much of the interest in what happened out here that night? The jet-ski alien abduction?"

"Not aliens, I decided. The '*gami-manitous.*'"

"Lake spirits," she said.

He *had* noticed, of course. It was great timing. Really took the heat off. But he knew to say nothing else about it, just put his hands back on her solid hips and pull her in, a little closer.

77

THE COFFEE was still cooling inside—he'd told her it was his turn; he'd try his hand at this batch—and they were out on the lawn again, in the blazing midday sun, and he was telling her what he'd heard about the latest saucer sightings and how, with so many folks this summer proclaiming they had "open minds," you'd think church attendance would be up. And though she looked, physically, as if the sun had her complete attention, as if she were listening intently to the bright heavens, she was chuckling, really seeming to get it in a way that made her appear older, as if there'd been a mistake with her birthday, some sort of chronological slipup and she really had to be at least in grad school. Her head was lolled back in a way that exposed her neck and tipped her chin up at him, her mouth drowsily parted in a half-grin, half-stupor from the sun. Her skin glowed with the sweat that collected across her lazy-looking mouth.

It was all too much. He told her he had to go inside and do a little work.

She didn't question this, though what work she might think he had Gene could hardly imagine. It wasn't as if he would ever again be asked to compose a sermon. But he had become suddenly terrified that she would catch him looking at her in that way—at her neck, at her mouth, that mole on her clavicle like a lost chocolate chip, that silver cupcake topping in her tiny belly—and it would ruin everything between them. So he checked first on the coffee cooling in the sink, with a slight vapor of steam still rising, and looked out the window and snuck another peek. Even from that distance, he could see her lips were dry, the way she rolled them together like the sun was making her thirsty.

Stop it, he told himself, and retreated to the den and booted up the computer. He looked at the picture of Mary up on the shelf, nineteen years old, and tried to imagine a time when he was more turned on than right at this moment.

Lord, he prayed silently. Please, Lord. What burdens are you giving me? What tests are these?

He got online and went right to Ultrateen.com. The pictures emerged one after another like bullets from a Gatling gun; like magic boxes, all in a row, taunting him. He got up and closed the door and unzipped his fly.

He went through several rows of these pictures, clicking on each and waiting for them to download, stroking himself the whole time. This is better, he told himself, than hovering around out there and gawking like a pathetic old man. That's not what our friendship is and I refuse to make it that.

But these images just weren't doing it. He couldn't help it: he wanted to see the other ones, the ones that still haunted him from a few weeks back that looked so much like Kimberly. With a sense of defeat, he clicked on the history folder and sifted through it till he found that string of shots that could almost have been her, the head tipped back, mouth open like a baby bird feeding.

He went faster, more out of a desire to finish and be done with it than pure passion. But it wasn't working. It just wouldn't do when he knew she was right out there; that he could step into the other room and see her through the kitchen window. So finally, he did—fly still unzipped, bent slightly at the waist, stepping quickly and cautiously, like a cat-burglar, into the kitchen. He moved over to the window and stood to one side, hoping to remain hidden if she looked over at the house. But she was still resting, head tipped back, her neck exposed, her legs in front of her rubbing slightly together at the ankles, the toes fidgeting. Perhaps she was asleep now, perhaps her throat and lips were dry, but she seemed to be swallowing slightly, the movement there along her neck, and she was biting at her lips, her mouth slightly parted.

And as he stared at her out there, a single thought began to take hold of him, a strangely conceptual fascination: how far was it, exactly, from where he stood on the foam dishwashing mat with the birdhouse print in front of the kitchen sink, and that point out on the lawn where she was stretched out on her chair? It had to be less than a hundred feet, more like fifty, and the narrow divide terrified him. To think that only fifty feet separated him from a despicable, illegal and immoral connection made his fingers tremble with fear.

Still, he thought about it. He thought how there had to be a way to shorten the distance, to make the connection, the contact, without going to jail or hell or having her ever know.

He continued to tug at himself, knowing he couldn't safely do this for much longer. Glancing down at the sink again, he saw there was no longer any steam rising from the coffee. Soon she'd hop up and come in to check on how he was faring with the drinks. He looked out at her again, checking, and then down again at the pitcher of coffee cooling in the sink and saw there was a way. There was a way to connect.

Besides, he was so close, his breath catching, head swimming. He could do it. Right now he could do it.

With his left hand, he grasped the pitcher by the handle and lifted it out of the sink. It was full and heavy and he tried not to spill it as he lowered it to his fly. He focused on the line of her neck, the way she breathed through her mouth, her lips slightly parted. And then he was doing it, the back of his skull tingling, his breath raspy, the release, the dizziness, his lungs huffing, the sway and wobble as he tried to stay on his feet and oh dear Lord . . .

With the remorse already seeping in like poison, it was all he could do to sneak a peek, but he did, and he saw he'd done it, hit it dead-on. Three distinct white blobs, still afloat but sinking into the coffee. He set it back down in the sink and retreated to the bathroom, hobble-footed—his fly still open, pants slipping down—and cleaned himself up. The bathroom fan roared overhead as he went through the motions—washing his hands, straightening his pants. He inspected his flushed cheeks in the mirror; tried not to look himself in the eye. Returning to the kitchen, he stood over the sink, staring down at the pitcher of coffee, considering. Don't overthink it, he told himself. Act. Stop prolonging this and act and maybe then it will be over and you can get back to normal.

So he got the nondairy creamer from the fridge and poured it in, stirring it well, the murky black liquid turning beige. And he added another handful of ice and opened the cupboard and took down a tall glass, holding it up to the window to make sure it was clean—a habit of Mary's, to double-check anything that a guest would be putting their mouth on. He poured a glassful, holding it up to the light again to see if he could see anything out of the ordinary in it, then picked up the pitcher in the other hand and carried them to the mudroom door and put his back to it, pushing out. The light, blinding, almost caused him to lose his footing as he forced a smile and said, "Here you go. Service with a smile."

With her hair up in barrettes, he could see the muscles at the back of her neck as she sat up and swiveled, looking up at him over her sunglasses. There was that smile, the teeth, the lips, the intake of air flaring her nostrils and she slipped off the sunglasses and wiped her face with a towel and turned and reached for the glass, all in one motion, twisting in the chair. He brought it closer, held it out for her and she said thank you and brought it directly to her face. He watched the tipping of her hand, the frosty glass cloudy where she touched it with her sunwarmed fingers, and the creamy liquid tilted, the plane of it angled back, her lips parting at the edge of the glass, open. Her head was raised up, her neck bent in that exact position that had become, in this short time, just this summer, so familiar to him.

She drank it. She swallowed. He was inside her.

Her eyes closed just for a second in a gesture of appreciation. Her lips were slightly foamy and so she wiped them with the back of her hand. "Pretty good!" she said. "You're learning all kinds of new tricks!"

The whole yard—the line of trees, the swing set, the riverbank beyond—all shimmered with light, like August heat rising on asphalt. Everything was swimming—he felt a shiver climb his spine, up to the top of his scalp, tingling, flaring out along his shoulder blades, the back of his knees. He tried to brace himself against it, to stiffen himself, but that only seemed to spread the effect through his entire nervous system—heart attack, he thought, stroke. Seizure. I've been stung by a hornet—zinging through him like the shot they gave him the day Mary died.

"You're shivering," she said. "You feeling all right?" She reached out and touched him, grabbed him by the leg as if he were about to fall. "Gosh, maybe I should be waiting on *you,* huh? Here!" Hopping up, she motioned for him to take her place on the chair. "You think you're sick? Maybe we should make you a *hot* beverage instead?"

He wanted to say no, no, he was all right, he was just fine, but the words wouldn't come and, rather than collapsing, he just sat down where she'd indicated, and made little waving motions with his hand.

HE WAS LYING down in his bedroom when she stuck her head in to say goodbye. He raised his hand but stayed flat on the bed. The dizzy feeling had passed, but he couldn't face her now.

Shadows filled the yard outside the window and then the sun was gone, setting unseen on the other side of the house, out toward Lake Michigan. He lay there, looking out at the growing dim, and wondered how long he would have to lie there to starve to death. Would anyone come for him? How soon would his kids become concerned and phone someone to look in on him?

James 1:15, he thought, *James 1:15 . . . Then, when desire has conceived, it gives birth to sin; and sin, when it's full grown, brings forth death.*

The girl would check on him. She'd be there tomorrow. But of course.

She'd said something about pasta salad in the fridge, but he had no interest in food. He remembered there were actually some of the cupcakes from his birthday still left, too, and he regretted now not going for the birthday kiss that day. Perhaps that would have resolved the situation; satisfied his need to connect with her.

What finally roused him from bed was the memory of a very old bottle of Harveys Bristol Cream, in the cabinet under the hi-fi. It wasn't actually a bar; it seemed unseemly to have an actual bar in the parsonage, even though it was built in the late fifties, at a time when everyone had a bar in their home. In those days it was like having a TV, or now a smoke detector or a computer. During the cocktail party heyday, they'd served a drink or two but had kept the supply modest and didn't outfit the cabinet with a lot of paraphernalia like lemon squeezers and shakers and silver ice tongs. It was just the bare bones, meager enough to be considered Amish. This bottle, for example, had barely been opened. It still had a gift tag, tied with ribbons around the neck, that said *Merry Xmas from the Meehans.* The Meehans were divorced the year the *Challenger* exploded—whenever that was. Dust had caked up on the sticky neck of the bottle to form a sort of gum that made it impossible to open. He took it over to the sink and ran it under the hot water and still couldn't twist it off. But when he looked down in the sink and thought again what he'd done with the iced coffee, the shame gave him a burst of strength to finally wrench it off, the cap skittering around in the sink.

It smelled like syrup. He didn't bother with a glass but shoved the neck in his mouth and tipped.

He'd only been really drunk once in his life, when he was fifteen and, on a dare, snuck three or four nips off his father's stash of Tanqueray. He'd felt remorse after and prayed and, rather than cover his tracks by topping off the bottle with a little Lavoris, blubbered his confession to his mother.

Now he took the bottle into the den and turned on the computer. He needed to send an e-mail to the kids.

```
Dear Ben and Abbey
This is my last email. Sorry. This sins't working out.
In Christ's love,
your father
```

He did it the way Kimberly had shown him, adding both names to the address line. He hit *Send,* then closed out of there and hit *SHUT DOWN.* As usual, the box came up that said *What would you like the computer to do?* and listed several options. He stared at it, thinking that what he really wanted it to do wasn't listed there and so he just confirmed the one that again said *SHUT DOWN.* He stood there, wobbling, waiting for it to do what it said it would, then unplugged it from the power source and lugged it out into the yard and heaved it into the river.

It made a great splash, but as soon as he did it and the night breeze hit him in the face, he thought again about his sermon, about what he'd said about the Devil in the box and blaming the box and he realized he hadn't accomplished anything at all. The computer wasn't the problem. And all he'd done was pollute the Oh-John.

"Sorry," he said, and then louder, in the hope that someone might be out there and actually hear him, "Sorry. Really, really sorry."

78

THIS WAS WHERE he'd come with Mary, the first time, years ago. This very beach. It was years before they moved here, before the position with First Pres. Before they were married, in fact.

It was 1957. He was twenty-four, still in seminary school and attending a youth retreat at something called the Cliffhead Fellowship as a chaperone and group leader. Mary was assigned to his group, a high school junior from down in New Buffalo. She was seventeen.

And just as he was tonight, he heard, that night, too, James 1:12 repeating like a stuck LP in his head: "Blessed is the man who endures temptation . . ."

Looking back, it was easy to see how it happened. They were together all day for two weeks. It was something that evolved slowly, that eased into being. It wasn't a tawdry, soulless thing, sudden or careless. Inevitable, is how it felt afterward.

They snuck away the penultimate night of the retreat, down the path of terraced flagstone that traced the stone wall, zigzagging down to the beach. They swam, he remembered. In their underwear. It was the first time he'd ever seen a woman's slip, outside of the Sears catalogue or the painted kind on that pinup girl card deck he had back then. They swam out in the breakers and laughed hysterically, out of nervousness and the chill, out of a fear that they shouldn't laugh, that they had to keep it down or lights would appear up on the cliff and they'd be sent home, both of them, in shame.

He remembered that when they returned to shore, they were hand in hand, and it wasn't straight back to the bottom of the stairs but veering a little to the south, to what was now a neighbor's beach with an elaborate dock and some kind of nylon windsocks like carnival flags that flapped in the dark. But back then, it was just further unmarked beach where they could move back against the grassy curve of the cliff there, into the lee, both of them muttering how they needed to get out of the wind, both of them knowing full well what they were actually stepping away from.

Even now, he could see the image of her, afterward, standing, knees bent, in the surf, one hand hoisting her soggy slip, exposing to the moonlight and to him that place he'd never seen before in his life, her other hand scooping up water, splashing the blood away. She was beaming peacefully, her head tipped, hair hanging loose to one side, watching him watching her. He remembered how he couldn't breathe, how he sobbed and she seemed quietly confused by that, her joy broken by concern, and waded back to shore to touch his face, and they prayed together over what had happened. The shame he felt!—not for being with her, for she was beyond a doubt another part of him, some essential element that had been missing from his person and, he hoped, *he* was also something that had been absent in her. But he was ashamed for letting it occur in this way, for behaving like a regular Joe, for being cheap about it.

He'd once written a sermon, second year of seminary, that won that year's Witherspoon Award, and it was titled "The Sin of Being Normal." The gist was that it's the "regular Joes" who blithely fall into sin; that nonconformists are better suited for leading a righteous life because they are predisposed to questioning everything, even and especially their own actions. And what better way to weigh sin, to scrutinize it, and thus avoid it? A radical thought in Joe McCarthy's dust cloud, to champion nonconformity.

It was not unlike the time he got rip-roaring drunk and later determined: that's just not me. Neither was rolling around in the sand with jailbait, rutting like two beasts more interested in soft pink tissue than brain tissue and heart.

After they prayed over it, they decided they had something beautiful but it was not to be touched again. Not until marriage. And they didn't do it again. Not for two whole years, till 1959, when he was twenty-six, graduating from seminary with a position as an enlisted chaplain on the Wurtsmith Air Force Base, across the state, just above the Thumb, and she was the far more acceptable age of nineteen.

And then Ben was born soon after, in 1960—Ben Webster Reecher, because they went to see him play the night they figured they'd conceived. And Abbey followed in '63, and just as it looked like he was bound for a military life—which was a far more conformist life than he imagined ever falling into when he crafted that sermon about the "regular Joe" a decade before—an opportunity came their way that seemed heaven-sent, a sign, a way back to that special, water-trapped town where they'd walked into each other's lives, that dark shore where they'd first truly been man and wife.

It was 1969, a year in which the rest of the world seemed to be shuddering, but they were moving, with their scant belongings, back in time, to that cramped, outdated parsonage where only the shelf paper ever changed. And the congregation welcomed them, gathered round them, seemed so glad to have them, excited by their youth, their newness, wanting it to touch them and bless them back. They fawned over Mary that first day and teen girls swooped in as free baby-sitters, enough to handle five times the kids, taking them out into the yard, showing them the newly painted swing set and the river and the white-caps on Lake Michigan beyond. There was almost a buzz as they flitted like cartoon bluebirds, preparing the nest. There was an elaborate fondue, with several cheeses, and everyone dug in as they darted about the house, helping unpack. They were told to keep the fondue set: it was a housewarming present. Hal Markham, who was gone now—liver cancer in '84—donated a brand-new mattress, right out of his store window, and the men all helped carry it in and the women all giggled with Mary, whispered that they wanted their first night in the house to be special.

The secret was, despite all that, they didn't spend the night there. After all that toting and unpacking, that whirlwind day full of new people and new sights and charging around the neighborhood, learning which dogs to pet and which to avoid, Ben and Abbey were out like Lazarus. This was a safe town, they felt, where nothing would happen. And so they slipped away and spent the night back at the bootlegger's place, down on the beach, snug in the lee of the cliff, mostly talking, in low, awed tones, about the kind of life they were about to have, and the many lives their lives would touch, and what a wonderful place this was they were about to call home.

AND TONIGHT IT DIDN'T LOOK MUCH DIFFERENT than it had those earlier times, the smooth gloam of the beach and the darker roll of the waves and the distant glow—though much dimmer now, since the lighthouse collapse—far up the shore, at Sumac Point. The water seemed colder to his toes tonight, but he chalked that up to his trepidation and the scolding monitoring of his more mature mind. And the fact that he was alone. How much easier it would be to convince himself to turn away and go back home, with no one to prod him and tease him and double-dare him, no one for whom he could show off.

But no—he had to do this.

He was so absolutely, completely alone, it felt like he should yell something, or announce something—proclaim his sins out into the night, make a confessional of the crashing waves. He wasn't sure if he should be talking to Mary now or his Savior or whom and so he kept his mouth shut and told himself he was just going swimming.

The force of the waves was stronger than he imagined as he teetered out through the surf. And there were rocks underfoot, sporadic booby traps that collaborated with the waves to knock him off-balance. One large breaker caught him off-guard and he fell to one knee, stumbling, his hands splayed for support underwater, and he felt his shin scrape and a fingernail bend back against a rock. He got a big mouthful and thought for a second he would drown right there, not two yards from shore, but he sputtered and cleared his passageway of water and got himself back up on two legs.

Several more lurching, Frankenstein steps and he was out over his head and clear of the danger of the rocks. He paddled in place for a moment, turning his back to the whitecaps, and squinted back at the shore. He could just see the spire of the bootlegger's place, poking up above the cliff, could even imagine he saw someone back there, down on the beach—a couple huddled in the shadows, lovers, teens—and then he turned around and started swimming, a sharp-elbowed crawl, heading toward the deeper dark.

He'd forgotten how hard it was to swim in the dark when the waves were coming fast. There was no way to see them and gauge their height or time his breathing between them. Lake Michigan could not be described as calm tonight, and he marveled at the amount of activity that could be going on out here, with no human witness other than himself—how stirred up and wild it was and yet no one was there to confirm it was happening. The waves were whitecapping, cresting, the pounding roar a rhythmic hush in his ears, like a cradling mother lullabying, swing-lowing, sweet-charioting.

His body made only crude approximations of the motions he once knew. The strokes he made felt ludicrous. His timing was off and he got a mouthful of water and then another. And then the sobbing came, and more water in the mouth, because his breathing was off, too, ill-timed against the waves. But he kept going, struggling to put more distance between himself and the shore. "Oh God," he said, out loud, in a voice he barely recognized. It was the voice of someone in pain; a person who would normally come to him for help and now it was coming out of his own mouth. And then he saw, or thought he saw, a thin flash of light. But his eyes, pounded by a wave, squeezed shut and flickered against the water, and he wasn't sure what he'd seen.

He kept trying to pull forward, but his arms were weak now, no match for the waves, and so he treaded water, dog-paddling and gasping, churning in a circle as if caught in a whirlpool. Just getting my bearings, he told himself. Just catching my breath. I'm going to keep going. I'm going to do this . . . But now it was all mixed up. He wasn't clear which way was up, what was water, what was the black sky; if he was slipping under or simply besieged by pummeling waves.

And yes, there were lights. He burst out with a cry of laughter at the sight of them and got another mouthful of water in return. He'd expected lights, joyful lights, and they washed down upon him from on high, a white, shuddering light and he reached for it, his body sinking, down, away, as his arms came up, reaching for heaven.

79

JANEY WAS ON DUTY when the sensors went off at the bootlegger's place, so she drove out there to have a look. It was probably a deer or large raccoon setting it off, but Hatchert had promised the real estate guy, Barry Self, they'd hop up and check it out every time the stupid thing went off.

The sensors were new, hidden at key spots along the driveway ever since the night earlier in the summer when kids smashed a window in the basement servants' entry and broke in. Personally, Janey thought the sensors were stupid. Whoever eventually bought the place—if anyone ever did—would certainly have plenty to fix up or modernize, so the damage done by a few trespassing teens would be a drop in the bucket. It wasn't like the place was anywhere near its Cliffhead glory days. Besides, they hadn't stolen anything or vandalized anything last time—other than the door. She was sure it was just a boy and girl looking for a place to do it. She'd found a condom wrapper in the middle of the upstairs ballroom. But not the actual used condom, which made her feel they weren't rotten kids, whoever they were. They might break a little glass and have sex in an abandoned mansion, but they practiced safe sex and they didn't leave the gross condom lying around for people to find.

This time, when she pulled into the sweeping turnaround, circling the long-dry fountain, her lights caught the reflection of taillights and she thought, *Okay, either more teen shenanigans or fishermen . . .* The car looked familiar—a late-eighties Buick. She ran through the mental list of local fishermen who parked their cars in various favorite spots around town at different times, depending on what was running when. Though those fishing guys usually worked the river or Roger's lake . . .

Oh my God, she thought, dismayed at the way her mind was working. Lake Meenigeesis, I mean. It's not *Roger's* fucking lake . . .

Anyway, fishing the shore of Lake Michigan, in the middle of the night, that would be a little odd. Pivoting the side spot, she flashed it around the car: either empty or they were keeping their heads down, hoping she'd go away. It could be some fisherman's kid, on a hot date or a dare. Or somebody had boosted one of the old fishing guys' cars, though there had been no cars reported stolen, joyrides or otherwise, for most of the year. Then she realized why she was thinking *fisherman* and knew she was way off: it was the little stylized fish symbol in chrome on the side of the trunk lid. It meant *Christian,* of course, not *I subscribe to the Orvis catalogue.*

This was Reverend Gene's car.

She climbed out of the cruiser and she could hear it now, the music coming from the dash. He'd left the radio on, some sort of woman crooning jazz, sad and velvety like waves. Certainly it would run down his battery and then how would he get home? Something wasn't right.

She thought of the big to-do over some sermon he made recently. Some folks were outraged. They said he wasn't stable anymore.

Grabbing her big Maglite, she moved toward the crash of the lake, standing at the top of the steep steps that led down to the beach, and swept the solid beam down below. "Reverend Gene?" she called, several times. She told herself maybe it wasn't loud enough to be heard, but knew it was. The Maglite caught something wetly splayed near the water's edge, possibly pants. She'd have to go down there. She might have to radio in the Coast Guard boys for help, maybe a chopper search, but for now, she would have to do this herself.

She started down, a small acidic ache building in the center of her chest—a bad feeling about what she would find, or not find. But she told herself that the one consoling thing was that it was her shift tonight, that *she* was here to face this thing, not an outsider, a man who never knew Reverend Gene, wasn't held in his hands as a newborn at the baptismal font, never sat at his feet for the children's sermon or heard him belt out a slightly syncopated "Amazing Grace" through lungs that might now be filling with water. This was a thing for her; what she was supposed to be doing; the reason, after all, she was here.

80

HE DROVE UP to Camp Grayling on Saturday. Landry met him at the gatehouse, dressed in his fly vest and fishing cap and driving his own pickup, with an aluminum skiff in the bed. He said he was heading over to the Au Sable as soon as he got Roger set up. Roger called him Colonel Potter and Landry slugged him lightly in the solar plexus, then got in and led him around behind the administration buildings and the barracks and the gym where he taught the various pool classes, and then the basketball courts and the motor pool and all the rest, to a series of man-made hummocks in the earth, like the ancient mounds found among the Plains peoples. There was a fenced-off demolition range and a windowless shack, all bunkered with sandbags. They got out and Landry introduced him to the corporal on duty, then Roger stepped in to check out the inventory.

The smell hit him first. That fecund, diatomaceous musk like motor oil, so familiar. He hadn't smelled plastique in years and yet it did as it always had, taking him first back to that smell of cleaning guns, his Uncle Jimmy Two-Hands showing him how to maintain the old gallery gun after bagging rabbits. And playing with clay in art class and rubbing his boots with neat's-foot oil and the way it cured on the old woodstove, smoldering, one breath away, it seemed, from total combustion. Then motor oil and the service station he'd worked two summers, back when they really gave service—oil, air, windows, Green Stamps and a smile. And then, inevitably, sadly, the smell of the demo shack in Rach Soi and the unwashed greasy hair of Coots and Miller.

It never failed to surprise him, how that oily smell of plastique carried. Bomb-sniffing dogs did not impress him, not with that waft hitting him like a hard shove down memory lane. Jesus . . . It was all packaged tight and proper, of course, in blocks and sheets, way across the room from the coils of det wire and the caps and the rest of it; everything clearly labeled and separated by dividers that, frankly, wouldn't do shit if the place really blew. Still, it was a pretty neatly organized shack, all in all.

Behind him at the door, he heard Landry say, in a low voice to the corporal, "This guy was a SEAL in Nam—canal stuff. I don't think you need to hover. Get me?" So the corporal went back to the stoop to read something, probably a skin mag, and Landry left him to it, saying he'd say goodbye now; that he'd probably still be out fishing when Roger signed out off the base. Roger grunted, still trying to get a handle on what he was looking at, inventory-wise.

What *was* he looking at? None of the labels seemed familiar . . . The thing is, it wasn't like he'd been subscribing all these years to *Explosives Today*. He didn't go to demolition conventions or sit in chat rooms with chemists and paramilitary types. Other than the stump for Reenie Huff and the Petersons' jet-skis (and dock), both of which he jerry-rigged with clumsy homemade materials, he'd successfully avoided all this for decades. Some expert, he thought. It's amazing I'm not mistaken more often for Alfred Nobel . . .

Okay, it maybe *looked* different, but he told himself to hold on a second. The camp wouldn't be getting state-of-the-art stuff. This had to be the same old stuff he'd known before, only with different packaging, different classification numbers. He saw the letters *RDX* and thought, okay, that's C-4. I know what that is.

But a few things had definitely changed. For one thing, along with the claymores and plastique bricks and flexible Detasheet—all recognizable C-4 explosives—there was something else there stamped *PETN*, which he took to be Semtex. He knew very little about Semtex but understood it was used only for commercial demos and by terrorists, that the U.S. military didn't use it. The corporal's explanation sounded a little sketchy: "Colonel knows a guy, I think. I think on account of we're Reserves, not regulars, he can purchase some stuff through his own channels, not the Pentagon or whatever, so he buys some of this, his budget gets stretched a little further. Plus, he thinks we should start to get familiar with it, too. Get more 'well-rounded' or something . . ."

He saw now that it wasn't a skin mag the kid was reading but a paperback novel, something about terrorists blowing something up. *Nice,* Roger thought. *Guy's smack-dab in the center of Hemingway country here, instead he fills his head with that Hollywood fantasy crap . . .*

Outside, there was the log bunker where they set off the charges—a low sandbagged trench, not unlike a baseball dugout, except topped with a roof of knotty pine logs and camo mesh tarp and fitted out with a "hell box," where the switches were actually thrown. Then there was the demo range, a hard-packed grassless field, the no-man's-land between the bunker and the charges. At the end of the range, about two hundred meters back, there was a ditch, lined with tattered polyurethane to help retain the water. He went over and inspected. They'd set up some obstacles, sections of telephone pole or maybe pilings from an old dock, for him to experiment on. They'd already filled the ditch, from a hose snaking back to the bunker. It looked like about a meter deep of muddy water. He thought maybe they had a tank or a water hole somewhere on the base for the deeper stuff, the more advanced dive stuff that people thought of when they thought SEALs, but this would do for today.

He started small, breaking off just a thumb-sized crumb of a brick of C-4. Molding it into a ball, he waded into the water and felt around at the base of the first piling till he found a knothole and shoved it in, jamming the det cord in and unwinding it as he walked back to the bunker and attached it to the hell box mounted there.

"Clear," he said to the corporal, who repeated it back, and Roger flipped the safety and then the toggle and *boom,* there appeared, fanned out from the lip of the trough, a display of long shreddy toothpicks and a dark patch of dirt where the water had splashed.

He walked back over to the trench and acted like he was inspecting the damage. The results were about par with what he remembered from the same amount of C-4 in the old days. Maybe a *little* more powerful, but more or less the same. But he wasn't really checking the damage, he was checking himself, timing his pulse rate with his watch. He stood with his back to the bunker so the corporal wouldn't see his fingers at his wrist and maybe tell Landry.

But the pulse rate wasn't bad. He felt pretty calm, actually. Maybe he'd built this whole thing up in his mind for nothing. Sure, he hated loud noises when they took him by surprise, but maybe he was okay in a situation like this, when he knew each blast was coming. What the hell, he thought, and decided to try the other stuff, the Semtex. Being unfamiliar with it, he decided to use a smallish piece of flat Detasheet and see what it did and then work up from there. On the next piling, feeling around underwater, he found a splintering crack in the wood and slid the Semtex sheet about halfway in, then humped it back up out of the ditch and started back for the bunker, trailing the det cord.

He wasn't quite back to the bunker, just as far as the top step leading down inside, when the det cord felt snagged, caught short. It wasn't going to reach to attach to the hell box. He turned and squinted back and saw it was still coiled up way back at the trench, caught on a piece of wooden debris from the last blast. He gave the cord a tug. Rather than straightening, the whole charge pulled loose of the piling, up out of the water in a short hop, moving only maybe a meter closer than his initial placement, landing up on dry land. There was a hard blow to his chest, and then to his back and elbows and back of his head as the world tipped fast and turned white, which he soon realized was more of a light blue, really, and finally, he realized—though this took him considerably longer—that he was looking at the heavens.

The rest was gone. Just sky and a roar and nothing else until ceiling tile. Perforated institutional ceiling tile.

THE GOOD THING WAS, there'd been no breaks, no external injuries, no flying debris lodging anywhere on his body. The blow had been only concussive, knocking him to the ground with sound waves. The bad thing was it was still a big enough blast to severely diminish his hearing. It felt like he was underwater or in the hull of a ship. The Camp Grayling medics told him the loss might be temporary, or it might not be.

He was still trying to understand what had happened. He hadn't even plugged into the hell box yet, had he? So he'd jiggled the thing loose—big deal. The old C-4, the claymore mines, wouldn't have done that at all. He could have stamped on them, dropped them from a roof. Back in Nam, they'd shaved off pieces for a slow-burning cookfire, the stuff was so stable.

Landry, who'd been yanked back from the Au Sable and didn't look real thrilled not to be fishing, gave him some material to read while he lay in the cot, basics of Semtex and some of the newer innovations. Semtex, it turned out, was cheaper for a reason: it wasn't definitively any more powerful than military C-4, but it was more unstable. You couldn't throw it around or flop it onto the ground like you were landing a perch. Well, you learn something new every day, he thought. Though lessons like this one, he could do without.

Landry made him stay in the camp hospital ward for one night, under observation, before he would let him go. They had to write notes for him, holding up their questions on a dry eraser board.

The next day, Landry offered to drive him home, but Roger refused. Landry then asked, with a series of dialing pantomimes, if he could call someone to come get him and for a second, Roger thought of Janey—she could probably even make it look official, part of her job—but no, he didn't want to trouble her. Besides, he'd have to leave his truck here and come back for it later, so forget that.

He took the graveyard quiet home with him, that white noise still in his ears all the way down to Weneshkeen.

And now he was back home, sitting out on the porch on the cane rocker like an old man in Grandma Oshka's bathrobe, staring out at the lake, hearing nothing more than he would have heard a hundred years ago—less maybe. It sounded like a distant wind blowing in his ear, like the shush of water over rocks, his own pulse a steady *thwump-thwump* in his ear like a night bird taking flight. It actually made the lake look different, this lack of ruckus.

And because of this, there was no car door slam, no creak of leather, no footsteps on the porch. Because of this, the familiar white cardboard pie box with the vonBushberger's logo and the telltale C, for cherry, scrawled in red marker across it, and above it, the broad jaw and sad, wide, cockeyed smile of Janey as she came up the front steps, were the first signs he saw that he was no longer alone.

EPILOGUE:
SUMAC DAYS

THOUGH THE SEARCH for Reverend Gene had officially been called off, Reenie Huff had a few more ideas where to look and a way to proceed that would at least qualify as beneficial exercise. The boys had been too bullish and stumble-footed, she decided, out there with their huge boats, churning up the water. That was no way to find the man. Since the body hadn't turned up onshore or inland, through the Ninny John, chances were he'd gone out past the point of surf, out in the deeper calm where a body could float in pretty much any direction, willy-nilly, not just get pushed back to shore where it went in. She had no fish sonar nor apparatus with which to drag the depths, for heaven's sake—all that heavy gear the men had been using—but she had a feeling that might not be necessary. Gene was a spiritual man, light and heavenward-reaching, and she could almost picture him out there, still bobbing along. Just below the surface, perhaps, but buoyant, his corporal remnant resisting the descent.

And those boys with their speedboats and testosterone, their drive to produce results, could easily have chopped up the water so badly, no one could see a thing. They'd meant well, but still, she wasn't convinced that if he was actually out there, he couldn't still be found.

Rowing, was the way. She had her single—her lightweight ocean shell—that could glide along the surface in a manner far more subtle and surgical. It might not cover great areas at great speed, but it could be done with infinitely more care. This approach was a bit needle-in-the-haystack, surely, but at least she could look out at the lake when the winter finally came and know that she'd done her level best not to forget this man who'd lived among them and served them and deserved to be reclaimed by someone not a stranger—someone who knew who he was.

She had a rope and some Styrofoam buoys, tucked down in the hull at her feet, in case she found him. At her age, she was probably too frail to tow him back, but she'd at least be able to mark him better and point the authorities to the right spot. Bear Eckenrod had also lent her a portable GPS so she could pinpoint the spot, though she wasn't certain she could work the gizmo, if it came down to it. He'd apologized for not being able to help more, but he had a lot on his plate. The whole village was getting ready for the Sumac Days festivities. They needed to move on.

She put in at the Edgewater Road access, down past the old Lasco place, so she wouldn't have to struggle around the lighthouse rubble they were still trying to pull out of the channel. Getting beyond the surf, out into the calm, was the real workout, but once she was out there, it was a whole different, glassine world. Midday, the wind did little more than ripple and play twinkling tricks of light.

She was out a fair distance, the access road now a tiny paper cut in the gray-green haze that was the trees, when she brought it hard to port and headed south, parallel to the coastline. She would go till she could just make out a floating colon mark : on the horizon, which would be the black-and-white stripes of the next lighthouse, the behemoth Big Sable, then she would turn around and put in, and later in the week maybe try going north, maybe as far as Point Betsie, on the next day she had no appointments scheduled at the Planned Parenthood clinic in her garage.

A submerged log got her excited for a moment, before she realized what it was. Then a waterlogged makeshift anchor buoy: two battered milk jugs and a hank of sawed-off rope. But at least it was some indication of the quality of observation possible from her low line of sight, angled below the refraction of sunlight. She might have missed this detritus were she up in one of those big cabin cruisers or patrol boats, as all the volunteers and the Coast Guard had been. The clumsy clods . . . Frankly, she wondered if they'd all been a little too keen on coming off as heroes, after seeing the hoopla that surrounded Janey Struska's rescue of those kids. They probably all imagined themselves on TV, having their own brush with fame, getting the glory and the credit, and didn't stop to consider the prudent way to go about this task.

The Coast Guard even scrambled a helicopter when Janey first radioed it in. Would they have done that, Reenie wondered, before she'd gotten such notice for the lighthouse recovery? Maybe not. But they responded right away; flew low out in front of the bootlegger's place, shining their spotlights down into the chop. One Coast Guard fellow reportedly thought he saw something in the beam of his light, a hand reaching up. Maybe. Reenie wasn't convinced. She wondered how they could be sure *what* they were looking at, stirring up the water like they must have been, those big blades turning the lake into a churning washing machine and the spotlights shattering the crests into a million silvery mirror shards. They dropped a man down with his frogman getup but he saw no further sign of anything.

She was out for about a half-hour when something happened. If she told you about it, she'd say she was too focused on the water; on what was under the surface; scanning for anything that could be the Reverend. Or that her eyes were playing tricks on her. But truthfully, she'd grown distracted. She'd started watching her wake two points on port quarter, hypnotized by it a little; the silver ripple that paralleled the distant shore.

Snapping out of it, she turned to see she was startlingly close to another vessel—a three-masted square-rigger, anchored directly between her and the sun, looming suddenly like a pirate ship from a dream. The rigging shimmered silvery lances of sunlight in her direction and she had to squint and shield her eyes. She was coming alongside, about two points off the other's starboard bow. She thought of the Bermuda Triangle back in the seventies—whole ships supposedly vanishing without warning—and imagined the process reversed. She thought of the wild talk of late, of unexplained lights over the water. She thought of the dive camp schooner, but that should be anchored more to the north and would certainly be wrapping things up for the summer, this close to Sumac Days and with Roger Drinkwater unable to help right now. Diving would be out for a while, due to the condition of his ears. She thought, fantastically, of a secret scheme in which Gene Reecher was able to live out his retirement on this beautiful old yacht, cashing in on his own insurance policy and whooping it up, way out in Lake Michigan, with moonlight and twenty-year-old Scotch and his favorite old jazz records and none of those fools back home any the wiser.

She thought of all these things in a second of shimmering white sunlight and the time it took for the rigging to clang against the mast, loud and lonesome and real; a knell. And then she thought of her age and her stubbornness and the fact that, if she were honest about it, she sometimes let her principles rule over common sense and that she was perhaps getting a little too old for such shenanigans. The truth was, she probably hadn't been paying enough attention and almost plowed right into another vessel. The truth was, this was a task for a younger person whose mind might not be clouded by the light-headedness of low blood sugar.

"Ahoy!" a man called from the deck. A dark silhouette, one hand in the rigging, the other waggling in the white sun.

"Ahoy," she said quietly, in her librarian voice, and as she drew closer, into the shadowy lee of the ship, it shielded the sun and she was then able to make out colors and details of the man standing high above her. He wore a baggy Ball State sweatshirt and long khaki shorts and had a pair of binoculars slung from his neck. His cap was less baseball and more aviator, the bill squashed and arced into a frown. Wisps of gray and rust poked out around the ears. She guessed he was in his fifties. He stood motionless, looking down at her, grinning around the stub of a cigar.

He removed the cigar, becoming conspicuously gap-toothed. "What is that—a kayak?"

She was a bit preoccupied. She'd rapidly gotten in too close and was now trying to retract her starboard oar before it scraped against his hull. "It's an ocean shell," she said, struggling to hold herself at arm's length from the boat. "For rowing?"

He jabbed the cigar back into his grin, nodding, then removed it again. "You sure it's not a kayak?"

The man was a bit of a fool. She said, "I would admit it, I assure you, were it so." Was he possibly pulling her leg or did he really not understand the difference between oars and paddles? She glanced up again to see if he looked like a fool. It was hard to say.

He shrugged as if to allow that she was welcome to her opinions. "Looks pretty kayak-y." He had a sort of Hoosier accent, she thought. She wondered what he was doing way out here. He seemed to be alone or at least without family or friends. Generally, the bigger the vessel, the more crowded. But not in this case.

She was considering informing him that he should keep a lookout for the body of a drowned man, and wondering if such notice was truly necessary—is that something you'd overlook if you came upon it?—when he produced a small white box, the top an open nest of paper, and held it out in front of him, calling down to her, "Want some fudge? Last piece!"

"Thank you, no." As if this were a reasonable consideration, her mind automatically ran to the practical for justification: she was all set, food-wise. She had an apple and two PowerBars and some of Roger Drinkwater's Schmatzna-Gaskiwag® jerky. And what was she supposed to do—climb up to the deck and take a piece? Open her mouth and have him toss it to her as if this were SeaWorld?

Shrugging, he fished out the alleged last piece and stuffed it whole into his mouth, eyes wide, then dropped the box on the deck, slapping his hands together, dusting them off. He spoke with his mouth atrociously full. "Man alive, that's tasty stuff . . ." This she took as her cue to keep moving, inching the shell along by pulling, hand over hand, along the hull of the yacht. She could still hear him overhead chewing loudly and mumbling *mm-mm-mmmmm!* and it was sort of, though not entirely, amusing, in a way, and she thought, Who is this simpleton? He seemed familiar and the gulpy, dumb-guy voice he now put on, calling after her as she cleared his stern, seemed like something from TV: "Hey! Kayak lady! Know where I can get me some more fudge?"

Weneshkeen, she was about to say, but felt it would come out funny. It would sound the way the Indians had pronounced it, years ago, as if it were a question or a challenge.

Acknowledgments

Special thanks to the following for their assistance, support, advice and benevolence:

Bob & Connie Amick, my parents . . . plus Dr. Ken Abrams, Bruce Amick, Henry Amick, Jack Amick, James H. "Pappy" Amick, The Ann Arbor Public Library, Clark Beavans, Gwen Beavans, Joe David Bellamy, Millicent Bennett, The Benson Ford Research Center, Stan Bidlack, Juliet Cella Blumenthal, Joe Breakey, Fred Chase, Lois Colón, Matt Colón, Nancy Debassige, Mary Beth Doyle, The Elk Rapids District Library, Erik Esckilsen, Archie Ferguson, Deborah Garrison, Matt Garrison, Meilan Goller, Chris Gordon, Eric Grant, Joe Gray, Rich Griffith, Chris Hatin, Oogima Aakiin Ikwe, Roger Jankowski, Eric Kelly, Lauren Kingsley, Christine Kulcheski, Ilana Kurshan, The Lake Superior State University Native American Center, Travis Lampe, Joslyn Layne, Arek Majewski, Maria Massey, Greg McIntosh, Michigan Department of Natural Resources, Adrienne Miller, Farah Miller, James Monger, Pamela Narins, Pilar Queen, Jim Roll, Laura Roll, Stephanie Sabatine, David Scott, Richard Scullin, Dick Siegel, Joe Snapp, Jack Spack Jr., Elaine Spiliopoulos, Harold Stusnick, César Valdez, Katie Van Wert, Joe Veltre, Sally Vering, Brandon Wiard, Joe Pete Wilson, Brad Wurfel and Dave Zaret.

Miigwech to all of you.